EARTH IS NOT ALONE

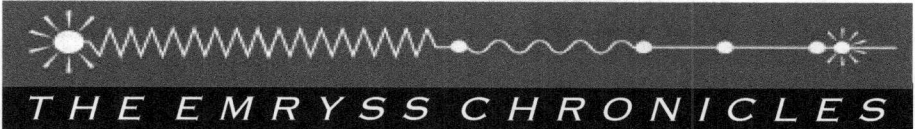

THE EMRYSS CHRONICLES

John Knapp II

EARTH IS NOT ALONE

EPHEMERON PRESS

"Love, romance, tragedy, and responsibility after…Earth's modern technology collapses. This tale has enough mystery to inspire readers — young and old — to discuss 'theories of truth and being' long into the night! Be prepared to travel to other worlds."

— *Gladys Hunt, author of Honey for a Teen's Heart*

"Reminiscent of Lewis, Tolkien and L'Engle, EARTH IS NOT ALONE… swept me away — laughing at the cleverness of the heroes and crying at their joys and defeats."

— *Stephanie Whitacre,*
Campus Life Director at Lackawanna Trail High School

"A nice job!… in the ballpark with Lawhead… I liked it even better [reading it] the second time!

— *Robert Newman, Ph.D.*
Astrophysicist and former prof, Biblical Theological Seminary

"EINA raises intriguing questions and makes… plausible conjectures about Christianity on other worlds. Answers to which we won't find until we make contact with aliens or arrive in heaven, but which are… fascinating for those of us waiting on Earth."

— *Jack Maynard, a software architect for aircraft systems*
who lives in the (future) Susquehanna Territory

"As a Fortune 500 software engineer who grew up in what becomes… 'the Susquehanna Territory,'… [this is] a riveting read that will keep you guessing with each twist. One note of caution: don't pick this up if you need to be well rested in the morning."

— *Eric Wood (whose old home is quite near "Big Bend")*

"Sci-fi and mystery… teen romance… the first book I've ever seen that truly tackles the concept of life in other worlds from within a Christian worldview."

— *Grace Bridges, New Zealand*
(www.titletrakk.com)

SUDDENLY, ALL REGULAR ELECTRIC
POWER IS GONE

ALL ELECTRONIC EQUIPMENT HAS
BEEN DESTROYED

PEOPLE ARE UNHARMED

318 DAYS LATER, AEMP YEAR 01

AT BIG BEND HIGH SCHOOL,
SUSQUEHANNA TERRITORY

NORTHEASTERN PENNSYVANIA

"Michael, you're 17,"said Mr. Cample, "and Triana, you're new here . . . and 16?" — she nodded — "and probably the most gifted student I've ever taught. And only months from a graduation everyone once thought impossible. Why throw it all away?" The teacher extended his arms. "How could you two have done something so stupid and obviously wrong?"

"Done what?" asked the boy, genuinely puzzled...

"Look... the world might be going to hell all around us but, though I'm hardly religious, it's not going to happen in my class! Understand?....You both claim you're Christians! ...I can count on your both telling me the truth? That's your Jesus way, isn't it?"

Michael... took the girl by the hand... seated her... and seated himself beside her. As Triana smoothed her lap, a matchbox-sized metal box with a tiny blinking blue light tumbled from her skirt pocket onto the floor... Instantly, Michael covered it with his foot, slid it back under his chair, at the same time dropping his pen. Bending to pick it up, he palmed the strange box and put it in his pants pocket.... Small beads of sweat rose on the girl's forehead.

✳ PART I: THE SUSQUEHANNA TERRITORY

Setting: Earth
Time: 11 BEMP – AEMP 01, Day 12

✳ PART II: THE ACCUSATION

Setting: Earth
Time: AEMP 01, Day 318

✳ PART III: DEATH IN A TAVERN

Setting: Emryss
Time: Soon After the Destruction of the
Kingdom of the Horse and Sword

✳ PART IV: THE SECRET OF ZAREBA

Setting: Emryss
Time: About 15 Years After
Events in Part III

✳ PART V: THE RESOLUTION

Setting: Earth
Time: AEMP 01, Day 319

ISBN 978-0-912290-31-7
3rd printing 2010

Address: ephemeronpress.com or contact may be made through the author's website johnknapp2.com

This story is a work of fiction. While it assumes certain scientific concepts and the acceptance of conservative Biblical interpretation, the author in no way insists that correct Biblical or scientific understanding must follow his reasoning that reaches beyond known science and looks into the future; instead, he holds only that Scripture might allow, and be congruent with, the logical interpretation given in the story if the events described actually happened. It in no way "replaces" commonly accepted Biblical end-time scenarios. Names, characters, places, and incidents either are the product of the author's imagination or are used fictitiously. While "The Susquehanna Territory" strongly resembles a portion of Susquehanna County, PA, where the author lives part time, and some actual places are named, such as "New Milford" and "The Montrose Bible Conference," there is a gentle but deliberate rearranging and renaming of certain locations, and recasting of facts, such as giving a different name to Montrose sports teams. Other than that, any resemblance to actual events, locales, organizations, or persons living or dead, is entirely coincidental and beyond the intent of either the author or publisher.

Cover art, illustrations, and layout design by Dominic Catalano

The few Scriptures cited, or alluded to, are from New International Version © 1973 by International Bible Society.

I wish to thank Dr. Inez Alfors, formerly of the English Dept. of SUNY-Oswego, for her detailed critiquing and editing of an earlier draft of this story; also my consultants: Jack Maynard, for input about electronics and EMP; Master Frank Schermerhorn for his teaching me Soo Bahk Do karate; and Joe Winkleblech for his input about archery. Any misguided use of what I believe to be their excellent knowedge and assistance is my own fault.

Thank you, Stephanie Whitacre, for your proofreading of the final manuscript.

For bottomless coffee and kind service in the early morning hours while I wrote and revised, I wish to thank Mimi's, Panera Bread, Bob Evans, and Denney's, (in Viera, FL); J & J's, Miss Penny's, Cindy's, and Lattner's McDonald's (in the"Susquehanna Territory," PA); and Townline and Port City Diners (in Oswego, NY). A special thanks, too, for the prayer and support of the Wed. AM worshippers of Prince of Peace (Anglican) Church (Viera, FL).

--John

This book is dedicated to my children, Ethan, Phoebe, Eli, and Andrew, who have been read to, or have read privately, most, but not quite all, of this volume, and who have helped with critiquing these pages. Without Ethan's detailed assistance, this book would be much less than it is.

And to my loving and very patient wife Karen.

And to members and attenders of **THE ENDLESS MOUNTAINS STORY CLUB** of Montrose, Pennsylvania, where I now live half-time. *All these people have heard aloud parts of this story, or related stories, and have left a signed record of attending club readings.* Names are grouped in ways the people here will understand.

Norm B., Dawn B.

Dave D., Chris D., Robbie D., Jessica D.

David D., Penny D., Ryan D.

Dave H., Elaine H.

Ray J., Shirley J., Roy J., Beckie J., Christina J.

Henrietta K., Arlene K., Laura K.

Bill M., Edie M., David M., Mark M., Tom M.

Jack M., Peggy M., Phil M., Becky M., Sarah M.

Larry S., Patti S., David S., Janelle S., Mechele S.

John K. Sr., Dodie K.

Chuck S., Martha S., Nadean S., Jessica S.

Dave S., Barb S.

Dave T., Renée T., Heléna T., Leah T.

Celia W., Jim W., Dan W.

Russ W., Mary W., Eric W., Sandy W., Leslie W.

Sarah W., Becca W.

Thomas D., Jane D., Piper F., Jessica F., Pat H., Margaret H-M., Fred K., Jill R-M., Jean R., Song T., Chika Y.

And Others Who Heard Including: My mother Eleanor (now 98), Matt C., Sarah F., Kaitlyn K., Christie L., Carolyn M.

☀ PART V – THE RESOLUTION

olktales. Are they ever more than just stories? Are any of them — some passed down for centuries — ever true? Historically true? Accurate in spite of thousands of retellings?

Also, do people — people created in God's image, if you will — live on other planets? People who are fallen? With similar DNA? People you could love — fall in love with? "The Bible doesn't say Yes or No," says Michael Hammond's adopted father Dr. Jonas Harwell and most others who have thought about this.

But what if — what if you had good reason to believe that someone from another planet, a fallen planet, had come to your world in your time and spoke your language? And spoke to you face to face? What would you say to him — or her — about God, and one's responsibility to God? Or, more specifically, how would you explain Christ's once-for-all-time death on Earth for all sin? About Adam and Eve? The Jewish connection?

And what if there was a "call" from this planet to help people there understand God? Partly, because of a strange prophecy given there (but not here)? And partly because stories about people there — that strongly resembled some of our own classic stories — had already "arrived" on Earth? And, even further, what if you could possibly go there?

Not a common problem in your world, you say.

But things were hardly common on Earth when this story begins…

CHAPTER I

SETTING THE STAGE

PLACE: *Science classroom, Big Bend High School,*
            Susquehanna Territory, PA
TIME: *Winter, early 21st century, AEMP 01, 318 days after*
            EMP has destroyed all electronic microcircuitry

"**M**eet me in the science classroom at 4:50.

"It will be dark," their English teacher added, "but everybody will be gone. I must see both of you immediately." Michael knew Mr. Cample thought highly of them—at least he once did—and that he didn't mince words.

Little did the senior suspect how long the next ten hours would be, and how life as he knew it had come to an end.

Michael made it up to the second floor, just as the soon-to-be valedictorian with shoulder-length dark blond hair, with predictable punctuality, entered the classroom door thirty feet ahead of him. Faint light from inside erased some of the blackness from the hallway. Quietly he sprinted to the door she'd left open to help anyone behind her get there more easily. A hint of her perfume lingered.

His ears met the sound of flapping wings. A large starling grazed the wire that ended in a lone 100-watt bulb hanging down from the twelve-foot high ceiling. Across the chalkboard and charts of the human body on the wall danced oversized, winged shadows of the trapped creature.

The girl, the only person there and legally blind, seemed not to notice. She stood far across the room facing the tall, single window, just behind and to the left of the teacher's long desk. Bending, she pulled at handles on the window. With surprising ease it slid up a foot from the paint-chipped sill, and a gust of cool air entered. Then she pivoted to the side and turned, her back pressing against the wall, facing the room as an artist might stand by a painting on canvas, waiting for critics to appear and ask for explanation. Since her glasses were off, Michael knew he hadn't been seen.

"Cour – a – cour – a — la - la - loo," the girl sang softly into the gray silence. A chill ran down Michael's back, yet he felt warm. He unzipped his black leather jacket. He tucked back down in the inner pocket the rolled-up science article, "The Sleeping Dragon," written years ago, but that only yesterday his adopted father had given him to read. The girl turned back to the window and, tracing circles in the air with her hand, pointed to the opening.

Instantly, the bird attached itself to the dangling cord. The light and its shadows danced faster. The creature cocked its head.

"Cour – a – cour – a - la - la— loo," the girl repeated, facing the window.

The bird fluttered down to the right of the desk and landed on an oversized knob to a door large enough to lead somewhere else larger than the small storage closet actually behind it. Again, the bird cocked its head. The girl tapped the sill with her finger. In an instant the creature was through the window and gone. She closed the window.

"You can come in now, Michael," she said just loud enough, without turning.

Just then their teacher arrived behind him. He was breathing deeply. Without speaking, the two entered and strode to the front of the room.

Cample dropped his angular frame into the chair behind the massive desk. Veins stood out on his neck above the open collar of his faded plaid shirt. His full head of black hair was shiny in the faint light.

"Sorry, I'm late," he said, "but Stanley and Feinsteck have had nothing but trouble from some bird in here all day—in the only room that still has light."

"It was only a starling, Mr. Cample," said Michael, running a hand through his dark curly hair. Oddly, two old-fashioned, left-handed student desks were closest to the desk across from the teacher. The girl lowered herself into one, Michael the other.

"*Why* did I ask you to come here now?" asked the teacher. "And neither of you can guess?"

"No sir, I've no idea," said Michael.

"Nor I," said the girl.

The troublesome bird was forgotten. Michael noticed the two moderately thick binders on the teacher's desk.

"Triana," he whispered, "he's got my story for the senior honors project up there! Is the other—"

"Sorry, Michael"—she pulled her hair to the side—"I just can't..."

Too late he'd realized the girl's glasses weren't on and the desk itself was probably as much a mystery as anything on it.

"Michael, you're 17, and have lived here all your life," said Mr. Cample, "and Triana, you're new...but 16?"—she nodded—"and probably the most gifted student I've ever taught. You're both only months from a graduation everyone once thought was impossible. Why throw it all away? May I be candid?"

"I'm almost 18, Mr. Cample," said Michael, "and about being candid—we expect you to say anything you want."

The girl nodded in agreement.

"Okay, I've heard how you and your church..." He paused.

"It's all right, Mr. Cample," said Michael. "Speak freely."

"How you and your church," the teacher continued, "preach *honesty*."

"Yes," said Michael.

"Well, then, how could you have done something so stupid and obviously wrong? And I'm not going to let you get away with it! I may not believe in God, at least in the way you do, but there is a right and wrong. And I'm going to make you realize that."

"What have we done?" asked Michael.

"Done what?" repeated the girl.

How in control she sounded, thought Michael. And looked. She sat straight, but though her skirt fell just over her knees, he sensed they were slightly shaking. He glanced away to the closed door, then up to the dark gray of the ceiling. He brushed back his hair, much darker than the girl's, and which fell just to his eyebrows. He mustn't be impatient. Despite Cample's dramatic way, he was usually fair. With resolve, Michael clutched the scarred top of his chair, leaned forward, and fixed his eyes on the teacher. He would look ready. But ready for what? Except for the dull roar of the generator two floors below, there was silence.

"You know," said Cample, ignoring their questions, "millions have died outside the Territory this year. Thank God we don't know how many! We've been fortunate—"

"Thank God we've been *blessed*!" interrupted Michael, immediately wondering why he'd said anything.

"God is a word today, Michael, that doesn't come boxed with deity. We in the Susquehanna Territory have been *fortunate*—call it what you will—but don't forget it! We've lost things that a year ago we never dreamed we'd give up. While we wait for THE PROBLEM, as it's called, for things to return to…uh…normal, we—"

Suddenly, the dull whirring of the generator ceased and the lightbulb flickered out. Fresh silence gave way to the rattling of a window by an icy breeze as a clouded winter sun surrendered its last light. Cample leaned over, raised the globe of his ever-present lamp, and lit the wick. A spiral of sooty smoke rose into the darkness. He lowered the glass and the room once again brightened.

The teacher focused on the boy and girl.

"While we wait for what comes next, we mustn't lose what we still have. Things that *really* matter! Things that make us what we truly are. If you think I'm misguided, or silly, to make such a big thing out of this, in a sense, you're probably right. Quite frankly, I can count on one hand the number of students I can talk to like I am now. But *integrity*, Michael, Triana, if people like you two and me"—he paused—"if we start *cheating* in things as inconsequential as this"—he pointed to the two binders on the desk—"what do we have left that matters beyond self-preservation? What dignity is there?"

"If," said Triana, "you're talking about our *separate* honors projects"—though Michael knew she couldn't see them, she turned toward where they lay—"our topic was hardly 'inconsequential'!"

"It was important to me," said Michael, "and I sure didn't cheat."

"So you deny it—both of you!" Cample smiled and for some reason the light within the glass chimney flickered. The boy and girl exchanged glances.

"Let me be clear. If you think I'm going to let this go, think again. I have ethical standards and I don't need God to help me out. And I don't care who thinks I'm blowing this all out of proportion. The school will side with me. And"—he looked at the girl—"I'm certain you don't want some of this to be made public!

"As you know, I've studied a lot of folktales—stories about other places and times long ago. But believe me, there are no stories, or I should say, stories *of this world*—which are like the two you handed in. I'm convinced you—you of all people—cheated. But even so, your stories are far from complete.

"And I think you'd like to know, I just may have some more things that you, especially you, Triana, would like to know right here" — he pointed to his briefcase — "information I think you know nothing about."

CHAPTER 2

"THE SLEEPING DRAGON"

Excerpts from "EMP: The Sleeping Dragon,"
An Editorial in *Science Weekly*
(Written April 17, 13 years BEMP)

In July 1962, a long-feared dragon awoke and crawled out of its lair....

Immediately following one of the last American nuclear explosions in the atmosphere...electrical systems in Honolulu, 800 miles from the blast, suddenly went dead....the secret of EMP, which had long terrified a handful of scientists, was broadcast to the world.

"Electromagnetic pulse" is the tremendous surge of electromagnetic energy that accompanies a nuclear explosion, and is especially severe when detonation occurs high above ground. Such fallout has very different effects from what we usually worry about with neutron bombs, for while leaving buildings and most physical objects intact, and people virtually unharmed, its invisible wave causes immediate "death" to electrical equipment that uses microcircuitry.

Then in the early part of the 21st century, soon after 9/11, came the development of non-nuclear explosives that could produce an even stronger electromagnetic pulse.

EMP had been known about for years, but not the extent of its power.

That it could cripple electrical power distribution and invisibly destroy sophisticated weaponry, as well as other technology, great distances away was alarming. Immediately, though the Federal Government played it down, building defenses against this powerful force became a highly classified priority.

And a scientific nightmare.

It also became a terrorist's dream: With great explosions at strategic points on the globe — that shed not a drop of blood — primitive third-world countries, with bursting populations, could exercise both physical and psychological muscle.

As early as 1963 the specter of EMP became, according to the League of Yale, "the third most likely plague that could destroy representative government in a country the size of the United States, if not the forward march of civilization itself."

If this were not enough, with each passing month newer, tinier, more delicate and much cheaper miniature circuitry of astonishing capabilities began to invade everything plugged in, or that ran off of batteries. Millions of microchips, too small to see, too delicate to repair, and too complex for most to understand were created and spread like a viral contagion around the planet. By the late 1980's the infection of their magic was everywhere, in briefcases, pants pockets, clipped onto belts, on every wrist. Fleeting time had even become hostage. And when people paused over their instant dinners to reflect, they wondered how they had ever lived *BMic* (before microwaves).

But will the virus ever die?

Will some cataclysm ever usher in a new age — AEMP, After Electromagnetic Pulse — when we will have plenty of pendulum-swinging, ticking time to look back and ponder how we live?

Automobiles also surrendered their primitive past, receiving improved ignition systems; their dashboards became electronic cockpits, information centers. Even bulky electrical hardware became fine-tuned with electronic grids of microcircuitry. One by one, power-generating and transmission companies surrendered to the new technology which seemed almost overnight to become faster, safer, and cheaper.

We had entered a new age. If there were bugs in the systems, time would take care of them. Hadn't it always?

But what to do to be really safe? Obviously "soft" and vulnerable parts had to be protected—"hardened." And so a reassuring new buzz word was born. But how hard is hard enough? And should "whole systems" be hardened or just "soft parts"? Experts argued vigorously behind closed doors and hotly disagreed. Consequently, science has followed both paths.

Then arrived glass and fiber optics which was hailed to be the answer by some, just another complication by others. Glass should be immune to EMP just as "large" vacuum tube technology with its soldered and taped copper wire connections had proved to be. But delicate microcircuitry was never far away from glass linkages.

Ironically, the age of atmospheric testing was over just as the magnitude of the problem was realized, so the newly developed highly touted defenses against EMP that the military says we now have developed, as well as the very questionable commercial "walls of protection" that industry has sold itself, have never been adequately tested.

"We accept them on faith," declares Roger Steinberg of M.I.T., "because we have no other choice."

"The hairless ape has made himself into a god," says Nobel laureate Harvey Mott, "but he lacks the most important traits of divinity. He, pretending to be something he is not, forgets the past. And he doesn't know the present. He is not all-powerful. And the worst of his kind has found a way to destroy the best, for Homo sapiens, depends upon tools—and now the ones on which he depends the most have wriggled out of his control."

In short, technology as we now know it may disappear like the dinosaur, and highly specialized modern man along with it.

Irving Miller
Editor and Publisher

✳   ✳   ✳

The quickest way to understand Michael and Triana and the confrontation with their teacher, and explain the horror about how their world suddenly and dramatically changed, is to examine several more brief printed records that seem of little consequence unless put side by side along with what happened on Day 1 of AEMP 01 and the days that followed.

All, except the last, were written at least 8 months before business as usual ceased:

> *– 11 brief (one only 2 lines) newspaper articles or*
> *   records from Kansas, New York, and Pennsylvania*
> *– 2 high school office memos exchanged by a teacher and*
> *   principal*
> *– A Sunday take-home letter prepared by a small-town*
> *   minister*

Put together, these paint just enough background of the peculiar, newly formed Susquehanna Territory of northeastern Pennsylvania. And reveal just enough about several important people who lived there.

Why?

To describe one of the strangest teacher-student-parent confrontations that ever took place. One in which four people put everything they believed in on the line. And where resolving what first seemed like an ordinary conflict would open a door to a whole new world.

Or, to be more precise, two new worlds.

PART I

THE SUSQUEHANNA TERRITORY

"... a measure of life, a moment of death — that's all that's certain ... None of the ancient prophecies... none of our novels or movies ever prepared us for what we have seen..."

Chapter 12

CHAPTER 3

A FLASH OF LIGHT

TIME: *April 1 - April 13 [11years BEMP]*

PLACE: *Elkton, Kansas*

News item at the bottom of p.1 of the April 1 *Dodge City Ledger:*

POSSIBLE METEOR STRIKE

Last night one light sleeper living just west of Elkton was treated to a rare celestial event as a large meteor plummeted to earth at 3:58 AM.

Reports Mary Prichard: "I awoke suddenly to a low howl of wind, just as if a storm were rising. Like a magnet I was pulled to my window. Outside, above a tall oak bordering my back fence, a yellow pen-shaped shaft of light glided over and down past the rise on the prairie behind our house. Then the howl itself ceased, though its echo still rang. A minute later an explosion — like those at nearby MacInroe Quarry rattled the window glass in front of me. Then all was quiet as a cloud of dust rose and darkened the full moon to blood red."

By 5 AM the area of impact was cordoned off by Baker Company, Panther Division of the U.S. Third Army which, "coincidentally," according to Capt. Jeremiah Trent, was bivouacked only two miles away. All roads within 20 miles of Elkton along U.S. 56 have been sealed off.

✳ ✳ ✳

Headline in the April 13 edition of *The American Enquirer:*

ALIENS SURVIVE CRASH LANDING
IN SOUTHWEST KANSAS!
3 FLEE BURNING UFO, ONE CARRYING CHILD
–Witness Forced to Undergo Psychiatric Exam–

On April 1, visitors from outer space survived a fiery landing just west of Elkton, Kansas, says Gilbert (last named withheld) who watched from less than a mile away in his stalled 18-wheeler.

"There was this light just south at US 56 — exactly at 4AM, because my dashboard clock and watch both stopped," said Gilbert. "All of a sudden my steering locks up, my engine stalls, and it's all I can do to get on the shoulder and stay there. When I finally stop, there's this explosion like dynamite. A plane crash, I figured. With my power window dead, I opened the door and the smell of hot metal stings my nose, and right across on the prairie, smoke rose like out of a chimney, making the full moon darken.

"Just as I got my wits back, I saw two guys that looked like adults, but I couldn't say how old, staggering away out of sight, each with what looked like a large white canvas bag slung over his shoulder. Then, a thin helmeted giant dressed in some kind of silvery-white space suit spattered with blood, with extra-wide silvery boots like nothing I've ever seen, comes toward me carrying what looked like a child — four, six, seven years old? Who could tell? — in the same kind of clothes, but with the helmet ripped away. Desperately, this kid is rubbing its eyes and gasping for breath like tasting earth air is something brand-new.

"Just then my heart begins to pound like it's gonna beat outta my chest and I'm terrified. Then, I'm sorry to say, I fainted dead away. Don't even remember hitting the pavement.

"Next thing I know a soldier is shaking me. When I start tellin' what I saw, suddenly I'm jerked away and pricked with needles and grilled for hours. Then they let me go. Somehow, and for some reason I can't explain, I never mentioned the two men I saw in that first instant—not until now. Perhaps seeing that tall man with the child pushed it outta my mind.

"Can't tell you just why, but I know they wasn't Americans and, even though their blood's as red as yours or mine, I'd lay ya a 100 to 1 they wasn't even from earth."

CHAPTER 4

HYSTERIA PUT TO REST

TIME: *April 16 – Sept. 5 [11 years BEMP]*

PLACE: *Elkton, Kansas*

Item on p. 3 in the April 16 issue of *The Topeka Sentinel:*

ALIENS LAND IN ELKTON?
'ABSOLUTELY NOT,' SAYS GOV

"**. . . N**ot one shred of evidence," said a spokesperson from the governor's office, "which unfortunately, won't help you sell papers." When asked about a story in a national tabloid reporting a truck driver encountering aliens along U.S. 56 early in the morning of April 1, the governor's office was curt: "Absolutely not. Consider the source. Besides, don't you guys use the calendars on those expensive watches?"

As to why the five square mile area was still cordoned off, came this response: "As best we can tell, a meteorite of some size did strike the earth, and as soon as our precautionary tests for radiation and other risk factors are complete, the area will be reopened for inspection to the public."

When Franklin Glarm, new editor of *The American Enquirer* was questioned, he offered no comment other than, "With the new truth-in-reporting law just passed by Congress, we take ourselves very seriously. In short, we stand by our story."

✳ ✳ ✳

Item on p.3 in the Sept. 5 issue of *The Topeka Sentinel:*

BASEBALL-SIZED METEORITE UNCOVERED

Finally, after five months of countless delays, "Alien Acres," as a patch of prairie near Elkton has been dubbed, has become open to the public and the Army Corps of Engineers has presented a brief report, along with fragments of a baseball sized iron-nickel meteorite. But the long-awaited report does not come without controversy. "At last we have the BB that killed an elephant," said Dr. Thomas Haggai, Chair of the Physics Dept. at Oral Roberts University. Says Dr. Spiro Ryland , relaxing at an off-season baseball practice of Kansas University Jayhawks in Lawrence: "Yeah, it's a meteorite, all right, a sky rock dumped on a million cubic meters of pawed-over sandbox sand. But by whom? And why? It's like a groundskeeper finding a quarter while raking the pitcher's mound. Whoever carries money there? Shake your fist, if you will, at mindless Mother Nature for holes in her heavenly purse. And on your way out send the vendor up with another cold one."

"With the wild stories that nearly ripped apart the Internet — even though few took them seriously — we had to go over everything with a fine-toothed comb," said an Army spokesperson.

Enough said...

CHAPTER 5

MICHAEL HAMMOND

TIME: *May 7 [ca 3 yr. BEMP]*

PLACE: *Big Bend, Pennsylvania*

News item from the May 7 *Susquehanna Voice:*

SCHOLAR-ATHLETE NAMED

The Harley Cather Junior High of Big Bend proudly announces the selection of Michael C. Hammond Jr. as scholar-athlete of the year. The son of Michael Sr. and Clara Rose Hammond of Big Bend, Michael, along with basketball team captain Ron Gorman, led the Junior Cougars to their first-ever Section V District Finals.

According to Coach Patrick Jensen who presented the award, "Michael is not your typical point guard, and he doesn't usually score in double figures, but rarely does anyone else without his help, for as playmaker he has the uncanny knack for being at the right place at the right time to rebound and find the open man. He is a team player without equal in my junior high coaching experience."

Said science teacher Mary Blanchard: "Michael is an example of someone who can excel and go far if he's willing to set his mind to his work and study hard."

Michael's hobbies include drawing, painting, and karate—he's presently a red belt—and science fiction. He plans to attend Big Bend High this fall.

CHAPTER 6

JONAS HARWELL

TIME: *July 18 – Feb.24 [ca 3 yr. BEMP]*
PLACE: *Big Bend, PA*

News item from p. 1 of the July 18 issue of
The Binghamton Press-Ledger:

FOUR DIE IN FIERY THREE-VEHICLE CRASH

For the second time in a month the scythe of death has cut across the foggy, rain-slickened stretch of I-81, ten miles south of Binghamton. According to witnesses, a truck from Helmon's Quarry traveling north at a high rate of speed, without warning crossed the median into the southbound lane, striking first a sport utility wagon in the passing lane and then a sedan in the right lane.

Dead at the scene were the driver of the sport utility wagon, Michael Hammond Sr., 37, his wife Clara Hammond, 35, both of Big Bend, Pennsylvania; Beverly Harwell, 51, of Santa Clara, California, who was a passenger in the sedan; and Herbert Morley, 23, of New Milford, driver of the truck. Treated at Binghamton City Hospital, and in guarded condition, is Michael Hammond Jr. who was returning from a karate tournament in Binghamton. Treated for minor cuts to his hands and later released was Dr. Jonas Harwell, 52, also from Santa Clara.

＊　＊　＊

News item in the July 19 *Susquehanna Voice:*

PROGRAM CANCELLED AT BIBLE CONFERENCE

Due to the tragic death yesterday of his wife Beverly, Dr. Jonas Harwell will not be speaking on "Science and the Bible" scheduled for Friday and Saturday nights at the Montrose Bible Conference. Dr. Harwell, who did graduate studies at Cornell, had accepted a pastoral post in Big Bend only last week, where he preached his first sermon at the Grace Missionary Alliance Church.

Dr. Harwell suffered only minor injuries in the accident on I-81 that claimed his wife. (Obit. and funeral arrangements on p.4.)

＊　＊　＊

Notice Feb. 24 (ca 7 months later) in the weekly *Susquehanna Voice:*

FORMAL ADOPTION

Michael Hammond Jr., 14, of 307 N. Ash St., Big Bend by Dr. Jonas Harwell of 411 Bagby Rd, Big Bend.

CHAPTER 7

MARVIN CAMPLE

TIME: *Aug. 3 (ca 5 months later) [ca 2 yr. BEMP]*
PLACE: *Big Bend, PA*

News item from the Aug. 3 *Susquehanna Voice:*

NEW ENGLISH TEACHER NAMED

Harry Slater, principal of Big Bend High, announces the appointment of Marvin Cample as a new teacher this fall. Cample, author of the book *Endless Mountains Folklore* and a volume of poetry, *New Gods in Old Worlds*, is no stranger to many Susquehannites. Born in Montrose, and educated at the University of Iowa and the University of Kansas, Cample says simply, "after seven years of study and research in the Midwest, I'm glad to be back where I belong — in Big Bend, and in the classroom." Cample is currently gathering a collection of previously unpublished folk tales.

CHAPTER 8

WATER TOWER NUMBER ONE

TIME: *Aug. 3 and 17 [ca 2 yr. BEMP]*
PLACE: *Big Bend, PA*

Another item in the same Aug. 3 issue of *Susquehanna Voice:*

EYESORE GETS NEW FACE

Thanks to the Grace Missionary Alliance Church, "Old Number One," erected in the 1920's as the first all-metal water tower in northeastern Pennsylvania, has a bright silver new face!

Last November, the tall, slender water tower that many mistake for a silo, built near the parsonage behind Grace Church experienced a bizarre accident. According to our best interpretation of a "highly classified *event*" in Big Bend nine months ago, an unidentified aircraft, probably from Fort Drum in New York, lost part of an engine or fuselage that fell with such surgical accuracy it smashed only the roof of Old Number One without seriously damaging the rest of the tower. For months the immediate area around the tower had been fenced off both electronically and with razor wire to all but the Army and the new pastor, Dr. Jonas Harwell, while the Air Force in its good time cleaned up the mess, collected fragments, and restored the roof, which we reported on in a May editorial, "Your Tax Dollars at Work."

"We thought at first of tearing her down," said Rev. Jonas Harwell, the new pastor at Grace Alliance, "but folks around here have developed a bit of attachment to her as a historical landmark. There's even talk about putting her on a heritage list! Besides, she's too good to destroy. Her pipes are still good. Who knows when she might be needed in an emergency."

Old Number One, presently not in use, is the only man-made enclosed water reservoir owned by a church in Pennsylvania.

✳ ✳ ✳

Note in the Aug. 17 issue of *Susquehanna Voice:*

WHERE DID ALL THE GLITTER GO?

No sooner did residents get used to the new metalic shine of Old Number One, than it was gone! "We had some complaints, especially from motorists," said Rev. Harwell of Grace Church that owns the land as well as the tower itself, so we decided to make it blend in more closely with the trees surrounding it."

For those who haven't recently looked unto the hills in Big Bend, Old Number One now sports a tasteful coat of dull silvery green. "Don't thank me," says Harwell, "Thank Michael Hammond, who's spent most of the past two scorching weeks on scaffolding. For the most part, the special paint had to be slowly applied by brush. This paint will last for years, and will make our tower more like it once looked, as well as making it gracefully blend in with the environment," said the pastor from Grace.

CHAPTER 9

TRIANA SIMMS

TIME: Aug. 24 and 27 [ca 1 yr. later, 8 mo. BEMP]
PLACE: Big Bend High School

Memo from Principal Harry Slater
to Teacher Marvin Cample:

To: Marvin
From: Harry
Re: New Transfer Student
Date: Aug. 24

Marv, I hate to dump this on you, but it can't be helped. I'd like to bypass the sea of paperwork at Guidance and keep this as quiet as I can. Hence no email on this—from or to me. Please destroy after reading.   I trust your confidentiality here.

Got a call from the Rev. Jonas Harwell about a new girl, I mean "brand-new," called Triana Simms, who'll be transferring in. Somehow either he or his church is sponsoring her and Harwell has become her legal guardian. Seems that she's blown in from nowhere, and all her records—grades, birth certificate, everything—have been lost or are on hold somewhere. Some kind of government protection program,

39

says Harwell, and the only thing he has for her is some letter from the U. S. Dept. of Education, giving her a Social Security number and Federal certification that she's free of all forms of AIDS, including Strains III and IV and, further, she's not from any of the three states tied up in the secessionist mess in the west.

She's 15, he says, and should be entering the junior class. Also, it seems, she's had some kind of nurse's training, and, to complicate things, as Harwell's legal ward she'll be living at the church parsonage and "helping with housework." You know there's talk about Harwell and some dying relative that's living with him, hidden away on the second floor. Makes a great story anyway. Stuart's sworn he's seen papers that the man's severely deformed and a hopeless mental case who's been hospitalized somewhere out west. Well, God's healing has its limits I suppose.

Marv, something smells! These church people sure have more faith than I do! Charley and I would swear out a warrant to find out what's going on there if we had anything solid to go on, but Harwell's too smooth. And I'll be darned if I want to get screwed up by the Feds now with all this stiff-handed Triage Doctrine stuff that grew out of the Great Earthquake. Thank God we're in the east!

Whatever Harwell is, he's no fool. And he can look you straight in the eye. Which I like. He's hard to hate. After the way he handled his wife's tragic death just after coming here, and even adopting the Hammond kid who was orphaned by the same accident, and has no family at all except for his aging great-aunt with whom he now lives, he's got quite a few church members worshiping more than just God above.

Marv, neither of us has lived here all our lives or was born yesterday, so keep your eyes open. Next Sunday I'm going to hear him preach. Ever hear a fundamentalist in person? And from Cornell of all places! Even taught some form of martial arts there it's rumored, and I've heard he's a great chess player. I've got nothing against him personally, but he's not going to hurt any of my kids if I can help it!

One more thing. This Triana Simms, whatever else she may be or not be, is severely visually handicapped—near-sighted, says Harwell. She's got a fistful of laws and do-gooders in Harrisburg behind her that say we can't fumble the ball here! Remember, board election this year.

Marv, all I want you to do is informally test the girl and give me an evaluation. Damn the standardized tests and paperwork. School starts in just, gosh, is it four days? Just tell me if she'll fit in and where. It's hard to think she'd be a junior at 15, but you decide. I'll trust your judgment all the way. We can fill in the blanks later. The last thing I want is another flap with Harrisburg—or maybe in this case, the Feds.

I'm stupid to put this all in writing, but I wanted to spell things out, and I've no time to see you. Please destroy this! I have to leave immediately for Harrisburg for a couple of days—now of all times!

41

Mary's talked to Harwell. She can arrange a meeting with Triana. Please get on this immediately. I'll owe you one. Thanks.

-- Harry

✳   ✳   ✳

Memo to Harry from Marv:

To: Harry
From: The friend you owe
Re: Triana Simms
Date: Aug. 27

Relax about Triana. At least for now. Never have I met a high-school student her equal in general knowledge—science, math, English, you name it! Even says she loves languages. When I asked her which ones, she simply smiled and said, "All I run into." But when I must have looked puzzled, she—as if to put me at ease—quickly added, "I enjoy Spanish." End of discussion about that.

She showed me some samples of her writing. If what she gave me was actually hers, I've never seen a high-school student with more talent. Oddly, she said she even enjoys translating, which I wish now I'd pursued but didn't. When I asked her about the three AIDS epidemics, the invasion of killer bees, the fifth amendment rights of suspected terrorists, and

recent arguments about state secession after our great
western disaster, she spoke intelligently, though briefly,
and made a thoughtful comparison of our country
today with the U. S. of yesterday (New Orleans) and
yesteryear (the Civil War). She was pleasant, cautious,
but well informed. Her worldview was remarkably
consistent for someone her age, though naïve and
heavily colored by religion, but what would you
expect? She also said she loved folklore, and I'm sure
she saw this pleased me. Her only noticeable weakness
was regional geography, which only confirms she's
not from around here. An alien, perhaps! If so, raid
the galaxy! Not only is she unnervingly self-assured
without a touch of arrogance—or else is the best
actress I've ever met—she's personable, polite, almost to
a fault.

Harry, she's definitely holding something back—
don't ask me what. But who says we have to tell
everything! I guarantee I haven't played all my cards
yet, so watch out! But thanks for your trust. I value
that. Triana Simms will make a fine junior and with
new guidelines about handicaps from the state, even
with two years in our school you'll have to consider
her for valedictorian—on that I'll wager. The
Holmes twins and Michael Hammond will just have
to move over. They're not even in her league. This
won't go well with Doc Holmes, but since he and both
Hammond and Simms are "Big Bend Grace Macs," or
"Big Macs," as the kids say, we know God can smooth
over any ruffled feathers.

One more thing. I sense the girl hasn't had it easy. One of the few personal things she let slip was that her former nickname was "Quartz," no doubt hung on her by classmates. And she does wear the thickest glasses I've ever seen on a child. But without them I'm convinced that she's nearly blind—as well as stunningly beautiful with blue eyes and naturally dark blond hair.

So shelve your doubts. Quartz Simms is a real gem!

I've done some other checking up as well. First, there's no department of religion at Cornell, and people in philosophy, English, and history say they've never heard of a Rev. Dr. Jonas Harwell. Thought you'd like to know that honesty at our Missionary Alliance Church doesn't exactly run along the straight and narrow.

Now, Harry, I've been too candid, as you know I usually am with people I trust. So it's no monitored e-mail return. Where has personal freedom gone? It's your turn to destroy some words.

I wonder how well he really does play chess. Maybe I'll just invite myself over and find out.

                                                    - Marv

CHAPTER 10

PUTTING IT ALL TOGETHER

To be accused of cheating is embarrassing. And the consequences can be devastating.

Especially if the evidence seems clearly against you. And you're honor students in your last year of high school.

In the story about to be told, one student or the other — or possibly both — had to be lying. Still, proof would be required for punishment, at least in ordinary times. Marvin Cample would be the first to insist upon that.

But when this story begins, times were far from ordinary. In fact, Cample's shocking accusation seems trivial in view of the world-changing events that took place after the school memos written only 8 months earlier.

How these events came about must be told next.

CHAPTER 11

THE INVISIBLE EXPLOSION

TIME: AEMP 01, Day 1
PLACE: Big Bend

On the warm, gray morning of Day 1, the sky suddenly turned white, and the long, rumbling thunder-like boom which immediately followed seemed to kick against everything in its path like a breaking wave.

It was early spring. Everyone's ears rang and rang, but even more haunting was the sudden urge, several confessed, to suck in deeply as if invisible hands pressed hard against their chests. Yet as soon as the push brought terror, it left. People looked up, toward each other, and when they tried to speak, words struggled to pierce the ringing.

Yet no building toppled, no healthy person fell.

However, as the thunder roll ended every TV set, cell phone, computer, every quaxy-pad music player and pocket Quedison, every land-line phone, refrigerator, freezer, modern automobile, power cycle, gasoline pump, electric light, and every other electrical appliance ceased functioning. At first, it seemed like the start of another electrical storm, no stranger to Big Bend. A time to gather in small children. A time to bathe in the quiet natural darkness and fresh country air that precede the wind and wetness of a spring storm. A time to stop and rest. With acts of God, work could wait.

But this was hardly an act of God, at least not an ordinary one. At least as far as anyone could tell.

And if a storm were on its way, there was not a trace of wetness, and after the washing of what seemed like a thick, rolling of air, there was no wind, not even a breeze.

Soon it was discovered that everything not "on," not plugged in, was also dead. Rare exceptions were flashlights, some, but not all, of the battery-powered emergency lights at the medical clinic and County National Bank. When almost every automobile in motion rolled to a halt—some in the middle of intersections—and the clocks and watches that hadn't gone completely blind froze forever at 10:19 AM, the effect was unnerving. People knew that something extraordinary had happened.

It was unusually warm, a summer-like Saturday morning. Here and there up and down Main St. tiny businesses that seemed left over from busier days—Mildred's Antiques, a wireless but now useless coffee and magazine shop, a carpet and floor vinyl store—mixed easily with tall frame houses, many which had a patch or two of green or white paint peeling off an eave or wall. Everywhere porches lay naked to the waiting trappings of spring.

On these porches, screen door after screen door snapped open and banged shut, punctuating the ringing and otherwise eerie calm. Mothers with small children spilled outside onto cracked sidewalk stones that had been in place for over a century, joining handfuls of shoppers and idlers staring in disbelief. From the middle of Main St. puzzled drivers emerged from their stalled cars.

Something terribly unusual must have happened.

Something new, very different, that ran far past the mountain.

The trouble wasn't just limited to electrical failure. One teenager wearing ear buds tuned to his Quedison was found dead on a steel sewer grating outside of Martin's Movie Palace. No sign of injury. At the library in Hillside Haven two senior citizens with implanted needle tuners toppled out of their chairs dead. Three other active seniors with older pacemakers were driven to their beds.

Overhead, an antique Piper Cub, now held hostage by an upgraded ignition system, attempted an emergency landing, but crashed, killing pilot and passenger. On the ground, automobiles, also controlled by electronic cockpits, rolled to their deaths, bending fenders and bringing more human injury, mostly minor. Others whose lives or livelihoods depended upon machines, lifts, elevators, and power tools suffered misfortune.

But all seemed to know—though none said so then—that if what suddenly happened in Big Bend had also happened in Philadelphia and nearby Binghamton, the consequences in those places must have been horrifying.

By nightfall it was clear that there would be no "bounce back," as had occurred in Hawaii more than a half century earlier. Electrical current had not just been punched down. It had died. And all that depended on it probably had been "melted" and was useless. To get things going again wouldn't be easy.

But not everything electrical was destroyed. Batteries and dry cells still functioned. Many gasoline-fueled generators, especially older ones, were unaffected. A few cars, those made before the early 1970's, and familiar in 4th of July parades, were unscathed.

Most exciting was finding that several large antique radios, made long before FM, still functioned. These radios with bulky vacuum tubes—instead of transistors, circuit boards, and microchips—were the first instruments in the 1940's to bring their owners live news of World War II. Time, of course, replaced them all. But throw them away? Not necessarily in Big Bend! The nooks and crannies of many large, sagging barns—too big to survive in cities or suburbia—would soon yield many treasures from the past.

Several antique radios, as some guessed, when properly grounded and connected to antennas and batteries or generators, would spring to life!

And so they did!

On the evening of Day 3, after hours of scanning the static-filled short-wave frequencies on a four-foot-high Philco radio made in the 1930's, that was set up in the narthex of Grace Church, and later the main auditorium, Rev. Harwell and Elder Amos Crandel stumbled across the voice of the President of the United States, broadcasting on an emergency frequency using vacuum-tube technology from some secret bunker below the White House or in Maryland.

Despite an attempt at bravado, the President sounded so impersonal, so helpless, it was embarrassing. The fiery rhetoric from his cleverly orchestrated and recent campaign had vanished. There had been no "foreign attack," he insisted. But there had been several "atmospheric explosions" — whether nuclear or non-nuclear undetermined, source also undetermined — said to be "harmless" to people, animals, and buildings, but fatal to *electronic* circuitry.

Power-generating plants, which had become totally dependent on digital equipment, were out everywhere. No "quick fix" was in sight. There was a near total blackout of communication. Computerized records and files everywhere were "down," and though he would not admit it, had probably been destroyed as well. Taxes, both state and federal, were "temporarily suspended," as well as welfare benefits, payment of interest or dividends, Social Security, or other pension plans. All federal and state transactions were "on hold until further notice." There would be "no bank checks, salary checks, foreclosures, or evictions from lack of payment."

What had happened was an "act of God," though he insisted that God was not "involved." His voice sounded measured, almost mechanical. "Nearly all motor vehicles, aircraft, and ships are useless," added the President, "so we're all in the same boat." The attempt at humor, if deliberate, failed to amuse. He tried to make clear that in spite of great tragedy — which appeared to involve so many — the

United States government was intact, and his family, his cabinet and their families, and other officials were alive and safe at undisclosed locations.

This same message, nearly 15-minutes long, was repeated at different times over the next four days, as if new listeners would be tuning in.

On the fifth day after the power failed, the President announced a set of guidelines "approved unanimously" by the U. S. Supreme Court that would govern American life for the foreseeable future. People in the narthex of Grace Church took care to write them down word for word.

FIVE GUIDING PRINCIPLES FOR THE NEW AGE

All American citizens, and others living in America, from this time forward until further notice, are to do the following:

1. Regard the day of explosions as AEMP 01, Day 1. <u>Regular calendar time for immediate practical reasons, in terms of business and ordinary law, is temporarily suspended</u>. When regular calendar time is restored by Presidential order, business obligations, ordinary law, and Constitutional guarantees would return to regular BEMP status.

2. <u>Everyone must stay where they are and organize</u>. Since everyone had suffered alike [which, of course, wasn't true], travel was counterproductive. People were to organize themselves into self-governing territories to be administered by provisional committees headed by elected governor-generals with war-power authority. To these leaders any nearby military units and service personnel were to report.

3. <u>Everyone must establish cottage industries and a temporary barter economy</u>. Skilled people, regardless of age, must quickly produce a variety of essential products and services; they must also

train others in an apprentice system, and establish a workable way to exchange products and services.

4. <u>Everyone must volunteer to help those with special needs</u>. Many of the old, sick, orphaned, or disabled would have special needs. Good Americans during the Age of AEMP would volunteer at least one day a week to serve such people, and provide other services for the common good, without expecting to receive compensation or remuneration of any kind.

5. <u>Everyone must pray</u>. Each person should pray to his or her own deity, regardless of denomination or creed, and seek to rise to his or her own divine potential. Further, there would be no persecution or intolerance of any kind for the religious beliefs of those who follow the above guidelines.

And so the Susquehanna Territory, about 25 miles long and 18 miles across—which included Montrose and New Milford—was born.

One of the happier notes amid the new confusion was how Susquehannites, especially the young, responded. After the dead were quickly buried, and the injured treated as well as possible, sorrow was quickly set aside—perhaps driven by a collective hidden fear. People banded together and sprang into action.

The five weeks of school that remained were cancelled, and everyone received automatic "passes" for incomplete and obviously unachieved schoolwork. Teenagers, already in the habit of school-day gathering, were organized into "bicycle brigades" reporting first to the schools, then to the 4-H, scout, and church leaders and to the new Governor-General and his officers.

Helping the hurting, assessing the damage, and carrying messages back and forth came first. Then arranging a meeting of mayors and councilmen in centrally located New Milford, to make rules, establish boundaries. Refugees could be expected immediately from nearby

Binghamton to the north, and probably eventually from Scranton, Philadelphia, and New York to the south and southeast.

This realization was viewed with terror, and perhaps more than anything else, cemented a surprising unity among often quarreling individualists.

In hours after the initial explosions, comparatively poor Susquehanna had probably become rich compared to her neighbors. At least everyone seemed to sense it. Though no war had been won — much less fought — citizens eyed their comparative bounty as spoil. Guns and ammunition; candles; batteries, both ordinary and the revolutionary sun-rechargeable ones — totally free of microcircuitry, fortunately — that had been developed and mass-produced only eighteen months earlier; gas and oil lamps; and oil of every kind which was plentiful in supply disappeared from stores in less than three days, to say nothing of foodstuffs — flour, bread, milk, canned goods (and manual can openers), cigarettes, tobacco, matches, liquor, salt, canning jars, pectin, sodium nitrate — that might be needed in the short term…and perhaps longer. Credit cards, no longer able to be processed by machines that had died, were useless, though handwritten notes of credit were — for some — extended to ridiculous limits. Paper money was still good and — at first — was taken at customary face value as thousands of dollars quickly exchanged hands. And for a few hours — but a few hours only — personal bank checks were accepted on the same basis as cash.

Then, as supplies of money ran low, prices began to skyrocket. It was then, more or less naturally, the barter system kicked in on its own. Tote bags, or "bank totes," or just "totes" as they were commonly called, made from canvas, heavy cloth, vinyl cord became standard traveling accessories if venturing more than a hundred feet from one's house. This spawned a new greeting: "Need any Xtras?" to which a passerby might reply, "Nothing really, thanks, but know anybody who'd trade some matches and seed corn for canning jars? If so, send 'em my way."

"Xtras," always spelled that way, and with "X" always capitalized with the respect given to deity, just as "Internet" always had been. Extra things to trade, things that others might need, became the new capital in AEMP.

There was a feverish attempt to preserve frozen food, especially meat. From the parking lot of Jiffy Supermarket downtown to the backyard of the remotest mountain cabin, backyard fires sprang up as people attempted to salt—even by crushing 50-lb. field blocks for cattle—and smoke and dry rapidly thawing meat.

Bicycle Brigaders (soon known as BB's) and 4-Hers on horseback proved invaluable. Frantically, they delivered pamphlets from the Cooperative Extension on techniques of preserving food—a skill not unfamiliar to many Susquehannites. With this literature soon exhausted and no copiers working (until several old manual mimeograph machines were resurrected), children, riding endlessly up and down winding mountain roads, relayed precious information they'd committed to memory.

Fortunately, it was spring and the beginning of an early summer. Seeds and fertilizers were abundant at the three Agway stores. Although few believed that a bounce back to normal wouldn't be too long around the corner, overnight, it seemed, there developed an overwhelming interest in gardening. Faith in the soil seemed to become a common bond and, somehow, lawns of fresh lumpy overturned soil became symbols of dignity and hope.

But weeks passed and things did not change. There was no invasion, at least not a foreign one, as some had feared. At least not yet. And if a nuclear explosion had caused their difficulties, nothing that lived seemed harmed.

However, for most people life had changed dramatically.

Commuters to Binghamton and many in local service jobs were stranded and without work. Salaries had ended and with skyrocketing prices paper money held little value or interest. Axes, saws, and garden tools became cherished possessions kept under lock and key. Bartering became a fine art, and people threw themselves into practical work which relieved frustrations and held meaning. Especially in a rural area like Susquehanna the matter of honor had to be at least superficially displayed. There was the matter of one's name and how it was regarded. At great risk was one branded a "laggard" or a "slacker" in temporary hard times.

And physical work was a way to pass the hours.

Surprisingly, law and order held. Perhaps because a strong and respected governor-general was quickly elected and he, his mayor-colonels, and council proved unusually wise. Perhaps because there was a renewed spiritual interest and prayer. Perhaps it was because of guilt and fear — guilt, because others were suffering more, fear that things in Susquehanna could get much worse.

This was reinforced by the steady flow of American refugees who had fled from the cities, bringing stories of starvation, murder, barbarism, and horrors beyond description. Thousands, perhaps millions had died within days. There had been outbreaks of disease, though the first outsiders said little about it, fearing their own banishment.

Opinion about what to do about the refugees was sharply divided. Supplies of everything were limited. Everyone was worried about food spoilage and disease. Rationing became necessary and everyone accepted it. But with a growing influx of refugees, especially people with no skills whatsoever about how to live off the land, tensions rose.

This led to several things:

The governor-general ordered a local census and Susquehannites were methodically counted, registered, and numbered. Numbers were memorized. To have a unique number in the Susquehanna Territory was a treasured possession. And stealing one's number and using it inappropriately was considered a felony. (Plenty of service people were available to do this and were willing to do so. And with the scarcity of manual typewriters — there were only a very few — legible handwriting quickly improved and became a fine art!)

Males 15 through 65 were organized into patriot military brigades of minutemen, with headquarters in the three main towns. All were under the command of the Governor-General and were expected to bear arms and give service at a moment's notice.

Hunting laws were suspended. The 4-H leaders were given the charge of organizing a pony express to deliver local messages.

Auto transportation, except for the Governor-General (who commandeered a 1964 red Volkswagen Beetle), his mayor-colonels, and certain emergency vehicles, were banned to conserve oil and gasoline. Most fortunate for Susquehannites was the installation in Montrose two years earlier of federal emergency reservoirs of diesel oil and kerosene which, if necessary, could be tapped mechanically without electrical power. A registry of auxiliary working generators owned by farmers and building contractors was made and a quartermaster corps was organized to regulate their use in hospitals and public buildings. An 11 PM curfew was put into effect.

Most important was the "Great Wall" that was hastily built. At first, in many places it was little more than a barbed wire fence, but day by day it was upgraded and improved. "If disease is to be kept out," said the Governor-General, "and if law and order is to be kept in, and we are to preserve what little we have for ourselves, a wall must be built and vigorously defended."

To define the new boundaries a strip of forest or field 100 feet wide was burned completely around the irregular 25-mile-long, slightly narrower, roughly oval area of countryside and mountains. This strip was continually patrolled by minutemen with standing orders to first warn, then shoot to kill anyone who attempted to cross.

This was highly controversial. But on this the Governor-General refused to budge and, right or wrong, the newly born Susquehanna Territory began to establish its own identity. It even flew its own flag—an American flag with all its stars removed from the field of blue, replaced by a golden S. Often this "temporary" flag was flown alongside the controversial newest American flag with 47 stars or the more familiar one with 50 stars. The flag of the Territory very soon, according to the newest refugees, became a respected emblem of a strong and safe mountain island surrounded by suspected anarchy, disease, and terror.

CHAPTER 12

THE EPISTLE TO BIG BEND

The following document, typed on a manual, nonelectric typewriter and crudely printed on a hastily restored hand-cranked mimeograph machine — both at least 60 years old — was handed out at the Grace Missionary Alliance Church of Big Bend, Pennsylvania, on a Sunday in May on Day 12, AEMP 01.

*   *   *

The Rev. Dr. Jonas Harwell, pastor by the will of God at the Grace Missionary Alliance Church at Big Bend, to all Christians and Other Fellow Citizens and Refugees of the newly formed Susquehanna Territory:

Grace and peace to you from God our Father through our Lord Jesus Christ during these difficult and disturbing times.

Praise be to God who has blessed us in the heavenly realms with every spiritual blessing in Christ.

In view of such blessing which is commonly recognized and accepted by believers who have received the Holy Spirit through salvation in Jesus Christ, I hope you won't consider me presumptuous to share my counsel, opinion, and feelings in the same manner as our spiritual father St. Paul. Not that I am an Apostle, certainly not! Nor do I claim any special inspiration for these words. But they do reflect a wisdom that God has let me gain that I believe is relevant for these troubled days.

Having studied science in my university days at Cornell University, I have some understanding about what I think has befallen us, and as a Christian, chosen by the Lord Jesus Christ, I care deeply about how we should think and act. Above all, we must remain calm, faithful, and Christ-like in these difficult times.

It is now the 12th day since our global catastrophe.

I say "global" deliberately, though I cannot prove it. After days of continually scanning shortwave bands on the 1930 vacuum-tube Philco radio we've placed in the narthex of our church, we have picked up only two signals in addition to the intermittent broadcasting through vacuum-tube technology of Radio USA from Maryland.

On Day 4 we received an unintelligible, garbled broadcast from Radio Jerusalem. And on Days 4, 5, and 7, we clearly heard news of unprecedented horror and tragedy from one of the most powerful stations in the world, HCJB in Ecuador. But all we learned was that, like here, all electrical power had failed and Quito, with its teeming hundreds of thousands, was in chaos. We have detected nothing whatever from the BBC, Radio Moscow, Radio Persia, or Radio Beijing. And nothing from anywhere beyond Day 10, except from our own American emergency station in Maryland.

While death has also touched our rural towns and townships, our suffering must be nothing compared to what has happened in our great cities.

We, and much—if not all—of the world, have been drained of our invisible life blood, regularly transmitted electricity, for 12 days, and I am convinced any transfusion to restore life as we knew it is very far off.

What has caused this? The culprit, I believe, is EMP or electromagnetic pulse.

Let me tell you what I think has happened:

Scientists have known about the effects of electromagnetic pulse for more than a half century. It wasn't until 1962, however, that we knew the strength of this electromagnetic surge, or "push," could be so powerful and crippling from nuclear explosions detonated high in the atmosphere. And as research from the 1990s showed, EMP was not only dangerous with nuclear blasts, but with nonnuclear ones as well.

And just what is the effect of EMP on delicate electrical connections? It may be compared to an invisible foot stepping into a shoe filled with grasshoppers. The marvelous, high-jumping creatures are instantly crushed, destroyed, even though after the foot is removed, insect parts are still recognizable and some grasshoppers may still look intact.

The discovering of the devastating force of EMP immediately led to decades of frantic, highly classified research in every civilized first-world country to find ways to shield and protect extremely tiny microcircuitry, which is sensitive to sudden electronic pulses. This was one major—but little publicized—objective of the Star Wars Defense initiative long ago in the Reagan-Bush years. Ironically, as research progressed a bewildering array of newer, faster, smaller, and even more delicate electronic systems became available. There seemed to be no end to human ingenuity.

These electronic wonders spurred an economic war which, to our embarrassment, Asia began slowly to win. There was no time to wait, to properly design adequate protection. Caution thrown to the winds. The strange new marvels of science invaded all technology like a virus. Everything became infected. In short, research at the Pentagon was always at least one step behind—if indeed it was on the right path. And large-scale realistic testing was out of the question. America couldn't keep up. But no country could.

At first, some thought that any effects from a surge of EMP would be temporary, but this was proved wrong.

What then could be done? There was the promise of "shielding." And the promise of materials like fiber optics which were said to be immune to EMP. But the digital electronics which joined nonmetal parts together was not. The long glass chain was riddled with weak links. Circuit-breaking devices were also developed, but many wondered if they would work since EMP was as fast as lightning, the age-old conqueror of nearly every conventional device.

For years we as everyday citizens have routinely handed the mysterious wizardry that controls our lives "across a counter" to be repaired, or more likely discarded and replaced by something from shelves of parts or whole devices that are newer, better, and faster. Now the magic has gone. The "fix-it shop" is out of business and the shelves of replacement materials are useless.

So what do we have left? We have ourselves and the God who made us. May you who read this never forget that God has saved us, and provided salvation from far greater tragedy.

When will everything be restored? I have no idea, except it will be a long, long time. The machines which made the machines which made our machines have also probably died. And so has most of the discarded materials of our older, pre-electronic technology. Science has routinely pushed away history like an ignorant, pesky child. Now the hands of technology have lost the present; to regain it we will have to relearn the past. And when our lost things once again start to reappear, if they do, lines will be long to claim them.

As to <u>what</u> or <u>who</u> is behind this—I have no idea.

I think we can rule out sunspots, comets, or anything natural, because there was no astrophysical warning.

And because of what seems like a huge global effect, a simple "accident" doesn't seem likely. The effect of EMP lessens with distance, so there must have been many explosions strategically spaced, or some chain reaction, so that just the way we live has been stripped away and not our lives themselves.

Then who's to blame? A foreign country? If so, things backfired and they hurt themselves—unless they consider their lives cheap and are counting on superior numbers to offset our superior weaponry.

Are we facing a terrorist threat? If so, no demands have been made—at least that we know about.

Was it the work of a madman? I doubt this could have been the work of a single person. The destruction was too vast and selective.

Have we been visited, or attacked, from another world? This can't be ruled out, though we've no direct reason to believe it. If such proves to be true, I urge you to remember that our Almighty God and Savior is author and ruler of <u>all</u> worlds and not just our own.

Is this the work of Satan and his demons? First, has not our great enemy already been at work among us? If he were <u>directly</u> behind this, at least we can say that he employed no device beyond our present scientific understanding.

Is this the beginning of the Great Tribulation prophesied in Scripture? Or the time of Christ's Second Coming? If so, we are not the first to ask such a question in the face of great tragedy. The apostles wondered about this two thousand years ago when they suffered.

And, more recently, the suffering of Christians in Holland, in Russia, in Ethiopia, in South Africa, in New Orleans, and recently on our western coast led to the asking of these questions. And the only answer has been silence. Christ will most definitely return a second time as He promised, but the time of His coming according to Holy Scripture was not known to St. Peter or St. Paul, or even to the heavenly host.

I am no exception.

Is what has happened a sign of the "end times" as some have suggested? If so, it is hard right now to say just why. While we live from day to day we must ask questions, search Scripture—the whole Scripture—but I cannot, yet, go further about what may happen next, for I do not know.

As Christians we have a blessed hope, a promise, a secure future. But on earth we may be called to suffer. We have just had dramatically impressed upon us the sober reality that a measure of life, a moment of death—that's all that's certain. Now everyone says so openly. None of the ancient prophecies told exactly how certain particulars would come to pass—indeed, there were no suitable words—and none of our novels or movies ever prepared us for what we have seen, and, even more important, have come to feel.

And no movie or television screens still live to take us around the world, or even our neighborhood. There are no projection screens to paint with words for worship, and no computers able to share needs and knowledge.

For our new-found silence, I ask you to make new songs for us to sing, as Scripture has always encouraged.

I ask you to look your neighbor in the eye and take his hand. When you must speak, do so slowly and loud enough to be heard.

There is much we do not know. There is much for us to discover. Much to rediscover.

I do, however, know this: Our Lord has told us that if we have two cloaks and our neighbor has none, we are to cheerfully give of our bounty, and our Father will reward us.

I ask you, brothers and sisters in Christ, to walk in the way of the One who gave Himself for us. Blessed is he who puts to death his own selfish interest on behalf of another. Be as wise as a serpent with your time and your talents, but always be generous and kind, reflecting God's love.

Pray for the President of the United States, who

only seven days ago gave us his "Five Guiding
Principles for the New Age." Pray that he and
our other leaders will seek only the God of Holy
Scripture.

Pray for your Governor-General and mayor-colonels,
who rule because of God's sovereign will.

Pray for each other continually, and cheerfully
bear one another's burdens in these unusual times.

Pray especially for those beyond our walls who
suffer far worse than we, and pray that kindness
will—with a greater force than electromagnetism—
melt away every barrier that separates us.

Above all, love God with all your heart, mind,
soul, and strength, which is the first and great
commandment.

Peace to you all from God the Father of all and the
Lord Jesus Christ.

I and those with me here at Grace Alliance remain
your servants. I trust you will circulate this
letter—in the spirit in which it was written—
to believers and all others living within the
Susquehanna Territory.

PART II

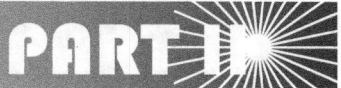

THE ACCUSATION

"The world may be going to hell all around us, but it's not going to happen in my class!"

Chapter. 13

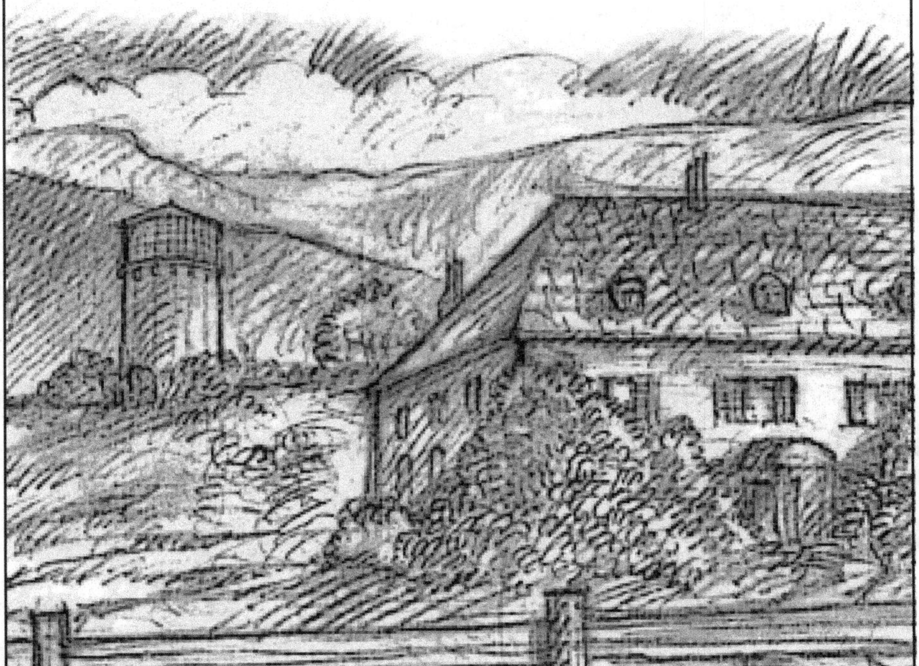

THE SINISTER CHAIRS

TIME: *AEMP 01, Day 318*

PLACE: *Second floor, science classroom,*

                Big Bend High School

arvin Cample is sitting behind his teacher's desk. On the front row at two battered, left-handed student desks Triana Simms and Michael Hammond sit side by side. It is late afternoon and, except for the three, the building is empty. The winter sky has just darkened. A single oil lamp lights the room. Cample has just accused Triana and Michael of cheating…

"So you both refuse to admit you've done anything wrong."

Cample's clothes were old and ordinary, in no way distinctive or defining. Veins stood out on his neck above the open collar of his faded plaid shirt. His slick black hair, showing no trace of gray, was combed back neatly. His angular frame perched on the edge of the shapeless oak chair that had endured generations behind a similar, massive oak desk. The echoing tick of a tinny wind-up alarm clock next to the oil lamp indicated 4:55. The teacher's obsidian eyes focused into the direction he aimed his words.

"Mr. Cample, I don't see the humor—" Michael struggled to match Triana's cool manner and knew he'd failed.

"Look, Michael, I know people, and I know you both well, so—"

"Obviously not well enough!" Michael interrupted.

"Michael, let him finish," said Triana, raising her voice just enough.

Uncharacteristically, Cample stood and, surrendering his obvious advantage, walked over to the window and stared outside.

The girl turned toward the boy and took off her glasses as she did on those rare occasions they talked to each other in class.

Michael's eyes met hers, and though his must appear fuzzy to her, that was in no way true the other way around. His mind raced.

A casual observer might say the girl preferred to be seen, rather than see things for herself which required special thick glasses. But classmates knew better. She just wasn't that way. Pondering at the expense of observing, yes, possibly, and listening instead of speaking, usually, but being aloof, hurtful, or dishonest—never.

He recalled those few times he'd gone to the church parsonage where Triana, his adopted father, and a housekeeper lived. If the girl ever saw him arrive, she'd slip away, and busy herself elsewhere in the rambling two-story building where she seemed to always be. She was fiercely private. Never had he spoken to her alone at the parsonage, and except for occasional expected chatter at church, rarely anywhere else.

Triana Simms, with unmistakably blue eyes that were hard to turn away from. And her distinctive perfume, with a story behind it, was pleasant.

Triana Simms. Without glasses nearly blind. But not without radar. Navigating the crowded downstairs hallway between classes seemed to come easy. Dim light, very common in AEMP time, didn't seem to bother her. Triana the brain. "The best in the test," according to Stacy Martin, obviously not expressing a compliment. Mysterious to be sure, out of the limelight by choice, "not easy to approach, but not unkind," said some, "a classic loner," seen mainly at school and church. And since she always backed away from favoritism and attention that teachers sometimes offer to the rare student that masters everything they teach, she had won grudging respect.

With his 20-20 vision Michael had watched the new girl's star rise for more than a year. If knowledge belonged to kings and queens, and there was a single throne in Big Bend, Michael knew she would sit on it. He and the Holmes twins, and probably a half dozen other wannabes, had been deposed. She was queen by default. And if she were a bit more open, it wouldn't take much imagination to see her play the part.

But palaces are large, and Michael knew he also had a key which he'd earned. And he wasn't about to throw it away.

Since his parents' deaths four years earlier, he'd lived in a drafty large frame house with his great-aunt Steffi, who worshipped the ground he walked on.

Rev. Harwell, his adopted father who lived three blocks away, most decidedly did not. But the busy minister was usually fair, Michael had to admit.

If things had been different, he might have walked away from the minister's generous kindness. Who was Harwell to tell him what to do? But he was now bonded to the man by blood — the blood of tragedy — since the accident that had killed both his parents and also the minister's wife. And this led to that Easter three years earlier when Michael heard again — really heard — the familiar story about the voluntary suffering of Jesus, and the boy publicly, but very quietly, decided to become a Christian.

And, until days ago, there was basketball and his steady girlfriend Stacy Martin, head cheerleader of the Cougars. But at 1:30 PM on Day 304, basketball ended for Michael when he became one-half of a foolish fight that erupted on court. The mayor-colonel himself, sitting in the bleachers, had stepped forward and banished both players from the sport permanently. There would be "no brawling in school of Susquehannites among themselves. We hang together or we hang one by one when the enemy comes," badly paraphrasing the famous quote. But so far, no enemy had come. The altercation had been nothing — and

70

would have amounted to little in the old days when games were played at night under lights, and not in the middle of the day. But the old days had passed. Since the incident, Stacy Martin hadn't spoken to him.

But with travel in the AEMP age so restricted, basketball had become little more than an intramural sport between the three Susquehanna Territory high schools, usually played outside, mainly on Saturday and Sunday afternoons, weather permitting. Seeing one's breath after making a touchdown was one thing, seeing it after a 3-point shot and crashing the boards for rebounds was another.

Who cares? Michael had said to himself, worrying more about his adopted father's reaction. He had been "calm and brave" was all that Harwell mentioned later, but the humiliation and unfairness lingered. For weeks now, with vague rumors of a coming war, with the rotating duty of armed men patrolling the "Great Wall" — as everyone called it — clearing land, cutting and distributing firewood, along with the pressures of the camps of refugees grandfathered in before the cutoff, with all this and a strange restlessness Susquehannites had begun to talk about — all this made sports, grades, even school seem almost trivial. But life went on. It always had.

And would. Though now some had fresh doubts...

Suddenly, Cample returned to his chair as if pulled by a cord. Once again he sat and leaned forward as if hinged at the waist.

"Look," said Cample, "the world may be going to hell all around us, but it's not going to happen in my class! Understand? I've got some questions and I want some straight answers. And I want the *truth!*" He paused.

No response.

"Christians. You both claim you're Christians, 'Big Bend Grace Macs,' or 'Big Macs' as they say."

Michael wanted to ask about the missing antecedent to "they," as they — the senior English class — had discussed with Cample only two

71

days ago. But he held it.

"Yes," said Triana.

"Yes, guilty!" said Michael, "That is, of being a Christian, and a 'Big Bend Grace Mac' — but *not* cheating!"

"So we can cut the foolishness, and I can count on your both telling me the truth? That's your Jesus way, isn't it?"

"Yes" — Michael hesitated — "yes, but..."

But before he could finish, Triana cut in.

"Mr. Cample, what *I* say will be true."

Her words were deliberate and dared questioning. But uncharacteristically, her hands began to tremble slightly. Michael shivered. He'd never seen her like that. Then, for the first time, he saw the silver medallion the size of a quarter hanging around her neck. On it was a large raised X which looked as if a small icicle hung at each point.

Michael sensed pressure building. Regardless of what Cample had against them, this was combat. And Cample — so far — had the edge. Something had to be done quickly — anything to neutralize their opponent's advantage.

Suddenly Michael stood, walked to the closest row, picked up two right-handed student desks, one with each hand, returned and, noticing that the medallion was now tucked out of sight, took the girl by the hand, brought her to her feet, seated her in the new chair, and seated himself beside her. As Triana smoothed her lap, a matchbox-sized metal box with a tiny blinking blue light tumbled from her skirt pocket onto the floor.

The box itself was strange, but most startling was that Michael hadn't seen anything so small, so delicate, so electronic *that worked* in more than ten months!

Instantly, Michael covered it with his foot, slid it back under his chair, at the same time deliberately dropping his pen. Bending to pick it up, he palmed the strange box and slipped it in his pocket. Without even glancing down, Triana studiously inspected her glasses. Small drops of sweat beaded her forehead. She knew. But had Cample seen? Michael slid his chair closer to hers. SSSRRRAAAWWK. When the girl reached up to brush back her hair, her hand touched Michael's. Lightly he clasped her fingers and held them. Cample arched his eyebrows.

"Should I even ask?" the teacher asked.

The advantage now had fallen to the boy and girl.

"Your seating plan was sinister," said Michael.

"Sinister?" said Cample.

Triana was unshaken. She broke into a gentle smile.

"Yes, Mr. Cample. Remember when we studied knights and heraldry in class?" she asked. "'Sinister' means 'left-handed.'"

"I know!" said Cample.

"Which neither of us is," said Michael.

"Neither?" Cample raised his eyebrows.

"Neither left-handed or evil," added Triana as if they were enjoying following a script they had practiced reading.

Michael started to slip his fingers away but the girl held fast. For the moment they had the upper hand. But "upper" over what? What was Cample up to?

Michael glanced toward the window. A dark cloud pushed across the dying light of the pale winter sunset. Bare limbs of the giant maples bordering the schoolyard tirelessly brushed the gray sky.

"I'll come right to the point," said Cample. Michael jerked back to attention. "Your honors class project instructions were simple and clear. Each of you was to locate and bring to class an 'old story' that best represented the values and hopes you consider important. *And no one, under penalty of failure, was to consult with, or discuss with, any other student or anyone else.* Am I correct?"

"Yes."

73

"Yes."

"And did both of you follow these guidelines?"

"Yes," said Michael.

"Yes," said Triana, "though, let me remind you, you refused my *first* choice, the Gospel of Matthew."

"And, Ms. Simms, you know fully well why I did — any biblical accounts that mention the resurrection of Jesus Christ..."

"OOOOOOOOOOOHHHHHHHHH!" came a sound from the corner of the room.

"...that mention Jesus Christ..."

"OOOOOOOOOOOOOHHHHHHHHH!"

"...have been judged inappropriate for the public classroom." Only Cample could keep a thought on track — in a hurricane or while having a heart attack! As he finished, all three found themselves standing, facing the large door of the storeroom, the knob of which the bird had earlier rested on. Someone — or something — was twisting and rattling the knob from the other side. But the door refused to open.

Michael felt the hair rise on his arms. Something had to be going wrong. He tiptoed across the floor stopping ten feet away. Triana put on her glasses and followed. Cample picked up a thick meterstick from the chalk tray and held it on his shoulder like a bat. He joined them.

Except for the knob and ticking clock, all was silent.

A minute passed.

As Cample eased sideways around to the front of the room, his slender six-foot frame cast a smaller and smaller shadow against the wall. He approached Michael, waved him back, and positioned himself a meter from the closet door.

"Come out!" he ordered. "We know you're in there! Come out!" Cample raised his stick but refused to go closer. "COME OUT!" The veins stood out on his neck. **"IN THE NAME OF *JESUS CHRIST*, COME OUT! DAMN IT!"**

74

Suddenly, the door exploded open with such force that the top hinge ripped away. Cample leaped back. A thin boy, barely five-and-a-half feet tall wearing jeans and an orange COUGARS sweatshirt stomped out and scraped his shoes on the floor as if wiping off mud. His longish hair was tangled over his pasty-looking forehead as if he were just waking up. His eyes, however, blazed. They fixed on Cample. He raised his arm and pointed to the teacher's chest. Cample began inching backward.

"**Forindal quaar veren!**" said the boy. "**FORINDAL QUAAR VEREN! FORINDAL QUAAR VEREN!**" The words were carefully articulated, but the voice was a man's, deep and guttural. Suddenly the boy sprang like a cat. Cample jumped back, raising his stick.

"ENGLISH, boy! Say it in ENGLISH! Who are you? What do you think you're doing? Eavesdropping? Get out! Or get expelled!"

"Mr. Cample," Michael whispered, "it's Jacky Fenton. I know him. A sophomore from South Milford. He tried out for junior varsity. Coach cut him 'cause believe it or not, he wasn't aggressive enough!"

Michael walked up to the boy and stuck out his hand.

"Jacky, get a hold of yourself! Nobody's going to hurt you! What's wrong?"

"**FORINDAL QUAAR VEREN!**"

Keeping his eyes riveted on Cample, as if the senior weren't even there, the boy flung his arm out sideways catching Michael on the side of his head, dropping him like a sawed-through tree. Cample's eyes bulged.

"That's my student and this is my classroom, kid!" declared Cample. He swung the meterstick down like a sword, but with perfect timing the boy's other arm shot up and out, parrying it away and snapping it in two.

Silently, Triana stepped into the boy's path, seeming to take him as well as the other two by surprise.

"Please, Mr. Cample." She nudged the teacher aside and faced the boy. Deliberate or not, the silver medallion with the X on it again was showing. Her words were slow and sounded carefully shaped. And the voice was her own.

"En Gallyin noma, dar ferrin meray!" she said.

"OOOOOOOHHHHHHHRR!   OOOOOOOOHHHHHHRRRR!" the boy responded. Was it a roar or a moan? Michael wondered. It sounded like both. Jacky fixed his eyes on the girl's medallion and backed away. "OOOOHHHHHRR. Ooooohhhhhrr."

"En Gallyin noma, dar ferrin meray," the girl repeated. Suddenly, the lamplight on the desk flickered and the boy began to twist and turn like a reptile shedding its skin. In seconds every trace of wildness was gone. He turned to Michael who'd made it back to his feet, then Cample. His eyes were now ordinary, but his white face had reddened.

"Wha...What's goin' on? I...I must've fallen asleep..." He rubbed his cheek as if waking. Michael sensed the boy was on the verge of tears.

"Where'd you learn that move!" Michael said, rubbing his jaw.

"Move? What move? Whaddya talkin' about? What? What am I doing here? I...I gotta go!" He turned and headed for the classroom door. When he got there, Rev. Harwell, almost invisible in his black suit and tie, was standing just outside holding a nearly empty canvas trader's tote that in earlier days would have badly clashed against his suit. The minister, well into middle age, had an athletic build. Light from the lamp reflected on his bald forehead.

"Jacky! Jacky, look at me!" he offered. "Can I help?"

"NO! I...I don't need no preacher. Don't need nuthin'. Let me by!" Harwell stepped aside and the boy tore past and disappeared.

Triana spoke first.

"Jonas, I'm sorry. But what else could I do? This is crazy. Michael and I were called in here after school and I still don't know what's going on."

"Mr....is it 'Dr.'...Cample?" asked Harwell. The minister entered the room and extended his hand.

"No PhD yet. If ever. Just 'Marvin'...or 'Marv.'"

"Well, Marvin, I'm Jonas, as you just heard, and almost everyone except very old ladies and newborns call me that. Good to meet you! Looks like you love these kids almost as much as I do." He paused. "I sure don't know what's going on, but these are my kids and I'd like to find out. How about a long talk—the four of us? But not here. How about back at the parsonage? It's suppertime, and Sally's been cooking shamelessly and you'd be doing her and my waistline a big favor if you"—he turned and faced the boy—"if all of you came and ate. If there's trouble, I want to get to the bottom of it. But first, let's eat."

"Supper? Uh...Okay, Jonas," said Cample. "Quite frankly, I've been wanting to meet you, maybe play chess...I, I hear you have this thing about truth. Well, Jonas, I warn you, I'm not religious, but so do I."

"Yet you call upon Jesus Christ," Harwell interrupted.

"I what?"

"Called upon Jesus Christ in front of the closet there." Harwell pointed.

"I...I did what? Jonas, you can't be serious! I...I was angry! You don't think I was trying to..."

"Marvin, have you ever been to Sunday school, attended confirmation class, done 'church time'?"

"Yes, when I was young I..."

"Then you should understand...understand that the name of Jesus Christ shouldn't be taken lightly."

"You mean...you really mean that when I said 'in Jesus' name come out' that...Come on, Jonas, everybody talks like...This is crazy! Go on back inside that closet and push. I'm sure you'll find wood, not a streetlamp covered with snow."

Harwell smiled. "Perhaps that's because our hands are too large.

Anyway, if we're going to talk about ideas, *wild* ideas, we'll both have to put some cherished beliefs on the table to look at. I'm willing. But only after dinner!"

"Okay, okay…I have plenty I want to say…about lots of things. But this afternoon—everything's happened so fast. What about those funny sounds, that *language*?" Cample spun around and faced Triana. "Hey, that medallion! Where'd it go?"

Just out of sight inside her shirt, thought Michael. Who, besides Triana, could hide things better in Big Bend?

"Jonas, Triana was wearing a medallion, a small pendant, a strange X thing. Now it's gone. And"—he pointed to the two binders on the desk—"*it's the same symbol that's in both Michael's and Triana's stories!* Doesn't Christianity, and I don't mean the modern kind that changes everything, doesn't Christianity believe in just one God over everything? One Jesus? One Spirit or power? Yet that kid didn't run from a cross. It was something else, something I've read about but never seen—not until a few minutes ago! Now as to folklore about religions, split personalities, spells, voodoo, witchcraft, even strange languages, and unknown tongues—I've read a lot. I'm sorry, Jonas, but something creepy is going on around here. Is your church some kind of cult?"

"Good for you, Marvin!" said Harwell. He leaned forward and focused on Cample. "I assure you we're Christians—all of us here— and not a cult. I wish everyone was just as concerned about purity of faith as you are."

"Jonas, in Kansas I met and came to respect several Tyndale Bible translators, but I told you I *don't* believe. I'm a scholar, a folklorist studying myths, fables, and folktales all my life. Now something here just doesn't fit—something is different, very different. And unless someone slipped some mushrooms in my lunch, you've got a lot to explain, *Dr.* Harwell. Am I still invited for dinner?"

"Absolutely!" returned Harwell. "I told Sally I might be bringing Michael, and she's always up for one more. Any objection, Triana? Michael?"

"No," said Michael. He looked at his adopted father. "I've done nothing, Jonas, nothing I know of. And…and I have some questions, too!…And I'm starved!"

Triana shook her head agreeing, but saying nothing.

"Jonas," said Cample, reaching down for his briefcase, "if everything's on the up and up, why would my two best students — who happen to attend *your* church — do something so obviously wrong?" He patted the briefcase with his other hand and gazed at the girl. His words, though strong, did not *sound* harsh. But the effect was eerie. "Triana, you can't hide forever. But okay, okay, dinner first — I've worked up an appetite — questions later, in honor of that almost forgotten Greek custom: the Law of Hospitality."

"Which," said Harwell, "was handed down from even older Jewish Law and Arab tradition to Christians."

"Go, you all get a head start," said Michael. "I'll blow out the lamp."

Cample briskly led the way out and down the long hall. It was dark and the smell of kerosene followed them. So as not to stumble, they ran their hands along the wall. The minister, Michael, and the girl held back.

"Triana," whispered Harwell, "whatever is Cample talking about?"

"Sorry, Jonas, I haven't a clue. It's got to be something about our projects, and, Jacky Fenton, I've never seen him before in my life. Even now, I can't even begin to tell you what he looked like."

"But you spoke to him and he understood!" said Harwell. "I got to the door just in time to see."

"Jonas, I didn't see him clearly, hardly at all, but I did hear him.

And he had to be answered. I think you understand what I mean."
She paused. "But this cheating thing. It beats me! I think Michael's as
puzzled as I am. Right, Michael?"

She turned and touched his arm. He had tried to follow quietly, but
without looking back she seemed to know exactly where he was. And
that he was listening.

"Triana, catch up with Cample and occupy him. I want to talk with
Michael." Without hesitation the girl shifted her book bag to her other
hand and disappeared up ahead. She obviously relied on more than
her eyes.

It was Michael's turn. He tugged at the zipper of this jacket. The
rolled-up science article crackled.

"Jonas, now you tell me what's going on. You know, Jacky freaking
out, this crazy conversation between him and Triana. You suddenly
appearing. What's happening?"

"Michael, I think we're all asking that. I sure am."

"And Jonas, there's this." Michael pulled the strange electronic box
from his pocket. The tiny blue light was still flashing.

"Where'd you get that?"

"Fell out of Triana's pocket. What is it?"

"It's why I'm here. May I have it?" Receiving it, Harwell pushed
an almost invisible button and the light stopped flashing. "Michael,
did Cample see this?"

"I don't think so, but if he didn't, it seems like about the only thing
he missed! I've never seen him so talkative."

Harwell looked at his adopted son. "You may learn much tonight,
more than you want to know. I need to tell you more, anyway. But
some secrecy will remain—for your own good. That's my decision.
However, that may soon change. I need some time. Please trust me.
I've trusted you more than you realize, perhaps more than anyone,
and I know you've trusted me. You were the best person to paint the

water tower without raising suspicion. To do it the way I said without questioning. That may matter a lot. Much is at stake.

"Michael, though you live with Aunt Steffi, you're my son—my only son. I love you and I probably haven't told you that enough. My daughters are married and gone, and now are alive or dead—I've no idea. Circumstances have cut us off. My wife is dead." He paused. "You're all the family that I know I have. You *must* continue to trust me. Pray to God. Test the spirits, as you've been taught. In time, you'll have to stand before God, not me. But Michael, I'd rather die than lead you astray. What Cample's up to tonight, I've no idea. But some important pieces to a certain puzzle are missing, and I think we all honestly feel that way. I'll tell you all I can—at the right time."

"Jonas, I hear you and believe you—so far—but you make me feel like an idiot!"

"An idiot you are *not*, Michael! In fact, besides Triana, there's no one—at any age—I can trust as well as you, for the way you think and act."

"That's heavy, Jonas."

"Then deal with it!" said the minister, matter-of-factly. "I need you," he added, almost whispering. Michael flinched. This was a defining moment about something. He would not let himself shake. But his eyes moistened. Everything from now on would be freighted with new responsibility. But about what? And in what way? He felt his father's arm around him. When had Jonas done that before?"

"Michael, you can help."

"How?"

"Pray...I think we'll all learn something important tonight. But Satan will be at work. Pray what happens will be right...for everybody. That God's will be done."

CHAPTER 14

THE AGREEMENT

s they left the school, Michael realized how little he really knew about his "home," the parsonage where his adopted father, Triana, and Sally the housekeeper, lived.

Grace Missionary Alliance Church was on the edge of town, a block from Main St., on Old Main or Bagby Road, a winding two-century-old highway not far from where a row of houses ended. Behind it and to the side, about a hundred feet back was the parsonage, and behind that still another hundred feet and to the side, where a grassy meadow surrendered uphill to a forest of ash, maple, and hemlock, stood the silvery green water tower. Easily mistaken for a silo, the tower rose high enough to spy over much of the town.

The parsonage was a two-and-a-half-story house with six tiny window gables that looked taller than it was. In front, by the entry to a winding driveway that wandered by a graveled parking lot was a small sign that declared the building a historic landmark, a stop in the underground railroad before the Civil War.

There were no streetlights AEMP, and their absence made picking one's way across six blocks of uneven, icy sidewalk stones a minor adventure, so reaching the destination made the prospect of a warm meal appealing.

Sixty-year-old Sally Ferguson, who cooked as well as cleaned, rarely disappointed any guest. To her, rationing and scarcity was a challenge—one she was up for—and her food was simple and ample, but tasty. According to Elder Amos Crandel, she had mastered her woodstove as well or better than Harwell his sermons, and a casserole by Sally was always "twice as good as it ought to be."

Before Harwell, Cample, and his two students had walked the three blocks from school, they neared a row of huge, sprawling pines as old as the town itself. Overhanging branches here and there cut dark lines across the vanishing grayness in the west. As they approached a weathered park bench, anchored as by a spell cast by the first tree, a dark hulking figure suddenly stepped into their path. Harwell waved the others back.

"What's in the tote?" The voice was thick, commanding. The man who spoke pointed to the minister's arm.

Without hesitation, the minister reached in and took out a jar. "Canned tomatoes." His voice was calm and steady. "That's it." He held out the bag to show it was empty.

The man struck a match. His clothes were rumpled. A stubble of hair, not quite a beard, darkened his face. When he saw the quart jar his eyes grew large.

"Tomatoes," Harwell repeated. "Now let's see what's in yours—now!" He pointed to the dirty bag on the bench, almost hidden in the darkness.

The man struck another match and looked at Harwell's face. Michael scraped a sidewalk stone with his shoe to make it clear to the man that his father wasn't alone. Before the match died, the man removed two huge potatoes from a bag that was obviously full.

"You've nothing to fear," said the minister. "Want to trade?"

Instead of answering, the man placed the two potatoes in Harwell's hand and reached for the jar. The minister pulled it back.

"Not so fast!" Harwell was firm. "These are canned tomatoes, but not tomatoes from a can."

The man held out another potato.

"According to the posted rate, it's four-for-one, isn't it? Now do you want to trade or not?"

Without another word the man handed the minister a fourth extra-sized potato, thrust the jar of tomatoes into his bag, and disappeared into the darkness.

"May God bless you," Harwell called after him.

"Jonas," said Triana, "You've not only lost Sally's jar, which you could have insisted he bring back, and with winter ending the rate is five-for-one soon to be six. Besides, we've bushels of potatoes already!"

"But he had no tomatoes. Did you see his look... Michael?"

The rest of the way to the parsonage passed without event.

Almost.

When they reached the winding driveway at Bagby Road, two children almost lost in the darkness were leaning against the old hitching rail next to the mailbox.

"Hi, Mindy. How's second grade?" Harwell held out his hand.

"Okay, I guess."

Mindy forced a smile. A raggedly dressed little girl about three held her hand. Their house, Harwell told them later, was a dilapidated sharecropper's building just out of sight around the corner.

"Your Aunt Effie?"

"Still abed, Rev. Jonas," said the girl. "But we're makin' it."

"I have a job for you, Mindy. Here's a potato for Aunt Effie, one for Carrie" — the little girl looked up — "and one for you."

"A job?" Mindy wrinkled her nose.

"Yes, there's one potato left. Give it to somebody else. That's it. Then bring me back my bag tomorrow and tell me what you did."

Without a word, the older girl accepted the bag with an air of seriousness and, taking her younger sister's hand, the two disappeared into the darkness.

The evening meal was delicious and uneventful, punctuated by small talk primarily by Harwell and Sally who sat with the others briefly, only to make trips back to the kitchen to refill dishes and cups. When the time for clearing the table came, Triana waved the others off as if the kitchen held some secret that needed guarding. In the dining room, shadows created by candlelight danced off the papered walls and the useless broad electric chandelier that hung down from the darkness like a circle of stalactites. Michael stared at the ceiling.

"And just what'r yah lookin' at up there, Michael?" asked the servant woman.

"An example of — should I say it Jonas? — Intelligent Design."

"But Michael" — the minister looked up — "what can it do?" He stretched out his arms in mock bewilderment. With hardly any expression, Triana looked down and slowly shook her head.

"What kin it do? My, my, it kin collect dirt, it kin!" offered Sally Ferguson .

"That's our cue!" said Harwell, pointing up without looking there. "Time to move to the study. Don't worry, hungry or not, more food will follow us to the next room."

The ceilings in Harwell's office were twelve feet high. The room was half again wider and twice as long. On all four walls shelves of books climbed to the ceiling, interrupted only by two narrow windows behind a massive desk that, unlike the rest of the room, was noticeably bare on top except for a large oil lamp, a small calendar, a notebook, and a worn Bible. Outside the windows a ragged yard sloped uphill to the water tower nearly twenty feet above a fringe of leafless trees.

Cample, briefcase in hand, walked to the window and stared out. The full moon brilliantly lit the cloudless sky. Michael noticed him almost imperceptibly stiffen.

"A bit eerie looking, isn't it!" said the minister. "That's the tower,

Old Number One. The first metal water reservoir in this part of the country. And we're never far from its shadow. It's always watching." Harwell chuckled.

"It's huge," said Cample without turning. "And in daylight it's green, isn't it?"

"Yes, silvery green." How odd, thought Michael. The man must have passed by many times. Why would he question the color?

For several seconds there was silence.

"And you can clearly see it from your window!" said Cample. The teacher caught himself, but Michael could tell something disturbed him. But what? He looked at Triana, but without her glasses on she seemed not to notice.

Suddenly, as if by deliberate choice, Cample turned and began inspecting a huge overstuffed leather chair to the right of the minister's desk.

"Try it," said Harwell. "You won't be disappointed." Michael marveled at how easily his teacher seemed to regain control.

Turning, Harwell struck a match and lit the lamp. Triana refilled everyone's cup with hot chicory — which for many had replaced coffee — from a pot that appeared from nowhere. And after Sally handed Michael a tray with a warm loaf of sourdough bread that had somehow escaped supper, along with a knife, a jar of jelly, a jar of honey, and a pitcher of milk, she disappeared pulling the heavy oak door of the study shut behind her. The minister groaned and shook his head. Michael knew how his father was embarrassed by such excess in these days.

Harwell found his place behind the desk, removed his coat and tie, and from a coat tree took and pulled on a gray, oversized sweater. He sank into his squeaky swivel chair and adjusted the lamp wick. The room brightened, masking any view of the tower through the window. Michael set the tray on a small table beside the desk.

Cample settled into the leather chair on the minister's left, facing the window, while the boy pulled up a padded office chair on his father's right, leaving a small formal wing chair between them for Triana. Before she sat, she pushed her chair an inch closer to Michael's as if to define sides.

"I beg your indulgence, Marvin, but I'd like to pray first," said Harwell. "Home-court advantage."

"As well as your position behind the desk," Cample replied, smiling. "A folklorist is sensitive and respectful to the culture he enters. But even more, I'll try to be open-minded for the sake of" — his raised his voice a bit hoping to be overheard — "Ms. Ferguson's cooking!"

"Another home-court advantage — I think! Thank you, Marvin for your candor and your caring. I wish more people I see were like that." Harwell glanced toward the bread on the small table. As he spoke a breeze stirred the bare maple just beyond their wall and a limb brushed the eave above the narrow windows.

Everyone bowed his head, but through his fingers Michael saw that Cample's eyes were riveted on the window. Then he saw why. Just outside the windowpane hovered a dark shadow, that for the want of better words, looked like a large bat-like creature! How the dim light magnified it! If he didn't know better, it looked like a tiny human with wings! If just for once they could snap on an electric light! Michael's skin tingled as the prayer continued and, oddly, he felt no fear.

Noiselessly, Cample stood, but just as he did the owl or crow, or whatever it was, darted away. Down he sank back into his chair, and even in dim light Michael saw sweat bead the man's forehead. His hands were shaking. Triana and Harwell had seen nothing. Michael felt the deep silence seem to roar as the prayer continued. He suspected, and rightly so, this would be an evening he would never forget.

"God, our Father, we come before you wanting to do only what is right in your eyes. May we get to the bottom of any trouble that lies before the four of us. We don't know what this evening will reveal, but you do, and above all, may you be glorified. May we be as wise as serpents but as innocent as doves. May your truth, which is the truth, not be compromised. May we be honest in all our words. May your people not suffer because of what we say. And may your presence be with us. In Jesus' name, Amen."

"A dangerous prayer, Jonas!" said Cample, discretely clenching his hands together. They no longer shook, but in the pale light his knuckles were white as bones. Slowly the minister raised his head and shifted backwards in his chair. "You see, Jonas, I'm no less interested in truth than you. And sometimes it isn't pretty as we will see."

Unlocking his fingers, he pointed to his briefcase while surveying each person's face.

"How strange it must seem with everything going on that I'm so concerned about cheating on one assignment. But Michael, Triana, Jonas, if we lose integrity and honor along with everything else, what's left? Why build and patrol our fence? Why be human?"

"I completely agree, Marvin." Harwell looked at the two on his right, then leaned back. The chair squeaked. "I've heard about your teaching, your passion for good stories and truth. I respect that."

"Truth, Jonas, does not belong to Christians." Cample uncrossed his legs and leaned forward. "Mind you, Christianity is a brilliant myth, I'll grant you, and…"

"Christianity is not a myth!" Michael interrupted.

"Son, let him finish…I'm sorry, Marvin, go on."

Son. The word cut deep. His father—his first father—used to call him that years ago. Now Harwell. Before, it seemed to always be just first names: "Michael and Jonas." Memories rushed back. The loss of his parents in the accident. The same time Jonas's wife was killed. And that first time he'd actually cried—when the minister, in his own quiet sorrow, asked him if he could be his father "…not your first one which you'll always treasure and keep, but your *second* father." And he'd agreed. His eyes watered. Michael drew a deep breath and glanced at Triana. She was staring at him, with almost a smile at the corner of her lips. Oddly, her glasses were in her lap. How much could she see?

"A folklorist," said Cample, "if he's honest, isn't just interested in stories for their own sakes, Jonas. He wants to know more. Not just where they come from, but what they mean. He wants to know why. It's hard for us to say out loud that we're searching for the Truth, so let's just…"

"A Postmodernist in the twenty-first century searching for *the Truth*!" interrupted Harwell. "Hmm. I'm impressed!"

"Jonas, don't play with words. Or stereotype modern scholarship. Or me, for that matter. Just hear me out, okay?"

"I'm sorry, Marvin. You're right, totally right. I apologize."

"Accepted…Now as I was saying," Cample continued, "let's just say we're trying to get as close to Truth as we can. I'm leveling with you, can't you see?"

"I can."

"Then you'll level with me?" Cample stared straight at the minister.

"Yes."

"Can't you see, Jonas, that by my honesty — my humility — I'm setting you up?"

"Yes."

"Then why do you agree?"

"Because I've decided to trust you."

"But, Jonas, I've told you I don't *believe*…"

"Perhaps," interrupted Harwell, "that's because you don't understand. And if that's true, maybe it's my fault — or partly my fault."

The minister paused. He raised his coffee cup, then put it down without drinking. Michael shivered. Once on TV he'd seen a poker game where a man lost everything he owned. Now, here by lantern light in his second father's office it seemed that more chips were being put on the table. The stakes seemed high in what might follow. Did Jonas know what he was doing?

The two men came from opposite viewpoints, but obviously had respect for each other. And while both seemed to enjoy sparring with words, neither seemed flustered or out of control. But was Cample simply biding his time, testing with short jabs, saving for some knockout punch at the right moment?

But Harwell was no stranger to the ring.

In fact, he had once taught karate, which Michael had studied in nearby Binghamton, and it was almost as if through an informal master-student relationship that he and Michael shared their grief. Michael had seen Harwell overcome weakness while he drank deeply the pain of loss. "I live each day because of Christ," he had told Michael, but Michael also suspected that long hours in the dojang had helped teach him discipline and balance.

Obviously his adopted father had hidden from him certain things. But what? And why? And what did Triana know that he didn't? And, with the world beyond the wall falling apart, why was Cample so insistent and patient? Could this puzzle that Jonas mentioned be the same for both of them?

And this "cheating"—whatever had they done?

"Marvin"—Harwell broke the silence—"you say you're a folklorist. Okay, I'll level with you. I'll be honest. And so will my children. But first grant me a boon."

"A boon? Okay. Up to 'half of my kingdom,' Jonas," said Cample, "but beware! My kingdom in AEMP is small. And I'll do nothing at all that hurts my students."

"The boon is this: Whatever I say will be true. Ask what you will, but on certain questions let me—and my children—refuse to answer.

And do not press me—or them."

My children. Michael smiled. It was hard to think of the strange girl as a child of anyone, much less as *any* kind of sister. And as to "refusing to answer," whatever did he know that was so secret or too precious and private to share? Those words were certainly not intended for him.

Harwell turned to the boy and girl.

"Will you go along with this? Or is there something serious here that I don't know about?" It was a request, not an order. Michael shifted his weight.

Triana nodded agreement.

Whatever was going on? Michael would hide his bewilderment as long as possible. Mechanically, he lowered and raised his head. The motion was judged satisfactory.

"One more thing," Harwell added. "Will you three consider whatever we say here to be privileged information and not let it leave this room—unless you are absolutely convinced it violates some specific law of the Territory or the will of God? If you all so promise, we can talk about many things. Marvin, Michael, Triana—will you agree?"

"Yes, I'll go along with that," said Cample. "You've not made it too hard for me to take things further."

"Yes," said Michael, not sure exactly what he was agreeing to.

"Yes," said Triana. "And, that includes *my* words, too, I take it?" Putting her glasses on she looked hard at the minister, as if looking for some signal. Then she focused on Cample.

"Certainly," said Harwell, "but be wise and brief."

Cample, for the first time, looked bewildered.

"Triana," he said, 'if you—all three of you—are confused, truly confused, about what's going on here, then rest assured, so am I. But with all these chips on the table I have no intention of folding my hand and walking away. I promise you that whether I find you guilty or innocent in this incident we must discuss, I will never repeat the details of what we say here, unless you file a protest to stop my failing you, or the school or the Territory formally demands it."

"Well," said Triana, "I still haven't the faintest idea of what you are up to, Mr. Cample, but rest assured I won't make a protest against you for any reason." Again, she took off her glasses and, for all that Michael could tell, retreated behind her familiar wall.

"Triana," said Cample, "don't be a fool! I've taught you better! Never surrender your rights without a fight!"

"Don't worry," said Michael, "*I* won't."

Harwell turned to the tray of food and picked up a knife.

"Sourdough bread anyone?"

CHAPTER 15

THE TELLTALE FOLKTALES

"Now, Marvin, what's all this about cheating?" Harwell wiped away crumbs from his mouth with the back of his hand.

Cample leaned forward, ramrod straight.

"In my special honors English class I simply asked each student to locate an old story that represents the values and hopes that one considers most important. Now beliefs are very personal things that should be arrived at *independently* — don't you agree, Jonas?"

"Uh…basically, yes…though I'm not sure I'm following you."

"So, since I wanted identification of, and eventually exchange of, real feelings and convictions, I emphasized *under penalty of failure no one was to discuss his or her choice with anyone else.*"

"And?" interrupted Harwell.

"Your two children turned in the same story!"

Michael spun around as if slapped. Slowly Triana brought her glasses to her face. She obviously knew something, but what? Michael turned to Cample and sensed the man was measuring their reaction.

"Actually, it wasn't *exactly* the same story," Cample confessed, "but two *connected* stories — stories unlike anything that's appeared and has been passed down in our world of folklore." He paused and uncrossed his legs. "These are your kids, Jonas. The stories are intriguing, singularly different from any other folktales in our world, but they're *obviously connected!* And, Jonas, as a Christian, I think you'd find parts of them confusing, if not downright disturbing!"

"You just said *not from our world*," interjected Triana. "What do you mean?"

"I meant exactly what I said!" said Cample, measuring each word.

"What are these stories?" asked Harwell. "Do they have titles?"

"They do, and I have them right here." Cample leaned over and opened his briefcase. "Here, see for yourself. 'Death in a Tavern'— that's Triana's; and 'The Secret of Zareba,' that's Michael's." He held up two sets of 8 ½-by-11 inch typed pages, the thinner one in a light gray binder and the thicker one in a Lincoln green binder. Quickly he returned them to the briefcase.

"'The Secret of Zareba!?'" Triana whispered just loud enough to be heard. She adjusted her glasses as if turning an invisible knob to lock in the right distance. She turned toward Harwell, but the minister's attention was riveted on Cample. Something had obviously caught her by surprise. Michael, who felt he knew less than anyone about what was going on, determined to hide his ignorance. At least for now.

"Just how are they alike?" asked Michael.

"You mean to say, Michael, that you deny you've ever seen 'Death in a Tavern,' or that you've talked to Triana about it?"

"Mr. Cample, I deny it completely! I've never even heard of 'Death in a Tavern' until this very minute."

"And"—Triana turned toward her teacher—"I've heard *of* Zareba, but…'Secrets of…of…'—whatever you said—I've never seen it…never heard of it."

"Don't try to fool me, Triana. You don't forget anything!"

"Thank you, Mr. Cample, that's very generous. '*The* Secret of Zareba,' I believe it was." Rarely did her dark golden hair shadow her eyes as it did now. "No, I've never seen this story before." Slowly she let her body settle back in her chair. This might sound impertinent from someone else, but not Triana. Michael knew this was her way of being factual, methodical, accurate without surrendering a syllable more than required.

Finally, he knew something she didn't!

At this point the conversation took an unusual turn.

"I don't like cheating," said Cample, his words sounding tamer than what they implied. "But it's only fair to say that it's not the cheating—I should say, *alleged* cheating—that I'm most interested in here, though it justifies our conversation." Slowly he surveyed each face. Harwell was ashen, but expressionless.

Cample seemed to be fighting an urge to charge ahead.

"You probably know I've collected and studied folklore in the West, as well as throughout the Endless Mountains and at the university. And"—he paused—"the two stories you turned in, though similar in many ways to classic folktales, in several ways they are not...

"In some ways they are very, very different. Different from our stories... *Earth* stories, that is." Harwell shifted in his chair and folded his hands. "But these stories do not exist by themselves...there are others like them!"

"*Other* stories?" Triana interjected. Harwell arched his eyebrows.

"From where?" she asked.

"Who knows?" Cample threw up his hands. "But they ended up in Kansas... southwest Kansas. Does that ring a bell?"

Triana dug her fingers into the chair arm. Her eyes grew moist. Michael was dumbfounded. Everybody seemed to know something that everyone else was dying to find out. Or was afraid someone would find out. Everyone except him. He was the ignorant one. But he wouldn't let on. Obviously, if these stories were what Cample was all excited about, he'd done nothing wrong. He'd nothing to fear. He would smile and play along. And get to the bottom of this. People had some explaining to do!

But with Triana—something was wrong. Before he let his brain offer a sensible objection, Michael reached over and for the second time let his hand fall on her fingers.

With not even a glance his way, she relaxed her grip on the chair arm and stared across the desk at Harwell. Somehow the flame flickered inside the glass chimney. The minister's shadow was huge and danced behind him on the wall of books.

It was Harwell's turn.

"Marvin, you teach an honors class. Let me join it." Suddenly the lamp sent up a sooty ribbon of smoke. Harwell adjusted the wick.

"Permission granted," said Cample, smiling.

"Here's the story I'll hand in," said Harwell. " 'Once upon a time in a faraway world a princess was born. Just when and where are unknown. But soon after her birth she was mysteriously confined to a narrow tower for several years. Never was she able to leave this tower and see any of the world around her. All her knowledge came from several well-meaning adults also trapped in the tower with her.'

"As strange as that seems, what I tell next will seem even more so. 'Through a spell of great magic, this tower had special chairs inside that allowed a person to sit upright regardless of how the tower moved— which it did—for outside it had wings that enabled it to not only move, but fly high in the air and far away! And fly away it did until the ground disappeared and nothing but darkness and pinpricks of light could be seen from the tower's windows, sitting, of course, in the special chair that allowed one to remain upright. Up in the sky flew the tower like a spear hurled by the gods. In a few years the baby princess became a young girl.

" 'Then one day the magic spell suddenly was broken and the tower sank and fell onto a completely different world and fell apart in flames. The young princess, who was injured, and at least two others survived.

" 'For years the princess was ill and could hardly see. For her protection she was passed from home to home, so many times that her experiences in the silver tower seemed no more than a strange dream. And when she began to study in her new world she learned that troubled children who encounter great hardship often create strange stories to give their lives meaning.

" 'But one part of her story was vividly detailed and she remembered it word for word. The adult who served as her primary teacher in the flying tower had reminded her over and over: "Always remember three things:

" ' "First, you are a princess by blood of ancient Emryss, home of a special Golden Sword and the last Flying Horse. But the Horse is dead, the Sword is forever lost, and the land itself has been destroyed. The royal blood in your veins is all that's left. You are in fact

the stolen daughter of the High Prince of Zareba
who was great-great-grandson of King Agnon the Great
who descended from King Merceon
who was anointed King centuries earlier
by Eldon, prophet of the
God of Heaven
to be First Royal Guardian of
the Golden Chest of Promise
in the Holy City.

" ' "Secondly, Your Majesty, you are also a daughter of still another world —" ' "

"Agnon the Great!... a Flying Horse!... the Golden Sword!" interrupted Cample, staring at his feet, his eyes large.

"Marvin, let me finish. ' "Secondly, Your Majesty, you are also a daughter of still another world. The blood of two worlds runs in your veins. And —" ' "

"And," interrupted Cample, looking up and staring out into the darkness between the water tower and the tall window, "thirdly, *when the blood of three worlds finally mingles in a child, my people will once again believe.*"

"You know that?" asked Harwell. "How did you find and read my story? And I know I certainly didn't cheat!"

"Nor did I, Jonas. Sorry. Is there more to your story?"

"No, Marvin. You took my last line. And the wind out of my sails. That's it."

"*Excuse me!*" — Michael's eyes were large — "Could somebody tell me what's going on?" So much for faking ignorance. "*What people?* Who are *my* people? And *three worlds*? Why is an odd spaceship story in 'tower-with-wings' language?" Obviously, Harwell had been up to something, but his minister/father had been caught some way. Cample had played a some kind of trump card and Michael knew it as well as his teacher. What strange knowledge did these two men — who seemed so different — share? And what did each know that the other did not?

" 'My people,' 'three worlds' — I suppose," said Cample, "these words can be made to mean many things. Such is the language of a good story. However, Jonas, I must admit that your story does sound a bit odd."

"Still," said Harwell, "you knew enough about it to say the last line!"

"That line," said Cample, "is apparently a motif, a theme if you will, to more than one story. Actually, even though I'd never heard of your tale — which I believe you're mostly inventing — I knew the line would fit."

The teacher stood, again pulled the two stories out of the briefcase, and handed them across the desk to the minister.

Michael was next.

"But Mr. Cample, as a folklorist what does Jonas's story mean? *Really* mean? And 'when the blood of three worlds mingles in a child, my people will once again believe?' Believe in what? And 'Emryss' and 'another world,' Mr. Cample. Are these *real* places?"

"What does anything mean, Michael? I care about many things, but right now it's the *story*—all the stories before us."

"Well, I care about more than that!" snapped Triana. Her face was pale, her body wooden. She continued: "What Mr. Cample said—about the blood of three worlds mingling in a child—came from my story, 'Death in a Tavern.' "

"Is that the story I'm supposed to know about, Mr. Cample?" asked Michael. "Well, if so, for the record, I've never heard of it before!"

"The two stories you just handed me, Marvin, came from this office." Harwell pointed to the bare top of his desk. "But, Michael, how did 'The Secret of Zareba' get to you?"

Michael uncrossed his legs and leaned forward.

"Well, 'The Secret of Zareba' I uh…"

"Speak freely, son," said Harwell.

"Well, one day I found a typed copy of it on a shelf over there." Michael pointed. "Jonas, you said I could borrow books, and, well, I know it's just hand-bound sheets of a story in a paper binder, but you said if I signed books out, so you'd know where they were, I could borrow them without asking. Look here." Walking to the shelf, he reached high up and pulled up a clipboard lying on a top row of books. "Here's my name and the title. It's a great story, in fact my all-time favorite, though it raises some questions about…well, that'll wait for now. But as for the other story, I swear I've never heard of it before in my life. And no, I never talked to Triana or anyone else about it."

Eyes turned back to the girl.

Large silent tears were rolling down her cheeks. Michael was frightened. He'd never seen her this way. Whatever was wrong, he could not — would not — let her be hurt. Never. Not if he could help it. He reached for her hand now in her lap and squeezed it. She removed her glasses, perhaps so she could better enter that private world that only she knew, perhaps because she was beautiful without them. Never before today had he as much as touched her. He held her hand gently. "Her turn" had come. In minutes, things would never again be the same. Michael knew it. But how would they change? He hadn't a clue. He started to slip his hand away to avoid embarrassing her, but without even glancing his way, she held his fingers tight. His hand had been accepted. It would not be given up.

At least not easily.

"Though I live in Michael's father's house," she continued, "and Michael does not" — her glance dared Cample to come up with some wrong idea about this — "I have never seen this novella, 'The Secret of Zareba,' though Jonas once told me he had *more information* I didn't know about." She paused and gave her foster father a wondering look. "As he knows, with my eyesight, I've never been one to pry about. Nor have I talked to Michael about *any* story. In fact, even though I'm holding his hand here" — Michael felt beads of sweat rise on his forehead — "I've hardly seen him in the past several weeks, except at church.

"Furthermore, I would never, NEVER take anything from this office without first asking Jonas." At this point she offered Michael an accusing glance punctuated by a split-second smile. She'd made no attempt to dry her cheeks, as if any distraction might derail her train of thought. How well could she see him? Michael wondered. Color rushed to his face.

With her free hand, she put her glasses back on and faced her teacher.

"But I did hand in 'Death in a Tavern,' Mr. Cample. I love this story. And why? It shows God's love for people everywhere, *even in other*

100

worlds. Nowhere else do I know of a story where a Bible character talks to people in other worlds.

"Mr. Cample, you put me in a terrible bind. At the last minute you rejected my first choice, the Gospel of Matthew. I love history — history that matters — and as a Christian, that record means more to me than…"

" 'History?' Triana," Cample interrupted. "Are you saying you value the history of the Gospel of Matthew more than the *history* of 'Death in a Tavern'? Is that what you mean?"

"Mr. Cample, you're trying to put words in my mouth."

Michael knew if he were in the hot seat, he'd value extra time to think. He reached for a cloth napkin from the nearly empty bread plate and tried to hand it to the girl, but she ignored him. With his free hand he dared to gently dry her cheeks, which she allowed but did not acknowledge, keeping her eyes riveted on her teacher.

Several seconds passed.

"Yes, Mr. Cample, I value Matthew more. Yes, I find both stories to give me meaning and hope — that was our assignment, wasn't it? And yes" — she glanced at the minister — "I consider both to be history."

"Did you…" Cample hesitated. "Did you by any chance type 'Death in a Tavern' yourself?"

"Yes."

"Was this story of your own creation, or did it previously exist?"
Silence.

"I said I considered it history, so it would not be a story of my 'own creation.' I did not make it up."

"Did you then read it — or perhaps hear it — in another language?"

"For the most part."

"But which — read or hear?"

Michael felt Triana's hand go stiff.

"For the most part it came from another language."

"But"—Cample almost whispered—"from what you *read* or what you *heard*?"

"For the most part it came from another language," Triana repeated.

"You wrote this in English?"

"Yes," Triana cut in, "English, which is what we speak!"

"English..." repeated Cample. "Did you translate this into English from the language of Emryss? And was that the language you spoke to Jacky Fenton earlier this afternoon?"

"Mr. Cample, *I'm not sure in what language that language was.*"

"Triana"—Cample scooted up on the edge of his chair—"Jonas said that both stories came from this room. You are saying you wrote, wrote down, one of them, translating it from a language you're not even sure what is. And further, you have heard *of* the other story but have never actually heard or seen it! Is that right?"

"That's right—except that I didn't know about that story, only that Jonas knew *more information* that I did not."

"And I'm supposed to believe that?"

"Yes."

"And why?"

"Because it's true," interrupted Harwell. "And that's my fault, not hers. Knowledge of some things carries a great burden with it. Triana probably will disagree, but I wasn't willing to put that burden on her—at least not yet. And why? Quite frankly there are important things I still don't know."

"Triana, Jonas—where did you get your information?"

"That's one question, Marvin," said Harwell, "we'll not answer right now."

"Okay, Jonas...okay, but remember, two can play that game! As well as an enchanting game of make-believe. I am certain that the 'Princess from Emryss' has some questions of her own that she'd like to have answers for."

"I suspect she does," said Triana, stiffly. "If *you* believe someone has come to Planet Earth from Planet Emryss, you're going to consider information that very few know about. And then stretch your imagination to the breaking point. If you're also going to believe this same person has also come from a second planet — for which there's not a shred of evidence — then you've more faith than the 'Princess' has, and you're going to have to look farther than this room! And...so is she!

"Have I made myself clear?"

"Yes," said Cample. "Yes, but" — he paused — "if one impossibility is allowed to stretch out in full view, a second impossible thing can sometimes ride on its back!"

Michael pulled himself up straight in his chair. In no way did Cample sound condescending, or seem to want to ridicule or laugh. He pulled his hand away from Triana's and peeled off his jacket which suddenly felt too warm for an office insulated by walls of books. What would come next?

The teacher's next words were totally unexpected.

"Well, I may have *some* of those answers — answers to questions I think the 'Princess' should ask!"

"How can you say that?" asked Harwell.

"Perhaps that's one question that *I* shouldn't answer right now," returned Cample, "but I'll tell you this much. I also have 'more information.' There aren't just two stories from — or about — Planet Emryss here on Earth. There are at least *four*."

"Four?"

Triana stood. Harwell leaned forward.

Michael could hold it no longer.

"What in the world, or should I say *this* world" — he extended his arms — "is going on? Zareba...Emryss are real places?! *Planet* Emryss?!"

"So some would have us believe," said Cample.

"Let's consider it a hypothesis," said Harwell. "This whole high school project thing has caught me by surprise. Marvin, it looks like we have read both stories — the two I know about, anyway — but it appears they haven't. I think the next thing is for each of them to read the other's story. Any objection to doing that now?"

"At this point — certainly not! No objection whatsoever. But now?"

"I think we can manage it," said Harwell. He glanced at the boy, then at the girl. "Considering the circumstances, yes. The longer story is the one Triana hasn't seen, and she reads almost as fast as some people turn pages."

Eyes turned toward Michael.

"Okay…the one I need to read is shorter…I know only yesterday I put away picture books for chapter books, but I'll try hard not to hold everyone up."

"Thank you, son! We'll be rooting for you." Harwell laughed. And though it was at his expense, Michael was glad to see the tension ease. "I'm sure you're hungry again — or will be!" The minister looked at the boy and smiled. "I'll look up Sally and see if I can get some more hot chicory and maybe some hot chocolate. Then we'll let you kids read and see what else you have to say. Are you two up to it?"

"Yes."

"Yes."

"And then, Marvin, you say you can answer some of their — especially the Princess's — questions? And even give her more questions that she should ask?"

"Some. Then I'll have a few more of my own — some especially for you, Jonas! We're still young! And they're much younger. I wouldn't end this evening now for all the world! or should I say 'all the worlds'!" Cample smiled.

"Fair enough," said Harwell, "but I think we may be in for a long night."

✳ ✳ ✳

HERE ENDS THE ACCOUNT OF WHAT HAPPENED
IN BIG BEND FOR THE TIME BEING. WHAT FOLLOWS
*ARE THE STORIES, **DEATH IN A TAVERN** AND*
***THE SECRET OF ZAREBA** GIVEN*
IN THEIR ENTIRETY.

Each story is followed by a brief discussion
among Michael, Triana, Marvin Cample, and Jonas Harwell
about how these stories may have come about;
and if they report real events from elsewhere,
and about how they arrived on Earth;
and what, if anything, they mean to the residents
of Big Bend, Pennsylvania in the early days AEMP.

(These two complete "folk" stories, while linked,
may be enjoyed in their own right, independent of
any understanding provided by the framework story.
To help in reading them that way, a dual
chapter numbering is included
for easy reference.)

106

PART 11

DEATH IN A TAVERN

A complete story

"By faith Abel . . . still speaks, even though he is dead."

Hebrews 11:4

CHAPTER 16

1
THREE
WORLDS
SPEAK

nce upon a time, a small boat was let down secretly from the side of a large sailing vessel. In it was a Queen, the granddaughter of King Agnon the Great, of the ancient House of Aeron, and her two grown sons.

For two days and two nights Crown Prince Gavin and his younger brother Fairold continually rowed, taking turns.

Their direction, West.

On the third day, clouds suddenly blackened and the wind rose. For this and the next day, the princes battled wind, waves, and rain, but could do little to keep a steady course. Finally, at the end of the fourth day, when their food and water were gone, both oars snapped in two at the oarlocks and the three were at the mercy of the sea.

When they could do no more, the Queen let down her thick dark brown hair streaked with silver, knelt at the center of the boat in front of a huge chest, filled with what was left of their former palace splendor, and committed their souls to the God of Heaven whom they all loved. Just when Prince Fairold thought all was lost, he raised his head to kiss his mother goodbye. He found the Queen's eyes studying the face of his older brother.

"Gavin, your father and others have ended their quest." Tears began filling her eyes. "The gentlest voice has just told me. But *if we stay with this boat, we'll safely reach shore.*"

Suddenly, a wave broke across the prow, mocking her words and soaking them with an icy wall of water. The Queen's head slammed down hard against the chest, and as she fell, Fairold caught her. Together they lay as dead men, clinging to one another in the rising pool of water in the bottom of the boat.

Then there was silence—how long, Fairold couldn't tell.

When Fairold came to, he smelled smoke. He struggled to remember where they were. There was the playful slap and pull of waves against wood. They'd stopped moving! He sat up, stared into a bright early morning sun and sneezed. His ears rang. The sky was a pale blue. He shivered. Though the first of Maenus, when light equals night, was three months past, the longer days of summery Solias hadn't quite muted the bite of spring.

Yards away the shore sloped up into a series of ridges, and just out of reach of the retreating tide were the glowing embers of a single log. But no one was in sight.

"Up! Up! We've landed!"

The Prince shook his mother, then his older brother, who slowly opened their eyes. He sprang from the boat only to have his aching legs collapse beneath him. Painfully, he made his way past the wrinkly sand to a thicket and returned with an armful of sticks and branches. How odd that they were dry! As gentle as eggs, he lay them one by one on the log, and from it rose the fingers of a welcome fire.

Now Prince Gavin was as skillful with bow and arrow as his father had been. In no time he'd chased a couple of rabbits from the freedom of the thicket to a couple of sizzling skewers above the fire. The air filled with the welcome aroma of roasting meat.

Automatically, the Princes located their swords, shields, and knives, and began to rub them dry while the Queen attended to her trunk. Her carefully wrapped books were dry. Surprisingly, little clothing was wet; nonetheless, the tall grass and scrubby bushes were soon capped with a rainbow of linen and silk rippling the warm breeze.

It was then that they divided their meat and ate—for strength and purpose: Their doomed country was behind them. They had obeyed God, they, as others before them, and fled west with only what they could carry. Although the storm had carried them far to the south, for the moment they were safe, as few probably were that landed even farther to the south. As far as they knew, they were the last of their ancient royal family.

The Queen stood, and though they numbered only three, made a formal announcement:

"I declare this to be a special Sabbath—to thank the God of Heaven, and rest."

No one disagreed. Hours slipped by.

Not far from the shore a ledge of rock projected out, under which was a shallow cave. The Princes moved their fire to the cave mouth, banked it, and made their mother comfortable on a bed of coats behind it. The long days on the sea finally exacted their toll. They lay side by side and in minutes were fast asleep. No one stood guard. The sun slid the rest of the way across the sky and disappeared in the west.

In the middle of the night, the Queen awoke to a strange sound.

"Gavin, wake up!" She shook her oldest son. "We have visitors! Someone's out there singing!"

Fairold leaped up and, forgetting the low ceiling, banged his head. Yards away at the water's edge stood a row of about fifty men and women in white tunics with emblems on their chests. Their hands were empty. The music was melodic, haunting, but unclear, and as they sang the stars overhead seem to brighten and fade, pulsing with the rhythm. The singers seemed twice as visible as the full moon should have allowed.

As each Prince drew his sword, three young men stepped out from the row and, as if pulled by air, glided effortlessly up to the far side of the smoking remains of blackened embers. Each pointed down and the smoking embers sprang to life.

With a single motion, the Princes dropped their swords and along with their mother fell to their knees.

"Stand up! We come in the name of the God of Heaven but are creatures just as you!" With their words, the singers' lips instantly stopped moving and the music became a soft but rich multi-octave humming.

The Queen, Gavin, and Fairold stood.

"Who are you?" asked the Queen. "Where are you from? You" — she pointed to the man on the left — "you even look like my...my other son!"

"I am your other son," he answered. A large red X with sharp points hanging down at each tip emblazoned his chest.

"But Colin I..."

"Mother, I am not Colin, for at the moment your youngest son still lives."

"But my other sons are here!"

"Are they? Did you not have four sons? Have you forgotten?"

"But Crispin died three days after his birth!"

"Yes *he* died...and died because certain evil took place long before you and your father were born.

"Does the Great Shepherd forget the least of his creatures? Mother, look at me. I am Crispin your son, and I am as I am, and *here* before you I look as I would have looked. And *how you will see me again.*"

111

"Crispin! That name is music! These are your brothers Gavin and Fairold. If I only had your ring! But I gave it to your brother Colin to give to anyone he found worthy while he journeyed. I had so little else to—"

"Mother"—the man in the brilliant white tunic smiled—"**I need no ring.**" Somehow a staff appeared in his hand and he scratched words in the sand. "**Step forward, Mother, but do not touch me.**"

The Queen stepped forward and read. She gasped and tears began running down her cheeks, though she made no sound.

Suddenly a breeze swirled through the fire blowing smoke into the Princes' faces and the words were erased.

"**Mother, that was the only way I was allowed to tell you, and it must be our secret. Your youngest son has only hours more in this world. And you can do nothing for him.** *However, your grandson is not safe! A witch has pledged to marry him. Warn your children!* **But I must talk of other things.**"

Though he was her son, he spoke with authority and it was obvious the Queen recognized it. She drew herself to full height and clasped her hands together. Only her fingers moved. The soft humming of haunting music still cradled the conversation.

"Crispin, who stands with you?"

"**I am Abel,**" said the man in the middle. A large red cross emblazoned his chest. "**Your third son, to whom you've just spoken**"— he nodded to Crispin—"**died unjustly because of forgotten sins of his ancestors. I am the second born of Adam and Eve, the first man and woman in a different world, and I** *died unjustly* **at the hands of my brother because I obeyed God. But God, the Great Shepherd, did not abandon me either.**"

Abel pointed to a taller, paler man at the right. His skin was nearly white. And on his chest was a red circle surrounding a red dot joined by four lines. The Queen looked at the strange symbol and wrinkled her brow.

"**Do not be perplexed, good Queen,**" said Abel. "**There is but one** way to God. **My cross is sacred only because of what the Son of God did upon it.**" The men beside him nodded in agreement. Gavin and Fairold exchanged puzzled glances. **"Please know that our signs vary. Yet there is much the same in our worlds. The minutes, hours, days, and weeks are identical, and so is the God who did not forget us."**

He pointed to the tall man wearing the red circle and red dot on his tunic. **"You see, the Great Shepherd did not abandon Vandor, who's from still another world, one that saw marvels and tragedy beyond the dreams and understanding of nearly all God's creation. Nevertheless, he *died unjustly* along with millions like him, at the hands of his parents because they destroyed his life before he was born."**

"Crispin, I'm puzzled," said the Queen. "According to our Holy Book there is one God-Maker, who is one with the God-Son; and there is one death — that of the God-Son — and one coming back to life for the forgiveness of sins, yet the cross and circles that Abel and Vandor wear are unfamiliar. Why do they not wear the stakes? Are there many God-Sons in the flesh and many holy deaths?"

To this the three responded with a loud melodic chant, and the Queen at last had to cover her ears.

"ONE GOD...ONE SON IN FLESH...ONE WORLD OF MANY WORLDS...ONE DEATH FOR SIN ONE TIME FOR ALL...PRAISE THE LORD...PRAISE THE LORD...PRAISE THE LORD!"

From those at the shoreline the words echoed. Their arms were lifted. Above them the stars seemed to dance. The music was joyful, pleasant, daring imitation, contradiction.

It was Vandor's time to speak. His voice was gentle, but strong enough so not a syllable was lost.

"My gracious Queen, there are many worlds which look the same, feel the same underfoot, and have similar plants and creatures on the ground and in the air. However, there are differences: In my world

there are two moons — one the size of yours here, and one smaller, like the moon in Abel's world. Our three suns, though, are mirror images of each other and our minutes, hours, days, and weeks — which are a special gift from Highest God — are exactly the same. 'Teach us to number these our days, O God, that we may serve you.'

"Now as to Emryss, the God of Heaven and his Son have come as the Holy Book bears witness.

"In Abel's world, the God-the-Father as they call him and God-the-Son have come and left a book that is very similar.

"And in my world, called Elphia," Vandor continued, "God and his Son have also come in the same manner; but years ago in a great act of evil, then called 'wisdom,' my people destroyed every copy of the I-Rex Code, the special Holy Word that God had given us. Almost everything from that book has been lost; nevertheless, one curious prophecy refused to die: 'Thus says the God of all worlds, in days to come many will fall away, but a remnant will be spared. *And after the blood of three worlds mingles in a child, my people will once again believe.'*

"My gracious Queen, from your children will come a child *who is also from my world,* who will return to my people with the lost message of the Son-of-the-Highest-God's great act of salvation, which is for everyone who will believe."

"I...I don't understand," said the Queen.

"You — all three of you — do not need to know more. You have been chosen. That is enough. Just remember four things and obey exactly what the three of us" — Abel and Crispin nodded agreement — "say because we speak by will of the God of Heaven."

Though her two sons stood closely at her side, Vandor directed his next words to the Queen as if she were alone:

"First, my dear Lady, your concern for purity of the faith has been

114

noticed on high. Further words will not be given to you. This very night angels, which we are not, will visit your two sons and show and tell them many things. When you arise, carefully hear the words of your two sons."

Gavin and Fairold glanced at each other.

"*Second,* your old kingdom is only hours from its promised destruction. Those of your people who have fled and settled near the shore in the south will be saved and prosper as promised. But the God of Heaven has further work for you. Dry your tears for your youngest son and go with your two remaining sons immediately and rapidly far west *for a great King on Emryss needs help from a remnant of your tiny kingdom.* The reputation of your royal family has traveled far.

"*Third,* the road you take will never be far from a great and beautiful river to the south. But do not stray from the road, or for any reason so much as touch the black ribbon bordering this water, for it and all the land south, except for the coast where remnants of your people live, is *twice cursed.*

"*Fourth,* you will pass a few inns where you may stop and eat. But do not enter without a naked blade in hand, and do not spend the night in any. Eventually, you will come to a tavern in which a local girl has just committed murder. Dear Lady, if this girl pleases your son, he may marry her, though it isn't required, and as a commoner she knows nothing about life in a royal court. But she has suffered enough to wear a royal tiara."

And so the words from Vandor ended.

"How will we know when we get where we're going?" asked the Queen.

It was Crispin who answered.

"Dear Mother and brothers, you will know."

Slowly the three, without seeming to move their feet, drifted backwards, growing smaller and smaller until they joined the others on the shore, just the opposite of the way they'd come.

"PRAISE THE LORD!...PRAISE THE LORD!...PRAISE THE LORD!" sang the men and women on the shore. The rhythm was regular and the words were clear.

CHAPTER 17

2
GAVIN'S
VISION

lowly Fairold sat up. The sky was showing its first color, rapidly brightening minute by minute. The fire was out. He rubbed the top of his head. His thick dark hair, resembling his mother's, had cushioned the bump the night before. Still it hurt.

"Gavin, Mother, it's morning! I had the strangest dream!"

"Dream?" said the Queen. She struggled to a sitting position.

"It was magnificent! There was a row of —"

"Men and women," interrupted Gavin, yawning, "dressed in white." He stretched his arms and banged his knuckles on the stone ceiling.

"And of the three who approached us," said the Queen, "one was my...my son." She raised her hands and struggled to rub life into her cheeks.

"And dead brother," added Gavin, running his fingers through his straight flaxen hair. His blue eyes widened.

"Do you both hear what you're saying?" asked Fairold. His curly hair was nearly black and his eyes were dark and deep, but without the sharp sparkle of his mother's. He sprang from the opening, nearly

117

banging his head again. He examined the sand on the other side of the fire. There were no footprints.

"It appears that we've had the same dream!" said Gavin, joining his brother. He ran his hand over his hair that refused to lie flat.

"It was so real!" said Fairold.

"We've had a vision," said the Queen, "sent by the God of Heaven."

The Princes turned to their mother, the Queen. The woman, well into middle age, was known for her fondness of the clothing and trappings that come by royal right. But that was deceptive. Love of appearance and comfort went only so far.

Once at great risk she'd undertaken a dangerous quest. She'd been tricked into marriage and had actually taken her wedding vows dressed in plain clothes. And she'd actually ruled on the throne of her tiny kingdom alone, briefly, in the midst of tragedy and death. Her beauty and wit had disarmed more than a few and, as her High Counselor once said, she "spent considerable time keeping those weapons sharp." If that was her weakness, then her fierce stubbornness, when properly aimed, was her iron.

Above all, she loved the God of Heaven. Loved him with the passion of a child.

"Visions are rare," said the Queen, "but they have come before — remember the story?"

Fairold did. A year before his mother had dreamed of a sword scratching a strange riddle on a wall. In the same night the one she had loved had been shown three changing pictures that prophesied doom to their kingdom, and had sent their youngest brother alone on a dangerous quest he was in no way prepared for. They had never seen him again.

If they were true visions, fulfillment had not yet come. The kingdom they'd fled had suffered, but still hadn't been destroyed as far as they knew. And their lost brother's mission — nothing was more impossible. Fairold was glad the awful task hadn't fallen to him. But, if what they'd been told last night was true, their brother was still alive, but not for long. Apparently, visions were rich in some details but not in what a person wanted to know most. Maybe that was merciful. Fairold knew he'd never want to know exactly when and how his life would end. Let things happen as they will.

"What now, Mother?" he asked.

"First," said the Queen, "we must rehearse what we've seen and heard over and over so we won't forget the slightest detail." She stood, and rubbing the great ring of her old kingdom that was on her left hand, she walked to where her dead son had so recently appeared. She gazed out over the sea.

"And?" interjected Gavin.

"And we must do what we were told."

"Just how will we travel?" asked Gavin. "We've no horses. And… and there's your trunk."

"Well," said the Queen, "the direction to go is west." Without looking, she pointed away from the sea to the back of their cave instead of up and beyond it. The gesture was comical. Gavin smiled. His mother did not. "Unless you can think of something better, Gavin, my feet are going to start walking that way!"

"And your clothes?" asked Gavin.

"That trunk and everything it holds is the Dragon's curse if it stands between me and the God of Heaven. And Gavin, if anything ever happens to me, give my ring — for I'll not be buried with it — and whatever few things I have left to that woman."

"The one in the vision? But she's a commoner!"

"And so was your father! Now sit down!"

Automatically, the two obeyed. Fairold felt like a child. The Queen herself descended upon a narrow ledge that extended from the cave opening and began slowly pulling a comb through her long, dark silver-streaked hair.

"Mother, I thought we were to go immediately?" said Gavin. Fairold didn't like his brother's smile. But what should they do? The choices seemed limited.

"Have you forgotten?" asked the Queen. "Or did we not have the same vision after all?"

The Princes looked at each other.

"First of all" — the Queen paused — "were we not told that *I* was to carefully hear what an angel later told each of you separately?... Isn't that correct? Or did I imagine this?"

"Oh." The Crown Prince shrugged his shoulders. "I almost forgot."

"Gavin, you were born to rule. You can't afford that. We've so little. We can't throw away the part we've been given." The Queen put down her comb, threw back her hair, and shifted to a more regal position. "Now what did you hear?"

Gavin shuffled his feet.

"Mother, I saw more than I heard. And what happened was so strange I don't have the right words."

"Well, give it your best," said the Queen.

"Well...the angel first spoke from a column of fire. Later he was invisible. I clearly heard his voice but I never saw his face." Gavin uncrossed his legs and extended his arms.

" 'Fly,' he told me and, as soon as I entertained that possiblity, I felt myself rising off the ground, very much against my will, through thick pink clouds that grew more and more red. When I could do nothing to hold myself back I stopped fighting and let myself soar.

"Soon the clouds thinned and I found myself gliding through a sea of air, studded with dozens of 'balls' below me, above me, on every side. Each was perfectly round — very small and moonlike — and far away. Each ball seemed to have islands, some large, some small, that seemed to float on the skin of water that covered them. To my surprise I could turn and dart through the air at tremendous speed wherever I wished.

"Oddly, most balls glowed a most perfect blue, and more than anything, I wished to land on an island of one of these and explore. I pushed hard toward the blue island that seemed closest, the wind stinging my face and screaming in my ears.

"As I braked and began to glide across the pale blue sky, I was stunned by mile after mile of luxuriant vegetation, winding rivers, towering waterfalls, and crystalline seas, a beauty I'd never seen. But the island was empty—empty of people. Oddest of all, whenever I tried to land, I was pushed away as if by an invisible hand.

"There were two other kinds of islands, however, though not as many.

"One kind glowed the most beautiful and palest of yellows. I changed direction and flew toward an island on a yellow ball, and found it much like the blue world I'd left—with one important exception. Here and there the land had been cleared. Trees, apparently planted and tended, were heavy with fruit. At last I found a handful of simple lodgings near a lake. And, of course, where there are lodgings there are people. Softly I descended and attempted to land.

" 'Do not land,' rang a voice in my ear. It was the same voice that had told me to fly. 'You are unclean.'

"I dared not disobey. As I felt slowly pulled away very much against my will, I heard singing that made my heart dance. Down below were people like myself, though not entirely. They...they moved about in ways a bit different, but still pleasing to see. As I pulled away, I wondered how they clung to a round world without falling off. But then I was flying like a bird with wings—you know how dreams, or visions, are.

"Sadly, as the yellow ball grew smaller, my curiosity turned toward the third kind of ball, which glowed red as if smeared with blood. There were several of these, though fewer than the yellow and blue ones.

"Strangely, as I neared the closest red ball, I sensed I'd been there before though I knew I hadn't. Around and around the great ball I circled, faster and faster until my vision blurred. Then I could see nothing. I was terrified that my head would explode. Then came that voice that seemed to be always near me: 'Do not fear. You have flown far, but also far back in time.' Then the spinning slowed, the air grew hot and slowly my vision returned. Down below again there were people, but by what magic they clung to the surface of that great ball without falling off I cannot tell. And, though I can't say why, I knew that something down there was wrong. Terribly wrong.

"As I broke through a red cloud to descend to the surface, the color faded. I was not flying over land, but a vast sea, its water hanging to the ball like glue without spilling away—but you know how dreams are.

"Below us sailed a large three-masted ship of strange design. As I flew lower, my eyes were drawn to a line of naked men and women with skins as brown as soil. Tied hand to hand with heads bowed, they were marched across the deck, driven like animals it seemed, while clothed men with much lighter skin stood by, one with a whip as if those before him were cattle. It was disgusting. I was horrified.

"Then one of the dark men pointed straight up toward me, and as I hovered not more than a hundred feet above, I examined myself to see if I were properly clothed. I was. Then everyone was looking up. To my amazement, I discovered my flapping batlike wings extended twenty feet from tip to tip.

"Then a clothed, pale-skinned, man on the boat deck pointed a long stick at me. Fire flashed, and right after it came a sound like a crack of thunder. I could have sworn a pebble or ball of some kind tore past my head. 'Save me!' I cried. Suddenly I felt myself shrink to a fraction of my former size. I willed myself to rise and leave. And so I did, but again spinning so fast that once again I couldn't see.

"When I thought I could stand it no longer, my eyes suddenly opened and I found myself back, high above the red world, and I sensed, though I was smaller, I'd returned to the place above the red world where I'd started.

" 'Where am I?' I said aloud.

" 'You have now sprung *years ahead*,' said my invisible companion.

" 'Many years?' I asked.

" 'Years,' he repeated in a tone daring me to ask more.

"Then, once again I quickly descended, and I saw…I saw something so amazing that I hardly know where to begin! Slightly above and ahead of me, about 200 feet away, was a large silver spear! It was smooth and shiny, as long as several houses, yet no thicker than a man's outstretched arms times two. Into the silvery smoothness of the spear's 'skin' were three or four small round windows, I think, and I sensed that people might be on the other side of them." Gavin paused and closed his eyes. "How it ever hung in the air alone without wings I'll never know. But you know how dreams are…

" 'Inside the spear is the blood of your people,' said the voice.

" 'My blood?' I asked.

" 'You are at the same place, but years ahead of where you were before,' said the voice, ignoring my question. But the more I studied what I saw, the more my head began to spin—faster and faster. I was afraid I would get sick, terrified I would fall. But fall to what? My brain pressed against the side of my skull and my mind broke from its moorings and began to swim."

"Your mind began to swim?" interrupted Fairold. He rolled his eyes and wrinkled his nose. "How could your mind—"

"Fairold, let him finish!" said the Queen. "We must hear, remember,

123

and understand everything the best we can." The Queen's eyes were riveted on her older son. The Crown Prince stopped, smiled condescendingly at his brother, and resumed gazing intently over their heads.

"That's just the best way I can explain it," said Gavin. "To someone who reads, *a figure, a figure of speech,* sometimes works better. It's not a lie. I am reporting a dream...and remember, in it I did have wings — real wings!"

Fairold felt his face burn.

"Go on," said the Queen. "Be as accurate as you can."

"Gradually the spinning slowed, and at last I could make my wings take some control.

"So on and against the hot wind I soared for minutes, hours, days, years — I cannot say — but when the wind died and I began to see what was below, I was no longer over ocean but land, land in this same red world though how I cannot explain. It was then, when I saw my batlike shadow cast against a smooth stone wall, I knew that, once again, though I was still small, I could be seen.

"Then as the sun set and the sky darkened I neared a valley in a rolling range of mountains. Houses checkered the land — some isolated and some in curving rows along endless black stonelike roads." Gavin paused and squeezed shut his eyes. "There's too much to tell and too few words to use, but oddest was this:

"At the side of many roads stood dozens and dozens of small brightly colored metal huts, booths, or street shops of some kind, with odd-shaped windows on every side, with pure glass, clearer than any at our old palace. Even stranger, at the foundation of each hut stood four dull black circles that looked like wheels, but never did one turn! And though a door with a strange knob seemed built into every metal wall, I didn't see any used.

"They must be coaches, I first thought, but not one had a place to attach horse or ox. Then I remembered the Dragon's Kind, and wondered if they were driven by invisible power not of that world. But whether these came from Dragon or God, the huts appeared unused and wholly neglected.

"It must have been cold since most trees had no leaves. At one high point near an open field where the trees were thin, a strange silvery-green, windowless tower caught my eye, and down the hill from it a large house with a peaked roof.

"Down I glided, breaking with my wings to hover before a tall narrow window. Through the glass, again the clearest I've ever seen, I saw by lamplight a man bent over a desk—praying, I would guess—and beyond him sitting side by side a boy and a girl similarly bent, holding their heads in their hands.

" 'Things are not right,' said the voice that had guided me. 'Still they worship the God of Heaven.'

"Suddenly, another man I hadn't seen before rose from a large overstuffed chair and began staring straight at me. Whether out of fear or wonder, I cannot say.

" 'But,' said the voice, 'not everyone who sees believes.'

"Before I could answer, I sensed myself being pulled away, soaring up, higher and higher until I could once again see this red world as a ball, and I was astonished so much of it was covered by water.

" 'I want to go home,' I heard myself saying.

"It was as if the words themselves were a trigger to a catapult. Up, up I was pulled, higher and higher, farther and farther away from where I had started. Once again I looked at the vast sea of air studded with hundreds, perhaps thousands of ball-shaped islands—mostly blue, some yellow, some red. The magic which kept them from falling I can't explain—

"But again dreams, and visions I suppose, are that way." Gavin paused, glanced at his mother, extended his arms, and looked out toward the sea at whose mercy they'd been for days. "But," he said, returning to his story, "much that appears at night cannot be measured by what we see in daylight.

" 'What does this mean?' I asked the voice, which had no body but never seemed to be far away.

" 'I have shown you the world that is,' said the voice.

" 'The world?' I asked.

" 'The world of worlds,' said the voice. 'The world that is known to the stars of heaven.'

"Once again I was pulled at a great speed that was independent of my wonderful wings. Slowly I approached my last island, another round world in the World of Worlds.

"It was also red.

" 'Not here! Not here! It is evil.' "

At this Gavin turned and faced his mother and brother. "I can't say why, but I knew then something was wrong, badly wrong with this world I was entering. 'Not here!' I cried.

"But the more I complained, the closer I came. The air became gritty and hot. I was scared.

" 'Where am I?' I screamed. 'Take me home!'

" 'You are home,' said the voice. And with his words and the tug of hot air, the vividness of all that had happened began to soften. I prayed for words to hold all the wonder, but none came, none beyond what I've told you.

"As my feet touched ground, the redness dissolved, and things looked as they always had. I could tell without touching that my wonderful wings were gone. My regular size had returned. I rubbed my eyes and a great weariness came over me. I lay down and immediately slept."

The dream — the vision, the story — was finally over.

"The next thing I heard was Fairold waking us up."

For a minute no one spoke. A broad wave spilled high on the beach and drained back.

"Rare is your experience, Prince Gavin," said his mother the Queen. "Whatever it means, know this: Emryss is not alone. There are other worlds beyond ours. Our God is a God of Gods, the God of every world, known in a similar way to each. The least we can do is obey the clear words we can understand."

"And so, Mother," said Gavin, apparently newly refreshed. "You want us to leave at once for the west?"

"No."

"No? Then what next?"

"Gavin, we must do *all* we've been told!"

"Meaning?"

"I haven't heard from your brother. Fairold, did you also dream?"

The Crown Prince sighed, collapsed on a rock, and stared out at the sea.

"Uh...my experience was nothing like Gavin's." Fairold paused. "There were just three things. Just three...two warnings and a...a...a declaration...First, as we were safe in the boat, we will be safe in the coach. Anyway, I think that's sort of a warning."

"Coach? What coach?" interrupted Gavin, extending his arms.

"Second, we must not touch the horse or its reins. If he eats or drinks, it will only be because he doesn't want to attract attention."

"Horse?" said Gavin.

"Third, when orange and green ride the eastern sky, many wonders will begin to cease."

For several seconds there was silence.

"What else?" asked Gavin. "Is that it? What did you see?"

"I saw nothing," said Fairold. "I was only given words. And I've just said them."

"They are wonderful and beautiful," said the Queen. "And we

won't forget them." Fairold felt his cheeks redden. His mother had been thorough as always. And this included being gracious and kind, even to the least in her kingdom. And just who was left, besides those few who'd fled to the south, other than the three of them?

The last loose thread, however tiny, had been tucked away. She stood and smoothed her dress.

"Now, Gavin, we are ready to leave."

CHAPTER 18

3
THE
COACH

ust past the thicket above their cave, a ridge blocked the view of everything to the west. No one had yet gone up that far, so as to what lay ahead, no one had a clue. And no one seemed eager to find out first.

Breakfast was the leftovers from supper. The Princes quickly bundled and packed their coats, a change of clothes, a small kettle, and other odds and ends that would make life less difficult. But what would their mother do? From the corner of their eyes they stole glances in her direction. Overhead, the sky seemed to darken. Squawking gulls began their gliding descent.

The Queen scurried from bush to bush gathering up the clothes she'd laid out to dry the night before. Quickly she folded them. She refused to look up. Everything from the huge trunk fell to the ground in neat piles. Memories from life at their old palace rushed back. Methodically, she folded three dresses around several books and pushed these along with scarves, underclothes, and stockings into a middle-sized leather bag. Everything else fell back into the trunk. As she closed the lid, raindrops began to fall.

"Stop watching me!" she ordered without looking up. Her voice dared challenge. Tears trickled down her cheeks. "We can't be held back. Hide this back in the cave." Together the Princes lifted the heavy trunk. Just as they ducked under the ledge, the Queen shouldered her bag and started up the hill in a run.

"MOTHER! WAIT!" called Gavin. "She's crazy, Fairold. Can't you see her running a kingdom?"

"She already has, Gavin. That's why we're here! Let her go—we'll catch her soon enough."

Grabbing their own things, they started for the top of the hill.
As they neared the top, they heard the neighing of a horse. The Princes dropped everything and ran. Rain began to fall.

At the very top, Fairold saw a sight he'd always remember. First, a road that ran straight west as far he could see. On either side of it were rolling dunes of sand and in the distance, unless a mirage deceived him, there was the promise of trees and forest.

But that wasn't all. Just a hundred feet away stood a magnificent white horse pawing the ground. He was half again larger than any horse Fairold had ever seen, and across its back and flanks lay a scarlet blanket fringed with gold.

But just as wonderful was the magnificent coach to which it was attached.

No one was in sight. How could a single horse move such a carriage?

The Queen was already there and had opened the door. How could she get there so fast? wondered Fairold. Keeping a safe distance from the great creature, she knelt praying, or pleading—he couldn't tell. She turned to her sons.

"RUN, GAVIN, FAIROLD!" When they doubled their pace, she stood and screamed. "NOT *THIS* WAY! THAT WAY!" She pointed back to the way they'd come.

The Princes stopped and stared at each other.

130

"THE HORSE WON'T GO BACK!"

Gavin scratched his head and, with his finger, drew the words in the air.

"The...horse...won't...go...back...??"

Fairold interrupted.

"Gavin, don't you get it? The horse is westward bound. But back east is —"

"Aha! Her trunk!" Gavin smiled.

"HURRY!" yelled the Queen.

"How can she change like that?" asked Gavin.

"*She* didn't change," said Fairold. "The circumstances did."

Then came the beginning of that rare downpour in the desert that caused invisible life to burst forth, sprinkling the sand with fragile color which, no sooner than it appeared, would begin melting away as the unforgiving sun once again burned down.

Back down the hill the Princes raced through sheets of rain. When at last they'd stevedored the clumsy trunk up the hill, gathered their own bags, and made it to the coach, the rain changed to hail. The Princes threw themselves inside, joining their mother, soaked and exhausted. Conversation was impossible.

"We must stake the horse and set the brakes," yelled Gavin.

But as soon as he touched the door handle, the coach began to move. The Queen pulled him back. Fairold pushed aside the curtain covering the window and watched the dunes alongside the road move faster and faster behind them. At last they were a blur. He collapsed with his mother and brother on the sumptuous leather seats.

"Who's driving?" shouted Gavin. His face was ashen.

"Why, the horse is," said the Queen. She folded her hands and automatically drew herself to full height. Fairold suspected she was holding something back.

"But...uh..."

The Crown Prince, a master with horses, looked utterly bewildered. He sat inside on the front seat facing the direction from which they'd come. Beside him sat the Queen claiming her seat as if it were a throne, as calm as if she were in control of what was happening. Of course acting in control, regardless of the facts, was taught to royalty from an early age. On the back seat, facing forward, Fairold sat studying her, his sturdy plain sword and bag beside him. On the floor between them rested the Queen's chest that would serve as a table.

Fairold also was bewildered. Bewildered about everything: the frenzied rescue of the trunk; the sudden appearance of the white horse and the magnificent, unoccupied coach being just at the right place at the right time; also the sudden pounding of the hail, and the hypnotic jouncing of the coach as they raced down a strange road for an unknown place. All this finally took its toll.

Fairold laughed.

And laughed. And laughed unable to stop. The sound was drowned out by the hail pelting the roof of the coach. Tears cascaded down his face. Every trace of fear melted away. Doubling over, he rolled to the floor.

The Crown Prince glared at his brother in disgust. Then came the Queen's turn. In seconds, her seriousness melted away, and she laughed as she'd eventually done long ago when at a young age she'd been tricked into marrying that mysterious boy who was now gone. Her cheeks were soon wet with tears. The Crown Prince, thinking his brother and then his mother had gone insane, sat stiffly struggling to keep a shred of dignity for all of them. Then when the coach hit a sudden bump, the lanky boy's head cracked against the roof of the coach. Then all three dissolved into laughter and tears. They couldn't remember a time they'd been happier.

"A king must know how — and when — to laugh," said the Queen, as Gavin, shaking his head, reclaimed his seat. "There's plenty of time —

far too much of it — to be serious."

Nothing for me to worry about, thought Fairold. His mind went back to what his brother had said about the blue, yellow, and red worlds that were shaped like balls — people living on huge balls! Yet his father wouldn't have been surprised. "The sky is filled with balls," he would say. "Just as Emryss is, I think, if we could see it from far away."

And what about the round happy yellow worlds the Crown Prince had seen? Would the people there ever have laughed so uncontrollably? Were they made to laugh that way? Was laughter ever important to the God of Heaven?

And what about a red world like their own? Could they ever please God by laughing? Laughing because they knew they'd made a wonderful start in spite of themselves? By stubbornly and almost blindly doing what they felt was right, but still didn't understand?

And what did they really know?

It seemed so little. And made little sense. Some great king in the west was said to need their help. But what could they offer?

So far, they'd been unusually protected. Perhaps because they'd done all they could do according to what they'd been told.

Fairold thought back to the three strange things he'd been told: First, *they would be safe in the coach.* Second, *they were not to touch the horse or its reins.* Third, and strangest of all, was the part about *wonders ceasing after orange and green ride the sky.*

But unexpected surprises in their strange quest were far from over. And, whether or not their laughter was proper, little did they know how soon everything would quickly change.

"To those who have been given much," says an old proverb, "it's no surprise when much is suddenly taken away."

Never would the Queen and her two sons laugh together again.

CHAPTER 19

4
THE
BLACK
RIBBON

he hail was soon followed by a fierce thunderstorm. Then the thunderstorm finally softened into a gentle rain. The hypnotic clomping of the horse's hooves, rhythmic jouncing of sturdy springs over the axles of the coach, and soft blankets made the next several hours come close to Heaven.

The walls of the coach were carved paneling, beautiful to the eye, smooth to touch. It was easy to feel safe in the coach.

And the horse? He seemed to be an extension of the coach itself and was tireless and forever going — it seemed — the right way. But where? Everyone was exhausted, too tired even to think. Soon sleep came once again. And just as well. No thinking or sharing of possibilities would have predicted what was soon to happen.

The Queen fell asleep humming a hymn of praise. The Crown Prince sat staring at his weapon, mechanically polishing over and over his long, beautiful, shining iron blade. Slowly, he returned the sword to its sheath and let his eyes close. On a seat by himself, the younger Prince, not a distinguished swordsman like his brother, and who was alone on his seat, lay down on it and stared at the ceiling, his weapon

134

out and never more than a few inches away.

It was an odd habit. In public, one hand always on or inches from the hilt.

"Don't be so afraid," Gavin had teased, "It's not how close you are to your blade, it's how quickly you can find it and put it into action." Fairold himself dismissed it as just a strange habit. And what difference did it make? He didn't have to set an example.

Finally, the rain stopped, and soon after it the horse. With the carriage suddenly still, everyone awoke. How many hours had passed? Fairold had no idea. Gavin opened the door and everyone tumbled outside. While putting on her shoes, the Queen discovered a basket of fruit under the seat that everyone had overlooked, and from it everyone began to eat.

Sunlight streamed down through the tall trees on either side and a puffy fog steamed up from the cooler ground. The horse stood in place at the side of the road, spattered by mud, showing no signs of weariness, twitching his ears and staring straight ahead with unblinking eyes. Not once did he look back or bend toward the glistening clumps of tall grass which leaned — almost reverently — into their hardened path.

The Queen stared at the great creature that wore the scarlet blanket across his back. Why the blanket? Fairold wondered. Was it some emblem? Or was it covering something?

Suddenly, his eyes caught a short thick scar on the horse's shoulder. His left hand dropped onto his sword hilt. The magic of the horse was not, or had not, been all-protecting.

The Queen moved close to the animal, careful not to touch him. She whispered into the creature's ear.

Gavin and Fairold looked at each other.

Though the horse didn't twitch a muscle, Fairold sensed that the Queen got some answer to whatever she was asking.

135

She turned sharply to the Crown Prince. "O son, deep words from this horse echo in my ear:

'Not of this world,
not of this world,
not of this world,
soon I must go,
soon I must go,
soon I must go.'

"I would give anything to pull away the scarlet blanket, and lean once again against his warm body and bury my face in his snowy mane! Remember the story in our book?"

Slowly Gavin nodded. He looked stunned but neither he nor Fairold said a word. The younger Prince turned to the coach. His hand squeezed the hilt of his sword that was now sheathed. His knees became soft and wobbly. The wood on the outside of the coach had been carefully crafted and painted. But now the beautiful sides and top were battered and bruised. Paint and even small pieces of wood here and there had been knocked away. It had been the hail. While the horse seemed unharmed, the beauty of the coach had been marred. The magic protecting them had limits.

"Don't worry," said Gavin. "It's okay. The coach is well built. Nothing's broken. Let's press on. A king is waiting!"

After they finished eating, Fairold helped his mother back up the steps and followed her into the coach. Gavin mounted the steps to the driver's seat. The splendidly tooled leather reins, which ran from the horse to the brake where they were neatly tied, dipped just enough so the animal had complete freedom.

"I will ride here," said the Crown Prince. "It will look more natural and not attract attention if someone sits in the driver's seat."

"Don't touch the reins!" said the Queen, leaning outside the window.

Off the coach went.

And so went two days of traveling like the wind. Gavin reported that whenever he spoke, the horse would slow down, and that by applying the brake—which he hadn't been forbidden to do—he could bring the coach to an even halt, even though using the brake hadn't seemed required for smooth stops earlier... But, he reassured his mother before she could ask, never did he touch the reins. Periodically, when the coach would stop, the Queen and Fairold would tumble out, refresh themselves, stretch their limbs, and eat fruit on a blanket in the grass before continuing on their way. After two days the fruit was gone.

As the seat could be changed into a bed, at night the Queen slept inside, Fairold on the ground underneath, and Gavin, under the stars high in the wide driver's seat which he'd claimed for himself. The horse, which apparently needed no rest, stood as if tied in place. One couldn't have a better watchman, thought Fairold, and after tossing around a bit each night, the younger Prince fell asleep.

On the third morning a great river, which they'd already once seen in the distance, was clearly visible to the south. At noon they encountered their first inn.

Prince Gavin, who strongly resembled his father, had the look of a king. When he strode though the door with a bare sword, as well as an obvious bag of coins, his mother and brother following, they received the best food, however simple, their host had to offer. Whisperings went on behind their backs, of course, but they encountered no difficulty.

Late that very afternoon Prince Fairold suddenly awoke inside the coach to the now-familiar screech of the brake. He smelled smoke. Horses were neighing wildly.

Instantly, he leaped to the door and turned the handle, his other hand on the hilt of his sword. Something straight ahead in the middle of the road was on fire! The coach quickly slowed. As soon as he dared, Fairold jumped, and rolling once, found his feet. The coach ground to a halt.

137

Blocking the road and facing them was another coach, hopelessly lost in flames. One wheel was broken and up in the driver's seat a man lay slumped to the side, an arrow protruding from his chest. Although the great white horse of their coach stood fast, seemingly indifferent to the flames, the two matching gray horses which pulled the other coach were rearing madly.

Fairold leaped up to the driver's seat of the burning coach, and not seconds too soon. Yanking the poor man's arm, he helped him to the ground. As the man fell, Gavin cut the horses free and away they ran. There was no entering or saving the coach—even seeing what, if anything, was inside. On his own, the white horse pulled his coach with the Queen to the side and beyond the fire, safely away.

"White powder," gasped the man. "Give me white powder!" Fairold offered him water from his flask. The man vigorously shook his head and grabbed Fairold's arm with a viselike grip that hurt. "POWDER!"

"Who did this?" ordered Gavin, pulling his brother safely away. Suddenly, the man, who seemed indifferent to burns on his scalp and other arm, tried to stand and, falling, his eyes grew large. Just as his lips parted, they seemed to lock open. With a scream he tipped backward and fell.

The Queen, now by her sons' side, pulled up the man's head.

But he was dead.

Gavin examined the arrow in the man's chest. And another that was in his shoulder.

"Look at these feathers! Solid black and tipped with blood—blood from the last kill, no doubt. 'Tis the work of Brown Dragoons, I'd say. I'd no idea they came this far west!"

"Or south," added Fairold. "Gavin, have you any idea where we are? How far west, or south, we've come? I don't think we've ever had dealings with anyone here, at least in a long, long time."

138

"Contact with anyone this far west has been forbidden for years," said the Queen, "because of disease...plague...I'm not sure. But now that's been changed—at least partly. We must stay close to the road and not go south to the river."

"But Mother..." Gavin held up an arrow. "We don't know wha..."

"We *do* know," interrupted the Queen, "what we've been told. So we press on."

"On? Just what do we do next?"

"Next? We must quickly bury this poor man and get back in the coach."

Fairold stared straight ahead to where the road disappeared in the west.

"I wonder," he asked, "how much farther the world goes this way. Would we come to the end of it? Or would we come back to where we started?"

"Only with the help of a boat," said Gavin.

"Only with the help of this coach," said the Queen, "will we get to where we're to be next."

A shovel and some other tools were found under the driver's seat, and the man was quickly put in a shallow grave. It was hot and dirty work. The Princes were smudged with soot.

No sooner was Gavin back in the driver's seat, with Fairold and the Queen drowsing inside the coach to the beat of the horse's slow gallop, than once again the coach came to a stop. This time it was the silence that brought Fairold to his senses. His mother was asleep on a pillow across from him. He pushed back the curtain. The sun had nested like a golden egg on the road ahead, casting long shadows behind them.

Fairold opened the door. The hinge gave a long, tired creak.

KA-SPLASH

A stone's throw from the road was the great river.

"COME IN. THE WATER'S FINE!" It was Gavin.

Instantly the Queen was awake. In what seemed like a single motion she was through the door. From the ground she grabbed Gavin's sword, which he'd left behind, and headed for the river.

"GAVIN! COME BACK!" Across the road and through a thicket of shrubs she ran. Suddenly she stopped. "GAVIN! THE GROUND IS BURNED BLACK! BLACK! COME BACK!"

But whether the Crown Prince did not hear, or ducked under the water to avoid it, Fairold never found out.

Cautiously, the Queen held out Gavin's sword and inched forward.

"MOTHER! COME BACK!" Fairold screamed.

The Queen spun around.

"STAY! FAIROLD! STAY WHERE YOU ARE! I ORDER IT!"

"Stay, come, go, return, heel…" Fairold muttered to himself. But, as usual, he obeyed.

Just then Gavin surfaced and climbed up on the bank. Most of the soot and grime he'd washed away. After wringing out his pant legs he headed up the gentle slope to the road. Fairold stood in the doorway of the coach with his hand on the hilt of his sword.

"AAAAAAARRRRRGGGGGHHHH!"

Suddenly Gavin kicked furiously and leaped. Then fell. Instantly, the Queen was at his side and drew him up. Foot by foot she worked her way back, sometimes pulling sometimes dragging her injured son. Then both fell.

Fairold sprang from the doorway, but as he leaped, his head—still tender from the night in the cave on the beach—caught the top of the doorway. He fell, rolling into a ball, then stretching as long as he could on his back. As his head throbbed, the words "DO NOT TOUCH THE RIVER. DO NOT TOUCH THE BLACK RIBBON OF GROUND," went over again and again in his mind.

Desperately, he struggled to his feet. The Queen was moving again and so was his brother. Just as Fairold thought they would make it, Gavin fell once more. The Queen struggled to lift him. Fairold raced to the edge of the burned land.

"STAY BACK!" The Queen's voice was still loud, but hoarse in a way Fairold never had heard before. "IN GOD'S NAME, STAY BACK!" said the Queen. "THE GROUND IS CURSED!"

Fairold threw himself to the ground and did the hardest thing he'd ever done in his life: *Nothing*. "Why? Why? Why? God of Heaven, look down! Look down! Bring them back! Have mercy! Have mercy!"

On the Queen pulled. Gavin had ceased to move. Fairold thought his heart would burst. How his muscles ached from holding back!

When the Queen had only feet to go crossing the black ribbon of ground, lightning cut across the whole sky, and many seconds afterwards a great explosion of thunder rolled in from the northeast. Fairold covered his ears and raised his eyes to what he believed was the direction of his old home. Far away a thick cloud rose from a point on a distant mountain. It was dark...dark green. Then it brightened with touches of yellow which quickly darkened to orange. It was green, green scrambled with orange, a mixture of color Fairold had never seen before in the sky.

Just as he glanced down to his mother, a second explosion pulled his eyes back up. The billowing green-and-orange cloud, instead of expanding, suddenly shrank into the shape of a pulsing morning sun, eerie by contrast to the real sun which had nearly set behind him. Darkness grew by the second.

Two more explosions illuminated the eastern sky, and with the last, the sun-like ball burst apart, spilling a shining thread of greenish orange from north to south across the horizon just above the skyline.

Regardless of where the cloud came from, Fairold sensed that although God had foretold destruction would come, it was nonetheless evil, hidden evil now exposed, perhaps destroyed. Perhaps, but perhaps not. Without a face, without a distinct shape, maybe now it had simply taken a new form.

Something less obvious, more ordinary.

Words flashed into his mind. Long ago when his father who'd once fought a dragon told him stories, he would say, "My son, when the unusual appears, it is often short-lived. So don't forget what you see. If you ever encounter anything strange, remember every detail and, then later carefully write it down."

Had the remains of their doomed kingdom finally been destroyed? Vandor had prophesied it just had "hours left" on the same night he'd received the strange words: "When green and orange ride the eastern sky, many wonders would begin to cease." Had those "hours" now been used up? There was no mistaking the colors that now forced his eyes to the sky. Fairold swallowed hard. Clearly, it was over. Their ancient kingdom was no more.

But that wasn't all.

Fairold glanced down and froze.

While he'd been entranced by the show in the sky, his mother had crawled on hands and knees, dragging his brother the last inches to safe ground. Both lay in the grass at his feet, covered with ashes and dirt.

Gavin's body did not move.

Fairold was horrified, then felt ashamed. Then he saw. Just below his brother's knee and buried to the roots of its fangs was a hideous writhing snake the exact color of the strange sky in the east. Swiftly, Fairold raised his sword and struck off the snake's head and the severed body frantically began to twist and turn. The Queen, eyes closed, rose to her knees and prayed, her lips moving but without any sound. As she prayed, she raised her hands and slipped off her royal ring of the kingdom, identical to the one worn by Fairold and every one else in the royal family. She held it loosely in her open palm. Fairold had never seen her hand bare. He was terrified. Why this? Carefully he pocketed the small treasure.

Suddenly, there was a loud hiss as if water were spilled on a hot kettle. Both the body and head of the snake began to fade. Was the darkening sky playing tricks? With a poof, the snake was gone and the stench of sulfur filled the air.

Fairold bent down. The Crown Prince's face was at peace.

But he was dead.

Then the Queen collapsed. Fairold put his ear to her chest. There was no heartbeat.

"MOTHER!"

There was no answer.

Then he saw the three red spots on her swollen ankle. From stings, not snakebite! But they'd been told the land had been "twice cursed." He would never forget. Then came the buzzing. Gently, he eased up the hem of her long dress and a half-dozen angry bees, unlike any he'd ever seen before dropped from her skirt and scrambled onto his arm. Oddly, none flew. Then the needle jabs began—at least five. Fairold's head began to twist and turn against his will. His arm burned with fire.

For some reason, the winged creatures could not, or would not, fly. The last thing he remembered was crushing them all with his bare hands.

CHAPTER 20

5 REINS FOR THE PRINCE

omething wet and cold touched Fairold's face. The Prince twisted his head. Gently, he was pushed back. He dragged his arm across his face. The creature standing above him edged backwards. It was a horse. Not the white one who'd disappeared, but a gray horse. A second gray horse stood nearby.

Fairold struggled to his feet. It was nearly dawn. A tranquil morning in a world turned unbearably ugly. The magic was gone. He rubbed his arm where he'd been stung. It ached, but not badly.

Slowly, he made himself look down. His mother and brother lay motionless only feet away.

His brother had died. Bitten by a snake, a snake that grew faint and disappeared into thin air before he could totally destroy it.

And his mother?

He knelt by her, but he knew...

The Queen, was also dead. But her face, too, seemed at peace.

"Mother, turn back the quilt of Heaven for soon I will join you."

The bees! The bees, not a snake, had killed her. Her but not him. Why? Because she had crossed the black ribbon of ground but not he?

Or was there some other reason?

His mother had saved his life. Or was it his faith? Or fear? These questions gnawed at his stomach. If it was fear, it had turned his will into iron. Now if he had to die next, so be it! And he'd take anything orange and green with him.

The wide strip of black ground ran both ways before disappearing behind trees. How did it protect? And protect from what? Snakes? And bees that can't fly?

To think was better than to feel.

Then blind anger began to take hold. He took a pick and shovel from the box under the driver's seat. Furiously he attacked the earth to do what had to come next. Several times he fell back in the pale grass panting, only to spring up and begin digging in the rocky soil again. The sun was high when his mother and brother lay deep under an oval mound of earth beside a towering pine. He had kissed them — the last people he loved and even knew — good-bye. And after removing Gavin's ring, he buried them. He collapsed, soaked in tears and sweat.

Oddly, the gray horses, rather than scurry away, stood close by, nuzzling the Prince whose brother had earlier saved their lives from the flaming coach. The wonderful white horse had disappeared along with the snake and everything else orange and green. For some reason the horses had followed them. Horses that touched him must be safe to touch back — and be harnessed. And in harness, they must receive signals from the reins. And stop to eat and rest.

With little difficulty the horses were put in place.

Fairold climbed into the driver's seat. Mumbling a quick prayer, he untied the forbidden reins. Where would he go? There was nothing to go back to. He couldn't stay where he was, wherever that was. The horses were already aimed to the west. As the second royal child, Fairold had lived in the shadow of the Crown Prince, and was far quieter than his sister or questing younger brother.

But now he was the only one left. He took the reins and the horses seemed glad to be on their way.

"Thank you, God, for these horses," Fairold prayed.

This time a team of two horses — ordinary ones — were pulling. The animals seemed eager enough, but they needed testing. Fairold made them speed up and slow down. He tested the brakes. The wonderful coach now required a driver and horses, and the horses certainly seemed willing enough. Of course their speed was not now what it once was, and stops for rest became more frequent. Fairold was careful to stop where the grass was thick and green. And at one place, after stopping to grease the wheels which had begun squeaking, Fairold found a pond — on the north side — where he could bathe and put on his second set of clothes.

High on the driver's seat, it helped to think about other things. To feel the marvelous suspension of the coach sink and rise under his shifting weight. To see the horses flick their tails in unison. To hear the wheels creak and scrunch against the occasional soft places in the road. Oddly, the coach encountered no traffic whatever.

Slowly, slowly, the sun sank, impaling itself on the tall pines lining the road far ahead. Soon the road veered slightly to the left and the first gray of dusk elbowed in. Fairold took out his sword. From his seat he gently swung at and parried the blades of imaginary enemies. Even just moving his arm helped hold back the tears that the shadows seemed to encourage. As the sun disappeared, a low, two-story rambling building on the left came into view. He laid his weapon down and slowed the horses. At the railing , just across the road from the building, stood a half-dozen horses bearing shields and military bags. The banner and coat of arms were unfamiliar.

It was a tavern, probably with rooms upstairs.

He stopped at the rail. Angry shouts rang out from inside. Some sort of argument was going on, but other than the cursing, he couldn't make out the words. The gray horses laid back their ears. He tied their reins next to the other horses.

Before Fairold had time to lay out much of a plan, curiosity and an uncharacteristic recklessness came over him. Bitterness and anger welled up. Let it all end here! He fought for control as he'd carefully been taught. Never could he explain what he did next. Quickly, he untied each strange horse at the rail, and with gentle prodding they bolted away. Holding forth the naked blade of his sword, he silently approached the heavy oak door.

If death were to come, let it come now and quickly, he prayed.

But little did Prince Fairold know that, not once but *twice* in a single day, his future would completely change. And in a way he would never have predicted.

The trouble inside the tavern, and what led up to it, Fairold learned about all too soon. That's what comes next. But what led up to the argument is better told by someone inside—someone whose life was in grave danger.

Her story begins an hour earlier.

CHAPTER 21

6
BOAR'S
HOOF
INN

ambith Letterbrook would not stand still. She flicked her thick brown braids over her shoulder and leaned over on one foot, extending her thin body across the top of a long table. She wiped the wide planks for the dozenth time. Simultaneously, she ran the fingers of her left hand just underneath the table edge as if trying to feel something hidden there.

It was late afternoon and the effect was odd. Partly because the table was already spotless, and partly because the left-handed girl seemed too young and thin to serve in a tavern. At least in such a deliberate, but breezy manner. The smell of roast pork was everywhere. Rosebeth and Baylene, the other two maids, were in and out of the kitchen preparing for the evening meal. The few customers already present were not the curious sort and had just begun drinking, the main reason they'd come. So no one was paying anyone much mind.

Lambith was counting on that.

The table's surface was smooth from the heavy traffic of endless plates and tankards, almost glowing in the fading light poking like a spear through a tiny window overhead.

It was here that the Lord Dr. Oxram would sit, for it was the best place in the room, where one could sit safely with his back to the wall. Oxram would settle for nothing less. Years ago Oxram had unfairly confiscated — "stolen" is the better word — Lambith's father's farm on the great river and had left the man penniless and dying.

Above the table, at the westernmost end of the room and far from the outside door, a low, sagging ceiling began, over which several small bedrooms looked up into a thick roof of thatch. The nearly windowless walls of the sprawling room with its dozen or so tables were smoky white, a few simple pictures hanging here and there. But that was all.

The table was also farthest from the hubub at the kitchen door on the far inside wall behind the long bar, that ran parallel to the road, directly across from the outside door, but a bit to the left. More important, the table rested on a row of crude flooring a step higher than everything else, like a stage so that when the serving maids approached with heavy pitchers and platters, they had to slow their pace and carefully lift their skirts to step up without tripping.

Lord Oxram liked that. With a little imagination, the pause amidst the hustle and bustle could pass for honor or respect, which nowadays, unlike the doctor's newest cure, a white powder, he had much too little of to suit his taste.

Not, of course, without reason.

With little imagination, the elevated table could pass for a judge's table, because behind it a drinker or diner could face anyone from a commanding position. Or, if need be, with a half dozen friends even defend oneself with weapons. And since the recent plague of walking bees, and the recent death of Lord Emberly and his entire family, certainly Oxram could be counted upon to take every precaution as well as every opportunity.

Oxram, next to Emberly, was the wealthiest man in the western end of the Emperor's domain. And he was a physician of some ability, though nowadays only desperation drove people to the man for his remedies.

With Lord Oxram things were not quite right, and while a few paid the man great attention as well as much money, many others found his latest cure very disturbing.

As to the barony itself, which had fallen to the Lord Doctor upon Lord Emberly's death, there was an uneasiness. The Boar's Hoof was located in the exact center of the barony but, modest as it was, the tavern did not belong to him. Still, it was here that important business often took place and local gossip was exchanged.

Now in the best of times Brown Dragoons, who were scattered far and wide in Emryss and were even known in Fairold's old kingdom, were simple outlaws who served only themselves. But that was changing, Fairold would soon learn. By ones and twos, robbers at least on the fringe of this gypsy group began turning to the Lord Doctor, and more and more fierce men now wore his strange coat of arms—which closely resembled the four stakes of the God-Son turned upside down.

And then there were the chilling, heavily armed warriors from Lord Oxram's palatial estate, who accompanied their master everywhere.

In the past few days the ugliness had reached a head. Eventually, Lambith was sure, the Emperor of the West, who she'd heard of but never seen, would finally arrive personally to sort things out. If only the people around her could hold on. But now once again, this very evening, Lord Oxram could be expected to arrive.

※　※　※

To better understand the desperate events about to happen, a week earlier an important conversation took place in this very room, and Lambith had been part of it.

In the wee hours of morning after every customer had left, the maids had finished their work, and it was silent upstairs, two men remained, sitting at the very table that Lambith later would be polishing. A burning candle stub stuck in a brown bottle dribbled wax and made shadows dance as Lambith, pitcher in hand, walked up and filled two half-empty cups and then her own which she'd brought. She pulled up a chair and sat.

"You may go now Lambie. It's been a long day. Everything looks fine," said her Uncle Merkle, a childless man, whose grandfather had built the Boar's Hoof. His lips moved behind a heavy gray, drooping mustache, that contrasted with thin strands of gray atop the bald head capping his stout frame.

The other man was Father Marc, Merkle's brother and Lambith's other uncle. The two had taken different roads; yet Father Marc's wandering path frequently crossed his brother's more predictable steps late at night under the sagging beams of the Boar's Hoof. This night was one of those times. The three sat nearly motionless before the flickering candle that exaggerated their silhouettes and made everyone seem like an eavesdropping intruder. A nearly dead fire still glowed on the hearth.

"I've no intention of *going* anywhere, my dear uncles," said Lambith, forcing a servant's smile. "But what are we to do?" Her large brown eyes were impossible to ignore. The slender girl sat straight and riveted her gaze on first one man, then the other. Slowly and mechanically she began undoing her braids.

"*Do?*" said Uncle Merkle, arching his bushy eyebrows. The thick hair left on the sides of his head matched his mustache.

"*We?*" said Father Marc. By contrast the dark-robed priest was slender, and his head was covered with dark hair that fell over his ears. "Do about what?"

"Don't play games with me, Father Marc! I'm hardly a child! We're in serious trouble here and I want to know what we ought to do about it!"

The priest stared at the girl he and Merkle had raised after Lambith's father had died, and then her mother who was the brothers' sister. Lambith respected the priest and what he stood for, but she refused to put him on a pedestal.

"The trouble," said Father Marc, collecting his thoughts, "runs far and wide...At its root...at its root is faith, lack of faith, lack of real faith, I'd say. Lack of true worship in the God of Heaven. Same problem as at a lot of places. That's the root. Now the trunk and the branches and the leaves...I'm not sure."

"*Uncle* Marc, look at me!" Lambith interrupted. The priest had a reputation for taking something simple like "tree" and growing a forest around it so that the tree he started with would disappear.

"Okay, Lambith" — Father Marc smiled — "Okay. There are some strange things going on. There's this new plague of walking bees..."

"Go on," interrupted Lambith.

"And there's been reports about serpents — orange and green ones that most people think only belong in storybooks."

"And?" said Lambith, fearing another digression.

"And there's those unexplained deaths, our own Baron Emberly, for one. And there's the Emperor who's 'far away' and, according to what I hear, may be seriously ill. Everywhere I go people seem restless. And the worship of God is neglected. Things are not good. Times are bad. And we who truly believe — we must be cautious; we're so few... so powerless."

"And *powderless* I hope," added Lambith. "Haven't you forgotten something important?"

"Yes, there's the doctor's powder, too," said Uncle Marc, "and..."

"Sssssshhhhh!" said Uncle Merkle, offering his first words. "The walls have ears these days — especially here!"

152

Lambith stared into the reddened eyes of her beloved Uncle Merkle and frowned. The black-robed priest had never been far away for long, but it was the bald tavern keeper who'd actually been her mother and father after her parents' untimely deaths. And he'd never complained. Besides Father Marc, Lambith was Merkle's only living relation. Someday, responsibility for the busy Boar's Hoof could fall to her.

The priest continued, turning his words up to the ceiling:

"O God" — the angular man folded his hands and looked up to the thick beam overhead — "make any evil ears nearby deaf to our words."

"Amen!" said Merkle, raising his eyes to Lambith while Marc lowered his to the girl.

"We must be quiet about the white powder and trust God," said Father Marc.

"And," interrupted Merkle, "we must wait for the Emperor. I have faith in the man, regardless of what you've heard. He can set things right. And he loves the God of Heaven. I'm sure of it!"

"In the meantime, I suppose," said Lambith, shuffling her feet, "we're to watch while everyone bows and scrapes to our new self-appointed protector, 'His Honor' the Lord Dr. Oxram and his thugs, and let him 'heal' us with his new 'powder of peace'! Right? Look around you. Soon everyone will be using it! Well, I for one would rather live 'unprotected' and die sick!"

"Sssshhhh, Lambie!" — Merkle wiped his hands on the apron that covered his ample paunch — "Oxram's powder is the only thing that's proven to cure the sting of the walking bees, and many say it cures boils, indigestion, nervousness, even the bite of the snakes..."

"And at what price, Merkie?" Father Marc extended his arms. "It's true, Ankor and Tyron's stableboy were stung several times and weeks later they're still alive, but have you seen them? Have you looked into their eyes? Their bodies live, but their eyes are glassy. Their minds seem to be wiped clean. They do nothing but call for more and more of the powder which Oxram sells for a higher and higher price! It's as if someone else lives in their bodies! And Ankor—no man was more kind or generous—remembers nothing, not even his own wife!"

"Not always a curse, Marc!"

"Merkie! I'm ashamed of you!" The feeble attempt at silence had failed. Father Marc poked his brother's paunch—"the powder is a curse! One that God must set right. Lambith is correct. It's straight from the Great Dragon himself! Don't ever touch it—for any reason. I've seen what it does to the people who use it and to the people around them. I tell you, the God of Heaven hates it!"

"But Marc, just where in the Holy Book does it say that? Has God, or prayer, or anything else ever had any effect on the stings – this plague brought upon us by the white Elphs, who the stings never hurt?

"And *why* aren't they hurt?

"And why do the Elphs, who except for their papery skin and height, resemble us in almost every way, ignore the Holy Book and always seem to know more than we do?

"And in spite of the awful bees that have followed them here, why are the 'peaceful' Elphs still sought out by kings to be counselors? Why? They don't even believe in God!" As he spoke, his cheeks began to redden, almost by the second. Sweat began to bead up on his face. His eyes rolled up to the ceiling. He grabbed the edge of the table before continuing.

So many words coming from her uncle! Lambith hardly recognized him. Something was not right.

"And Marc"—Merkle's eyes snapped down to the girl's face as if he sensed what she was thinking—"haven't you ever wondered if we've been 'given God' to keep us ignorant and satisfied, while kings, and even the emperor, know something more, something higher?" Merkle's face was now dark red. He glanced at his brother then began oddly staring at his feet. A drop of sweat fell from his nose.

"Lambie, dear" — his voice faded, then leaped back to full strength — "you'd better leave. It's just my headache, or I wouldn't be spouting off so. You really shouldn't be hearing this…"

"And why not?" The girl who'd just finished undoing her braids, tossed her head and her long, crinkled tresses whipped at the candle flame nearly extinguishing it. The effect was dramatic coming from the almost frail-looking girl. Her next words leaped out at the tavern keeper:

"I shouldn't be hearing this because…because I'm a child? A child you personally raised and taught year after year? A child who now teaches our maids everything they need to know to serve any kind of customer? Or is it because I'm a woman? Maybe the Elphs aren't the problem at all!" Then her voice softened. "Please, Uncle Merkie, I have eyes and ears! I'm not dumb! And you know I'm with you to the end."

"End of what?" Merkle jumped up. The effect was odd. He was sweating profusely. "Do you know something I don't?"

"Merkie, the girl stays as long as she likes. God only knows what you'd do without her — though I'm truly, truly sorry she has to live *here*. If her mother and father only…"

"Excuse me, *Father* Marc," Lambith interrupted, deliberately not choosing the word 'uncle,' "what goes on here, and how it affects my uncle and me is something between Uncle Merkie and me — it is our business, and the God of Heaven's who's listening to our silly words…O Dear God, forgive me…"

"Lambith," said the priest, "Your Uncle Marc" — he pointed to her chest — "will have a long talk with you later! I'm also family. Your… attitude…leaves something to be desired. You think you live in a 'palace' and can say anything you want? Well, wake up and thank God that you don't! These days, love for God in royal courts is hardly

155

the fashion, and with our low birth, slopping pigs is more honest than wearing a crown!"

The priest smiled and once again studied the ceiling, seeming to reach for a lesson if not a whole parable. "But God is merciful: pigs are a lot safer and more appreciative than people these days! You have the best of both worlds: the world of Emryss here as well as the promise of Heaven to come."

Lambith puzzled at where the priest was going with all this.

"Father Marc — Uncle Marc — I'm hardly slopping pigs..."

"Well," said the priest, "you could have fooled me!" His arm swept the room with its dozen tables. He pushed back his chair and laughed. "Your great-grandfather knew what he was doing when he named this place!"

"Uncle Marc" — Lambith's voice was uncharacteristically soft — "I'm confused." She glanced to the counter. "Please explain to me: Am I or am I not 'suited' for this 'sty' called the 'Boar's Hoof'? Do I not get the letters right? There are only nine of them! See, not only can I read, but I can count!" She pointed to the letters at the sign behind the counter,

BOAR'S HOOF

then sat up stiffly and dropped her hands into her lap.

"I certainly hope," she added, "that my other uncle here who lets you fill his stomach with what I bring you to eat doesn't think you're commenting on his food! Here, have something more to drink, something pigs wouldn't touch."

Before either uncle could refuse, with a single motion her slender arm lifted the heavy pitcher and refilled both cups. Both men looked at each other, shook their heads — Merkle smiling for the first time — and while each took a long drink, Lambith dropped both her fists to the table and continued:

156

"Really, Uncle Marc, I'm sorry, really sorry. I know you're a priest — a true one — but even if I'm ignorant of books, it's plain to see that things are really terrible here. And the one thing that's obviously evil through and through is the white powder, Lord Dr. Oxram's powder."

She turned and stared at Merkle.

"People swear by it, will give anything for it, and the more they get, the more they want. I've seen it day in and day out. At least one of Oxram's armed henchmen is always nearby. Last week more money has changed hands across our tables for white powder than ale! Oxram's got people eating — literally eating — out of the palm of his hand."

The priest turned to his brother.

"Merkie, is this true?" There was silence. "Merkie, remember the questions you asked? First, you've wondered why this powder is evil. Yes, the Holy Book says nothing about it, and little about any remedies. But think — do you know of anyone who's been completely cured by it? Anyone who's taken it and is better off than before? True, a few have lived longer than expected, but none were better off. Not one person.

"Second, you asked, 'Has God protected us in any way from the stings?' Quite frankly, I don't know anyone to be cured by prayer. But God, through the Elphs, if you will, has taught us clearly how to *avoid* the walking bees. Burn 20-feet-wide strips east to west — and keep the land blackened — just north of the river. Yes, we're without water from there, but water is plentiful from the north. And you know, we've become careless about that. In several places grass grew up over the burned spots, and bees were able to travel over new grass. For that we must blame ourselves.

"Third — are you still with me, Merkie? — you asked about the Elphs: 'Why aren't they hurt by the stings? Why don't they believe in the God of Heaven?' They have said over and over, that not long ago they came from 'far away,' from a place we've never been, and that the bees came with them, bees that mated with bees in this country. They are 'used to' such bees, they say, and have been for generations, so the stings have little effect on them.

"In all fairness, several Elphs have tried their magic on us by marking several of us with arm scratches to shield us from the bees' magic power. Unfortunately, this was not widely done because of fear. And as you know, the priests are divided about whether this should be done."

At these words Merkle's face grew even darker red and his eyes became fierce.

"No Elph will ever scratch me and live!" said the tavern keeper. He wiped his face with his sleeve. Lambith leaned forward and again put her elbows on the table and cradled her chin. Her eyes were riveted on the priest.

The priest, ignoring this, continued:

"As to what the few Elphs among us *believe*, most, it is true, still reject God. 'Primitive superstitution,' they insist, but their words are rarely unkind. Some, in fact, read the Holy Book. Never have they been openly hostile to holy things as have been our own Brown Dragoons.

"One Elph told me, 'We've learned deep things about which Emryssites know nothing. We know by what must seem to be great magic that the world *suddenly* began *billions* of years ago, and will eventually end. But why? And how did life begin? How did simple things become complicated things? We've never found out. And how can Elphs and Emryssites marry each other and have children as some do?' About such matters like this a few Elphs have found our Holy Book to be quite profound."

"Elph nonsense!" exclaimed Merkle.

"Nonetheless, Merkie, our kings eagerly seek those few Elphs among us to be advisors. They know things that can make our lives better. And they're hardly a threat in combat because of the weakness of their pale skins to face too much sunlight.

"And Merkie, you asked, too, if 'we've been "given God" to keep us ignorant and satisfied' while others live by some greater truth. For me that is the easiest…"

Suddenly, Merkle kicked back his chair and stood. Sweat poured from his forehead. His shirt was soaking wet.

"Don't…I don't want to hear it…no…no, not now!" Merkle turned his back to the table and frantically dug into a pocket beneath his huge apron. Suddenly, his hand emerged and flew to his face. Father Marc leaped to his feet and grabbed him from behind. Merkle drove an elbow back into the priest's stomach, doubling him over. The tavern keeper himself collapsed on the floor.

Instantly, Lambith was at his side. She pried apart his fingers and screamed:

"White powder!" She struggled to force open his mouth. His tongue was white. "Uncle Merkie, how could you! How long have you been eating this? Why?"

But consciousness had slipped away, and other than Father Marc's struggle to regain his breath, the room was silent. Never had Lambith talked so sharply with her uncles. Now the conversation was over.

✳   ✳   ✳

Of course, this all took place a week earlier — before the tavern maid carefully prepared her table for an expected guest. Yes, trouble was no stranger to the Boar's Hoof Tavern — both inside and out. But the worst was yet to come.

CHAPTER 22

7
LORD
DOCTOR
OXRAM

 en-year-old Kerky Greenwald always carried a stout stick, and if anyone were crazy — harmless crazy, though one couldn't be sure — it was he. Of course, Millie Gatewood, a red-haired orphan a year-and-a-half younger, sharply disagreed.

Millie worked in the kitchen of the Boar's Hoof, and lived in a tiny room of her own behind the great oven and next to a larger room that was Lambith's home. There was no mistaking that Millie worshiped the ground Kerky walked on.

Not because she'd ever talked with him, because she hadn't. This despite endlessly chattering with anyone who frequented the tavern. And why not Kerky, who always wore leather leggings and a coarse goatskin shirt with the stakes of the God-son burned into the front?

Because he never spoke to anyone, not so much as a word. Millie, of course, had talked to him, but never *with* him. And was the boy even capable of speech? Opinion was divided.

Kerky's silence was hardly a problem to Millie, who had plenty words of her own ready when the strange orphan would drop in with bags of wild fruits and spices to trade. These he'd gathered from the woods where, as far as anyone knew, he lived by himself. More than once he'd patch in new thatch over the small upstairs gables at the tavern, and in exchange, Uncle Merkle would give the boy loaves of sourdough bread and other foods hard to come by.

Always before Millie let him escape, she'd force him into a corner of the kitchen — only she could get away with this — and stuff him like a goose with every possible kind of food. Then filled, he would suddenly slip away as if entering the tavern were a necessary evil for business, and not a place to while away time.

✳   ✳   ✳

Very soon before Fairold's arrival, and soon after Lambith polished the table a last time, the moment she was waiting for had come. But before Lord Oxram's appearance, Father Marc arrived. It had been a long week since his brother had collapsed under the spell of the white powder.

Uncle Merkle had revived, of course, but barely so. All he could do was some of the simplest work. Nothing more. He was a changed man, mumbling to himself, and spending long periods wearing a clean apron sitting behind the bar on a bench, staring vacantly at where the wall seemed to join the ceiling across the dining room. So Lambith took charge. Rosebeth, Baylene, Millie, and Chargan the cook made no objection, customers were told the tavern keeper was ill, and life went on as before.

At last, when the room was half full, there came the pounding of horses' hooves. Then an exchange of curses. Rosebeth and Baylene noticeably stiffened, and the three maids exchanged glances. Millie peered in from just inside the kitchen where she stood peeling a potato with an oversized knife.

Suddenly, the great door burst open, and six armed men, wearing mail, helmets, and light armor, entered in a deliberate single file. Lord Dr. Oxram, a stout man though muscular and tall, was fourth; and just behind him was a soldier carrying a conspicuous bulging canvas bag over his shoulder.

Without breaking pace, all but the first man who remained by the door, made their way to the far table that Lambith, with difficulty, had kept empty. Oxram claimed the center chair on the back side and descended upon it. All but the Lord Doctor removed their helmets. The soldiers at either end, on cue, unsheathed their swords and lay them across the ends of the polished table top.

The entry was a pattern Oxram had devised. In these difficult times when many needed his "services," he was not one to take chances.

But neither were the serving maids—in bad times or good. After all, the inn was mainly a tavern.

Rosebeth was an attractive widow nearly twice Lambith's age. She struggled to avert her eyes and remain calm. Nervously she tucked in a curl that had escaped the bandana that hid her luxurious auburn hair. Her hand fell to the cloth belt tied around her waist and fingered the short, sharp dagger that she always carried.

If Rosebeth were slender beneath her bulky dress, Baylene, the second maid was not. Four years older than Lambith, she was stout and clearly the strongest of the serving women. Her blonde hair cascaded over her shoulders when not tied back. She, too, as others in her profession, carried a hidden weapon.

Both looked at Lambith as if waiting direction. For the moment she ignored them. Lambith's carefully braided brown hair and simple homespun dress allowed no folds or secret places. The dress fell to a foot from the floor and the narrow tie around her waist allowed no room for weapons. Nor did she carry any.

Lambith, facing the men, busily polished a plate she held. She glanced over it and studied the Lord Doctor. The chain mail across his chest rose to a thick leather collar under his chin. The thin silver-edged helmet sloped down to his heavy brows and, except for ear holes, descended on the sides and back to within an inch of the leather collar. A bright silver band crossed the helmet hiding the bridge of his nose. Only the eyes and an area about the mouth were exposed.

It was unusual to wear inside even an ornate dress helmet, as this was, but these were unusual times. A royal blue cape fell from Oxram's shoulders. On his chest was the defiant, X-shaped emblem of four arrowheads pointing up, which with little imagination appeared to be an inverted symbol of the stakes of the God-Son.

Lambith received a tray of tankards from the kitchen and delivered it personally. When she leaned across the table to hand the first tankard to Oxram, he reached out and grabbed one of her braids.

"Just one minute, Lassie!" He raised the tankard to her lips and forced her to drink, spilling a generous portion down her dress. Lambith, unable to move, stiffened without wincing as the cold liquid sloshed on the floor. Oxram waited a full minute to see the effect on the girl. When convinced the drink was safe, he shoved the tray to his men and took a long drink. Still holding the girl's braid, he wiped his mouth with the back of his hand.

Suddenly, he pulled and drew her face to his. Everyone turned and stared.

"Aye, a pretty lass like you shouldn't waste her life in a pig sty like this!" His lips curled into a smile. "Sorry about your dress. Here, get another." With his free hand he found a large copper coin and tossed it, striking the girl on the neck. For an instant the coin stuck before sliding down her dress out of sight. "Come," said the Lord Doctor, "come back with me and I'll make you a lady!" One soldier beside him muffled a laugh.

Lambith heard footsteps behind her. The soldiers on each end raised their swords. She forced herself to giggle. She dropped her hand on Oxram's wrist and squeezed. The instant he relaxed his grip she broke free.

She turned to the priest behind her and glared. She motioned to him to step away. Father Marc raised his eyebrows and eased backwards. Lambith spun back to Oxram.

"Oh...you honor me, Lord Doctor!" Slipping back out of his reach, she bowed, then with an eye on the edge of the platform, she deliberately stumbled and fell into the arms of her uncle.

"Father Marc, I'm okay," she whispered. "Get back and leave me alone!" She tore away from his grasp as if offended and looked shocked. The men laughed. She turned to Oxram and extended her arms.

"Me...be a lady?" It was her turn to laugh. "You don't really know me, Lord Doctor! I'd be nothing but trouble! Besides, I'm too young and clumsy, and still in the service of my uncle."

Too late she realized she'd said too much. Lambith scanned the room. There were several unfamiliar faces, faces with eyes only on the canvas bag that lay in plain view on the table. One man unconsciously licked his lips. Uncle Merkle was staring. Lambith swallowed a groan.

Suddenly, Merkle rose and, with his hands out as if sleepwalking, he approached the bag. Lambith moved into his path. His eyes were vacant and he was soaked with sweat.

"Uncle Merkie, NO!"

"So that's the uncle you serve!" Oxram smiled. "Come here, Uncle Merkie. I have something for you." From inside his pocket he drew out a small vial. He held it out like a bone to a dog. The tavern keeper staggered forward with quickness that Lambith hadn't seen in years. Brusquely, he pushed her aside and snatched the bottle.

"Slowly, Uncle Merkie," said Oxram, teasing.

Whether her uncle knew or simply didn't care, Lambith never

knew. Out came the cork, and in front of everyone, Merkle tipped back his head and downed all the powdery contents.

Why powder from the vial and not the bag? the tavern maid wondered.

Just then the outside door flew open and nearly smacked the soldier standing there in the face. In stepped Kerky Greenwald with his walking stick in one hand and a bag of his own in the other.

"Well, look what the cat dragged in!" said Oxram. "And look at what he's wearing on his chest—the stakes of the God-Son!" Oxram stood. "And a staff, too! I think we have a prophet here. Speak, boy. Give us a message from God!" From his pocket Oxram drew another copper coin and flipped it toward the boy. Kerky ignored it and headed straight for the kitchen.

"Speak to me, boy! I'm talking to you! If you wear the stakes of the God-Son, you tell us poor sinners what he says!" Oxram's men laughed. "Roland"—the Lord Doctor turned to the soldier at the door—"cut the emblem off that prophet boy's shirt! The little faker's got nothing to say!"

The guard's sword was out in a flash. He walked toward the boy.

"Kerky, he's right behind you!" Millie screamed from the kitchen. She dropped her potato, but not the knife, and sprang into the room.

At the sight of the girl, Kerky dropped his bag and turned mechanically. As the soldier came within reach and extended his sword, Kerky, without showing a trace of fear, humbly bowed his head. Puzzled, the soldier lowered his weapon.

"What the...?"

These were the last words he said for some time, for just as he spoke, Kerky jerked his staff up between the soldier's legs. As the man screamed and doubled over, his body twisted so his backside faced Millie. The girl aimed the knife and threw with all her might. The second scream was louder than the first.

Roland fell, writhing in agony.

Kerky grabbed the fallen man's sword, held it over the fallen man, at the same time pushing Millie behind him into the kitchen.

Lord Oxram roared with laughter and, on cue, so did the rest of the men. None dared move from the table without Oxram's order, as they'd been trained.

Father Marc made his way to Lambith's side.

"Your Uncle Merkie's been poisoned!" he whispered. "You're in big trouble! You have no uncle left to serve! Quick, slip out the back through the kitchen. I'll calm them down."

"With what, Father Marc, just words?" Tears welled up in her eyes. She wiped them away and refused to look down. If anyone leaves, it's you, Uncle Marc!" The priest's jaw dropped. "Father Marc" — she fought back more tears — "the powder in that bag on the table is all that there is. I know it. And the recipe — only Oxram knows it. He always carries the powder with him. He trusts no one. He won't even help one of his own who's wounded. He's always surrounded by soldiers who fear their families will be killed if anything happens to him. He's said to have royal blood.

"Listen, Uncle Marc. Tend to Merkie, but first take Roland into the kitchen before he recovers and tie and gag him...and bring back his sword."

"But, Lambith..."

"Do it!"

She turned from the priest as if he wasn't there, and nodded to her maids, another tray of tankards appeared, and she spun around to face the Lord Doctor. Mercifully, someone pulled her uncle away behind the bar. The hardest thing she'd ever done was now to ignore her dying uncle and pretend. Her stomach knotted.

"More ale! We'll dress your comrade's wounds, so drink up! This round's on the house!"

"But the boy and girl are in that room!" said Oxram, pointing.

"They are in my service and will be dealt with, Lord Doctor." Father Marc returned from the kitchen with the soldier's sword. Lambith nodded and the priest handed it to the soldier on the end. She bowed to the doctor. "Are we not already in your hands?"

CHAPTER 23

8

A
SURPRISE
GUEST

he felling of one of Lord Oxram's soldiers by a stick swung by a mute, skinny ten-year-old boy caused no small stir. Everyone was whispering. As Lambith recalled later, fear could be smelled, but oddly not a person present left. Oddest of all was the almost total ignoring of Merkle, who most probably thought was sleeping off whatever had suddenly come over him.

But his sleep was an eternal one. And apparently only Father Marc knew, and Lambith suspected but refused to think about it.

Which was fine with Lord Oxram.

Several drinkers with flushed faces — mostly strangers in the two dozen or so present — seemed riveted to the pillow-shaped bag. Oxram's "patients" must have learned of his whereabouts and followed him to the Boar's Hoof. But if some present were victims of the powder, others, mainly regular customers, were held hostage by their own curiosity. Whatever would come next?

As Lambith again leaned over and down with her tray, she saw that the other maids were easing their way with trays to each end of the table.

But the Lord Doctor was also waiting.

As soon as a braid fell within reach, Oxram grabbed it with his left hand. With his right he whipped out a knife.

"How dare you make light of one of my men being harmed?" he snarled.

Lambith screamed. Oxram pressed the braid on the table and began slowly sawing it with his knife. He laughed as strand after strand of brown hair fell away. Now Lambith, after years of serving, was much stronger than she looked. Frantically, she grabbed Oxram's right hand and instead of shoving it away, pushed it down, severing the braid completely and for an instant pinned the man's hand to the table.

The tavern maid's left hand darted under the table. With a jerk, she pulled away the long heavy knife wedged in the crack where she'd hidden it. With a flick of her arm she drew the weapon behind her back. There was one unprotected inch of neck below the helmet and above the chest of mail. No room for error. No second try.

As the crunch meant the braid was completely cut, Oxram rolled his hand over the girl's, pinning her instead. Ripping away the severed braid with his left hand, he held the trophy up, threw back his head and roared with laughter.

It couldn't have been more perfect!

With every ounce of strength she ever had, Lambith swung furiously from the left in a wide arc all the way to the right. Only the Lord Doctor's neck was in between.

The sideways attack from the *left* was so sudden, so unexpected, so powerful, and so accurate (for the girl was left-handed) that Oxram never knew what hit him. If it weren't for his neck bone, his head might have dropped off backward to the floor.

The soldiers couldn't have been more surprised. As those on each end found their naked blades already on the table and stood facing the girl, the weapons suddenly clattered to the floor, and each man fell forward across the polished wood, joining their master. A knife rose in each man's back. Rosebeth and Baylene had also struck. Chargan the cook slipped from the kitchen doorway with a huge meat cleaver and edged toward the table.

This left only the two soldiers next to Oxram on either side. Each struggled to draw his sword. Lambith knew she must act fast. Her return swing was too low, missing the one on Oxram's right and giving only a glancing blow to the one on the left. Furious, she drew back and stabbed forward. The thin knifepoint found a chink in the mail, and blood immediately appeared in the shallow wound.

As Lambith lunged again, the soldier on the right caught her hand and the blade fell. Instantly he was over the table, pinning the girl down by the throat.

Then two unusual things happened:

First, a stranger transfixed by the bag of white powder ever since he entered, finally found his chance. Like a gazelle he was over a table, overturning oil lamps on either end. Three others followed and, ignoring the poor tavern maid, one seized a fallen sword and slashed open the bag. A cloud of white rose from the floor. All at once a dozen men were upon the bag in a frenzy. More tables were overturned. More lamps and candles fell. Since the powder was quite flammable, several greasy trenchers and jackets and benches were soon smoldering while the white cloud thickened. Then the powder in the air ignited and sparks danced like fireflies.

Secondly, the outside door opened once again. In the doorway stood a young man in royal clothing holding a sword. On his scarlet cloak was the coat of arms of a kingdom not known to Lambith's people, but across his tunic was the golden X-shaped emblem of the stakes of the God-Son.

That marking, however, was very familiar .

CHAPTER 24

9

A
DECISIVE
MOVE

rince Fairold knew he'd walked into the middle of deadly conflict. And instantly, he knew it was no accident he was there. Death lay before him. He could smell it, along with other troubling smells.

But the horror of death was now no stranger. Under his fingernails, though he'd scrubbed them till they nearly bled, was the soil from burying his mother and brother that morning.

But now the girl on the floor held his attention. A soldier was at her throat. Why would a dozen able-bodied men ignore her struggle?

Then he saw the white powder. It was everywhere, with men kneeling in it and scooping it up like sand.

White powder.

"White powder" had been the dying driver's last words. The last words of a bleeding man with parched lips. If anything seemed clearly evil, this was it.

It was time to act.

He surveyed the smoky room. A tiny man—a cook, most likely—held a cleaver, and a small boy with a stick like a spear, and a girl with

171

a knife—much too small for all this—were coughing and inching their way toward two furious seasoned soldiers, one slightly wounded it seemed, and the other holding the girl. Nearby, two maids, with blood on their aprons, stood terrified. Three fallen men lay without moving across a long table, the one in the middle lying in a pool of blood. Who were they? Then he caught sight of one soldier's breastplate with the stakes of the God-Son—but wait! The stakes were upside down in mockery!

This made it more clear.

But why were the wide-eyed men, not in the powder, hiding under tables or back against the wall? Bystanders or cowards. Probably not enemies. Waiting to side with who would win.

Fairold could understand. He hated fighting, even the practice field.

What would Gavin do? In palace games he would needle him. "Fairold, you must *announce sides, eye everyone, be clear, be loud, show no fear, act fast, end well.*" He may not be able to fight, but he had a good memory.

But his brother was dead. Dead...Dead.

He looked at the poor girl. Anger welled up. He strode to the center of the room.

"IN THE NAME OF THE GOD OF HEAVEN, EVERYONE STAND BACK!" He waved his sword. Let death come. So what!

The boy with the stick sprang forward and knelt before him. The true stakes of the God-Son were burned into his leather shirt. The small girl followed.

"I, Kerky, am with you, Sir Knight."

"And I, Millie," said the girl.

If the Prince had been looking for a surprise for an edge, this was it, though he didn't know it.

"He...he...he speaks!" exclaimed someone from under a table.

172

There was a buzz of whispering.

"What's going on, boy?" said Fairold, not taking his eyes off the girl being held.

"HE'S GOING TO KILL HER!" screamed Millie.

"RELEASE HER!" ordered Fairold.

"NEVER! JUST ONE STEP CLOSER AND SHE'S DEAD!" said the soldier. The man was huge, a giant. The second man, leaning against a table and holding his hand over his chest, smiled, and gingerly raised his sword.

The Prince's memorized training raced back.

"COWARD! DO GOD HATERS NEED A WOMAN'S SKIRT TO HIDE BEHIND? TOUCH ONE HAIR OF HER HEAD AND I'LL KILL YOU...I'LL KILL YOU ONE INCH AT A TIME!" The words were out before he realized how foolish they sounded.

The soldier sneered.

"WHAT, AND CUT ME DOWN TO YOUR SIZE?" He laughed and, still holding the girl, stepped to the side exposing the repulsive emblem of the upside down stakes, and with his free hand thrust forward the stump of the girl's severed braid. "HER HAIR'S ALREADY BEEN TOUCHED, YOU FOOL! SO WHAT ARE YOU GOING TO DO ABOUT IT?"

It was now or never.

"Boy," Fairold whispered to Kerky, "you and the cook keep the bleeding one away, but be careful!"

Slowly, he approached the giant. In the smoky haze the huge man looked terrifying. But if the soldier had any doubts about the Prince's resolve, Fairold would remove them. And if the soldier had any chance to stay alive, he must at once abandon his dagger and draw his sword. And if he killed the girl he was holding, he must face not only the Prince — whose skill he was unsure of — but all his unbridled fury.

And if he were to kill her, he must not hesitate.

He hesitated.

At the moment he relaxed his grip, Lambith jerked her head down and darted through a cloud of smoke under a table. The second soldier, perhaps not thinking clearly, thrust his uncertain sword down hard, just missing the girl's leg, but pinning the hem of her skirt to the floor. With a loud rip, Lambith pulled free.

With both hands he struggled to pull back his sword. Kerky, seeing an opening, stepped forward and swung his stick sideways with all his might catching the wounded soldier in the side of the head. Whether this or the tankard Baylene brought down on his head actually killed the man, no one was sure. He fell across Lambith's legs, pinning her momentarily, and moved no more.

This left the giant.

As the man glanced at his falling comrade, Fairold sprang forward and swung, striking only his blade and running down it onto his sword arm. The giant was furious! With a flick of his wrist he parried away the offending blade. Fairold stared straight ahead, swallowing his fear. He was no match for this enemy. His acting was about to be discovered. Quickly he pulled back his blade.

The man smiled. And then made his second mistake.

Since he wore chain mail, and his challenger wore none, he lowered his sword just enough to inspect the blood dribbling from the superficial cut on his arm.

Fairold had one important secret. His sword. But was it good enough for his only chance?

Do or die.

Instantly, without allowing for a defensive parry, he lunged straight ahead, weapon first, like a spear. The giant, knowing his sword would arrive too late, shot his left arm up to protect his neck.

But the plain, heavy sword favored by the Second Prince was aimed lower for the midsection. The point hammered into the light iron mail, parting it on the blade's way into the man's stomach. He groaned going down, though his late sword grazed Fairold's left arm.

The Prince's wound was slight, the giant's fatal.

It was over.

The Boar's Hoof was a mess. Blood and oil everywhere. It was difficult to breathe. Floorboards now blazed where lamps had been spilled. At first, the fire seemed manageable, but the smoke had grown thicker and thicker, nauseating people who remained inside. One man stuffing his pockets with powder grew angry, and when he blocked someone's exit, others shoved him away and began throwing handful after handful of the "precious remedy" into the fire.

WHOOSH!

The flame widened. Rancid greenish-orange smoke filled the air. There was coughing and choking.

Chargan, the cook, led Lambith outside, coughing. Millie disappeared into the smoke-filled kitchen.

Father Marc did his best to pull away men still clawing at the burning sack of powder. It was sickening. There were great hacking coughs. One man vomited, only to cram more powder in his mouth. Pockets bulged. Beards were dusted white. Many acted as if not a handful of their precious salvation should be left behind. Later four men were found missing.

Lambith ordered Chargan, over his protests, to rescue the remaining soldier who was tied in the kitchen. At last he stumbled outside, his hands tied behind him. Chargan pushed him down in front of a long watering trough across the road, near where the gray horses and coach had been tied.

With the tavern doors open, flame leaped to the ceiling. Soon the thatch was ablaze. Lambith stared one last time at the tavern and inn that had been in her family for four generations, and was her only home as long as she could remember.

The uncle who'd raised her was dead, and his body burning up, without a moment to think about it. All her belongings, everything she possessed, all she'd ever known was turning to ash.

Memory and ash—the soil for new things to come.

CHAPTER 25

10

7000 DAYS,
1000 WEEKS,
200 MONTHS

ambith buried her face in her hands. Suddenly, as if someone were watching, she pulled them away and wiped them on her torn dress. She said nothing. She tossed back her head and stood with her hands at her side.

The eyes of three dozen or so — the fire was attracting a crowd — quickly turned to Millie, who everyone had forgotten in the confusion. At the last possible second, she exploded out of the doorway, a tongue of fire following her. In her hands were two large bags of Lambith's and her possessions.

The crowd eyed the strange Prince still holding his bloody sword. Father Marc whispered briefly to him and took charge while Chargan tied the remaining soldier to a tree. Still holding his cleaver he returned and stood beside the Prince.

Father Marc surveyed the crowd.

"This stranger...Prince...uh..."

"Fairold," whispered Fairold, "from the Kingdom of the Horse and Sword at Aeron."

"This stranger, Prince Fairold," said the priest, "from the kingdom...

at Aeron, has finally brought a measure of needed peace to our barony."
Suddenly burning thatch began to crackle loudly as darkness set
in. Father Marc raised his voice. "But several have died, including
Lord Dr. Oxram" — to this, several applauded, and much whispering
began — "and my brother who owned this tavern, may God rest his
soul. There's still important business here that needs to be finished.
And I want everyone to stay around until we're done."

Of course, no one was about to leave.

"First, there's the white powder. We priests have seen the effects
of the Lord Doctor's so-called new 'cure.' The small amount of good it
sometimes does is overcome by the overwhelming bad. I tell you, *the
powder is evil.* It's an insult to the God of Heaven. Now the powder is
gone. Gone forever!"

Fairold heard a few groans. One red-faced man even fell to the
ground and swore, and when someone put a foot in his ribs the applause
was overwhelming. Father Marc pointed to a half dozen nearby men
who he trusted. Chargan was among them. As they came forward,
each bowed low to the Prince. One even fell to his knees and wept.
Fairold bowed in return. Never was he more embarrassed. For an
instant he wrinkled his brow and squeezed his eyes shut. Then he
caught himself. He glanced at the tavern maid a few feet away.

She saw.

Wiping away her tears, she looked at him and for the smallest
instant squeezed her eyes shut like he did.

She knew.

Tears from her great loss made her dark eyes glisten. But whenever
their eyes would meet, Fairold would swear that she was holding back
a smile. A kind one.

But it was no time to grow soft. He must be royal as before. Why?
That he would figure out later.

The priest asked the faithful men he'd called to turn and face everyone else. Father Marc took a deep breath.

"Now," said the priest, "In the name of God I want every person with as much as a grain of this powder on his clothes or body, even under his fingernails, to come forward. **Now!** And if any try to run away, I want them stopped!"

At this, other men who secretly hated the powder quickly came, and bowing before the Prince they'd just met, and shaking the hand of the priest, they joined those already called. Sides had been clearly taken.

Men who'd hidden away some of the Lord Doctor's cure didn't stand a chance. All were identified. Some surrendered peacefully. Others resisted. Handful after handful of the collected powder burst into flame as it was thrown into the inferno that once was Lambith's home. A few reluctant men with bulging pockets had their shirts ripped off their backs and burned. At least two disappeared into the darkness completely naked and screaming. The orange and green air made several sick to their stomachs.

There was the sound of crying. It was sad to see those held by the powder's spell shed tears, and see the few who refused to cooperate be tackled, bound, gagged, and stripped.

The huge watering trough across the road was full, and everyone who had touched the powder washed. And washed and washed.

"Know this," declared Father Marc, standing over several broken men weeping at his feet, "the end of the powder you ate is death and only death, death in soul and body — and it still may kill you! And you may find yourself wishing you were dead. But very likely you will live. The only cure for this 'cure' is to stop. To stop and pray."

"Prayer will do you nothing!" screamed the surviving soldier from the tree where he was tied. **"You are dead men!"**

"Not hardly," said Father Marc. "And God is my witness." He lifted his hands to Heaven. "Dear God, for your name's sake, restore

179

these men." There was a chorus of Amens.

The soldier screamed for a chance to speak.

"Listen everyone! And listen good! Lambith Letterbrook has taken the law into her own hands and has killed royal blood! The Lord Oxram is a blood relative of the Emperor himself! And, as a cousin to Oxram, so am I! Further, THE LORD DOCTOR AND I ARE IN THE SERVICE OF THE EMPEROR AS YOU WILL SOON LEARN! Remember the law: *Any commoner who kills anyone of royal blood — without permission of the Emperor himself — must forfeit his life!*

"Lambith" — he smiled — "think you're above the law? You're as good as dead! What do you think of that?"

Lambith walked to the tree. Several followed.

"Well, Sir Pig…"

"Roland is my name, girl."

"Well, Sir Roland Pig, know this: I love and serve the God of Heaven. What do you think of that?" Her words were distinct, measured, clear. "You should do the same. Further, I think you're a liar. The Emperor would have nothing to do with swine like you. Now I've just one question: How many times can a person die?"

The soldier stuck up a finger.

"God saw that! And if you also mean 'one,' then I don't have anything to worry about, do I?" The tavern maid tilted her head, which made her remaining braid appear longer, and looked the soldier straight in the eye. Before he could answer, she awkwardly reached down the front of her dress and pulled up the large copper coin that had landed there earlier. In her other hand was a dagger. She held it at his throat. "Open your mouth, Sir Roland Pig, cousin of the Emperor." When he hesitated she pricked him. His jaw flew open. "You're forgetting that your uncle just killed my uncle, Mr. Pig! So you answer to me! Now eat! Or join those inside!" She pointed to the burning tavern.

He closed his eyes and she popped the coin in. She held the dagger under his chin as he tried to work the coin down. When he started to gag, she yanked out his shirt — his chain mail being already stripped away — and while his lips held tight, his eyes bulged in terror. With her knife she stabbed his shirt, stopping just short of cutting the skin. Deftly, she cut away the evil emblem from the front of the shirt that all Oxram's soldiers wore. With knees shaking, the soldier swallowed and the coin disappeared. He belched loudly and several laughed.

"We don't take blood money," she hissed. "So carry it back to your sty where you can give it back!" There was applause.

The girl walked over to her Uncle Marc.

"It's going much better than expected," whispered the priest, "but, Prince Fairold, we're still left with a serious problem. The Law is clear. And Lambith has broken it. A commoner on his, or her, own can never take the life of anyone of royal blood. For any reason. The life of a royal can only be taken by other royalty. Word of this killing will certainly reach the Emperor's ear."

Fairold smiled.

"Did you ever hear about the wonders of prophecy, dear priest?" The priest arched an eyebrow. "Father Marc, I'm going to ask you a favor."

Fairold leaned over and whispered. The man looked stunned. Like most priests, he could ponder a situation from every possible angle, and then probaby delay the simplest of decisions for "further study."

But that was for ordinary things.

Of which this was not.

If he could find only one honest way out of a mess, especially to save a life, he could change gears with blinding speed and risk everything, as he'd just done with the white powder.

By now the sky was black, though light from the burning tavern made even a large gathering still possible. It was perfect for what came next.

The Prince reached into his pocket with one hand, and out towards Lambith with the other. He took her hand. Before she realized what was happening, he slipped an elegant golden ring on her finger.

Fairold turned and faced as many as he could. Except for the snapping flames of burning thatch and the occasional collapse of something in the tavern, it was silent. Many here, Fairold guessed, must love the God of Heaven, and he would—he must—assume the mysterious missing Emperor did so as well. Was the Emperor the "great king" in their vision? Except for the tavern's name he knew nothing about where he was, the region, or the barony—not even their names! He must not let on. He must speak deliberately, but carefully and *clearly* as his brother Gavin would say.

"Dear friends, I am Prince Fairold of Aeron, descendant of King Agnon the Great, and heir to the throne of the ancient kingdom of the Horse and Sword. More important, I am a follower of the God of Heaven, and am on my way to meet the Emperor." He paused to let this sink in. He could play-act with the best. Words had always been friends. But using them in public! That was new. Real action? That was his dead brother's gift.

But no one else seemed to have healing words except for the priest.

And a tavern maid.

One whose life he'd saved. She'd let him take her hand. Her fingers were hard and strong. But warm. Her jaw fell as she examined the ring and raised her large eyes back to the Prince, who raised his own hand to show her he wore a similar ring. He did not look away and neither did she. His words to everyone gathered were clear:

"For valor in defending her land, I give this lady a royal ring, last worn by my mother, the Queen of our ancient kingdom. May I present to you, Lady Lambith Letterbrook of Aeron, the Kingdom of the Horse and Sword."

There was loud cheering for…well, no one was quite sure.

But the play couldn't end here. It was Lambith's turn. And the new Lady did not disappoint. She let the Prince hold up her hand for all to see, and broke into a friendly smile. Feelings, words, and understandings would follow. But what would she say?

Then came the loud whispering.

"This is impossible! She's not lived 1000 weeks" said a man who'd lost his shirt to the fire. "No one can be made a Lady, Lord, or Knight before that age! That's the Law—the Emperor's Law!"

"She's just a maid, a tavern maid!" said another. "Not old enough by a twelve-month or two, I'd say!"

"Who cares what the Law says?" said another.

"I care!" said Fairold. "I care for the Law…and I care for this girl! The Laws of my Kingdom do not require a set age for Ladyhood." He paused. His mind raced. What to do next? The priest on his other side raised his hand to his face and whispered:

"I must remind you, Prince Fairold, that you're in the Emperor's realm."

What realm? If he only knew this place's name, he could be much more believable! He must hide this ignorance. His brother would… but now the Crown Prince was dead. But the Crown—as invisible as it was—still lived on! As did his memory of the vision on the beach!

Lambith still hadn't said a word.

Fairold still held her hand. He bent down and spoke just above a whisper:

"Lambith, will you marry me?"

"Will I…I…what? Is this because…"

"Marry me. Marry me now. I…I…love you."

"You what?" she asked.

"I love you," he said more strongly, not taking his eyes away.

"Like this?" Her torn dress was filthy from the spilled ale and soot.

She fingered her cut braid.

"Yes."

Silence.

She raised her hand to his cheek.

"Let me look at you, Prince Fairold." She touched his cheek, his forehead, and the dark curly hair that fell down from it, as if she were inspecting a statue. For several seconds she said nothing. "Do you love God, *really*?"

"I do," said the Prince. "I love him with all I am and have...which isn't much anymore. But...I know this sounds strange...my dead mother — whose ring you wear — my dead brother, and I had a vision... that...that was *partly about you*." Tears filled his eyes and he struggled to keep them in. She refused to look away, but he sensed her soften. "I must leave immediately. Come with me!"

She reached over and touched his eyelid, and when water trickled out, she swept it away with her finger and wiped it dry on her own cheek.

"I love you, Prince-Whoever-You-Are."

Fairold raised his hand to his mouth to keep his next words private.

"My mother, my brother, and I were on a quest for the God of Heaven. We're to meet a 'great king' in the west. Where I'm not sure. Why I'm not sure. But now I'm the only one left. I no longer have houses or land. My kingdom far to the east has been destroyed and the few people left are scattered. I've no soldiers or servants. But I am the heir. I must finish our job. By royal right — regardless of what they say — I can make you a Lady. And even more. "

"But why me?"

"First, you love the God of Heaven. So do I."

"How do you know I do?"

"Your sermon to Sir Roland Pig. You wouldn't lie about all that.

184

Or to me."

"But my words were crude...I...I'm not the princess type."

"You'll make a PERFECT princess" — he extended his arms — "with a little help, of course."

"From the staff of your royal court, I take it."

"Yes, and right now the whole staff at your feet — so to speak!"

"You aren't crazy, are you?" Her smiling eyes drilled into him.

"Because I love you?" said Fairold. "Maybe — no, not because of that." His face reddened.

She pulled her hand from his and from somewhere pulled out a knife. While her uncle sucked in and held a deep breath, she sawed off the longer braid and undid her hair. She handed the weapon to Millie, behind her, who immediately began to saw and cut the rest of her hair to even things up.

"This is my dowry" — she handed him the newly cut braid — "It's all I have!"

"Not quite," added Millie. But nobody was listening.

"You are old enough to marry, aren't you? To marry in this place? Do I have to ask someone?" Fairold asked, as if he'd forgotten something.

"Old enough?" — she paused — "I'm certainly not as old as you!" Again, the Prince reddened. What would his brother have said to that? He'd answers for everything. For the first time Lambith looked away, more serious than he'd ever seen her. "I'm not sure. I think if I were as old as I ought to be, I wouldn't." She looked at the large golden ring she'd received. On it was a tiny picture of a horse flying over a large sword. The ring fit her work-hardened finger perfectly. She smiled, took his hand again, and quietly began crying.

"Lady Lambith Letterbrook has already accepted your ring," she said, loud enough for everyone to hear. "You've already accepted her dowry. She would be delighted to marry you. Besides" — she whispered behind her hand — "I must hear all about this vision I'm supposed to

185

be in—every detail—and since you're immediately leaving, I have to come. You realize, don't you, this is the only way I'd come with you?" The former tavern maid bowed respectfully. Behind her cheering indicated agreement to whatever was going on.

"I...I'm a bit new at this," said Fairold, ignoring her question. He bowed in return to the former tavern maid, prompting more cheering. "Now who should I ask about..."

"There's only Father Marc to ask and he already agrees," she interrupted.

"I...uh...what?" said the priest, his jaw dropping.

"Since you give permission, Father Marc, say the words of the ceremony!" said Fairold.

"Not so fast!" This time Millie barked the orders, and this time she was heard. "Closer! Closer! Bring everyone closer and sit in the grass," she said, waving her hands. "And do something—like pray! Lambith"—she pulled at the older girl's filthy dress—"will not be married in that! We'll be right back." Together they ran back into the darkness.

Privately, Fairold talked with the priest. He handed him some gold coins.

Minutes later the two reappeared, Lambith in a fresh cream-colored homespun dress, hair shorter but even and combed, sandals on her feet, and the magnificent golden ring from the ancient Royal House of Aeron on her finger. Fairold's jaw dropped. She smiled back. Light from the burning tavern was still bright, the air was warm, and shadows magically danced. At the watering trough the gray horses had been hitched to Fairold's magnificent coach, and Lambith's belongings were put inside.

Any play-acting was over.

Father Marc stood before those seated on the grass.

"Today is an ending as well as a beginning," he said. "There are several things we must settle. Pass on the truth about what you've heard and seen. Before they say the vows, please understand that Prince Fairold of the Royal House of Aeron and the new Princess by marriage, Lady Lambith Letterbrook, now also of the House of Aeron — the two of them — will be leaving to finish a quest ordained by the God of Heaven. Prince Fairold has given a ring, and Lady Lambith has presented her last worldly possession, a braid of hair to…"

"Not so!" interrupted Millie. "Lambith has a bag of clothes in the coach. And she has me! I'm Lady Letterbrook's personal maid. She's not going anywhere without me!"

"And" interrupted Kerky, "I'm already in Prince Fairold's service." He turned to the Prince. "Wherever you go, I go. It's the law here." Several laughed. If anyone were looking for a miracle to show God's approval of all this, it was the mute boy speaking.

"And your parents?" asked Prince Fairold.

"Kerky and I have no parents," offered Millie, certain Kerky had used up all his words for the day, "so you don't have to ask."

"What exactly is the Law about Knighthood and Ladyhood in this land?" asked Prince Fairold.

Father Marc turned and spoke loud enough for everyone to hear:

"Prince Fairold, our Law is quite clear. No child, regardless of heritage or deed accomplished may be titled 'Sir,' 'Lord,' or 'Lady' until he or she has valiantly proven himself or herself, and *has seen the light of 7000 days* — or as it's sometimes said, 1000 weeks, or 200 months which is the same thing. That Law, by the way, is a good one that ended much abuse of privilege."

"And I take it," said Fairold, "there's one legal exception to this that's known everywhere, including here?"

"Right." The priest sighed. "A princess by birth or marriage *of any age* is legally a Lady."

Only whispering broke the silence that followed.

Fairold turned and raised his hand. The whispering ceased. Oh, what were these people called? He still didn't know! He was learning their laws. He had to. Could he make it to the end of this? Would they stand by him?

"Dear friends" — at least they spoke the same language — "What's left of the Royal House of the Horse and Sword at Aeron far to the east extends its best wishes to you. And we ask for your prayers.

"Behold Maid Millie, who on this day has entered Lady Letterbrook's service. How old are you Millie?"

"In three months, on Solun 35, the eve before Aulius 1 — when day's just as long as night," beamed Millie, obviously enjoying parading special facts about herself to such an attentive audience, "I will be 100 months. That will be on the last worship day — the day my birthday and month day is always on."

"Let it be known," announced the Prince, "that today Maid Millie has courageously distinguished herself in battle — when many of her countrymen who were older and stronger were hiding under tables. If she remains faithfully in the service of Lady Letterbrook 103 more months, *and learns to read and write*, on the last day of her 200th month and thereafter, she shall be called Lady Millie" — he looked at the girl — "your other name, please?"

"Gatewood," she said.

"Lady Millie Gatewood of the Royal House of Aeron," said Fairold. He turned to Kerky.

"Your age?"

"120 or 10, Sir, as of the last day this week."

"Also a worship day," interjected Millie, as if it really mattered.

"Let it further be known that for bravery in battle today, if Kerky continues in faithful service to me and learns to read and write, that in 80 months, on the last day of that week, he shall be known as — your last name please?"

"Greenwald, Sir."

"He shall be known as Sir Kerky Greenwald of the Royal House of Aeron."

Loud whispering again broke the silence.

He dared not slow down. He drew a deep breath.

"As to Lady Lambith Letterbrook, she has promised to become my wife."

Without even asking, everyone stood.

"Father Marc, say the words."

Without hesitation, the priest of the barony (or perhaps one of the priests, Fairold had no idea), took measure of what was happening, and without further discussion he stepped forward and changed the destiny of this little part of the world for years to come.

Everyone was asked to circle the five of them—Millie standing by Lambith, Kerky by Fairold, the priest in the middle—and join hands. To do so, he said, meant they were asking God's blessing on the Prince and the tavern maid, as well as on themselves. Everyone joined the circle.

He began with a prayer.

"O God of Heaven, may all the events of this day, this night, tomorrow, and all tomorrows that follow as a result of this marriage, and those of us left behind, be for your glory. Amen."

"Do you, Prince Fairold, promise to love the God of Heaven and this woman as long as you live?"

"I do."

"Do you, Lady Lambith Letterbrook, promise to love the God of Heaven and this man as long as you live?"

"I do."

"Then by the authority given me by the God of Heaven, I pronounce you husband and wife, and Prince and Princess of the Royal House of Aeron." Whether he could add the last part no one knew or cared. But let it be repeated that way to the family of Lord Oxram as he knew it would be.

For the first time Fairold took the girl in his arms.

They kissed.

Once.

And once again.

Then, as if a curtain had been drawn on a stage, those making up the circle cheered. Was this the end of the play, or was there another scene to come?

There was.

Behind the circle, tied to a tree, the surviving soldier sneered.

Fairold and Lambith walked to where he was tied.

"Sir Roland — if you be 'sir' — let me present to you *Princess* Lady Lambith. By royal decree she's become a Lady; by marriage she's become Royal, and member of the House of Aeron, a royal family older than the Emperor's." Fairold prayed that this was true. Would the Emperor be offended? Would this come back to haunt him?

"So," he continued, "when news of this day spreads, tell why and how your beloved Lord Oxram was sent to his just reward, not by a commoner, but by a Princess — as well as a Lady, who a Princess is at any age.

"We leave immediately to meet the Emperor, who waits for us. Is that clear?" The "great king" had to be the Emperor. He would assume so until proven otherwise.

The soldier stared but said nothing. Fairold drew his sword.

"Speak!"

"You…whoever you are…you just don't know what you're saying. The Emperor is on our side."

"That remains to be seen," said the Prince. "Now when we untie your ropes, go and tell your people what has…"

"The heck I will! How can I go anywhere?" the soldier said angrily.

"It's pitch black. I can't get anywhere! The horses and everything is gone!"

Fairold looked around at the smoldering ruins.

"Soldier, you've made your point. Thanks to you, everything here's destroyed. Leave him tied."

"**NO!**"

"Don't worry, good soldier, your people will find out where you are and come and release you, or what's left of you. You can tell them how you let your master and the others die and explain why you're still alive."

"**NO!**"

"And tell your people about us."

The man screamed. Fairold told the priest to cut free the man soon after they were gone. He was to tell him that the Prince ordered this and insisted his life be spared.

"I think you've had an effect on me," the Prince whispered to his new wife.

"It's only the beginning!" she said smiling. "And, I think it may be the effect of the ring. You must tell me about your mother."

Tears suddenly began to roll down Fairold's cheeks.

"I'm so, so sorry," she said. "So much I don't know." Tears of her own began. She put her arms around him and helped him into the coach. From somewhere, someone had brought baskets of food and other provisions. Kerky—perhaps it was the effect of Millie—had declared that he was no stranger to horses, and that he, knowing well the road ahead, and having "done too little to help," would drive the team west, with Millie of course at his side, long into the night, leaving the inside of the coach to the Prince and new Princess. Fairold agreed.

The horses seemed eager to be off, and within minutes the coach was out of sight.

For the first time in several hours nothing was urgent, so Lambith

191

told her husband where they were and the names of everything. She cried when she told about how her Uncle Merkie and his brother had lovingly raised her.

For Fairold, telling about himself was much harder. When he asked her why she had so many questions, she said tavern maids had to "know things" to stay alive.

"It's no different for Princes," he said.

"And I'll bet it's even harder for Princesses," she replied. "Now here's what we'll do: Say what you will, long or short, and then stop. Isn't that fair? Then I'll give you some quiet. But when I kiss you" — which they both found easier and easier to do — "you must tell me more."

More new rules! But easy to break when no one was watching.

And, as Kerky drove long, long into the night, there was plenty of time to cry.

That night the Princess learned much about the ancient kingdom she'd just become a part of.

Fairold's sword, as always, was in easy reach, but the turning and groaning of the great wheels, the rhythmic clomping of hooves, the hypnotic jouncing on the springs under each axle, the warmth of the girl he gladly held, and her arms that were reluctant to let him go brought him to the end of the last page of the first book of his life.

Book Two would open for its first line the next morning.

The End

CHAPTER 26

A Critique of Death in a Tavern

THE STORY EXAMINED

TIME: *AEMP 01, early Day 319*

PLACE: *Dr. Harwell's study,*

                         Susquehanna Territory, northeastern PA

(This chapter picks up where Chapter 15 ended on p. 105.)

"**J**onas, do you see what's here?!"

Michael Hammond lay down the copy of "Death in a Tavern" he'd started reading more than two hours ago. He and his teacher were where they'd first sat. Triana and Harwell stood in the doorway, returning from down the hall. "The Secret of Zareba" was twice as long as the story he'd just completed, but Triana had already finished it. She and her foster father had been speaking privately. Her eyes were red — odd for the girl usually so in control. She tried to look unconcerned though it was obvious she'd been crying.

Something had disturbed her nerves of steel. He would say nothing now. He focused on his full sheet of scribbled notes.

"This is really strange!" he announced. "This story almost gets lost in the end with numbers! Look at how it treats ages and time!"

"Once again, Michael," interrupted the English teacher, "you're saying you never saw this story, or even heard of it before tonight?"

"Once again, no, Mr. Cample!" He turned and eyed them one by one. "Now may I go on?"

The three nodded.

"Look at how these people refer to the time of coming of age: '7000 days,' '1000 weeks,' '200 months' — three ways of saying the same length of time!"

"Right!" interrupted Cample, "Nothing is like this in our folklore — Earth folklore, that is."

"But couldn't this just be made-up?" asked Michael. "You know... like in fantasy or science fiction?"

"Everyone I know would assume that," said Cample.

"But," Triana interrupted, "although the story's long and more detailed than most folklore, it *sounds* like our folklore, don't you think? You know, magic, visions, strange creatures?" She looked at Michael and methodically crossed her legs.

"Folklore?...Yes" — it was Harwell's turn — "but doesn't the story become realistic from the death of the Queen and Crown Prince on? You know, the magic seems to disappear at that point."

"Yes," said Cample, inching forward in his overstuffed chair, "*if* you can accept the idea that Fairold walked right into the fulfillment of a specific prophecy."

"Still," said the minister, "a lot of loose ends are still hanging out." He stopped, Michael sensed, to measure the teacher's reaction. "There's plenty of mystery — in both stories. In 'Death in a Tavern,' for example, just who is the Emperor and where is he? We have to wait later for that."

"That's partly why I'm upset," said Cample. "This long 'folktale' is quite weak as a story in several ways. For all its monotonous details, it starts and ends too abruptly — like the Iliad, by the way — leaving the reader frustrated, for example, about whose side the Emperor is on. And that's important in the big picture of things. Also there are too many details about the marriage, as well as the odd distraction about

194

the number of days, weeks, and so on, to measure time.

"Now Michael, 'The Secret of Zareba' — the story you handed in — picks up years later where this one leaves off. Weren't you curious about what came before?"

"Yes, but that doesn't mean I looked around for anything else!"

Triana looked straight at their teacher.

"Well I'm not sure that the Emperor was most important in either story. I think the relationships between several of the characters and what they did was key. And the most interesting. That set the tone for everything." Triana lowered her eyes and removed her glasses.

"Perhaps," said Michael. He brushed back his curly brown hair. Was it Triana's fixation on the love aspect? Or something else? "I'm fascinated," he continued, "in some of what you call weaknesses: for example, the spelling out of similarities and differences between..."

"Excuse me, Michael," said Cample. "Before we look at those, note the words of Vandor, who was a..."

"*Person*," interjected Triana, "though never born alive."

"Whatever..." said Cample. "For now I'll let that pass." He shifted in his chair. "Remember, Triana, in class reading about the Rosetta Stone?"

"Yes." She smiled. Michael knew about her uncanny, savant skill in languages. "The Rosetta Stone," she continued, "was a black...a basalt stone found in Greece...no, I think Egypt...that had the same thing written on it in three different scripts — two Egyptian and one Greek. This helped people understand hieroglyphics and how to compare words and translate them from one language to another."

"Exactly!" Cample smiled. "I think that same idea's at work here. Look at what Crispin, Abel, and Vandor say. If we take them seriously, I think if we stretch things a bit for both stories, we have a 'Rosetta Stone' here, not just for words, but for the *ideas* and *numbers*. And for understanding the big picture."

"And perhaps," said Harwell, looking closely at Cample, "the *story* of a life in this room."

"Perhaps," said the teacher. Michael scooted to the edge of his chair. "But let me go on. According to Vandor, *the minutes, hours, and days in all three worlds, or planets, are 'exactly the same'; the suns are 'mirror images,' or the same; the moons, however, are slightly different and not one but two of them orbit his planet.* Also he says that the plants and animals are similar, and the 'feel underfoot' — or 'gravity' — was the same. Crispen and Abel repeat and confirm some details, as well as the Crown Prince recalling his vision the next morning."

"And," interrupted Michael, "though they have the idea of 'months' and 'years,' <u>nowhere are the months said to be the same!</u> *The lengths of months and years on the three worlds must vary!* And I think we can figure out just how they do from the story. Let me go further: It may be important. And make both stories we read more believable." He paused, scratched his head, and looked up. There was no objection.

"Look at this." Michael held up a piece of paper. "As I first mentioned, the same amount of time is expressed three ways:

7000 days = 1000 weeks = 200 months.

"That's the key part, but not the only one, of our Rosetta Stone. Now what does that tell us?" Without waiting for an answer he went on. "The first part is easy, if we accept the declaration that days and weeks are the same in all three places, and use an Earth calendar as a model. **Their weeks each have 7 days** because 7000/1000, given here, indicates 7 days per week. **But their months** — at least on the average — **have 5 full weeks** (1000/200).

"But let me go further. I'm going to argue that **each month is exactly the same, and has 5 full weeks that could fit into a perfect rectangle that's**

the same for each of their 12 months, and I'll show why it's 12 in a minute.

"First, I'm going to take two very tiny pieces from the second story. The angry young climber in it, who can't read but can do shockingly fast paperless math, declares in a fit of rage that '100,000 minutes' equals 'only 2 months' — any months, I'd say — 'minus a little more than half a day.' That's only true with a 35-day month. I multiplied that out to get 100,800 minutes (60 min. X 24 hr. X 35 days X 2 months = 100,800). If half a day, or 12 hours, is 720 minutes (12 X 60 = 720), then it would take just 80 minutes more to make 100,000. Of course, feeling I was right to start with, I started with 35 to check this.

"Also, in that story, we're told that 'five enemy soldiers died' trying to enter the mountain through the river tunnel during the month of Aulius 'at the rate of one per week.'

"To get to 'years,' which they also have but use less, we have to go to other parts of the story. When Kerky is asked his age, he says he's '120 or 10' which would have to be 'months' and 'years' respectively. Further, Lambith is accused of being too young to qualify for Ladyhood because she's not reached '1000 weeks' (or 200 months), by at least 'a 12-month or two.' That has to be the way of saying 'one or two years.'

"And when Kerky enters the story he's called a '10-year-old,' and in the second story Galen is said to be 14.

"Now why in the world — our world, anyway — does any of this matter? First, I think it's important to realize that years are much longer on Emryss than on Earth. In fact, with 12 months of 35 days each, there are **420 days in each year on Emryss** (12 X 35 = 420). But if this sounds confusing, look at how incredibly simple their month must be. That is, *every* month.

A MONTH ON EMRYSS

1	2	3	4	5	6	Worship Day 7
8	9	10	11	12	13	14
15	16	17	18	19	20	21
22	23	24	25	26	27	28
29	30	31	32	33	34	35

"I hope I'm not boring you. But it does connect with some science about this planet, and the calendar reveals interesting religious details about 'worship days,' or Sabbaths, and the beliefs and celebrations of the people. After saying a bit more about this pattern, I want to say just a bit more about years." Michael paused and glanced around.

Both men nodded agreement.

"Please do," offered Triana, matter-of-factly.

Michael tried to look surprised. The men exchanged puzzled looks.

"I'm *not* Stacy Martin, Michael," the girl continued. It was rare for her to let slip anything unrehearsed, but the hour was late. It was true his old girlfriend never could've endured all this, regardless of consequences.

But this sounded nothing like the girl with glasses in her lap. She was up to something. He must play along. He leaned toward her face, squinted, and tilted his head.

"Sta...cy... hmm? I'd almost forgotten..."

"Well, you don't have to remember *everything*. That's my job, remember?" Her dark blond hair fell to the side so the lamplight shadowed half her face. So quick and so focused! And back on track! Michael felt goose bumps rise on his arms. She smiled. "Keep going, Michael, I like to see you enjoying yourself."

Harwell and Cample exchanged puzzled looks.

She leaned over, and cupping her hand, whispered, "They're wondering, Michael. Good work. Keep them guessing." She forced a stern face. She was up to something.

And he was enjoying himself. Her eyes were no longer red.

He continued.

"If you look at the rectangle with 5 weeks of 35 days, you will notice that there are 5 Sabbaths every month: on the 7th, the 14th, the 21st, the 28th, and the 35th. How does that fit the story? Talkative little Millie is the key here. When asked her age at the end of the story she declares, and I wrote it down:

> 'In 3 months, on Solun 35, the eve before Aulius 1 — when day's exactly as long as night — I will be 100 months. That will be on the last worship day — the day my birthday and month day is *always* on.'

The 35th is the 'last' day before the 1st which starts the next month. That 'fixes' the rectangle.

"Further, when Kerky says his birthday is *'the last day of this* week,' Millie declares that it's also 'on a worship day.' Further, in the other story the '28th of Solun' is declared to be a Sabbath, eight days before Aulius 1. Also the 'middle Sabbath,' which I'd say was the 21st, seemed to be a fixed calendar marker.

"More from both stories can support my theory, but let me just add this: Maenus 1 is the Spring Equinox (day and night are said to be the same), Resurrection Day, and New Year's Day, and Aulius 1 is the Fall Equinox (again equal day and night), the first day of the 7th month, and the traditional God-Son's birthday. Whereas their use of months is awkward to us, the actual months and dates are very easy to understand. Our pattern of months and calendars would seem primitive and complex to them.

"So what do we learn from this? It strongly suggests that Emryss tilts on an axis like Earth and has similar seasons. This is also confirmed by the discussion about 'The Walk of Monks' in the other story."

Triana put her glasses on.

"I'm impressed, Michael—as no other girl your age would be, you understand—but does it mean anything more important than that?" From her tone Michael could tell she was hiding something. To let her know he understood, he let his hand fall again on hers.

"I've rambled on for one main reason: the characters in both stories just seem too young for much of what they do. But that's in Emryss years which are 420 days long. Let me give you another number. **Each year in Emryss = 1.15 Earth years** (420/365).

"This helps us take what's presented as 'facts' more seriously. First, the characters are a little older—in number of days lived—than their ages suggest. For example, 10-year-old Kerky says he's '120' or '10.' If the 10 is Emryss years, then he would be 11½ Earth years which helps us better understand his resourcefulness.

"Similarly, clever little Millie, when she gets to '100 months,' she'd be 8 years 4 months (100/12). In Earth years that's about 9.58 years, or"—Michael scribbled with his pencil—"almost exactly 9 years 7 months (420/365 X 8), which makes her contribution more believable. However, Millie is..."—he turned to Triana.

"Only 97 months old." She smiled.

"Which makes it harder to multiply," he replied. "I'm glad you're keeping up!"

"Michael, I really do like your calendar."

Michael slipped his hand away and Harwell and Cample exchanged glances.

He pressed on.

"Just one more thing about this age stuff. People thought of coming of age in terms of months—200 of them—and not in years as we do. In Emryss years that's 16 years 8 months, in Earth years, a bit more than

19 years 2 months. Lambith was said to be less than that, but we never find out how much. She might have married young, but she wasn't exactly a child bride.

"And if Millie had said much more, the balance of this story would have been even more uneven."

"As is this discussion," interjected Harwell. "I'm amazed, I must say, that without calculators anymore, how well you figure this by hand!"

Michael smiled. He flexed his fingers and examined his palm.

"I do have *my* gifts. But just one more thing—because I know Triana can *handle* it." He resisted glancing her way, but could tell she'd covered her mouth. "My real conclusion of all this is to say that I think someone, at some time, in some place, has taken real pains to tell us more than a story—or a once-upon-a-time folktale that is simply a made-up story."

"Meaning what?" asked Triana. "Since I've already confessed to writing this down, what did I say?"

"You said you *translated* this, right?" asked Cample.

"Yes, but…"

"The original storyteller," said Michael, "might be trying to say this really *happened*! Now I'm done…"

"You've done well, Michael!" said their teacher. "I agree completely. And already having spent some time on this story, I've come up with almost the same results—though I must confess, I missed your calendar connections. I wish I was as quick as you with numbers—without machines!"

"You did!" Michael dropped his notes in his lap. "Then why did you let me go on like this without stopping me?"

"With something this strange, Michael, I just had to hear how someone else saw it."

The teacher turned to Harwell.

"The thing that really puzzles me though is religion. Jonas, you say you're a Christian. What about this X-shaped symbol—the same charm, by the way, I saw Triana wearing earlier—and mention of the 'stakes of the God-Son'? And the Abel of Genesis appearing alongside of a character called 'Crispin' from a real world called Emryss and 'Vandor' from a real world called 'Elphia'? Doesn't that bother you?"

"It *concerns* me, Marvin," said the minister.

"And furthermore," said Cample, "this Queen on Emryss who received the vision was concerned about the existence of life on other worlds because of her 'Holy Book,' and she was especially concerned about the unfamiliar symbols—including your cross—because of her faith in a 'God of Heaven.' "

"An excellent question!" said Harwell, "especially from one who..."

"One who," interrupted Cample, "is simply asking questions."

Harwell reached for his Bible, his expression deadly serious. Again, Michael reached for and received the girl's hand. It was warm.

"Marvin"—Harwell scooted his chair back—"let me make some things perfectly clear before we go further. First, I accept the Bible as God's inspired Word and our final source in matters of Truth and responsibility. I do so by faith—"

"By *faith*," interrupted Cample, as if to underline the word.

"By faith," continued Harwell, "supported by good reasons, scientific reasons and philosophic reasons which I encountered during my academic training."

At this moment Marvin Cample decided to play a trump card.

"Jonas, it's been said in print that you studied at Cornell."

"That's right."

"But there's no department of religion at Cornell, and the next closest thing, the Philosophy department, says they've never heard of you! And neither has English or History!"

Triana and Michael glanced at each other, then at Cample beaming with satisfaction, then at Harwell. The minister leaned farther back in his chair, still holding his Bible. He smiled and glanced toward the wall of books closest to him as if scanning for some title. Slowly he turned back and faced the teacher. He looked dead serious.

"Most people don't check up on things like that," said Harwell. Squaaawwwk. The minister shifted his weight, propelling his chair forward. "And to be frank, they should!"

"And?" interrupted Cample.

"And when they do, they should be more careful!"

"Meaning?"

"I never studied religion at Cornell. And never said I did. My doctorate there is in something else." He paused as if looking for the right words. Michael was fascinated. This time his father was up to something. Trump cards — there's usually more than one in every game he knew. And often they don't have the same value!

"Not in philosophy, English, or history?" said the teacher.

"No, my doctorate is in astrophysics."

"In science?!"

"Marvin, I received theology training in Illinois and even here in Pennsylvania. Perhaps you've overlooked it, but Christians are taking science more seriously now, as many scientists are the Bible."

Cample took a deep breath and settled back.

"Marvin, let me go back to what I was saying. I said I accepted the Bible as God's Word by faith, supported — as I believe — by good scientific and philosophic reasons.

"Let me go further. I believe that human life on Earth is created in the image of God. Now even further than that. As far as I can tell — even though it's been argued both ways — I believe the Bible is silent about whether life exists on other planets.

"Also, I'm convinced that Jesus Christ is the Son of God, and is the Lord and Creator of all the universe — including other worlds of people, if they exist."

"But," interjected Cample, "what about the God-Son of Emryss?"

"If you don't believe," said Triana, "why does mention of the God-Son even matter to you?"

"The problem," returned Cample, "is not mine, Triana. It's Jonas's, Michael's, and yours. I know enough about the Bible from childhood to know that in Christianity — true Biblical Christianity — there's only one God, existing as one Father, one Son, one Holy Spirit. How can you have one Son of God being born, living, dying, and rising again in more than one place? That makes no sense at all! If we lose logic and common sense, what do we have left? Without logic, Jonas, even science would fail."

"Marvin, you astound me!" Harwell smiled. "Rarely have I met someone who got so quickly to the heart of an issue! You must have had excellent training!"

"Jonas, I read, I care. I 'believe' too, as we all do — in something. And I don't take my beliefs lightly."

"Marvin, would you 'believe' that I completely agree with everything you've said so far! Does that surprise you? And yes, philosophically and logically, the problem is mine — and my children's. In particular, I agree that Jesus being born, living, dying, and rising again over and over in different places seems ludicrous." He reached out and put his hand on the Bible.

"In fact, if I were to share one passage, it would come from Hebrews 9 and 10 in the New Testament. Over and over it says there that Jesus died *once for everyone everywhere.* And more than that, I believe that Jesus would *return for everyone who belonged to him at one time.* And if this story, 'Death in a Tavern,' is true — actual history, not a parable or fiction — then I must somehow respond to this seeming dilemma. And eventually I will. Or at least try."

"Just what is the problem?" asked Michael.

"Let's look at it this way," said the minister. He laid his palms on the desk. "Let's suppose other people in other places are created in the image of God — people like us."

"People like me," interjected Triana. Her glasses were back in her lap. She squeezed Michael's hand and stared into his eyes. "Would you still love me?"

Cample arched his brow and again exchanged glances with Harwell.

Michael was stunned. Love? What was she saying? Or *seeing*? There were different Bible words that had been translated 'love' that he'd learned about in church.

"I mean," Triana continued, gently shaking his arm, "if I were different, from somewhere light-years away, but our DNA was similar, could you...would you love me?"

"Of course!" declared Michael, determining not to be outdone. "After all, I'm a Christian. I have to! And would." He was sure there was a 'safe' synonym for 'Bible love,' though he couldn't recall it, that he could fall back on if he had to. "Triana, you sound like, like..."

"Like Lambith?...Well, maybe that isn't a coincidence!"

Michael leaned into her face. After all this time a hint of her distinctive perfume still lingered.

"Tri...Triana," he whispered, "are you crazy?"

"For letting you love me?" she said aloud. "Probably." She leaned up to his ear and cupped her hand. "Michael, I'm trying to disarm him. Cample is up to something, so let's keep him guessing. Help me. And Michael, pray. Especially for Jonas. Big things may soon happen and someone just might get hurt. And it's okay..."

"What's okay?"

"That you love me," she said just loud enough for all to hear.

Gently she pushed him away.

Harwell cleared his throat.

"Excusing me for whispering, but it was private." She offered a quick smile before again looking dead serious.

The minister continued.

"As I was...uh...saying before all this, what if there were people like us on other planets created in the image of God..."

"With similar DNA," interjected Cample, glancing at the girl.

"People," continued Harwell, "who had fallen into sin and also needed a Savior. What would God do?"

"I hope he'd be fair," offered Cample.

"Now just as to what God could do, or would do, the Bible is silent." Harwell studied the back of his hands. "Perhaps it's not for us to say. That is, when we don't have to. But it seems to me that as a Bible-believing Christian on Earth, we must start at one key point: Jesus died once for all at one time for the sins of the whole world—the whole universe. Just as the angelic creatures—though not real angels—in the story chanted, He is one, one person, one Lord, one Savior of all.

"Now if that's so, and others have the same opportunity we have, then it seems that one of two things must occur: Either people from those places must come here to learn about Jesus, or—somehow—*Jesus must have gone to other places at **the same point in cosmic time as he did on Earth and experience birth, life, death, and resurrection.**"

"Impossible!" said Cample.

"Perhaps I'm wrong, Marvin. But sometimes we have to think beyond things we understand. And this may be another one of those times."

"Can I have another example?" asked Michael.

"Michael, explain 'resurrection from the dead,' 'omnipresence of God,' the 'Trinity,' or fulfilled prophecy in a way we can all understand—even though we believe we have reasons, though not scientific evidence, for these things."

Cample smiled. "Quite a job, I'd say!"

"Okay, Marvin, since you profess not to believe, that is, not to believe Christian things, let's look at some complicated history apart from religion:

"Let's go back to our country's founding—just a sliver of Earth time, by the way. Think about television; antibiotics; microchips full of encyclopedias, novels, street addresses, and thousands of pictures and songs; air travel from the Atlantic coast to the Pacific coast that arrives an hour before you took off; and space travel to Mars where once a colony was being planned.

"Could Washington or Jefferson, people like us, people whose faces are on the money we use to pay for these things ever understand any of them?

"Could we expect the people of 200 years ago to understand plate tectonics? And the piling up of natural disasters three years ago that led three entire western states to go bankrupt and secede? And the federal government, or the other 47 states, facing the need to provide trillions of dollars of immediate aid, to accept their leaving the Union without the firing of a shot? And later our threatening Japan and China with annihilation if they even approached our western coast?

"Most Americans, of course, thought that with time this disaster could be fixed.

"Then EMP came along.

"Would Washington and Jefferson have understood how, until nearly a year ago, technology determined almost everything about how we lived, how we were entertained, and how we think? And how our country could barely survive without it?

"Perhaps there are attributes of God and characteristics of complex things only he could cause, the Big Bang, for example, that began our dimension of *time*, that we're a hundred years too backward to understand. And may always be. Oddly, though our mind can't grasp it now, we can show with numbers that there were once at least *six dimensions in addition to the four we now know.*

"Extradimensionality can show us how God *might* do or have done certain things like hear everyone's prayers at once. Of course, we can't say God does it that way, nor can we even visualize it."

"But," interrupted Cample, "aren't you running way beyond science to justify what you want to believe? And is that fair?"

"Yes and No. Realize, Marvin, though most haven't thought about it, it's nearly universally accepted by scientists that *the dimension of time travels in a straight line, and has a beginning and an end.*"

"But," said Cample, "what do they think about time before the 'beginning' and after the 'end'?"

"They don't—that is they can't think beyond those limits, as *scientists,* because there's no evidence time exists there. The one thing almost all agree on, however, is that there's no 'bounce-back' or 'recycling' of matter and energy in a never-ending way as suggested by many eastern religions, but not the Bible. This honest limitation of modern science is why I and many others are willing to think 'outside the box,' and at least consider information that comes from other sources."

"Other worlds?"

"Perhaps...but, Marvin, that's *not* my point here. Think about this: Science cannot answer some of our most important questions. It would be hard pressed to explain why we're having this conversation. Or *if* we should even be having it. Science can't tell us what's right or wrong. We have to look elsewhere to determine values.

"And I look to the Bible...for a lot of good reasons."

"Which I'd like you to explain to me—at another time."

"Thanks for the break, Marvin, because I want to go in a different direction in our discussion. For the moment, let me risk oversimplifying. God gave a moral code—the Bible—to enable people on Earth to lead the right kind of lives. Now *if* he created people in his image elsewhere,

I'm convinced he'd do something very similar for them.

"And while this 'Bible' for others might vary in many details, I feel sure it would be remarkably the same about birth, life, death, resurrection, and coming again of the Savior who is the Son of God, as well as in other key ideas.

"Let's first consider some possible differences in these worlds, assuming they exist. If fallen people live there, isn't it reasonable some would be at different stages of knowledge and understanding than people on Earth? Some more advanced, and some less as on Emryss?"

"Like people in Fairold's primitive world," interrupted Cample, "speculating about a spherical planet?"

"Exactly!"

"Or," continued Cample, "how about a more advanced people on Earth being puzzled by a large unidentified bat-like creature hovering outside their window?"

"What?... I'm not following you, Marvin. The bat-like creature was Prince Gavin in a dream on Emryss...?"

"Let's skip that for now," said the teacher, carefully studying the minister.

Michael and Triana glanced at each other.

"One thing you brought up, Marvin, holds my attention very keenly," said the minister, "and that's the symbols and signs. In the vision in the story, the strange X with the stakes and the strange circles seemed to serve in the same way as our cross. This is serious. If this is a true story undistorted by evil, then these signs must represent how Jesus died in other places—and I'm convinced, at the *same-once-for-all-instant* in time. If otherwise, I'd probably have to reject the whole story."

"Why?" said Cample. "Because the story is a fabrication, or because it's..."

"Evil?" offered Michael.

"That's what I think—now—on the basis of all I know. I may be too narrow here—and I've been wrong before—but I'm convinced that *Jesus died at one particular moment in cosmic time, though perhaps in different ways, for everyone anywhere.*

"Similarly, at one particular cosmic moment he arose, and at one particular cosmic moment he will return again to Earth, Emryss, Elphia—wherever he came the first time and lived to provide salvation where it was needed."

"Perhaps, Jonas, you're taking this all too seriously."

"Not if you know what I know, Marvin."

"I'm not sure what you mean, Jonas, but whatever you're coming up with, believe it or not, I think I can add to it!" The teacher tapped his briefcase. "And since we've come this far, I don't want to stop until we've faced some more very unusual things."

Michael felt Triana nudge his foot. It was time for a change of pace.

"You know," said the boy, "we've said hardly a word about 'The Secret of Zareba.' That's where religion really becomes important. Some parallels there with the Bible are unbelievable!"

"Before we do that"—Harwell looked at his foster daughter—"Triana, the story 'Death in a Tavern' that you turned in, the one that you *actually wrote down*, well, you've said very little about it! Anything more to add before we take up the second story?"

"Yes...I'll say a little now...more later, after we've discussed the other story." She looked thoughtfully at the window.

"As you know, I'm intrigued about the **genealogy** part and the names mentioned. Unfortunately, the Queen and her husband are never mentioned by name. And my source was silent. And the Queen was said to have a daughter, also not named, as well as four sons: *Colin*, who disappeared on some strange quest—and was probably dead, or soon to die; *Crispin,* who appeared in the vision and who died soon after birth; *Gavin, the Crown Prince,* the oldest who was killed by the snake; and *Fairold,* the second and last remaining son who ended up marrying Lambith.

"According to the story, Fairold who descended from the *House of Aeron* and the *Kingdom of the Horse and Sword* becomes the unexpected centerpiece of much that happens in Emryss somewhere in the 'west.'" She smiled.

"Now what does this mean and what do I think of it?

"Well, first of all, the 'short story' that Jonas told earlier comes from me — from things I've been told. And we'll let questions about that wait for a while. Am I a princess from the royal line of another planet? Or am I simply a character in a fantasy of my own creation? And 'kept away' most of my life for everyone's good. I'll let questions about that wait too." Her eyes began to moisten. Michael squeezed her hand. She welcomed it, and he found Harwell staring her way.

"Oh, don't worry, Jonas, I only let Michael get away with this. And he doesn't mind." She raised his hand and gave his fingers a light kiss and forced a business-as-usual look.

Michael didn't mind.

She flashed Harwell a quick smile and, caught off guard, the minister returned it. Her composure returned, showing strength that seemed to dare protecting.

The teacher was the next to surprise everyone.

"Triana, I want you to know that I take you very seriously, and I respect you more than you realize. I won't laugh at you — unless you and Michael laugh first! You are safe with me. But please realize where I'm coming from. Many, many things here I just don't understand."

"Thank you! Mr. Cample. And please realize" — she adjusted her glasses and seemed to study each face — "there's much here I don't understand, though I must face certain curious facts that are hard to deny."

"Such as?" Cample encouraged.

She raised her free hand.

"Let me say this much. The blood of two worlds is supposed to flow in the Princess's veins. When I was very, very young, in some place that's fuzzy to me, I have vivid memories of being told again and again that this princess was me.

"Proving the 'Planet **Emryss** connection' to anyone outside of an institution is hard enough, but the part about having ancestors from a second planet called **Elphia** is even more difficult. Other than Vandor's general comment in the vision—with no details given—I have no evidence at all for that! And, the strange 'man from outer space,' the 'man in the spaceship' that may have stolen me from Emryss as I've just learned from reading, insists that he, and nobody else with him was related to me!"

"Maybe I can clear some of that up!" offered Cample.

"Like what?" said Triana.

"Not yet, please," offered Cample, smiling.

"Really?"

"Yes, really." He pointed to his briefcase. "And, Triana, please notice I'm not laughing! But I promised nothing about smiling!"

"That can wait," declared Harwell. Michael sensed the minister was struggling to mask his eagerness. "We can't leave until we've discussed 'The Secret of Zareba.' I think Triana might have read too fast. I think she may have overlooked some of the pieces of the puzzle."

The End of Part III

WHAT FOLLOWS IS
THE SECRET OF ZAREBA
GIVEN IN ITS ENTIRETY

214

PART IV

THE SECRET OF ZAREBA

A complete story

"The secret things belong to the Lord our God, but the things revealed belong to us..."

Deuteronomy 29:29

CHAPTER 27

1
THE WALK
OF MONKS

areba was the "center of the world," Galen's father had told him. But that just began the confusion.

There were three "Zarebas": Most important was the ancient and tired, but enchanted, city of Zareba that had been long important for its history and for religious reasons. Twenty miles to the north, where it was more arid was the tiny unwalled village of Zareba, home of the famous weavers, with barely a hundred people living in comparative isolation.

And just east of the village, slightly south, was uninhabited Mt. Zareba. For all of his 14 years slender, sandy-haired Galen, the only child of Lord Fairold and Lady Lambith, lived with his family in Zareba Village at the base of Mt. Zareba.

Less than a hundred yards from the village, the mountain stood like a giant, desolate, sloping watchtower over the stubbly fields, arid plain, and nearby village. Over 300 feet high, the flat-topped "mountain" was too tall to have been built, its base too wide, and — though difficult to explain — its appearance demanded that somehow it had to have formed naturally. Because of its isolation and small size it wasn't a true mountain, but the name had stuck.

The mountain was also home to a number of peculiarities.

Over the years, thin clouds occasionally rose from the mountain's roughly circular flat top, which sloped very steeply downhill at those places where the cliff face did not run straight up and down. It was as if a cork or a plug were thrust down into the plain, with the narrow part on top. The main irregularity was one slender rock spire — like an icicle upside-down — that rose to within a dozen feet from the top from attachment on the west near the base. An unbroken stone wall circled the rim at the top.

Then there was the "tip" on the western side that was the highest point of the mountain. A tall slender flagpole capped a circular tower of some kind just inside the wall on the west, though no one in the village had memory of a flag ever flying there.

As to what caused the clouds, or who made the walls, the tower, and the pole, no one knew. The history had been lost, so only legend and rumors offered reasons as to what the place was and why no one lived there. Some said it was an ancient altar to winged demons, while others declared it once was a true center of worship of the God of Heaven.

But no one could get up there and find out. For more than a century Mt. Zareba had proven impregnable. Its sides were too hard and steep to be scaled. It simply couldn't be entered.

That is, until Galen's great discovery.

At the mountain's base on the west, facing Zareba Village an old "entryway" — if that's what it really was — was filled with a dangerous high pile of round boulders that somehow had to have come from the inside. Several people had been killed trying to pull them away. So since the God of Heaven might be showing disapproval, entry from the western side was no longer attempted.

There was one other possible way inside.

On the north side of Mt. Zareba, oddly, a cave opening seemed to forever swallow water from the deep bed of the Ember River that aimed straight towards it from a zigzagging stream slightly uphill from the north. Rather than water running or trickling down to the river, it was as if the small mountain "pressed down," pulling the river to it.

Curiously, as the water struck the mountain, instead of diverting or damming it, it plunged slightly down to some tunnel under it and disappeared, some believed to a secret caldren of Hell, eventually to thrust itself up, warm and bubbling from some underwater opening on the opposite side.

Trying to enter Mt. Zareba by way of the river had also been deadly.

The current was swift and the water deep enough at the base that once anyone disappeared under the small mountain, there was no turning back. Within minutes, the corpse of the person who dared enter the passageway would reappear, battered and lifeless in a warm pool on the opposite side. If some opening in the river tunnel led to the mountaintop, no one had found it.

So Mt. Zareba remained a desolate place full of mystery and sorrow, doing little more than marking off the pathway of the seldom-used Walk of Monks which soon will be explained.

That is, until late one unusual summer.

Galen's discovery followed a very dry summer, which followed a dry spring, which followed a snow-free winter.

But two other life-changing events in the boy's life came first.

For reasons which will soon be clear, the Emperor had made the boy's father Fairold, a prince from a destroyed eastern kingdom, lord over Zareba Village.

As to the humble village, Lord Fairold, as he was called, had reasons for living there, not least of which was that his talented and loving wife, Lady Lambith, who'd risen from a low station in life, couldn't have been happier anywhere else.

And though small, the village was far from ordinary. Knowing why helps one understand the strange events soon to come.

A half-dozen master weavers and dyers under direction of a lean, swarthy, wiry-haired Master Weft lived there, as did Master Maleg, a nearly bald stonemason who was crippled from the waist down. With Maleg lived his strong flaxen-haired twin sons, Saren and Soren, who'd apprenticed themselves to their father's work.

The land around Zareba Village, arid except near the river, managed little more than brambles and stubbly grass, but the kind that sheep and goats would welcome, so nearly every villager had something to do with these patient creatures — whether shepherding, carding and dyeing wool, spinning yarn, or making cloth. Skillful work from village looms was known far and wide. Even the most modest village homes boasted colorful blankets, curtains, and rugs, as well as clothing that contrasted pleasantly with the dusty streets and nearly barren countryside.

Part of the village's fame came from the geography.

The unusual stony neck of Mt. Zareba that was thrust up just east and a bit south, overlooked the village like a looming watchman, casting a deep, cool shadow over much of the village for the early parts of most sunny days. The "tip" of this huge shadow, that on a clear day ran from the pole atop the tower, down the tower, all the way to the base of the mountain, extended to the village streets and far beyond, moving slowly each day as regular as the hand of a giant clock.

In some forgotten time, the shadow's tip served as a finger to determine the pathway of a constantly changing *Walk of Monks and Kings* at the base of the mountain. And, quite frankly, since no one recalled a king ever following it in a Sabbath of meditation, it was usually just called the "Walk of Monks," even though monks seemed just as rare when the events that follow took place.

The unusual thing about this strange path was that in sunlight the

219

walkway itself was "alive" and always moving over a sizable area! And, to stay on it one had to continually move physically as well as think and pray!

Traditionally, one would stand as close as possible to the shadow's tip. Then in a dusty field near the entrance to the village (if one began early), with one's back always to the sun—which wasn't the object of worship—one would continually move slowly backwards or sideways, always glancing down, as the shadow slowly made an arc along the ground. A person would keep as close as possible to the changing path, with one's mind on the Maker of Emryss and a special object of meditation if there was one. If absolutely alone, two people could whisper or pray together as they moved along. A pilgrim could begin this walk early, late, or at any point and continue for a whole day, an hour, or even a few minutes, as long as one desired.

In summer, with the sun at its highest, the distance of The Walk was shorter and slower and the shadows were crisper and easier to follow. Six months later in winter, with the sun at its lowest, the path was quite longer and was much harder to see. Over the years, stones had been placed to show months and weeks to approximate the path for the seasons on days when the skies would cloud over.

By the year of this story's events, however, use of the moving pathway for any religious reason almost never happened. In fact, "Why was such a silly pathway even needed?" some asked. And "Was the God of Heaven even pleased or just amused by its use?" Nowhere was this tradition mentioned in the Holy Book.

The light and shadows, however, affected not only worshipers, but the weavers. Sudden crisp and contrasting light and dark encouraged experimentation and a distinctive blending of colorful yarns against the rough gray of stone, the sandy tans and browns of the desert, and the dusky green of the hardy prairie grass.

And there were those times in the morning when the bright sun would burst from behind the mountain suddenly but slowly dispelling the light grayness house by house, in an instant setting the tapestries visible through the windows ablaze with color. It was a rebirth of hues and tints as if the village were born anew. It was a time to stop and, with a steaming pot of tea, meditate for a few moments upon whatever mattered.

Apart from Mt. Zareba, the land was flat, except where it gently rolled, sloping almost imperceptively to the south toward Zareba City with its religious trappings, age-old legends, and rich traditions. It was said that many hundreds of years earlier the God-Son had ended his public ministry there, had been killed, and — according to the Holy Book — three days later had risen from the dead and ascended into Heaven.

But times and fortunes had changed often since then, and several times Zareba City had been destroyed, captured, recaptured, and rebuilt — as well as nearby towns and villages. Just where the God-Son had actually preached, died, and had been buried wasn't absolutely certain. Nevertheless, by dreams and visions, one by one old places in the city where important events had taken place were rediscovered. Over these, shrines and houses of worship were built.

Most important was finding the stone tomb said to have briefly housed the body of the God-Son. Next was finding the foundation of the first Great Temple. Over this foundation a Shrine to the lost Golden Chest of Promise was built. In it a replica of the sacred box covered with highly polished brass was displayed, and in which were placed copies of the first laws that God had given his people. The original chest had been captured and destroyed many, many years earlier, even before the days of the God-Son. The new shrine showed that God was still faithful, said some. As long as it remained in the hands of God's people, God would protect them.

This, of course, was good for business, and next to farming the rich, well-watered land surrounding the city, the endless comings and goings of pilgrims and travelers gave Zareba City a measure of importance and prosperity.

The city at the time of these events had a king given to religion, formality, and ceremony, though the Emperor limited the king's rule to within the recently restored city walls—and not an inch beyond. Zareba was not the largest city in the Emperor's domain. But it did have a unique history. And some said an important future because according to certain prophecies in the Holy Book, in the "last days" the God-Son himself would return and, for a time, "rule Emryss from Zareba." Hence the Emperor gave Zareba City his special attention.

Especially during the year Galen reached manhood, as his father Fairold would soon privately declare.

That was at a time when peace in the Emperor's realm began to turn sour.

Perhaps the unrest began when more and more people began to question aloud the old truths of the Holy Book, which no one seemed eager to defend. Or perhaps it was when rumblings came from the far south about a growing confederation of small rogue, but usually poorly ruled, kingdoms in the Empire, kingdoms of people who ordinarily wouldn't speak to those outside of their immediate boundaries.

A difficult moment arrived when a mysterious notice was found nailed to the door of the Shrine of the Golden Chest of Promise. It read:

> *"The day of old myths is past*
> *and so is our support for a city*
> *of false priests and monks*
> *who use our money to*
> *perpetuate old lies."*

At the bottom were the alleged signatures of half a dozen southern kings.

The long drought did not help matters. Many poor Zarebites suffered, and their pleas for aid seemed to fall on deaf ears.

Peace with southern kings never came easy, but usually the Emperor found a way to keep them appeased.

No longer.

Never had the southern kings pushed so far north with such force. And according to frantic messengers, something new was afoot. The alliance was an odd mixture: Along with the usual soldiers motivated by duty, greed, or guilt, were certain "God-believers" who seemed eager to attach new meanings to old truths; and brown-hooded worshipers of Emryss who openly practiced witchcraft and took advantage of the superstitious.

Then a messenger from Zareba City arrived at Zareba Village with a sealed personal letter for Lord Fairold.

It was from the Emperor.

CHAPTER 28

2
THE EMPEROR'S LETTER

rom where he sat, Lord Fairold's coal-black eyes locked upon his thin but nearly full-grown son.

"Prince Galen, I have news of gravest import."

Prince — the word echoed in the ears of his only child. How long since his father had called him that? In fact, had he ever? And why now? There'd been some connection of his family with the Royal House of Aeron, and there'd been news of remnants of their destroyed kingdom even settling on the coast far to the east, so why did his parents and he wind up here? His parents were usually so open, but why had they been silent about their own past? And his? What was there to hide? There were "reasons," his mother had told him. And when the time was right, he would be told. He'd waited years.

Galen sensed that time was now.

Lord Fairold leaned across the massive table where he conducted village business, in the front room of their simple home. Wide boards, well worn, covered the floor. The walls were plain white plaster, and an elegant tapestry displaying the Great Flying Horse and the Golden Sword of his grandfather's kingdom hung on the wall behind him.

The story of his grandparents ruling there before the Great Destruction seemed like a fairy tale. Galen had read that story. And he'd heard about how his Uncle Colin's great quest had begun.

And then how it seemed to have ended, though the details had never been filled in. Galen had become convinced that even his parents didn't know.

Lord Fairold's thick, dark curly hair with a touch of gray resembled his mother's, and seemed heavy on his lean frame. He seemed hardly a warrior, though he was said to have been one. His words when he offered them, however, were sure and commanded attention.

By contrast, Galen had blue eyes and sandy brown hair. Brushing it back, he automatically turned and slid the bolt into the lock on the door behind him. A beam of morning light just escaping the shield of the mountain, pierced the window in the shadowy room, and fell like a pointer across the letter Lord Fairold was holding. It had come in a roll and bore the seal of the Emperor.

Galen strode to the table, meeting his father's gaze straight on, as was proper, he'd been taught, when serious matters were afoot. Galen took the letter, which curled down from his fingers, and held it to the light.

Once before he'd seen the steady, deliberate writing of the Emperor, as well as his signature on documents that came to his father from time to time. This was composed by no scribe; it was from the High King's own hand.

Without being told, Galen began reading aloud.

My dearest Fairold, Prince of Aeron, Lord of Zareba, descendent of the kingly line that gave us the mother of the God-Son, and servant of the God of Heaven:

225

Greetings to you, to lovely Lady Lambith, and to your
most trusted servants Sir Kerky and Lady Millicent,
and lastly, to your son Prince Galen. I consider none greater
than you five in the Empire God has placed in my trust for
the few years we walk the beautiful, lonely paths of Emryss.

I have not forgotten how I and our great alliance of kings
are forever in your debt — a debt which now will increase.

For I bring you terrible news.

For months we have heard rumblings of unrest to the
south, miles beyond the borders under our care. But since the
petty southern kings have long only fought among themselves,
they have posed us little threat.

Now all that has changed.

A monstrous warlord named King Stulk, under the banner
of "New Times, New World" has done the impossible: unite
nearly a dozen quarreling kings into a powerful fighting force.

The assault has been so sudden that our losses have been
overwhelming. As you know, in the name of peace our alliance
of kings has kept only a small standing army. In retrospect, we
have made a tragic mistake. This has been perceived as a great
weakness and King Stulk has leaped upon it.

Lord Fairold, as of this writing my palace, though many miles
from Zareba City, has been stormed and lost. My son and daughters

Lucia and Lemerah have managed to escape, though my precious wife Brilena, personally directing our palace defenses in my absence, perished. Half of our standing army has been destroyed.

The strike from the south has come like lightning. Our only chance is to retreat to the north and wait for reinforcements from our allies in the east and west. But I am convinced that if we can hold on, this ungodly southern alliance will crumble, for they are their own worst enemy, and we can defeat them.

Lord Fairold, I have two favors to ask:

As you know, Zareba is precious to believers of the Holy Book. And also to me. I am certain King Stulk, who mocks the old ways as foolish superstition, is bent upon destroying Zareba, both to break our spirit and establish his own godless "New World."

You can do nothing about his next target, Zareba City. Others will try to defend the Holy Places there. But as to Zareba Village with its ancient guild of weavers and Mt. Zareba—I wish to have them spared if at all possible. From what I have learned, I am concerned that King Stulk may attempt to find a way to do what we have never done: breach the mountain's cliff walls and claim the ancient High Place for his own purposes.

Regardless of what good or evil is actually there, he will attempt to fly his evil flag above that tower on top, which is as much a mystery to him as to us, as a sign that the words of the Holy Book have passed away, and a New World of his own making has come to take its place.

227

My greatest prayer is that Mt. Zareba, whatever it is or was, will never be taken. Do what you can to prevent it, but not at the expense of the lives of the weavers and their families.

If you have no other choice, save them and flee. You will do so with my blessing.

Secondly, there is the matter of my children. My plan is to send them north separately for their own protection. One will come to you. (I am being vague deliberately.) Please take care of my child as you would your own. I remind you of the promise you made to me more than 15 years ago.

My child will bring you a thick book about your people, that I've not had time to read. Sadly, the brave man who risked his life to bring it died just after arriving and the day before we had to flee. He finished the book, he said, after your brother was no longer able.

I wish I could bring better news, and I pray the day will soon come when I can.

May God watch over you five, and those from my family soon to arrive—all of whom love the God of Heaven. There are none I love more than my own family—and you.

Your servant in His name,
(signed) Charlayn III,
Emperor of the United Kings of Emryss
by will of the God of Heaven.

Prince Galen put down the letter and looked across the table. His father's eyes were still fast upon him. But there were tears — tears Galen had never seen before — on his cheeks.

"Today, my son, I declare you have come of age. I'm sorry the formal time will not wait."

"Father, I don't understand!"

"Galen, I must tell you certain things that you do not know. And you may ask me questions — any questions. You are nearly the size of a man. Now I hereby declare you to be one. I expect you to be faithful to the God of Heaven as I have been. And I expect you to be faithful to your mother and me, to the ancient royal family from which you have come, and to the village where we live..."

"And," interrupted Galen, "to the mountain?" He ran his fingers through his sandy hair.

"*And to the mountain,*" repeated his father. "O How I wish I could do something about that. The Emperor can dream impossible things... We must do what we can do. All of us must quickly leave."

"As God is my witness," said Galen, "I will do all you've asked, even unto death." He felt his knees tremble. He still held his father's gaze. His own eyes resembled neither parent exactly except for their intensity.

"Father, much about this letter is so puzzling. Why does the Emperor care so much for *you*?... For Mother?... Millicent?... Kerky?... For even me?" He pointed to the paper. "Look, he even mentions me by name, even knows I haven't come of age! And all these words...they're to us, the five of us, except for the part about the promise you made. He's never even seen me! How does he know my name? And...whatever promise did you make?

"Oh, but he has seen you! He's even read the book we have that tells the story about your grandparents."

"When?"

"When you were a baby — he came here, came to the village."

"To see Master Weft and the weavers, I suppose?"

"Yes, he came to see them, but not just for that. Be patient. I will get there. He also came for other reasons."

"Father, the Emperor mentions two daughters, Lucia and Lemerah, but also a son — whose name he doesn't mention. I never knew the Emperor even had a son!"

Lord Fairold glanced at the window. In the short time they'd talked, the sun had risen, moving across the table to the floor and Galen's short boots. For several seconds silence ruled the shadows.

"I never knew he had a son either."

Galen was puzzled. How could the Emperor, himself a ruler over dozens of kings and hundreds of lords and barons think so highly of his father, who was a prince without a kingdom, and who looked hardly a warrior, and was now only lord over a tiny village? And if the Emperor and his father were friends, why didn't his father know about the Emperor's son?

There was a knock at the door.

Fairold nodded and Galen opened it. His mother, Lady Lambith, entered with a large tray of bowls of steaming oatmeal, a plate of sliced buttered bread, a piece of honeycomb, and cups of tea. Though well-dressed in clothes that could be worked in, and well-mannered to a fault when she wanted to be, Lady Lambith handled the heavy tray with ease and, laying out the plates and bowls, she served her son and his father at places set across the table from each other. Her companion, Lady Millicent, with a head of abundant fiery red hair, and who was almost 10 years older than Galen, whisked a chair into place for the man, newly declared-to-be. Fairold glanced up. Both ladies offered I-dare-you-to-object-to-our-presence smiles, gave impish little bows, spun quickly on their heels, and left.

Galen could see the three shared some secret he knew nothing about—one that he suspected before, but had—stubbornly, perhaps—refused to show any interest in. But why when they were so open about everything else? Fairold's eyes followed the two ladies to the door that led to the rest of the house. When the latch clicked, he turned back to his son.

"Let's eat, Galen. I've a story to tell you." He took a bite of oatmeal and turned his head to the window. "And this story involves people—real people. And it will take some time."

"Does it tie in with the letter?" asked Galen.

"It certainly does. Why the Emperor cares for you? Sit and listen. You will wonder no longer."

CHAPTER 29

3
HELP FOR
A DYING
MAN

 alen, you know how the old stories have magic and power —
often telling the Truth better than a school lesson." The
boy nodded. Fairold drained all but the last swallow from
his cup of tea. Laying the palms of his hands flat on the
table, he sat up straight.

"Father, I'm ready."

Without further fanfare, Fairold began.

DEATH OF A KING

Once upon a time a godly Queen and her two sons had an unusual vision.
Fairold's eyes drilled into his son. A gust of wind brushed a tree limb against
the wall outside and Galen could almost hear the veil of secrecy begin to tear.

*In the vision a heavenly messenger said that a Great King in the west
needed help — their help — so in a splendid coach the three headed in that
direction. On the way the Queen and the Crown Prince died most tragically,
and the surviving Prince, all alone, had to dig graves and bury them. He was
terrified — and angry. This anger more than anything drove him to continue
the quest alone, and to be vigilant and brave as he had never been before.*

232

For he was the last of his ancient royal family.

The very evening after digging the graves he came to a small barony called Ashbrook, a place he'd never heard of. There, in an inn beside a river, he met a beautiful tavern maid who he quickly rescued from misfortune, fell in love with, and married all in the same day. With his new wife, as well as two orphan children, a boy ten and a girl a bit more than eight, who became their servants, once again the Prince continued westward.

On the four traveled for nearly two weeks, stopping at occasional taverns along the road and living off the land. But nowhere did they encounter a king of any kind, or anyone who seemed to be looking for them as prophesied.

And God protected them.

"But," Galen interrupted, "excuse me, Father, but after his mother died, how did the surviving Prince, who was not the Crown Prince, know that *he* was the one was the one to do this great undertaking? Perhaps the Queen and Crown Prince had forfeited their…"

"As far as *I* know, Galen," said Lord Fairold, "the prince didn't know. But he was scared and very angry. That much is certain. 'God needed, or desired, *them* to help,' the messenger had said, and even though the surviving Prince had always lived in the shadow of both his brothers, he still had the royal ring of his kingdom, signifying authority and responsibility. And until God told him differently — which God did not — he would continue until he succeeded, or died, after which he would gladly join the rest of his family."

"But wasn't his new wife also family? What about…"

Fairold shifted in his chair, his eyes still on his son.

"*Prince* Galen, let me continue!"

"Yes, Father."

At the end of the second week of their journey, just as the sun was about to disappear, an axle pin on their coach suddenly snapped and a wheel came off.

The coach ground to a halt, everyone got out, and with a whole lot of pushing and pulling the four moved the coach out of sight behind a large thicket. With the onset of darkness, they refreshed themselves and spent the night there.

The next morning the Prince was awakened by a scream. Sword in hand, he tumbled out of the coach into the gray mist of morning and was startled to discover that they had camped alongside a beautiful lake. And also that they weren't alone.

A hundred feet away stood three men.

The largest one, with hair as black as a raven, was struggling between the other two with, it seemed, his hands tied behind him. Suddenly he swore and swung an elbow, knocking one captor back. The third man countered in an unusual way: Instead of a sword, he held a large fowling net. Up and over the large man's head it went, and down in a tangle of cord he fell. Instantly, the third man was upon him with more rope. The man swore and screamed piteously.

The Prince ran to the scene, his new servant boy at his heels. He stopped about twenty feet away. He could tell from the man's clothes that he was a person of means, and his captors who had to be bandits of some kind, were more plainly dressed, and were armed only with daggers. Never had the Prince seen such poorly armed outlaws. Each went for his knife.

"In the name of the God of Heaven, let him go!" yelled the Prince, holding out his sword, and the boy, his trusty staff.

"In the name of God, leave us alone!" shouted the first captor.

"God...?" The Prince paused. Now what?

The men seemed hardly like outlaws. But he doubted not for a second their resolve to risk everything to keep their prisoner. Frantically, the large man struggled to escape the net. In his fury, the ropes around his wrists came loose. With a great leap he was up and gone.

"After him!" shouted one captor, ignoring the Prince, who despite his challenge looked hardly a threat. Immediately, the captors were in hot pursuit, the Prince and his servant not far behind. No more than fifty paces beyond the bush, near the water's edge, stood a splendid coach, and just as the Prince saw it, the raven-haired man disappeared inside the door. Immediately, he came back out carrying a cushion.

With a knife in hand, he slashed it. In went his fist and feathers flew. Suddenly, his hand emerged holding a small vial. Removing the cork with his teeth, he emptied its contents into his mouth. White powder flecked his beard.

By this time the captors were at his side. The large man's jet-black eyes bulged with fury. Angrily, with one arm he violently brushed both men away, sending the smaller of the two sprawling in the dust. The second captor turned to the Prince.

"Stranger, if you truly love the God whose sign you wear on your chest, please help us!"

"LEAVE US ALONE!" roared the large man. His voice was terrifying. Muscles bulged on his neck and thick arms.

As the Prince moved closer, he noticed for the first time the X-shaped emblem of stakes on the large man's chest. The Prince's anger boiled over in childlike rage.

"Where did you steal that shirt?" His voice cracked on the last word.

The huge man's eyes grew large. As he lunged forward, the Prince, holding back his sword, stepped sideways and the man stumbled and fell. Slowly he rose, his body swaying. When the Prince met his gaze head-on, the large man's dark eyes rolled up into whiteness. Then he fell again. The smaller captor, waiting for just the right moment, leaped from where he lay, pulled away the large man's hand, and put his ear close to the man's face.

"He's still breathing!" he said.

The second captor looked at the Prince. His eyes were pleading.

"You must understand, he's our master...and we love him."

"Then we must help him," said a woman's voice. From nowhere the Prince's new wife, now a Princess by marriage, was beside her husband with her servant girl. The sudden presence of the young woman and her servant

235

took the large man's servants by surprise.

Then the story came forth — at least part of it. The servants' master, the Prince was told, had recently returned from a trip to the east. There he'd become ill, and to cure him, a physician had given him a new remedy — a white powder. At first it worked like magic: the illness disappeared and he recovered. But afterwards, came an insatiable craving for the remedy itself! And the more he ate of it, the more he desired. Before returning home he bought huge quantities of the powder at an enormous cost.

But the man was nothing like his former self. Friends and servants tried everything to cure him of his new cure, but all failed; for the man, it appears, had ingeniously hidden small quantities of the powder everywhere. Just as he would calm down and seem normal again, an hour later he'd be found unconscious, nearly dead with white flakes dusting his mustache and beard.

This once faithful and kind man began to ignore his responsibilities. At first, family, friends, and servants covered for him. Then as they earnestly began searching for, finding, and secretly destroying his cure, the man became even more creative in his concealment. His very profitable business began to fall apart. If the Emperor had learned of the man's foolishness and how he'd affected others by his behavior, said the smaller servant, he would have been imprisoned, if not executed outright!

Something drastic had to be done. Finally at his wife's frantic request, two trusted servants bound their master very much against his will and took him far away from anyone who knew him to find some way — any way — to cure him.

"And I'm one of those two men, and here we are," said the smaller servant.

"Then we must cure him," said the new Princess. She glanced at her husband, who held his tongue, searching for the right words.

"And how?" asked the servant.

"That remains to be seen," said the Princess, "but those who've worked in taverns have their ways. Besides, we've seen this powder before. But" — she

236

raised her hand and pointed at her questioner – " if you allow my husband and me to help, you must promise not to interfere."

"You have our word," said the smaller servant. The other man nodded. "Only promise you'll spare his life!"

"I'm sorry, but God takes promises very seriously. We can't promise that," said the Princess. "All we can promise is that we'll do what we can. He may suffer, even die, mind you, but he should live."

"Cure him! Heal him! We'll pay you anything."

"We want no money," said Princess. "There's nothing…"

"Wait!" interrupted the Prince. "There's one thing you can do…no, two things."

"Name them!" said the smaller servant, the obvious leader of the two.

"First, we have a wheel on our coach that needs repairing, and second, we need information. We're new here and we're seeking the Emperor."

The large man on the ground rolled over and looked terrified. His servants glanced at each other. They stepped to the side and the larger of the two whispered to his companion. The Prince wondered if his words seemed foolish.

"Heal our master, and even though the Emperor may kill him if he catches up with him, we'll take you to the High King personally."

"You can do that?" asked the Prince.

"There's some risk, but we can," said the smaller servant. The man on the ground groaned.

"Then we have a deal?" asked the Princess. She looked at the men, then back to her husband. He nodded approval of he knew not what, and she offered him a small bow. The Prince hid his surprise.

"We do have a 'deal,' as you say. We agree to everything." The man on the ground groaned again. The girl looked at him with disgust.

"Okay…since my husband agrees, we're already wasting time. Take your disgraced master, remove his shirt bearing the emblem of the stakes of the God-Son – whose name he's blasphemed – and tie him under your coach. Tie each

237

hand and foot to a separate wheel. And make sure to set the brake on the coach tightly.

The men's eyes grew large.

"You, you would stretch him out in the manner of the God-Son?!"

"If," said the Princess, "it reminds him of what the God-Son did for him and the rest of us, so much the better. But that's not the main reason. Don't worry, we aren't going to pin him down with the stakes and kill him. If he dies, it will be because of all the powder he's eaten." She looked at the man staring stupidly from where he lay. "But I think he's too stubborn to die."

As soon as the man was tightly tied as the Princess instructed, he revived enough to find his voice and curse. Next to the coach was a large bucket of icy water that had been drawn for drinking. Without a moment's hesitation, she raised the bucket just high enough and dumped half the water over the man's head. When he cursed again even louder, he received the rest of the water. The more the man thrashed, the more the ground under him turned to mud.

At last came silence.

But just for a moment. The Princess stood as close as she could get, hands on hips, and measuring her words as carefully as a seamstress would purple fabric, she responded in a fury:

"You may yell and scream anything you want, and you may hate God with all your heart, but you will NOT curse the God of Heaven in the presence of a Princess of Aeron! Have I made myself clear?"

The two men's jaws fell to their chests. Their eyes were like saucers. The Prince himself felt his knees weaken, but he hid it and stood firm. Never, from a girl, had he seen such fire! But how glad he was that she was there. Very glad! His wife looked at the two men and pointed to the bucket.

"Now show your master that you agree with me! Go, fill up this bucket again for we may need more."

The men gladly disappeared with the empty bucket.

The large man, now wide awake, was silent. And covered with mud. He stared up at the bottom of the coach as if in a trance. The Prince had never seen *a person's eyes look so sorrowful.*

Now the Princess had a young servant girl, who'd refused to let the tavern maid-turned-Princess leave her, and so served as "her personal royal maid." The Princess accepted her because they loved each other, and the very able little girl had no family. Though at this time she was only 97 ½ months and counting, she'd seen more trouble and grief than most do in a lifetime. Her shell was hard and tongue sharp, but they protected a tender heart.

She stared at the poor man under the coach. She and the boy servant – 120, or 10 years old as I said earlier, but already a tested warrior – were fiercely loyal and uncommonly wary. The girl asked the boy for a rag, and receiving one as well as some water and a small measure of soap, washed the man's face and dried him off a bit with a towel. The Princess told the boy loud enough for everyone to hear that if the man harmed one hair on the girl's head, he was to kill him. For the boy, also without any other family, and who was a self-appointed royal servant to the Prince, this order was unnecessary.

Few knew the sobering details of the "Drunkard's Last Walk," but the Princess was one who did. It began with a quiet request of a family member or trusted friend, with the secret consent of a few others, after everything else had failed. On this "walk" a hopeless, violent, continual drunk was bound and spirited away into the forest for weeks of "treatment," which was never discussed. Half such people died; half walked out sober never to touch ale again.

But the large man, despite his problem, was no drunk.

The Princess's plan, and she had one, was simple. And startling.

The man was to be tied at all times, no matter how he protested, or what he said. He was to be doused with water for any blasphemy (and this only happened once more). He was to be brought food and water at regular intervals – which he refused, but only at first. He could "exercise," but only from under the coach, and then only one limb at a time – as he was always to be secured by three ropes, and then with a guard watching. His servants, with the Prince on guard, would attend to the man's physical needs. The tied man would stay there as long as the Princess thought necessary.

The Prince suggested that, to pass time, all should take turns reading long sections of the Holy Book within earshot of their captive. A problem arose when he learned that only he and the man's servants could read, though the Princess insisted that she could read some — since it was assumed royalty could read — the Holy Book proved too difficult. This made her, and the two child servants, more eager to read and write words than ever. And, with help of the Prince, the time had come to learn. So, "school" began for the visiting royal party, and the man under the coach attended class, like it or not.

And oddly, perhaps, there was no objection.

Day followed long day, and four weeks passed. Fortunately, the boy and the man's servants were excellent hunters and cooks. Food was never scarce.

Then came an interesting turn of events. All except the young servant girl had left the coach for a couple of hours, to fish, to wash, to gather wild things to eat. It was a beautiful day. Quietly, the Prince returned with an armload of firewood. As he came near, something made him stop short and duck behind a tree. Under the coach the large man held the Prince's precious Holy Book. The man himself was reading aloud, which he'd never done in their presence, and he was pointing to words as he read. Close to his side sat the servant girl, who now and then would grab his arm and stop him, apparently puzzling over some word. Then the Prince saw the man's arms and legs.

The ever-present ropes were off! The Prince drew his sword.

"Please stop!" yelled the servant girl. "He's already died! The Holy Book says so!"

"Aye, but I live again as a new man!" said the man. "The Holy Book says that too. Missy, better tie me back up." The girl scampered to the ropes.

"You were free but you stayed," said the Prince.

"I am free," said the man, as the girl retied his legs.

"And you stayed," said the Prince.

"I stay until the Princess of Aeron forgives me for cursing and says I may go — and you make me one promise."

Suddenly, the Princess stepped into view.

"The matter of cursing," she said, "is between you and the God of Heaven. As for me, I forgive you." In seconds it seemed everyone had returned. Then she knelt without embarrassment and prayed loud enough for everyone to hear, "O God of Heaven, we thank you for your mercy upon this man. We ask you that if he ever so much as touches this evil powder, or anything like it, that he will vomit until he can no longer stand. Amen.

"Now with my husband's permission, you are free to go."

The Prince nodded.

The servant girl again began untying the ropes.

"I will not leave until you and your husband make me one promise." The man, still under the coach, spoke with new, strange authority. His voice was rich and strong. "You must promise me that your firstborn will marry one of my children."

"But we have no children!" said the Princess.

"I have a baby girl and my wife is expecting another child," said the man. "The future holds many things!"

"We...barely know you!" said the Prince. "Besides, we have nothing other than what you've seen. And..."

"But they have the royal rings!" interrupted the servant girl. The Princess motioned to her to be quiet.

"Also," continued the Prince, "we're on our way to meet the Emperor. We have no idea what the future will..."

It was the small man's turn to break in. His cheeks were wet.

"We promised that if you cured our master that we would introduce you to the Emperor."

"The sooner the better!" said the Prince. "We've spent far too long here!"

"On this you are quite mistaken, dear Prince. Everything we've told you about our master is true except for one thing. The Emperor does not seek this man's life, for he is far from being an ordinary citizen." The smaller man drew himself to his full height. There was a full minute of silence, even from the usually noisy birds nearby. "It gives me great pleasure to introduce you to the Emperor of the United Kings of Emryss, Charlayn III." The man under the coach slowly crawled out. His legs wobbling, he struggled to his feet. He leaned back against the coach.

Everyone from the Royal House of Aeron — following the Prince's example — slowly dropped to his knees, as did the Emperor's servants.

"Stand! Stand! All of you!" said the Emperor. "I should be bowing to you, though if I did, I doubt I'd be able to get back up!" All six stood. "You've saved my life, all of you." He turned and gazed into the eyes of each one. "Please unstrap the trunk on the back of the coach and put it on the ground," he told one of his men. Without a word the larger servant did. The Emperor rummaged to the bottom of the huge box, then asked the Princess to step forward. Her hands were shaking. "There," he said, pointing down to a small bag. "That's the last of my powder. Take it! I dare not touch the bag lest I start vomiting."

The Prince chuckled quietly. How long since he'd last done that! The Princess, however, did not. She reached in, pulled out the bag, and holding it away from her with two fingers like a dead rat, carried it to the fire, and dropped it in. Once on the glowing coals an orange-green flame leaped up and a sharp sour odor replaced the outdoor freshness. The Emperor's eyes grew large and he started to gag. The Princess stepped forward and, though he was filthy, hugged the great man and kissed his cheek.

"It will be okay," she said. The feeling passed and the man smiled.

"There is one thing more," said the Prince, "something we must tell you before anyone one else does."

"And that is…?" said the Emperor.

"My wife, recently a maid in the Boar's Hoof Inn, many miles east on this very road, and now who is a Princess of Aeron by marriage, killed the Lord Doctor Oxram who created this evil powder. Further, we have destroyed much, perhaps all of this powder, along with the doctor, all his armed bodyguards except one, and his recipe, and, unfortunately, a fine tavern that burned in this *battle. The doctor's surviving bodyguard claimed that Oxram had royal blood and was related to you. And that..." He paused.*

It was the Emperor's turn to interrupt.

"You and your wife must be fearsome warriors! The two of you, with your servants' help no doubt, killed Oxram? Remarkable! Killed his bodyguards and destroyed the powder? I'm amazed!"

"No more than I am, Your Majesty," said the Prince. "We did have a bit of help from other serving maids, but my words are true."

"And," said the Emperor, "After these weeks...I don't doubt them. I will hear more about this later. But as of this moment I have five things I must say, and my servants will put down what matters in writing.

"FIRST. I now love the God of Heaven with all my heart. I have begged Him to forgive me for the horrible things I've said — and I believe He has. I beg you to do the same, to forgive and forget — and I hope you will.

"SECOND. I wondered where the white powder actually came from. Anyone who rid the Empire of it and its creator has done Emryss a great service.

"THIRD. You see that horse?" — he pointed to one of the creatures that pulled his coach — "that horse has more royal blood than that jackal Oxram. And royal records can prove it. He's a deceiver and a liar and has been no end of trouble to me. Doubtless, somehow he saw that I got his powder so I would die in disgrace."

The Emperor paused, and told his servant to carefully record what he would say next.

"FOURTH. The Princess here has kissed me, which is not public behavior of commoners in my realm, though it occasionally is for royalty. Recognize then, that I accept this lady who wears a ring of the important Royal House of Aeron, that now only exists in people's minds, as a royal Princess by marriage. I declare that she and her companions are innocent, and guiltless, of any of the recent deaths at the Boar's Hoof Inn. And to seal these words, she shall receive special instruction in palace ways and traditions from women I will send, and

on this day six months hence, she shall be declared a 'Lady of the Empire,' our highest rank for women.

"But only on one condition." He paused.

"What is that, Your Majesty?" asked the Prince.

"That she learn to read and write—and to my personal satisfaction! Wearing the tiara of Lady of the Empire is a great honor, which few have received, but those who do must be able to read and write—and they must do it very well!"

"I will not disappoint you," said the Princess.

Without even a glance her way, the Emperor continued. That he could think and act so quickly was startling, and that he expected obedience was obvious.

And it was obvious he was well.

"Now let me finish—

"FIFTH. You said a tavern was destroyed. It will be rebuilt in fine style at my expense in memory of the House of Aeron."

"Excuse me Your Majesty," interrupted the Prince, "but you said you were sending women from your palace—just where will you send them? I've no place of my own besides my coach, and I've little money and nowhere to go. My quest from God has ended."

"Oh yes, there is that detail — I almost forgot," said the Emperor. "My brain, I fear, is still covered with mud. There is a place, my dear Prince, that I'd like you to go and govern for me—at least for a while. It's a small village 20 miles from the Holy City, and is a fitting place now for a Prince of Aeron. It's called Zareba, the same name as the Holy City, and it lies in the shadow of a small, tower-like mountain also of the same name. Both of these places are very important to me."

❋   ❋   ❋

"And, Prince Galen," said his father, "so ends the story about the Emperor, your mother, Lady Millicent, Sir Kerky, and me."

244

CHAPTER 30

4
A PROMISE
TO KEEP

ather! Why have you kept all this from me? And...and you still haven't finished your story! I am your and Lady Lambith's son, am I not?"

"You certainly are!" answered Lord Fairold.

"What about the Emperor's 'request' in his letter, and the 'promise' in the story?" Galen stood, and glanced at the empty dishes before again meeting his father's gaze.

"Well, you see, we came here — and stayed."

"No, Father. About the promise about your 'firstborn,' especially when you had no children to offer? Am I not your firstborn?"

"You are."

"And?"

"I've waited more than fourteen years to tell you this for several reasons. You see, the time was not right."

"And it is now?"

For several seconds there was silence.

"Yes, unfortunately. Few know about what happened when the Emperor was cured. For one thing, he was terribly embarrassed for his weakness, and especially for blaspheming the God of Heaven before

Millicent, Kerky, and the rest of us. Yes, he does truly, passionately love God. And, yes I did promise 'you' to 'one of his children,' but"—he paused and raised his finger—"I agreed only if later we *both* still believed God willed it."

"I, just a villager, marry the daughter of an Emperor?"

"Why not?—in time, of course, when you come of age."

" 'Come of age,' " said Galen. "Didn't you say earlier that's now happened?"

Lord Fairold looked down, and finding a piece of bread on his plate, popped it into his mouth. He finished his last cold swallow of tea. He looked up at his son.

"If I were the Emperor, I'd be pleased."

"You honor me Father, but I've never been to a royal court. The only home I know is here. My skill with a sword is weak…"

"As is my own skill," Lord Fairold interrupted, "so you must practice more! But, you're also your mother's son. You've already learned to stand tall and listen when you know nothing, and even now, at your age—I've heard you alone at play—you can fence with words, a valuable skill much safer than fighting, and quite effective if done with kindness."

"And, if married to the right woman!" said a new voice. His mother, the 'Princess' of the story, had tiptoed into the room unnoticed. Lady Millicent stood in her shadow. Lady Lambith smiled at her husband, and spoke respectfully in a whisper just loud enough for the boy to hear, "Dear husband, are you still glad I'm here? *Very glad?*"

"Dear wife, how long did you hold your glass against the door listening?"

"Dear husband, a tavern maid, if she's to live, hears everything. A 'glass to the door' is hardly necessary in this case though, right, Lady Millicent?" The young woman with fiery red hair nodded. "You know, dear husband, if you'd asked me not to, I would have obeyed. But you did not, so I had to make sure you got things right." She turned to the boy-declared-to-be-a-man. "See how one talks in a royal court? Gently and logically."

Lord Fairold grimaced and looked away.

"But, Galen," said his mother, shaking her finger, "don't get married the same day you meet a beautiful girl! Oh, the very idea!" She rolled her eyes.

"Unless it can't be helped," interjected Lady Millicent, with her first words. "And she's as wonderful as your mother!" She seemed to be forcing herself not to laugh.

Lord Fairold stood and glared.

"Prince Galen, my son, as you can see, sometimes it's hard to break free from your past! Look at the beautiful ladies standing before you! Neither has set foot in a palace, yet if they could master their tongues, they could grace any royal court. I was born into one. I can tell you that important things happen inside a palace, as well as outside its walls. It's not unlike God and us. *True worship* happens inside us, and true service is done outside our bodies. Only the skin separates one from the..."

"From the other," Galen interrupted. "You've told me before, Father, and I learn quickly. But as to girls and ladies and such" — he glanced at the window — "I ..."

"He will do as he ought, Lord Fairold," Lady Millicent interrupted, "because Kerky and I ..."

"And his mother," Lady Lambith interrupted.

"Will see," Lady Millicent interrupted again, "that the outside part, and the inside part, whatever, is just as it should be." She gave a little curtsy and bowed.

"And we are blessed, Prince Galen," said Lord Fairold, still focused on his son, "that these brilliant words are trapped by these walls."

"With your permission, Lord Fairold" — Lady Lambith's voice was unnaturally soft, and to Galen, scary — "I would like to 'return' to the palace, which, of course I learned about through special tutoring, and *reading — a lot of reading…*"

"And, Lord Fairold," interrupted Lady Millicent, "as to reading, I was taught by the Emperor *personally* — how many can say that? Pardon me, Lady Lambith."

"And in that reading," Lady Lambith continued, "I learned that from the two greatest commandments, which I think your father is trying to explain, to love the God of Heaven first, and then love others — from these, all good manners and good behavior follow."

Lord Fairold glanced at her from the corner of his eye.

"And one of these," said Lord Fairold, "is not interrupting important conversations."

"I pardon you for interrupting *our* interruptions, my husband. A few more words, Your Honor" — she gave a slight bow — "and I'll be done. It's true that certain ladies who know more about taverns than palaces have a lot to learn.

"But sometimes they, too, must teach! Modesty, a sense of propriety, and restraint as a Lady of the Empire forbid my going further." With that, she curtsied delicately and deferred once again to her husband. Galen's eyes grew large. He had seen his mother and father spar with words, even play with them, but never quite like this.

Then to Galen she curtsied as well.

"My son, make no mistake. There are fine distinctions in the degree and angle and manner of how and to whom to show respect. Sometimes you must bow to a frog — which your father definitely is not! — but not low. You must never grovel! Don't forget that. Your father, usually with more important things on his mind, sometimes muddles some details around the edges. And now, so you don't misunderstand what I mean, please observe.

"Please stand, dear husband."

Lord Fairold gritted his teeth, rose from his chair, and took several steps forward. She moved until she stood facing him. Slowly and gracefully, she curtsied deeply, holding her dress to the side. Rising, she extended her hand which he drew to his lips and kissed. She circled him with her arms, drew his head down, and kissed him lightly on the lips.

"I love you," she whispered.

Then, holding her husband's hand, she turned to face her son.

"Now Galen, that was a bit more than what's called for in a royal court. But how much more? You'll have to decide. But oh dear, Galen, remember you're in the presence of a lady — two in fact, though they're not usually on display here. So tip back your head and close your mouth! Good, you learn quickly. It's important to be taught by those who know, and no one can teach you what Lady Millicent and I can. We've both had excellent training from the owner of a famous tavern, where every kind of business took place, not to mention training we've had from the Emperor himself. This was our good fortune, and yours.

"My son," she said, pulling up a chair, "now it's time to be family." Millicent brought up another chair and sat, as did Fairold and Galen.

"Now, my dear husband, tell our son what else he needs to know."

"Prince Galen, be thankful that the tavern maids' words have been 'brief.' We are here today because I missed the chance to go on an important quest by lingering too long at my morning prayers. We've said nothing about it yet, but that 'book' that the Emperor's child is said to be bringing may explain more.

"But I can never forget that, because of my preoccupation, my youngest brother Colin undertook an impossible quest he was least qualified for. But I'm sure that somehow he did much before his untimely end."

"I think," said Galen, "there's more to that than what you've just said."

"Yes, Galen," said his mother, "there is!"

"You realize," said his father, "that you can ask such a question because I missed that particular chance" — he looked at his wife — "and, later, took another!"

"Measure your words, dear husband!"

"God works in mysterious ways!" offered Lady Millicent, extending her arms. Her voice was lilting, so unlike the everyday Millie Galen knew. Goosebumps rose on his arms. What was she up to? "You see, Prince Galen, I'm here, too — another obvious proof! And I've not only learned from your father and mother" — her voice turned deadly serious — "but from reading the Holy Book and the history of your grandparents!"

"You've read *The Fourth Prince?*" asked Galen.

"Of course!" she replied, "many times, and I read very quickly, thank you! And I'll bet this 'new' book being brought by the Emperor's child, whether long or short, will fill in some missing pieces."

"If she — or he — arrives," said Lord Fairold. He paused. "I'd give a lot to know what happened to Colin. It was awful what he was trapped into doing."

Lady Lambith stood and then knelt by her husband's side. She took his hand.

"It was not an accident, dear husband. And neither am I!" Lady Lambith stood and returned to her chair. "And, from what you told me, he was hardly a child. Your place, dear husband, is here with your people, and with me because you saved my life and I must return the favor! You prayed for God's will then. Do it now. Just remember the prophecies that you and your mother received on the seashore. They weren't casually given. You were to help a 'great king,' and if brave enough, to marry me! You've done the last part, and here's our son Galen" — she pointed to the Prince — "*but now I'm convinced that your 'helping a great king' is far from over*!

"And, remember, the prophecy now includes us.

"Come, Lady Millicent," said Zareba Village's Lady of the Empire, "someone has to clear away these things." With a sweep of her hand, the dishes and cups methodically fell into the tray, and Millicent followed with a towel, so in a bat of the eye the table was ready for whatever was next. "The Holy Book is clear: 'She who is the greatest servant on Emryss shall be greatest in the Kingdom of God.' "

"The word is 'he,'!" said Lord Fairold, shaking his head. But the women having disappeared through the door neither saw nor heard. "Galen, bolt the door! Now back to where we started. Yes, I—that is, your mother and I—promised you, if God seemed to agree, to marry one of the Emperor's daughters, though which of the two, I have no idea. Of course many things could change that."

"Me, marry an Emperor's daughter?—You've got to be kidding!"

"Well, it's not impossible," said Lord Fairold, "and let's stop wasting words. When you're older, we'll talk about this again."

Suddenly, there was a loud knocking on the outside door. Galen unbolted it, and two men burst into the room.

"FIRE! FIRE!" There were shouts and the sound of many footsteps outside.

"Lord Fairold," said one of the men. "It's burning! Zareba City is ablaze!"

The streets filled with people, and everyone moved to where Mt. Zareba didn't block the southern view. The entire rise of land on the horizon was covered with thick black smoke. In several places fingers of fire and smoke reached up toward the clouds as if holding them to the ground as by ragged strings. Everyone was speechless. If flames looked this high from a distance, the fire must be great indeed!

Galen didn't have to ask. Zareba City was quickly coming to its end. The village would be next.

And soon.

CHAPTER 31

5
TWO
CATS

atching what looked like the wholesale destruction of the Holy City mobilized the entire village. Lord Fairold, his son quickly learned, had long planned for a variety of possible misfortunes before the Emperor's letter had arrived.

The ferocity and success of the attack upon the walled city suggested a large, well-organized enemy, one that was no match for a village without a wall, without soldiers—except for Sir Kerky Greenwald, who was in Lord Fairold's personal service. Also in Zareba Village were many women and children as well as the old.

No attempt would be made to defend the village.

At best, said Fairold, they would have two days, possibly a bit longer, before the first of the enemy arrived. His plan called for two caravans of horses and wagons—one headed east, the other west, with half of the villagers in each. Perhaps one, maybe both groups could be saved. They would leave in wagons that very afternoon. The shepherds, driving as many sheep and goats as they could, would leave at once. Time was precious, and as much distance as possible was needed to escape.

Most things had to be left behind.

As the appointed time to leave approached, a serious argument

252

broke out. Master Weft, the oldest weaver, flatly refused to go. His life was already spent, he said, and he would stay until the last minute hiding the huge supply of tapestries awaiting sale, and burying some of the looms if possible. His weavers, of course, must go, but he would die before seeing their precious work in the hands of godless kings.

Master Maleg, the stone mason, also refused to go. He'd lived his life and while he still had powerful arms, he'd been crippled by an accident and was unable to walk without crutches. He would not slow anyone down, he said. This led to further complication because his twin sons Saren and Soren, who were two strong but silent apprentices, refused to leave their father.

But Lord Fairold was adamant. The time had come. He would not wait.

He took Galen, Lady Lambith, Lady Millicent, Sir Kerky and — at the last second — Saren and Soren aside.

"Prince Galen" — for the first time in public he said "Prince" — "I need your help. Sir Kerky and I must be off at once. I am ordering, asking really, you to stay one more day. I'm leaving a wagon and four horses. Stay and do what you can to persuade Masters Weft and Maleg to change their minds. Regardless of your success, you are to leave in exactly one day and join Sir Kerky in the east. I and my group will head west. God willing, we'll meet again before long."

By this time a crowd had gathered. Lord Fairold jumped to the back of a dangerously overloaded wagon so all could see. Though shy by nature, the ruler of the village had learned long ago there were times to act boldly in public — even at the risk of being wrong. He pulled up his son.

"This is Prince Galen, my only son, my heir and the last of the Royal House of Aeron." This wasn't news to the villagers, only the way it was loudly announced. "Sir Kerky and I leave now, he to the east and I the west. My son will follow tomorrow. He serves God, the Emperor, and me. With my departure, he rules what's left of this village."

With a single motion he pulled the great golden ring from his finger — the last object he owned that indicated his royal lineage — and held it high. He pulled his son's hand up and placed the ring on his finger. His dark eyes scanned every face, daring anyone to contradict him. He looked down at his son.

"I'm taking all swords and spears, though you may have two bows and two quivers of arrows. Don't be foolish and attempt to fight." His father was a man of few words, but when he took action, it was down to the smallest detail. "And, though I fear it's too late, we give another day for some of the Emperor's family to arrive."

Lord Fairold looked down to Saren and Soren who stood nearby. He spoke just above a whisper: "Please help my son, and leave with him."

"I'll gladly stay, Father," said Galen, who was friends of the brothers. "We'll watch for the Emperor's coach...and we'll be careful." The twins nodded in agreement. Tears trickled down Lady Lambith's cheeks. She hugged her son but said nothing. Lady Millicent leaned over to her husband, whispered in his ear, circled her arms around his neck, and kissed him. Sir Kerky's stony eyes betrayed a moment of anguish.

Suddenly, someone said there was the dust of hoofbeats on the southern horizon, and though it was a false alarm, it was just what was needed to get everyone moving.

Off due north sped the two caravans side by side. A few even tried to touch or join hands in adjacent wagons, and some of the younger men, to lighten the wagons for a faster start, began running alongside. One-half mile ahead the northern road ran into the great road that connected east and west. There, Lord Fairold turned sharply west, while Sir Kerky, without pause, headed the opposite way. It was as if the caravan were a piece of twisted cord, beginning at a point, only to grow longer and longer until it suddenly began to unravel into equal pieces and pull more and more apart until the pieces separated and disappeared in opposite directions.

The plan also called for killing any animals left behind and torching what was left of the village, but with the confusion of those staying behind, the abundance of what was left, no one had the heart to begin.

As soon as the caravans were gone, Master Weft returned to his shop and locked himself inside. Galen watched and shook his head. It was then Lady Millicent slipped out of a doorway where she'd been hiding, wearing a simple linen dress instead of her earlier finery.

"Leave him alone, Galen. He'll come around." The boy jumped. "If you think I'm staying behind because your mother is worried, you're partly right. But partly wrong. I wanted to help. And Kerky let me." Galen glared, masking his surprise. But deep down he was glad. And Kerky had "let her"? Galen doubted her husband had much say in the matter...

"I'm going to walk over to the mountain, Millie."

Somehow, for reasons he couldn't quite explain, he felt the mountain's pull. Tracing even a portion of the Walk of the Monks was out of the question; nonetheless, he must have a few moments to think before anything more. Perhaps somewhere in the rocks at the foot of the mountain a few things could be safely hidden away. He picked up a coil of rope that had fallen off a wagon and looped it over his shoulder — why, later he could never say. In his hand he carried his greatest treasure, an Elphian spyglass.

"I'm coming along," called Millicent after him. "But I'll try not to come close."

Galen groaned, but only outwardly. The chatty tavern maid-turned-lady, though not quite 120 months older than he, had been like a second mother. And he sensed she respected him. She was a wellspring of information, especially about certain things his mother probably also knew but wasn't likely to tell him. He was glad she'd stayed.

"If you're going to pray," she called ahead, "sometimes two are better than one." Only Millicent could get away with saying something like that. And she knew it.

Pray.

Only yards from the base of the mountain he sat on a smooth sloping rock and lay back. Galen would pray, but with his eyes open. He tried to concentrate, but only the simplest words came.

"God help us!"

Yards behind him, Lady Millicent also sat and appeared to be praying.

Galen's eyes rose to the mysterious tower whose top could just barely be seen beyond the ribbon of wall capping the mountain.

Suddenly, at the point where the wall intersected the shadow of the tower, something moved! Galen raised his spyglass. At first his hand shook so hard he almost dropped it. Drawing a deep breath, he steadied himself.

It was a cat, a snow-white cat pacing the top of the wall only inches from the edge!

For a full minute Galen followed the creature until it moved out of sight. Then, lowering the glass, he traced a line down the mountain to its base, the point at which the river gurgled underground in the narrow tunnel out of sight.

There at the base, more movement! Another snow-white cat! Galen watched the creature tiptoe dangerously near the deadly tunnel. Suddenly, it leaped straight toward the water, but instead of splashing in, it landed on a log! A log wedged under the opening! By the time Galen raised his spyglass, it was gone!

CHAPTER 32

6
THE
GREAT
DISCOVERY

n seconds Galen stood on the bank at the tunnel opening.

How many times had he and everyone else been here —
picnicking, playing as a kid? In bed at night how he'd
wondered about the mysterious mountain! Was it really
an ancient shrine to the God-Son? Or, perhaps, earlier a home to the
ancient people God chose and gave his first set of Laws? Was it from the
Mountain, or the City, that the mother of the God-Son had eventually
fled back east to his father's old kingdom?

Or was something up there totally the opposite, a pagan shrine to
everything God hated? Did King Stulk know something they didn't?
Was that why he was so eager to come to Zareba?

And if it weren't evil, why, when his father tried so hard to get
someone to the top five years ago, did six courageous villagers have to
die tragically in the attempt?

As to scaling the outside, three brave climbers with pitons, hooks,
and ropes had almost succeeded before the bottom climber slipped and
pulled all three to their deaths.

Galen shuddered when he remembered the enemy was on its way.
Mountains were common in the South, and several southerners were

said to have reputations as skillful climbers.

Several others from Zareba—both village and city—had contemplated attempting an underwater entry using ropes. But two died when their ropes snapped. Minutes later their bodies appeared, broken and bruised, on the other side of the mountain where the river made its exit. Another had been pulled back drowned. Two others— the only ones to have made the attempt and lived—were pulled back with broken limbs. The current, they said, was too strong, the riverbed too slippery, and nowhere did they find any ceiling or opening in the tunnel, or any place to hold onto to stop one's forward movement.

Lord Fairold had called off the quest, and at first posted guards to discourage more adventurers. The mountain was declared off limits, except to look at and dream about. And dream the children did! Being thrown into the tunnel was openly confessed as a common nightmare. And certain parents didn't help by threatening their children with this as punishment.

Conquering the mountain, of course, was a common dream.

But lingering too much near the tunnel's mouth, attempting to climb the sides, or even so much as stepping a foot into the old "main entrance," if that's what it was and not just a series of traps, was a punishable offense administered by Lord Fairold himself. Idlers caught in the forbidden territory soon found themselves busy shoveling out sheep pens until their arms ached, or worse, and so the shepherds had become excellent watchmen!

But now Prince Galen was Lord of the mountain as well as what was left of the village.

How long since he'd last stared at the tunnel opening where the river disappeared? He squinted his eyes. The riverbed at the mountain base narrowed to only six feet wide where the water disappeared. And shouldn't the water have run the other way, away from the mountain as on the other side? Could the rock somehow have pushed up through the riverbed when the river was much larger, and then sunk back? Was the mountain hollow inside?

Now with the drought reducing the amount of water, there seemed to be a natural archway six-feet wide, rising to almost a point five feet above the stream and, judging from the stone edges just above the water level, at least two feet thick. Could it have once been an entry? If so, it was blocked by a huge sheet of rock inside, which seemed to curve down underwater toward the center from the edges, leaving a small open gap on each side. Could this be some sort of "wheel" that covered a larger opening? If so, could it be moved? The gap on the left was where the cat had disappeared.

But if so, no one had ever made that "inner" rock budge. It was just beyond where the river entered that it plunged down and disappeared until bubbling up on the other — south — side of the mountain. The problem, said one survivor, was that once under the strange, inner edge of rock, there was no place to catch hold to come up to breathe before being swept away.

But now the river was low, lower than Galen had ever seen, and the curved edges of rock were about four inches above water! And, on the left, a rare log almost 10 feet long was wedged! The cat must have jumped inside from the log.

Upstream, if forded carefully, the water was no more than thigh deep. Galen began making his way to the left side. When he reached the log, he lay aside the spyglass and rope and slipped down the stone bank into the churning, waist-deep water.

"WAIT!"

Galen turned. Lady Millicent had just crossed the stream where he had, but not quite as successfully. She had fallen and lost her shoes. Lifting the hem of her dripping dress she scrambled to his side.

"I thought you were going to stay away!" said the boy.

"So did I!" said Millicent. "Here, take the rope. You can't afford to make an even bigger fool of yourself! A dead fool. Tie this around your waist. No, that's the wrong kind of knot! It'll cut you in two! Do it this way." Quickly, she redid Galen's knot. She kicked the log with her bare foot. When she was convinced it was firmly wedged, she slipped all the way into the water, wrapped herself around the end of the log farthest from the mountain, tied her end of the rope securely to the log, and held on. "OK!"

"Get out!" ordered Galen.

"No, the water's fine. I'm OK. Don't"—she raked a handful of red hair out of her mouth—"sound so smug! I'm not the one being stupid!"

"Are you sure? Well, thanks anyway!" Galen slipped away until the water was up to his chin. "Thanks, Millie. I really mean it."

"What?" said Millicent, "for being here?"

"Just thanks…" He coughed and spat out a mouthful of water.

"Galen, be careful."

"Here goes!"

He took a shallow breath and ducked under the edge of rock. Up came his head. THWACK! This would hurt later. But no air! The water tore at him. His feet flew up and away. He was at the mercy of the rope. Millicent had saved his life. Slowly, slowly somehow she pulled him back. He found the end of the log. He eased up his head. THWACK! He tried again. There must be a place for his fingers!

Gasping because he couldn't help himself, cool air along with water filled his mouth and started toward his lungs. So little room to maneuver. Again, his feet began to slide. He coughed, propelling his hands up. THWACK! His knuckles hit rock. Then a crack. There had to be one. If a cat could…then his fingers found a crevice. He held on. SKWRAAAAK. A rock above him slid back, but just an inch. A precious inch.

Desperately he pushed one way then another. At last the stone slid—an inch, then another and another and another! Raising his mouth to the crack, he sucked in deeply. With a great heave, the rock slid at least a foot. Thrusting his whole body up, he shoved sideways with all his might.

As he coughed till he thought he could cough no more, he found himself sitting on the edge of a slab of rock. Cool air struck his face.

Gathering his strength, he tried to stand but was almost jerked back by the rope. Water rushed by under his feet. He was inside Mt. Zareba and was still alive!

"MILLIE, I'M IN! I'M TAKING OFF THE ROPE!" But the thick stone and echo of rushing, falling water was too loud. With some difficulty he untied the rope, not realizing the effect it would have on his companion.

At first Galen thought he wouldn't see anything, but dim light rose from the blue water under him and slowly his eyes adjusted. Details became clearer. He was in a cave, how large, he wasn't sure. The flat floor was cut in two by what he soon learned was a six-foot-wide canal which led no more than ten feet straight ahead to a wall, where underneath the water once again dropped and disappeared. Bridging this carefully cut canal was a row of six carefully cut stone slabs—each two inches thick and more than a foot longer than the canal's width.

Fortunately, the first slab had a broken corner caused by earlier debris from storms. The brave cat—perhaps deaf to the rushing water—must have entered unaided, giving the boy hope to attempt entry. Galen's slight build had saved him. Saren or Soren, despite their strength, would've been doomed because of their broad shoulders.

The first thing Galen saw was about twenty more identical hand-cut slabs lying stacked nearby. Stones just light enough for two men to carry. He looked to where the "archway" must be outside. There before him stood the answer to a long-asked question, a twelve-foot high circular stone—a wheel of some sort it had to be. A door that could be rolled to the side. But how?

Galen looked behind him, then overhead. From somewhere he heard water trickling down the back wall. Slowly he made his way to it. Warm water, almost hot! Then he saw the strange beam — or what he thought was a beam — that ran from the back wall up and over the great stone on the right side. At the wall, rising up to the beam were steps, cut into the stone and covered with slippery moss. Up he went. At the top, at right angles to the beam, ran a shallow canal, or sluice of hot water.

Where the canal intersected the beam — which wasn't a beam at all but an empty sluice, or trough, made of sections of split-longways open glazed pipe — a small shield-like slab of rock was fitted with grooves on either side. A sluice gate! But almost sealed shut from disuse. Galen sat in the nearly scalding water and kicked and kicked the gate. At last it broke free. Up it slid and down the empty pathway water raced, only to spill out on the top at the right side of the wheel.

How long since the sluice gate last been used? Could such a tiny waterfall ever turn such a large wheel? But then there was not just the weight of the water but its temperature.

What Galen saw and heard next made his heart pound. Instead of simply running down the wheel, for more than a minute the water disappeared into it! There were holes in the edge. Large, deep holes, how deep he couldn't guess. He couldn't imagine the time and difficulty for stone workers to create this! After several minutes, there was a loud grinding that seemed to echo even louder. Would there be another avalanche like the one that some said filled the western entry? Galen trembled.

Suddenly the round stone moved! Apparently the water filling the holes had increased the weight just enough to throw it off balance. As the stone rolled, new holes in the top received water. Again it turned! This time Galen was blinded by light. Light from the outside! The entryway was partly open. On the stone rolled until with a final groan, that almost sounded human, the stone came to the side wall and stopped. Sunlight poured in! Steamy air puffed out.

But could the door ever be moved back? And how? Galen didn't have long to think. Holes were also in the left side of the top of the wheel and now water was pouring into them. The wheel could "collect" water on either side! He must stop it before the wheel returned! But would the sluice gate ever move back? At last he managed to slide it back down, and just as suddenly as the water started, it stopped. Once again the sluice was empty. The mountain was open!

"MILLIE! MILLIE! I'M ALL RIGHT!"

The sudden light from the sun was blinding, and all he could see was the form of a woman standing motionless on the bank. She said nothing. At last it dawned upon Galen that from where he was he couldn't be seen. Or heard because of the falling water. Slowly he worked his way down the stone stairway.

At the bottom he spied a row of five holes in the narrow lip of rock just after the last stone slab. It must have held in place a fence, or grating. At least before it rusted away. Dropping iron rods through the holes should remove the threat of being carried off by the underground river.

"MILLIE! MILLIE! GET SAREN AND SOREN! HAVE THEM BRING MASTER MALEG'S IRON BARS! HURRY!"

Galen moved out onto the first stone slab, the one closest to the outside. A steamy cloud preceded him. He raked back his sandy hair. He didn't realize until later how frightening he must have appeared!

"MILLIE, ARE YOU ALL RIGHT? Though soaking wet, she stood on the bank like a statue. Galen could see she'd been crying. Over the years he'd seen her in almost every kind of situation, but never with tears. She stood as a statue, ashen, still holding the rope. The unattached end danced aimlessly in the churning water. Something was very different about her, but what?

"Is that you, Galen? Her voice sounded light and unnatural, just loud enough to be heard above the falling water.

"It's me, Millie! I'm OK," Galen said, also just loud enough. She continued to stare, not moving a muscle. **"Come on, Millie! Snap out of it! Get back! It's still dangerous! Not safe for me to jump back! We need Master Maleg's iron bars immediately! To protect ourselves from the river!"**

"I love you, Galen. God is my witness. I love you — in the right way, you understand."

"Of course I understand. And I'm sure Kerky does, too. Now go! GO! The iron bars! There's no time to lose!"

She dropped the rope and smiled. Tears unabashedly again began to fall. Like a child she fell to her knees and whispered a short prayer. Praying this way, with or without an audience never embarrassed or frightened her. But, just like with his mother, ignoring God did. In a flash she sprang up and ran.

As she turned, Galen saw. Her hair. Once it was fiery red. No more. In a few short minutes of terror she would never speak about, it had turned beautiful silvery white!

CHAPTER 33

7
STAIRWAY
TO THE
TOP

hough barefoot, Millicent ran. Crossing the stream she fell twice, only to recover her footing and redouble her efforts. When safely across, Galen returned to the back of the cave. From somewhere up high hot water was dripping, even running down on the cooler stones below, causing pillows of steamy clouds to puff out the entrance, obscuring his view.

Quickly, he must explore! With such an elaborate entrance, there must be a way up.

Slowly, Galen moved toward what he thought was the back wall, just below where the sluice pipe began. To his surprise, there the wall curved to the right, and while the mountain wasn't everywhere hollow, a wandering pathway, with an uncertain ceiling overhead, led to a tunnel that had to have been dug. At first the darkness inside was almost total, but a sturdy handrail on the side was reassuring. Slowly the light brightened ahead.

When he'd gone four times the distance of the opening to the back wall, the tunnel widened and suddenly began sharply circling ever upward, with many steps cut into the stone floor. The source of light was now overhead. Here and there the side of the tunnel opened to a hollow core that was brighter. But when Galen leaned over to look down, he could detect no bottom. The drop-off was sheer and terrifying. In places the side opposite the railing just seemed to disappear. To fall would mean certain death. Any protection once there had rusted or rotted away. He clung to the railing that snaked forever upward, and hurried as fast as he dared.

To Galen it was like being inside a gigantic old tree that had rotted on the inside. But instead of soft wood, everything was hard, and often slippery wet stone.

Up, up, up he went, pushing himself, in the partly natural, partly carved tunnel that ingeniously elbowed this way and that through cracks and fissures. Galen so hated heights he refused to look down. And looking up was often just as unsettling with a ceiling, if there was one, lost in darkness. No time to see. No time to think. He must reach the top, make a decision, and get back. Down below, Saren and Soren might rush things, unaware of the danger he'd faced.

Could they possibly hide and survive here? Even bring the tapestries, weavings, looms, and other supplies into the mountain? Could the mountain provide days of safety? Weeks or longer? Or would it become their tomb? He must hurry—very carefully!

The light became brighter and brighter.

At last the tunnel opened into an explosion of light.

He was on top.

He knelt on the last step and closed his eyes. He thought of how Lady Millicent wouldn't hesitate to risk making a spectacle of herself in unusual circumstances.

"O God," he prayed, "where are we? Should we be here, or should we avoid this place at all costs? Show me."

He stood, rubbed his eyes, and walked into the sunlight. The opening was near the northern wall. The flat circular mountaintop before him resembled a very stony flat field, not unlike one 300 feet below. Except it was more lush. How soil had formed up here he'd no idea, but water, warm water, even in a time of drought, lay in the bottom of shallow pools here and there. The afternoon sun blazed down. His eyes struggled to adjust. There was a warm breeze. He was higher than he'd ever been.

Details came into focus. The ground on top was covered with stones, but was not hard to walk upon. And in several places were trees — fruit trees and miniature mountain olives, the smallest he'd ever seen! Obviously, they'd been planted years ago. And there were patches of tall and thick grass. To his right, tall weeds surrounded and ran up the sides of — Galen gasped — the mysterious tower on the northwestern side, whose shadow marked the ever-changing Walk of Monks! And the tower's walls and roof, made of fired bricks and tiles, were still intact! As was a great wooden door at its base. How long had he and his friends stared up in wonder at the quill-sized tower capped by its "ink-line" pole — stared and dreamed!

He ran to the tower and ran his fingers along the brick.

He turned. A similar tower stood near the wall in the southwest, but made of stone. Now it overlooked the dark rising smoke from far-off Zareba City. On the eastern side, 200 feet away, were a heap of stones and rubble that once was probably a third tower. Just past the rubble was the eastern wall, about eight feet high, as in the west and everywhere else, with a raised wooden platform inside it about three-and-a-half feet lower. And both wall and platform, as far as he could tell, were in excellent condition. On it a guard could patrol the whole mountain as if it were a castle.

Near the center of the top was a rectangular, flat, one-story structure. Back in the west, between the two towers though farther from the wall, stood a fourth and final building that had a high peaked roof, but was a little more than half the size of a typical house in the village. These last two buildings were puzzling. How long since they'd last been occupied? Last seen?

Then on the faraway south wall a white cat walked into view from behind the peaked roof of the building which was much closer.

It was the building that settled things.

He'd prayed for a sign. And there it was!

Now he must act! He could explore later. He must go back before anyone else tried to enter this new world. He prayed he wouldn't be too late!

The return trip was far more difficult than going up!

CHAPTER 34

8

THE
EMPEROR'S
COACH

hen Galen appeared at the opening, there was great cheering. Every remaining villager was sitting on the bank.

"Well done, Prince Galen!" declared Master Weft. The weaver, uncharacteristically, was beaming. Weft, of all people, the first to acknowledge his empty title!

Saren and Soren had a dozen or so assorted iron rods and bars by their feet.

How had Master Maleg been carried there so quickly?

Beside him stood Millicent.

"Mt. Zareba is ours!" declared Galen. "I'm claiming this mountain and everything in it for the Emperor and the God of Heaven!" How easily and childishly the words came. What would have his father have thought?

But no one laughed. Nor offered a syllable of challenge. Not even Master Maleg or Master Weft, who Galen knew were filled with questions. Instead, perhaps because of the horror of all that was happening, this offered a glimmer of hope. The cheering was over. He must go on.

"We're going inside!" announced Galen. "And we're going to stay here until the Emperor comes! And we're going to take in everything we can" — he paused — "working day and night, not stopping until we hear hoofbeats or see dust rising in the south!"

The plan called for first putting iron rods though the five holes to keep anyone from being washed away to his death. Then the rearmost stone slab was to be removed so if anyone did slip into the dangerous canal — which Soren soon did — he would stop at the rods, be pulled out bruised and soaked but otherwise safe. Next, with Master Maleg's advice, the twins placed the extra stone slabs carefully on rocks from the opening to the bank.

Entrance to the mountain was easy now — for friend or enemy.

Before he even realized it, Galen was answering questions and giving orders.

Yes, water was plentiful — both hot and cold, even enough to bathe in.

Yes, there was a way to the top, and it was suitable to live there. Or so he hoped! But they mustn't waste time going up now.

Galen — though he could hardly believe himself — rapidly began to tick off what must be brought in, and in what order. Never had he been shy, but never so loud, so pushy. Only three or four times did Master Maleg or Master Weft interrupt, but then only with details. If they succeeded in doing what he said, then what? Would things be better? If he failed, it would be his fault. They would die — or worse. Enough about that! He would think about it later.

Whatever weapons were left and food were to come in first. Especially the kegs of smoked and salted meats that had been left because they were too heavy for the wagons. And seeds would be needed, he emphasized. Was he crazy? Would they be there that long? With grass at the top, wasn't there soil enough for vegetables? All the grain that had been left behind must be taken for flour. And all oil, of which there had been several kegs, for baking and lamps. And pots, cooking utensils, plates and cups that had been left or discarded. All these must be brought.

Next were to come tools, but except for a few shovels and hoes and Master Maleg's heavy stone-cutting bars and chisels, not much had been left.

It was only after that they would bring the tapestries, blankets, cloth, yarns, and dyes. And the dye vats and looms — all of the weavers' materials were to be saved if possible. The cave at ground level seemed large enough. And things could be stacked.

Then, at least a dozen sheep, that had been too old or weak that had been abandoned by the shepherds. And goats. Every goat that had been left behind, and at least a dozen were found, were to be brought in. This would provide milk, and if the grass were overgrazed, the animals, starting with the sheep, could be slaughtered for meat.

After this, any of the books and archives that remained, and to Galen's surprise, in the haste of leaving, a surprising number of written materials had been overlooked. Galen insisted these all be taken.

Then, if any time remained, any furniture, clothes, or household effects.

Immediately, they began.

Master Maleg, unable to walk, was stationed inside the cave to organize what came in, and insist that the right things arrive in the right order. Galen insisted they work continuously day and night, so Master Maleg was also put in charge of trimming the lamps and preparing food.

The wagon was key to the plan. As soon as it was loaded in the village, off the horses would go the quarter mile or so to the mountain entrance. Those who grew weary loading and unloading took turns at driving, and, under Master Maleg's direction, stacking and arranging everything that was brought.

By early nightfall, food had been gotten, but absolutely no weapons were found. Everyone then concentrated on the tapestries and looms. Soon two huge piles of tapestries, rugs, and bolts of cloth rose as high as Master Weft himself. The dyeing vats, spinning wheels, and looms all by themselves crowded one side of the cave. Next to these were stacked the clothes. How to get all this up the stairs no one dared ask.

The horses, showing weariness, plodded on. Then at last the creatures were stopped so they could eat, Millicent watched them, and Saren and Soren went for the sheep and goats. Galen and Weft set out in the street a few pieces of furniture that the boy thought could be carried up the steps.

At the first light of dawn a black fist of cloud seemed to have punched into the western sky. The second load of furniture slowly creaked out of the village, the horses scarcely able to put one leg in front of the other. Saren cracked his whip angrily and Millicent walking alongside tried to calm him.

It was then that Soren yelled.

It had been his turn to run just far enough from the village to inspect the southern horizon. At one point, dust was rising, he said. Galen checked with his spyglass. A single coach, an elegant one, was being driven at breakneck speed! The Emperor's coach with some of his family! And farther beyond, more dust rose. Several horsemen in pursuit!

At this point the black fist of cloud began to rapidly spread its fingers east. There was a flash of lightning, then thunder.

The furniture on the wagon, said Galen, would be the last load. The stone slabs in front of the opening would be brought inside and all tracks near the entrance would be rubbed out. The last slab inside would remain off, and rugs and cloth would wrap the iron bars to pad them for cushioning a last-minute entry. Then on the inside Weft, Maleg, and Millicent would roll the great stone back while Galen and the twins remained outside. There the three would move the wagon far from the opening, release the horses, send them off, and then wait with such weapons as they had until the last possible moment. Then, after rescuing the Emperor's family, they would all enter through the underground waterway, be pulled up by those inside, and lay down the final stone slab.

As simple as that! It may not work, but it was a plan and no one objected.

Trouble came when the huge stone, after filling again with water, would not roll back into place! For several minutes, water overflowed the holes. The door just had to move back. Why hadn't they tested it? Now the horses were gone, and the cave, filled with everything they had, was a perfect target! They were trapped, trapped by their — no, his — foolish enthusiasm. They had trusted him. After all, he'd seen the top.

Now this.

Galen felt sick. They'd overstayed by half a day. Now all would be lost.

Lady Millicent pulled Master Maleg to the back of the great stone wheel and handed him one of his wonderful iron bars. Master Weft slid a great stone behind him. The crippled man flexed his massive arms. At last the wheel began to angrily grind its way back to where it had rested undisturbed for uncounted years.

KERBLAM! The final jolt was sudden. Galen, outside, was amazed at how once again the mountain looked as it always had.

Then his eyes were pulled to the south. The coach now could be seen without his spyglass. Its roof was afire! Galen raised the spyglass. The driver was slumped over in his seat and the reins were dragging the ground. The horses were galloping on their own. Only yards behind raced three horsemen.

Suddenly, the nearest one leaped from his horse to the back of the coach. Gingerly he crawled across the burning roof and down to the dead driver's seat. Flicking the whip he was able to draw back the reins.

By then, the second horseman pulled alongside the coach. In a flash he leaped from his horse to the door and was inside. Galen knew he and the twins were no match for these men. He must use a plan he'd dreamed up earlier but prayed he'd never have to use. There was no other choice.

At one place along the road from city to village, two large boulders stood like doorposts—one on each side of where travelers must pass. The coach would have to go between them. Galen positioned a twin behind each boulder, drew his dagger—his only weapon—and stood just ahead of the boulders.

And waited.

Lightning flashed and thunder rolled. The rain gently began. Very dry weather had led to discovering of the mountain entrance. Perhaps wet weather would help in war!

Just as Galen claimed this spark of hope, a sickening thing happened.

The door of the coach, thirty yards away, exploded off its hinges and fell away. A dark-haired girl in a beautiful purple-and-white dress tumbled after it, followed by the soldier. He rolled to his feet and ran to where she lay. Galen raised his spyglass. He wore a leather battle shirt under the light mail worn by horsemen from the south.

The soldier driving the coach didn't see this. On he raced, and finally seeing a boy in his path, frantically waving his hands, he glared, then grinned. Cracking the whip, he urged the weary horses faster. Galen slowly edged backwards. At the last second he screamed and dove to the side. The soldier laughed. As the Prince hit the ground, Soren stepped out with a long thin iron bar and swung, catching the forward-moving soldier squarely in the neck. He was dead before he hit the ground.

Galen flew toward the Princess, slowing to a walk as he neared.

274

The soldier, kneeling by her, turned toward him, his bare sword within easy reach. Lightning flashed and thunder rolled. Hiding both his dagger and rage, Galen let his eyes grow wide with horror. He mustn't let the man fear him. Holding out empty hands, he inched closer. The soldier's eyes were riveted on the girl. He lifted her limp hand.

"Boy, ever see an Emperor's daughter? The first one to get 'er can have 'er — first, says King Stulk. Now" — he winked at the shaking boy, and seeing nothing to fear, his eyes fell back to the girl — "what's left is hardly as good." The girl was motionless. He grabbed the hem of her dress with both hands and started to tear it away.

The ripping cloth tore away any real fear Galen had. Quietly, he raced forward and leaped. As the surprised soldier turned, Galen's right foot, held back in the jump, shot straight forward, striking the kneeling man sideways squarely in the jaw. There was a loud snap, and the soldier fell back, howling. Dazed, he fumbled blindly for his sword which proved a mistake. The Prince's hated lessons came back. *If you must strike with deadly force, don't do it once, but thrice — and very quickly.* Galen sprang to his feet and jumped again, stomping again on the man's face. In a flash the boy's dagger was out and he fell upon the man's chest. Up and down he stabbed, breaking through an opening in the top of the armor.

A strong arm pulled him up.

"Prince Galen, we aren't done!" It was Saren. Yards away, Soren struggled to free the horses from the burning coach.

The sharp edge of the third soldier's sword was raised high. Just as his horse galloped within reach, Saren shoved Galen back down on the man he'd just killed, and swung a wide arc with his own bar. But the stone-cutter's tool was heavy and Saren tripped. Galen would remember what happened next as long as he lived.

As the bar swung low, instead of hitting the rider, it came straight upon the horse's legs, and with two loud snaps the beast stumbled, sending rider and his sword separately several feet through the air.

Galen stared into the open eyes of the soldier he'd killed. Both of their clothes were covered with blood. He rose to his knees. His stomach turned. He gagged and found he couldn't stand. The sound of killing came from behind him as Saren finished off the dying soldier that had been thrown. And then the horse. He heard the clink of metal as the twins claimed the dead men's excellent swords and scabbards. He must do the same. He pulled off the belt and scabbard of the man he'd slain. Into it he pushed the man's fine sword. He'd made a promise to his father. But did the God of Heaven require this?

Then he turned and knelt. The Princess, perfect where she lay in the morning light, was in fact dead. He lifted and held her perfect hands. An older woman in servant's clothes knelt by the girl's side and, crying, covered the girl's face with a cloth. Galen took out his sword and threw it away. Quiet tears came and he didn't fight them. Saren, without asking, returned Galen's new sword to the scabbard.

Once again, Galen felt hands on his back. But these were soft.

It was a girl in a servant's dress. Like the Princess, she had deep brown eyes and long dark brown hair, almost black. Over her shoulder, hung a small leather bag that seemed to be sewn shut. Her dark eyes were red, but he sensed a backbone of iron inside her thin frame. Her hands trembled. Her cheeks also were wet. How painful this must seem for her. He felt numb.

She helped him up. With a scarf she automatically began to wipe away the blood on his clothes. She inspected his hands and arms for wounds. A large, young-looking man with thick curly hair and a boyish face stood over the dead girl and continually rubbed his hands. At his feet were several bags and a small chest that smelled of smoke. Beside him sat a large handsome black dog with short, sleek hair rapidly panting. Oddly, the creature seemed to question no one. Rain began to increase.

Galen studied them. The servant girl resembled the dead Princess! Perhaps... just perhaps in his haste the Emperor had...

"Milady," said Galen, "is this your...your *sister*?"

The girl and the woman began quietly sobbing.

"I...I'm Prince Galen, son of Lord Fairold and Lady Lambith and I'm — presently — Lord of Zareba Village and this mountain. I'm ready to help you — and anyone the Emperor sends us."

"Prince Galen" — the girl's voice was like fine linen, soft, careful words — "I swear by the God of Heaven that this dead girl is not...not my sister." She stopped to cry again... but caught herself. "I...I'm Mira, a servant of the Princess in the Palace, and I'm not worthy to walk on the same ground that this girl did." She turned to the older woman. "This is Maid Mara. No one is more trusted by the Emperor's family. This boy" — she pointed to the large young man — "is called Pinrut. He thinks slowly, but he's very strong and dependable. God loves him, and I assure you, so does the Emperor. The dog is his and is well mannered." She dipped her head in a short servant's bow. "Prince Galen, we are in your hands, but I beg you ask me no more."

At this point Soren ran up. He jabbed his finger south.

"Galen, look!"

The drizzling rain began to gather more force. The sky was darkening by the second. Thunder rumbled from the west and south — but not just from the sky. Stretched out as far as the eye could see were two columns of galloping horses the size of ants.

"There's only one way to keep them from defiling the Princess's body," said Soren, "and, since there's already a flaming lamp inside the coach, my brother and I will take care of that. Now go, Prince Galen!" It was the clever boy's first suggestion, and Galen wasn't about to object.

Without a word, he and Pinrut picked up the heavy chest and started back to the river, the girl and the woman following with as much as they could carry. Halfway, Galen stopped and looked back. In spite of rain, the coach with the Princess's body was already lost to flames, and the twins were running toward them.

Everyone was so soaked as they reached the river, they willingly entered the water perhaps to wash away the evil left behind. After the twins kicked away the log Galen had first seen, with his instruction and Saren's courageous lead, they formed a chain, and inched toward the hidden opening, now just above water at the side of the great stone wheel. One by one each ducked his head and disappeared under the stone. How Pinrut managed the dog, no one quite knew, but after he took his turn, the dog followed without hesitation. Lastly, after Soren, came the baggage and chest, and finally the Prince himself, who cut his hand on a stone as he scrambled up to safety. When Galen appeared, everyone cheered.

Maleg was waiting with hot soup, a small fire of burning oil in a cooking pot, and Millicent gave everyone warm blankets, of which there were plenty. Outside, the storm soon became fierce, making the damp cave even cozier. Even the sheep and goats seemed at peace, bleating out of sight in the darkness. The water beneath the slabs became swift and turbulent. The twins lowered the last rectangular stone and raised the iron rods, sealing everyone inside, as well as the fate of anyone foolish enough to try following.

They were safe for a while. The time had come for sleep — at least for a few hours — before anything else. If death were to come, it shouldn't be from sheer exhaustion. As they silently sat in a circle around the burning pot of oil, the servant girl found herself at Galen's side. Without asking, she began to tend to his hand. Cleaning and wrapping it, she held it with both of hers to keep the bandage in place. Galen smiled, but said nothing.

Millicent whispered into the boy's ear. He nodded and shook off an overpowering weariness:

"One thing," said the Prince, "will not happen on this mountain: We will not forget God who safely brought us here. As you must suspect, there's a way to the top, one I just found, but it's dangerous. I beg you not to go up ahead of me." Then bowing his head, he offered a short prayer of thanks. As he began, the girl eased her hands away; then her body, almost imperceptibly seemed to slide inches away as if someone were pulling her. But no one was, or even saw this except Galen, who stole a glance.

"Amen," said everyone at the end of the prayer.

"Beyond our stone door," said Lady Millicent, "the storm must be fierce. God is washing away not only our footprints but much of the evil we've seen. Inside, Master Maleg has refreshed us with food. Now we're all tired—as we ought to be. Before any of us goes one step further, we must rest. Sleep—which those of us here haven't done in two days. Right, Prince Galen?"

Though framed as a request, her words were taken as an order that no one challenged. Sleep. Never had the idea of sleep been so welcome. The word itself was suggestive. Galen's arms could hardly move. Everyone must have questions but that could wait.

But for one thing Maid Mira would not.

The servant girl eased back again to Galen's side and with trembling hands put her sealskin bag in the boy's hands. Her wet hair was pulled straight back and tied by a scarf. Her dark eyes were easy to look upon. He pushed back his own stubborn wet hair and rubbed his eyes, which adjusted to the single fire in the center of them. As he stared at the bag, she slipped off a leather cord from around her neck. On it was a large golden ring. She laid the cord and the ring, as if it were an egg, on top of the bag. Suddenly, her hands stopped trembling.

"What's this?" he asked.

"A ring you know and a book you do not," she whispered. "There were two books, but the Emperor knows you already have a copy of

279

The Fourth Prince."

"What's this one?"

"It's called *Inside the Hollow Spear*. It mentions your father, but it's mainly about your uncle and what happened to him. The Emperor told the Princess to give it to you."

"About Colin?!"

The girl nodded.

At long last he would find out what happened to his missing uncle, and learn about the ring on the bag, that was like his, and that must have belonged to him.

"The story was so unusual," said Mira, "the strangest tale my mistress ever let me read, so it had to be believed. And since your uncle wasn't able to finish his story, a false Prince near your father's old home named Andelwan had to do it for him. And" — the maid paused for a quick breath — "many years later Andelwan himself, just before he died, only days ago, personally delivered the story to the Emperor. Whether he knew of you or your father, I do not know.

"But, Prince Galen, let me assure you that this story has nothing to do with the Emperor's present difficulties — and ours." She stopped just as suddenly as she had started and, changing position, sat cross-legged without moving. She folded her hands in front of her. Tears began to leak from the corner of her eyes.

Without looking at the sealskin bag, Galen held it close. He looked deep into the girl's large brown eyes until she returned his gaze and surrendered the hint of a smile. What was she hiding? He handed the bag to Millicent whose hand, somehow, seemed waiting to receive it.

"You said you read this story and if so, you must have read it quickly," said Galen. "So you do…"

"Read? Yes, Prince Galen, I do read, and rather quickly. If one lives or works in the central Palace, one must read. The Emperor insists upon it. We're hardly a provincial kingdom!"

"Hmm…'hardly a provincial kingdom,' you say," Galen returned. He paused, letting silence do its work as his father would have done if someone had overstepped a courtesy. The girl flinched, as Maid Mara, next to her, seemed to prod her with her elbow. Maid Mira's face reddened. Awkwardly, she dipped her head in what could pass as a short bow.

"A thousand apologies, My Lord! I…I didn't mean to…"

"A *thousand*?" said Galen. "Sounds a bit excessive, don't you think? Especially since there's never been enough of us here to qualify for any kind of kingdom before…before…before…Maid Mira, you've given me an idea! A great idea! And you're just the one to help me pull it off!" Extending his hands, he stretched, leaned back, and closed his eyes.

"Prince Galen! Prince Galen!" Maid Mira paused. Only falling water from the other side of stones broke the silence. "Prince Galen, aren't you going to say more?"

Galen's eyes half-opened.

"Say more? Well, everyone of us from Zareba Village knows how to work, to do his or her part…"

"And?" asked Mira.

"And everyone knows how to read."

The Prince closed his eyes and sleep became the new victor. Somehow, he and his army of eight — soon to slightly increase — must at whatever cost, occupy and defend this mountain.

And the defenders? Besides **Galen** there was **Millicent**, the talented tavern maid-turned lady, though without formal appointment, soon to become High Counselor; **Weft**, the fiercely independent old master weaver; **Maleg**, the strong above the waist but crippled master stone mason; **Saren** and **Soren**, his strong sons; and now **Maid Mara**, said to be a highly respected older servant of the Emperor; **Pinrut**, a strong but feebleminded young man of uncertain origin; and lastly **Maid Mira**, a pretty, but headstrong servant girl grieving her mistress's murder and, perhaps, hiding some tragic secrets.

They were on their own. Nine people and a dog in a mysterious mountain — too small, it seemed, to be considered a true mountain — that hadn't been occupied since, oddly, no one could remember. Their job: to stay alive and repel a hostile army that had sacked and probably destroyed Zareba City, and now was bearing down on the Village and Mountain.

Their first encounter the next day would be one no one could have predicted.

CHAPTER 35

9
MILLICENT'S CHILD

alen awoke to the smell of hot tea. He jumped up with a start. Everyone else was already stirring. Soren sprang to his side.

"Galen, I had a dream and I believe it's from God."

"A…a dream?"

"Yes, a dream! The details are…are a little strange, but these words keep ringing over and over:

> *'The olive trees will bear four-fold,*
>
> *The olive trees will bear four-fold,*
>
> *But not again till the second year,*
>
> *But not again till the second year'"*

"Olive trees?" said Galen, rubbing his eyes. "That's it?"

"That's all I can remember — except that the trees were unusually short, half again taller than a man. Isn't that strange, to dream of small olive trees in a mountain of stone? Oh, and there was also this:

> *'If the olive trees need protecting,*
>
> *The leader must do it himself.'"*

Soren had come to him…Galen…the leader. Or at least Soren

283

thought so. But so had Millicent, Weft, and Maleg…so far…so, so, so far. Hmm. Olive trees. Goose bumps rose on his arms.

How could that be? He'd never have dreamed of that three days ago, regardless of what his father had said. Maybe the others were too sensible to try what he'd done. But things had worked out—so far.

But the future!

He'd no idea what was possible. In bringing everything inside and hiding here he'd sounded so sure. Now Soren had given him miniature olive trees—that he'd already seen!

"How long was I asleep?" He stared back into the darkness. Everything was gray. Gradually he realized that a faint hint of light was coming from the swift river under them through cracks between the stone slabs.

"Just a few hours—it's midafternoon, I'd say," said Millicent from somewhere behind him.

Galen ignored her.

"We must get to the top—without delay!" He reached down and fumbled with tying the laces at the top of his short boots.

"But I can tell from the sound it's been hardly an hour since it stopped raining," said Master Weft. "No one climbs mountains in the rain, not even southerners. Besides, they don't even know we're here."

"The soldiers," said Galen, "can't help but learn that we were recently in the village, and that some people must have escaped from the burned coach. And when they don't find anyone, they must realize we're hiding—and where else but in here? And, they may have seen us from a distance. Besides, when has someone been offered an Emperor's daughter as a prize? Come, we must get to the top with swords!" He fumbled at drawing his own weapon. How much better he'd done this alone at play! How childish he must sound! How could they ever follow him?

But they did.

He glanced at his sword. It was a fine weapon though he'd hardly looked at it. He'd taken it in battle. From a person he'd killed. The blade of the sword was clean. But the dead man's blood was still on his clothes. He put the sword back in its scabbard. Two free hands were better for the steps.

"Follow me, but be careful. It's slippery and the railing's not strong in places and there are terrible drop-offs." Heights — how he hated them! Fortunately Soren fashioned a small torch for Millicent to carry. Galen's stomach churned as again he climbed past dangerous openings that this time he could see. The sleek black dog followed panting, his toenails clicking on the stone steps. The twins, who almost carried their father, were close behind. Minutes later Galen was at the top standing in the blinding afternoon sun. There was the echo of deep breathing behind him.

Just as Galen's vision cleared, his attention was drawn to the western wall. The sun glistened just above it. But underneath, a long knife of shadow cut across stones and grass almost to the base of the eastern wall, and in this shadow something moved. At first Galen suspected a cat.

Then he saw the snakelike line that fell from the top of the wall. The dog — Silk was his name — growled and bounded ahead. The sound of scraping against stone broke the silence. Galen raced toward the chest-high platform. Finding steps, he climbed up and drew his sword. It came out smoothly.

The snake was a rope.

At the end was a fist-like bob of four iron hooks which apparently had been thrown over the wall and had wrapped around a rotting post next to the stairs. Galen squint his eyes and slowly peered over the edge. Ten feet below a man dangled from a rope that fell twenty feet further to the bridge of rock that jutted out two yards and joined the narrow pinnacle that ran up almost to the top of the mountain, the pinnacle that was the only projection that interrupted the nearly vertical rock.

How could anyone have gotten so high so quickly on wet rocks? Especially since no Zarebite had ever done it? Galen fought dizziness. He felt hands around his waist to steady him. The climber was from the South. Had to be. He must not be allowed up—at all costs. But more killing? He shivered. He mustn't show fear. Leaning over as far as he dared, he yelled:

"You want the end of your rope wrapped around a rotting post?" His stomach knotted. He smacked the taut line with the flat of his sword and nearly lost his balance.

"AAAAAAARRRRRRGH!" The man tossed back his head and looked up. His burly fingers and white knuckles strangled the cord. His eyes grew large. How could anyone have been brave enough to do this? His life must be spared.

"Really," said Galen, raising his voice, **"your rope is dangerously fastened up here! Want me to retie it?"** He smacked the cord again.

"NO NO NO NO NO!"

"Then, in the name of the God of Heaven"—Galen spat out the words—**"you must go immediately back down and never try this again. Do you promise?"**

The man cursed. **"What are you, a group of children?"**

Lady Millicent, as if she knew what was coming, appeared from nowhere and emptied a waterskin over the climber's head.

"STOP! Are you **FOOLS?"** Then he cursed again. His words bit into the silence.

For a second, Galen closed his eyes. Then he stared after the droplets of spray which splashed out and away from the steep wall where his enemy clung like an insect. He remembered how he'd had to close his eyes whenever climbing a ladder. He forced himself to open them now.

The hands tightened around his waist.

" 'Fools,' you say!" It was Millicent's turn. **"Look in a mirror! This mountain belongs to the God of Heaven, so we are careful to keep its walls clean from filth! Curse God one more time and we'll wash your dirty mouth all the way back to Zareba City! Perhaps you'd like us to oil your rope to speed you on your way!"** From nowhere she produced a bottle and started to pour its contents down the cord.

"NOOOOOOO! We...we...I thought no one lived up here!"

"Well, now you know better!" said Millicent. **"Tell your leader that..."**

"That's enough, Millie," whispered Galen. He glanced down, prayed he wouldn't throw up, and barked an order:

"Climb down NOW and tell your Godless king that this mountain belongs to me, Prince Galen of Zareba and the House of Aeron, to the Emperor, and to the God of Heaven. Got that? The next person who comes here uninvited will answer to..." At that moment both Saren and Soren poked their faces over the side.

"To us! Do you understand?"

"Yes."

"That's 'YES SIR,' " Millicent yelled through her teeth. Somehow she squeezed more water out of the waterskin.

"YES SIR!" cried the man. Without looking up, the man wrapped his arms and legs around the rope and down he began to slide in measured bursts. Galen was amazed at how fast he descended while still controlling his speed. Climbing with ropes was not a skill practiced in Zareba.

As the man reached the bridge connecting the pinnacle thirty feet below them, Galen was startled to see a young boy slip out from a recess in the rock. So there were two of them! Were they father and son? Suddenly, an argument broke out between the two but Galen couldn't make out the words. A second and longer rope circled the pinnacle and fell not quite a hundred feet farther down to where the mountain wall sloped a bit, meeting still another rope fastened below it. Galen marveled at the skill which had secured these ropes, and so soon after bad weather.

Down the man continued, but taking more time as the going became rougher. The boy, however, stayed where he was. As the man neared the bottom, he yelled words Galen couldn't make out to dozens of soldiers who'd gathered where he would land.

"They're getting the message!" said Millicent.

"I wish I could hear it," said Galen.

Suddenly there was a scream. The Prince jerked up his spyglass, nearly dropping it.

"They're shooting him!" he gasped. "His body is filling with arrows!" The man cried piteously and let go, falling the last fifty feet to the bottom. Soldiers raced to his body and began stomping it.

The boy on the ledge looked up. He wore a large leather cap unfamiliar in Zareba. Whatever was he doing up here?

"Want to come up?" Galen yelled down.

"Will you kill me?" the boy yelled up.

"That depends," said Galen, biting his tongue. **"But if we were going to, that would be pretty easy right now, wouldn't it?"** He glanced back at his companions. No one seemed to object.

"I can jump," yelled the boy, but his words were hardly convincing.

"Do it!" yelled Saren. His brother and Millicent glared at him. It was the first time Galen had seen the brothers disagree.

"Whose side are you on?" asked the Prince.

"The side that's not theirs!" the boy yelled. Even from thirty feet away Galen could see tears trickling down his cheeks.

"What god do you worship?" yelled Galen.

"The god that's against them!"

"Come up," ordered Galen. The boy leaned over and with a knife slashed the rope below him.

"He certainly can decide quickly," said Millicent.

The small climber seemed no more than eleven, perhaps twelve. How fast he scurried up the rope! In seconds, like a cat he was over the wall. He leaped recklessly from the platform, rolled over in the grass, and for several seconds lay on his back with his hands over his eyes sobbing. His sides heaved as he sucked in air.

Everyone circled him. Slowly he rose, and glancing at the Prince, fell on his face.

"I am in your service, Prince Ga...Ga...Ga..."

"Galen," said Galen.

"Galen," said the boy. His high-pitched voice was both surprising and clear.

"Your name?" asked the Prince.

"Storie." The young climber dragged a sleeve across his face.

"Storie?" returned the Prince, surrendering a smile. "Please stand."

"Yes, Your Majesty."

"Storie, I am not 'Your Majesty.' No one calls me that. And no one will."

Millicent interrupted:

"But make no mistake that Prince Galen rules this mountain! And he does in the name of God and the Emperor."

"Then I will serve Prince Galen, the Emperor, and the God of Heaven until the day I die," said Storie. Slowly he raised his head.

"So you think it's that easy?" said Millicent. "You cannot serve the God of Heaven, or anyone for that matter, until you really know him. But that's a problem we can solve."

"We will take you at your word," said Galen. "But know this: I rule—in the absence of my father. Further, we are all servants, and we all intend to defend this mountain until we die if need be. It's my will, the will of my father, and the will of the Emperor." Galen got goose bumps hearing his own words. He had play-acted before, but never in public. But this was no game. He must be firm, but why so formal? Millie or Master Weft or Master Maleg were expressionless, but said nothing. Did they think him a fool? "Are you still willing to join us in this?"

"I am."

"Why such a sudden change in heart?" asked Galen. "Because you had no other choice?"

"No...I could have jumped. What's death? After all, I've climbed often with Master Alpin and have faced death at his side. We've placed our lives in each other's hands several times."

"You've climbed many times?" asked Galen.

"Several times. In the South a master climber often apprentices strong children to learn his art—not only how to tie ropes but how to make them. In many mountains, like this one, there are niches, crevasses, and cracks that only a smaller body can get through. With his eye, Master Alpin found the 'path' up here from down below, but it was I who climbed and tied the long rope around the pinnacle." He paused. Several defenders glanced at each other, but no one spoke. "We often climb with our masters. At times we can do things they cannot."

"Are you ever afraid?" asked Galen.

"Sometimes."

"And your parents?" asked Millicent.

"I have no parents. All climbing apprentices must be orphans without families."

"And your change of heart? Why join and help us?" asked Galen.

"They just killed my master." The climber paused, fighting tears. "Master Alpin took me when no one else would, when everyone else just laughed at me. Master Alpin was the best. He patiently taught me everything. And they killed him simply because he didn't reach the top, and...and even saved their lives by warning them about you. King Stulk is a fool. Only three or four other climbers are with them, but none approach Master Alpin's skill. I...I don't think you'll have much to fear from the others, but I'll have to always check all around the mountain to be sure.

"But that's not the only reason I'm with you." The young boy turned and stared at Millicent, then at Mira, the servant girl. Saren and Soren exchanged glances.

"Then what is it?" asked Galen.

"King Stulk found the Emperor's burned coach with a charred body inside, and he's convinced the Emperor's daughters left Zareba City in it. And his daughters' beauty was the subject of much talk. Stulk is convinced that if he could capture one of the..." At this point the young climber's eyes turned to Maid Mira, who'd said nothing. "My lady, you look like a Princess...Princess Lucia. Yet your face, your clothes..."

"You flatter me." The servant girl bowed. "I...I've been in a palace, but I'm just a maid, a servant of the finest girl that..." She could go no further.

Galen remembered that the climber and the others probably had no idea the Emperor had separated his daughters in their escape. He hoped Maid Mira would keep that secret until they knew more.

The boy dropped to his knees in front of her.

"I'm sorry, missy, forgive me." Then he stood and dusted off his pants and shirt. Again, he methodically surveyed everyone.

"Your soldiers? Where are they?" Saren and Soren touched the hilts of their swords and smiled. "You mean you have no soldiers?" In a flash, the twins' swords were out. "I...I mean only two soldiers!" From nowhere Millicent flashed a long knife.

291

"Do you have trouble counting?" chided Millicent.

"There are nine soldiers—and you," said Galen. "Does that make a difference in what you promised?"

"There are now *ten* soldiers, Prince Galen!" Storie paused and fingered the hilt of a nearly hidden dagger. "King Stulk is a monster and a fool! I've overheard plenty! Things you should know. Stulk greatly admires the tapestries and curtains made in your village. Merchants have convinced him that this mountain has been unoccupied for years, and if anyone's up here now, it's only a handful of soldiers guarding one or more of the Emperor's children—in addition to the treasure."

"The *treasure*?" said Galen. "Storie, that's rumor, a rumor that grows with distance from its source. Most of us have been raised at the foot of this mountain and none of us believe that. Besides, deadly walking bees infest the bottom on the eastern side, and several villagers have already been killed trying to climb—"

"But Prince Galen, please realize what Master Alpin and I almost did. Of course, he was absolutely the most skilled. And"—he paused—"and somehow you have found a way to get in here. Perhaps, Prince Galen, you live too close to—"

"Perhaps," interrupted Millicent, "you've lived too far away." Her tone dared contradiction.

"I...I'm sorry. Forgive me." Again the climber dropped to his knees. "I shouldn't have said—"

"No, no," said Millicent. "Stand, please! You were right to tell us. As part of our army you must tell us everything you know! And think! And what you think they think! The more we know, the better off we are."

"One thing," said Storie. "King Stulk is determined to have the Emperor's daughter, at least one of them. You know what I mean. He's sure it will break the Emperor's spirit and make him surrender. And besides, he's dying of curiosity to find out what's up here. And to fly

292

his flag from that tower." The climber pointed to the pole that rose above the tower and was the highest point on the mountain.

Galen shuddered.

"I wonder how long it would take!" exclaimed Soren, offering his first words.

"What take?" asked Millicent.

"For King Stulk to die of curiosity," said Soren. For the first time Master Maleg broke into a smile.

"I think," said Storie, "it would really be hard for King Stulk to leave this place without trying every possible way to get up here. And, what's up here, anyway? And why are you...?" He stopped.

"We don't know," said Galen, forgetting that he might be saying too much. "We arrived, only minutes before you did." Everyone's eyes were on Storie to see the effect of these words.

"Then ten soldiers have just arrived!" The newcomer, so full of words that perhaps only Millicent could appreciate, recalling her own childhood. The young climber stiffened and stood tall. Surprises from him were hardly over. "Want to know why Master Alpin risked his life to get here? And the most important reason I've joined your side?"

"You mean Alpin wasn't really on King Stulk's side?" asked Galen.

"Not hardly," said Storie. "Master Alpin was definitely in the service of King Stulk — though he wasn't bad through and through like the monster he serves. You see, only he would take me in when I had no one. And he trusted me with his life. But today he foolishly risked his life for a prize."

"A prize?" asked Millicent.

"As I said, King Stulk is sure at least one of the Emperor's daughters is somewhere nearby, and if not down there, then up here. Just yesterday he said that whoever conquered Mt. Zareba first could have her first. 'But only first,' the King said. Then he and his soldiers laughed. From that moment I hated him."

"If King Stulk's so bad, and you followed him anyway, why did this upset you so?" asked Millicent. Masters Weft and Maleg exchanged puzzled glances. Maid Mara turned their way and whispered just loud enough for Galen to hear:"I think you're just about to get your answer."

"My master followed him," said Storie. "My *dead* master who, by the way, never touched me."

"So?" said Millicent. "Please finish!"

The climber's hand sprang to the strange leather cap and, pulling it off, flung it high over the wall. For several seconds Galen and everyone watched the cap spiral high before it disappeared from sight.

Then everyone turned to Storie. Long light-brown hair fell to just past her shoulders. Defiantly, she looked at Saren, then the others, and lastly Soren.

"He's a GIRL!" exclaimed Saren. "*She's* a girl," exclaimed his brother.

"So!? Girls can climb as well as boys. Now who...who will 'have me' first? Is that what everyone wants? It's what *they* want." She pointed back to the wall. It's all they ever talk about!" She was incensed. Or at least trying to be. But her fire was gone. She began to shake and again she fell to her knees. Once again tears came. "I've never cried before today," she said.

"Didn't your mother tell you about tears?" asked Millicent.

"I'm 13 — climbers never use months — and I've never had a mother," said the girl, "at least one I can remember."

"Will you have one now?" asked Millicent.

"You're asking me? ME?" The girl pointed to her scarred leather jacket, her leggings, heavy shoes, and filthy shirt. "My master is dead. I come from nowhere. No one would have me!" She laughed.

"I will," said Millicent. "Will you be my daughter?"

"You?! A Lady?! Want me?!"

"I do. But just while you're still a child. Don't you want to be a Lady also — someday?"

"Me, a LADY?!"

"Oh, it's not impossible. If you know how to work hard — as Ladies do in Zareba. If you're brave enough to climb, perhaps you're brave enough to become a Lady — that is, after you've proven yourself as a soldier. And learned to read and write. Ladies in this realm aren't quite what you might think.

"But if you want to be my daughter, you" — she pointed to the girl who was still on her knees — "you must decide. No one will make you. But I warn you, if you say yes, and Prince Galen declares you to be my daughter, the decision is irreversible. You must obey me and your new father — a man not here now, but one you can trust — when he comes back." With a graceful flourish Millicent dropped her hand to her own dagger, flashed it out to the side, and just as quickly tucked it back behind the large belt where it had been hidden. "Do you understand me?"

Galen was speechless, as was everyone else, though Maid Mira and Maid Mara seemed to be holding back smiles.

Millicent, herself, had not always been a Lady.

The girl stood.

"I can work hard, harder than anyone!"

"Then you agree?" said Millicent.

"YES!"

"And you will never lie to me?"

"NO! I will never lie to you."

"Then I accept you. Galen, say the words."

The words. The right words. Words that would seal this arrangement. As a Prince, if he was good at anything, it was mustering words. He must not fail here. Everyone was looking. He would invent.

"I declare…I as Prince of Mt. Zareba, declare to everyone present that the girl Storie is now the adopted daughter of Lady Millicent and Sir Kerky Greenwald, and that Storie… now Storie Greenwald has all the privileges and obligations" — Galen paused, searching for an ending — "that go with being their child and a citizen of Zareba."

"Storie," said Millicent, "hand your dagger to Mara." The girl immediately obeyed.

Millicent handed over her dagger to the older servant woman as well. The girl flung herself into Millicent's arms. Great sobs of joy broke the silence that only minutes ago had welcomed its first conversation in years. Millicent's eyes were wet as well. At last Millicent gently pushed the girl away and looked deep into her eyes.

"There's nothing wrong with tears, as long as you cry over the right things. And make no mistake, you will cry again." A puff of wind lifted her newly whitened hair, at a distance easily mistaken for blonde, at both sides of her face. The new beauty of the former redheaded tavern maid, now Lady, was singular and spellbinding.

"Now about someone *having* you, my daughter, please know that I now have you, and though I'll always be your mother, and you must obey until I tell you when; you're only on loan from God for so many days. You probably won't understand this yet, but the God of Heaven has me — first, second, and forever. And if you let Him, He will have you. We'll talk about it later. You've much to learn."

"Much?"

"Yes, you've clearly shown that girls *can* be stronger than boys" — she glanced at Galen, dropping her voice to almost a whisper — "but you must realize that girls must also be smarter."

"Smarter? Why?"

"Because they can and must be. For one thing, it helps boys — and men — rise up and do extraordinary things." She glanced at their

296

new leader, who was suddenly whispering something in Weft's ear. Together the two laughed. Let Millicent wonder, thought Galen. And let Storie Greenwald, who was taking it all in, figure it out. Millicent, as if reading his mind, reined herself in without backing up an inch. "But make no mistake, my daughter, Prince Galen rules here."

"You're *both* making fun of me," said Storie, for the first time smiling.

"No, Storie, she's talking about me." Galen struggled to look as if he considered Millicent's words nothing more than idle chatter. Which, of course, many weren't. Time to quickly move on. "Millicent, Storie, take back your knives. I don't want anyone unarmed. I don't care how far away the enemy is." No one challenged him.

Somehow Master Maleg moved on his crutches to within a foot of the new mother and daughter.

"Missy, the air's a bit thin up here. Carefully weigh every word that floats by! But watch your tongue!"

Storie balled up her fists and jammed them against both sides of her waist. Never had Galen seen such young hands so heavily calloused.

"Then...then you're saying my mother is wrong? Or that she's not my mother at all?" Up shot her chin, the muscles tightening in her neck. Everyone tried—with limited success—not to laugh, which seemed to bother her. *Mother.* Galen stopped silently praying and marveled how easily the word fell from the girl's lips.

"Oh no, Miss Storie," said Maleg, "we've all been witnesses to what's been said, and so is God, so we're all going to have to live with it! Prince Galen said so. But make no mistake: we'll all be forming opinions about that! Now about ideas—in Zareba you'll have to sort out many things for yourself. At least that's what boys do. And some things"—he glanced at Millicent, daring contradiction—"need time to sort out." He shifted on his crutches. Saren steadied him. "And if we can figure out how to defend ourselves, we'll have plenty of time to think."

297

"You see, Storie," said Millicent, "if you really want to be one of us, you've much to learn. And learn quickly. And don't forget to use your ears. No one's better with stones and iron than Master Maleg and his sons. But that's not all they know about." She turned and adjusted the dagger back to its proper location in her belt.

"Maleg, you think we're safe for the time being?" said Master Weft, finally speaking for the first time.

"We are if we triple the number of slabs over the tunnel opening downstairs. There's no way they can get in from below. And if we keep watch on the walls with piles of rocks handy."

"For now, we've plenty of rocks," said Saren. He pointed to the center of the land where they now stood. Galen could make out little in the lengthening shadows. Nothing made of stone missed the keen eyes of the twins.

"You can take it from me," said Storie, "they won't climb at night, or anytime soon."

Millicent turned to Galen. He nodded.

"Now that we've taken care of 'outsiders,' " she said, "we must do two important things: first, soldiers are below, and more may be on their way — we can study this later — but we must establish guard responsibilities, at least do a quick check each hour." Soren would be first with Storie joining him. The Lady of the Empire glanced back at the small, but unusually tall building that Galen had seen on his first trip up. Above the peaked roof rose a small steeple capped by a rusted X made of iron rods. The low, afternoon sun now hidden because of the wall, made a buttery glow on the underside of the X and on the spikes that hung from each of its tips. They were the stakes of the God-Son, the symbol on Galen's leather jacket. The building, not yet entered, had to be a chapel, a place of worship. True worship.

The steeple had been Galen's sign to stay.

In the tall grass, under the large trees bulging with fruit, in front of the tiny chapel, all ten joined hands in a circle—Galen to Millicent to Storie to Soren to Maleg to Saren to Weft to Mara to Pinrut to Mira and back to Galen—and knelt. And so began a new custom to be repeated often. Galen leading, Storie carefully following, they bowed their heads and prayed silently—or at least appeared to—while three or four took turns praying aloud.

Galen offered thanks—for safety and for the addition of Storie Greenwald. From the corner of his eye he studied Maid Mira, whose hand he held. First it was warm, then wooden. While seeming to want to be part of the circle, he sensed at other times she wanted to be anywhere else. Was his mind playing tricks?

When finished, Galen turned to Millicent:

"Dear advisor"—the Lady bowed gently and returned the Prince's hint of a smile—"you said there were *two* things to do. And the second thing is…"

"Why, run up the flags, of course!"

"Run up the flags?"

"Galen, we were to leave nearly two days ago. Your mother and father and my Kerky are now sick with worry. Right now, somewhere out there Kerky has Mt. Zareba and the village in the sights of an Elphian spyglass, wondering what's happened. The next most likely person over our wall is him if he doesn't find me."

"And how do we do that?"

"We run up the flags—we're certainly not short of them!" She pointed to the pitted iron pole above the tower that on bright days determined the ever-changing path on the Monk's Walk far below. "Raising flags will tell any Zarebite looking this way that Mt. Zareba is in our hands and…"

"And," Galen continued, "that we—at least some of us—are safe."

"And infuriate King Stulk!" added Master Weft.

"There's nothing I'd rather do more!" said Galen. "We must keep

King Stulk here as long as we can." Maids Mira and Mara looked puzzled. "The longer Stulk's army is here," he continued, "the better the chance our villagers can make good their escape."

When Millicent produced the flags, which she'd somehow kept nearby, everyone except Maleg and Mara climbed the five flights of stairs to the top of the tower. Fifty feet above ground, the roof was flat with a low wall around it, offering an open view of every direction far below, except for the actual sides of the mountain and the immediate land around the base. The sturdy pole ran twenty feet up from the wall, but any cords for running up flags were long gone. Galen frowned. He looked at Millicent.

But Storie couldn't have looked happier.

"Mother, give me your flags—and your bottle of oil," she said, bowing, just as she'd seen Millicent do. "This is something *I* can do for the Emperor!"

The pole swayed as Storie effortlessly made her way to the top.

"Be careful!"

The girl said nothing back. Methodically she tied each flag in place—the Emperor's flag over the flag of the House of Aeron. With one hand she somehow freed the frozen pulley, applied oil to it, and took note of how to thread it later with new rope. Without her cap, the girl's hair trailed out in the gentle breeze toward the road taken by the fleeing villagers. In the blink of an eye she was back down.

"The rising wind is good, Mother. They'll see our flags." She gently tipped her head to Millicent, then Galen. Weft rolled his eyes.

"Well done!" called Master Maleg from down below.

To those looking up in the fading sunlight, and wondering about who was on top of the mysterious mountain, the colorful flags would offer some answers. But only some. Never would Galen forget this evening.

Raising the flags took away some secrecy, but to those below, "sides" had been declared. Perhaps, thought Galen, the enemy would think the Emperor's daughters, even the Emperor himself was with them. And they would think that whoever was up here was counting on the southern army, usually restless raiders, to move on somewhere else.

Hundreds of Stulk's soldiers were rapidly pitching tents, mainly in the west between village and mountain, because the pinnacle made that side easier to climb. The village was on that side too, which could provide comfortable shelter for the King and his officers, as well as safety from the deadly walking bees they'd probably heard about, which were abundant in the east.

Just how far they'd moved north or south around the mountain during the drought was anybody's guess. Another guess was how much food, water, and fuel the defenders who'd suddenly entered the mountain had, and how soon they might become desperate enough to try to leave.

However, the soldiers would be weary after their lightning attack on Zareba City, and their dusty ride—till the recent storm—to the Village and Mountain. And this was hardly a band of restless raiders. They had a strong patient leader. According to Storie, they would wait and rest. Food wagons were plentiful, she said, with more on the way. Waiting and resting would be welcome. But how long would they stay?

For the time being, the fleeing villagers probably were safe, King Stulk was still clueless about his enemy above him, and reinforcements brought by the Emperor would be a long time coming.

Everyone descended the tower stairs to the first floor. Smoked mutton strips were sizzling over a flame in the fireplace. How quickly Maleg and Mara had laid out food!

Everyone picked up something to eat. With the sun about to set, the air still warm, they gathered outside, collapsed on the damp grass, and leaned back against the tower. From somewhere, Mara produced ten containers of every size and shape, and from a large bottle poured everyone a small amount of ale.

A curtain of silence fell. A silence very natural for where they were. But a silence unusual for the tiny army of defenders.

CHAPTER 36

10

THE EMPEROR'S DAUGHTER

alen," Millicent whispered, "before the sun sets, you must give us directions and purpose. Don't worry about making mistakes. I'll help you."

The Prince stood and wiped his mouth on the back of his sleeve. He stared off in the growing blackness now under the platform that surrounded the wall. Over the wall and down below there were dozens of campfires and the smell of roasting meat. The first direction he thought of was for Millicent, but he pushed it aside. She was wise, often much more than she sounded.

And she was right.

"God help us," said Galen, glancing quickly at everyone as his father would have done. Soren shuffled his feet and looked at his father. "And I mean that as a prayer," Galen emphasized. "Counting the tents and campfires below, and stream of soldiers' food wagons still coming in, I'd say we're outnumbered 100 to 1. Please understand that. And understand that I will hold this mountain—that we still haven't explored—for the God of Heaven, for the Emperor, and for my father as long as I can. Hold it until I die. And, quite frankly, I don't want to die—like this man whose blood is still on my clothes." He shifted to

303

a more comfortable position the scabbard holding his new, and only, sword that he'd put on for the first time hours ago.

How silly he must sound. But he meant every word.

Storie stared at him in wonder. Maid Mira was expressionless. Weft smiled but held his tongue. Could the wise master weaver have offered anything better? Galen would ask later.

"I know, and you know, there's a lot I don't know. But this mountain is important to the Emperor. And I'll do all I can to hold it for him. I welcome your help. But we'll have to work hard, very hard. Now I want to know right now, who else is with me?"

He glanced at Millicent during the silence that followed.

"Help me!" boomed Master Maleg. Immediately the twins brought him to his feet. Galen loved how this tough old man never complained. The stone worker stared at Weft. **"I'm here till I die!"** Maleg boomed.

Storie jumped up grabbing Millicent's hand as she herself was rising. Then almost in unison, everyone else sprang to his feet, no one wanting to be last.

"Once again, the God of Heaven is our witness!" declared the Prince. He raised his hand and paused to let the words sink in.

"Now the second day after tomorrow is the Sabbath and I want us to stop then, put on our finest clothes, and honor God by worshipping together in the chapel and then eating together at high noon. That day — the entire day — will be a day of holy rest. Until then, let's carry everything up by day, and make things ready up here by lamplight at night. When we need minutes or hours to rest, we sleep in the kitchen, or out here in the open. And we must patrol the wall. Other than that, I want us to work every minute we can — day and night — until the Sabbath arrives."

Galen gave a "how's that?" glance to Millicent. "You're a tyrant!" she whispered.

"Let's get moving," ordered Maleg.

"We can do two more trips down tonight," offered Weft.

"Thank you," whispered Galen, to no one in particular.

✳   ✳   ✳

Near morning, rain began which made trips up and down even more risky and caused the twins and Storie to improvise railings with the rope she'd brought. On top of the mountain, the defenders were quick to find shelter for what they'd brought as well as themselves. Patrolling the wall was not needed. The long drought that had led to the finding of the secret entrance had broken, making it much harder to discover, and even more than that, it was turning the enemy camp, which had spilled far beyond the village, into a sea of mud. There would be no immediate confrontation.

On top, dozens of discoveries accompanied the bone-weary work.

The eight-foot high wall was found to be in excellent shape, as well as the platforms made of split wood and stone that ran just inside it. The 300-foot-high nearly vertical cliffs seemed unclimbable in even the best of weather — even though they'd already proved that to be wrong.

If climbing up actually happened, said Storie, it would be at the western wall, where she'd made her entrance. Sheer cliffs on the other sides, as well as the possibility of the bees there, would discourage any other route. Still, they would take no chances and regularly circle the platform. It was a welcome relief from the other tedious work.

Their first job was to make sure the slabs covered the water entry below, and that the stone wheel that blocked the opening was firmly in place. And that there was easy access to water. Then began the dozens of back-breaking trips up and down, first bringing the food and eventually the looms — which Master Weft insisted would be ruined by dampness if they delayed.

And dangerous it was! One of the sheep, sure-footed as these creatures usually are, tumbled into the airy darkness to its death, nudged by a companion at the edge of a step. The twins retrieved its body and quickly butchered it. Their first Sabbath dinner would include fresh mutton.

Master Maleg and Maid Mara, who were unable to repeatedly climb steps, methodically scrubbed out and set up the kitchen on the first floor of the tower they'd entered the day before.

The round five-story brick tower proved to be both ingenious and well preserved. Twenty feet across at the kitchen, with ceilings half as high, it tapered slightly inward at each higher level. After a good cleaning on the first four levels, which Mara insisted upon, the building almost seemed livable, the kitchen perfect. Narrow brick and wooden stairs wound around the inside walls to the second floor and each floor above that.

Since a long table was found on the second floor, the dining room was established there. And after rummaging through all the buildings, ten usable chairs or stools of various shapes were located.

The third floor, which had a stone bathing tub built into the wall, Millicent claimed for the women before Galen could say otherwise. On the top floor was a similar tub, but larger, along with several spigots which could be turned to deliver *hot* as well as cooler water. (Hot water, they learned later, after a bit of repair, could be delivered to the kitchen.) Above the top floor was an ingenious system of baked clay pipes which ran from a cistern—now nearly empty—and in times of abundant rain could collect and deliver water. In drier times, water— often quite hot—from somewhere far below would collect in a shallow stone pool at the base of the tower, which in turn could be drawn up by buckets tied with ropes to windows of rooms with the tubs for steamy baths!

Galen and the others marveled. So old it had to be! Yet they'd never seen anything like it...

Oddest and most delightful about Mt. Zareba was that apparently deep inside the mountain the rock had to be very hot. Somehow pressure from below squeezed tiny streams of hot groundwater and steam from below up and out tiny crevices all the way to the top. No one had seen anything like this before, but in time Maleg and his sons eventually managed to get the water systems working in the two bedrooms and kitchen. And with the new rain, the cleaned-out cistern slowly began to gather water.

On the fourth floor the twins set up an old chiming clock which their father had somehow stashed away and brought. With colorful rugs — of which they had plenty — the fourth floor became an observation room, library, a place to meet and plan apart from meals.

The top floor with its ornate high-beamed ceiling; its stone bathing tub; tiny fireplace; its large canopied bed, with remnants of grayed curtains hanging in ghostly tatters; its bare table; its desk, bookcase, wardrobe, and chests — all empty — was as elegant as it was covered with grime. Whoever had ruled Mt. Zareba must have lived here, but had thoroughly packed up before moving away.

The room would be gradually cleaned and repaired. But, according to Galen, he would not live there. It would be occupied only by the next legitimate ruler of Mt. Zareba, whether the Emperor, his father, or someone else. The room would be slowly beautified to present to that person.

In days or weeks to come the painstaking restoration of the "King's Room" as it came to be called, would symbolize expectation of the Emperor's return. And of hope. Hope that they could hold on. Hope that it came before food ran out.

The second tower, the stone one in the southwest, resembled the first in many ways, though there was no running water, and it was nearly empty of furniture, and was more badly damaged by the evident century or so of neglect. There Galen and the men would sleep on the floor or in makeshift beds on the second and third floors.

East of the first tower was the large, nearly flat-roofed building, empty of nearly everything useful, except along one side wall where from floor to ceiling four rows of precious firewood had been collected and stacked years ago. Though the roof leaked here and there, Master Weft claimed the structure for his spinning wheels, looms, and dyeing vats. Here, if time allowed, the business of Zareba would resume, and those who wished to learn his craft could pass the time to do so.

And, on one side, Master Maleg claimed a place for making weapons.

The third tower, located at the eastern side, was little more than a pile of rubble — why, the defenders couldn't decide.

Then there was the tiny chapel — 15 feet high, 12 feet wide, and 30 feet long — between the first and second western towers, though a bit closer to the second. Its massive wooden door under a tiny clear window faced east, and led inside to rows of grimy short and narrow wooden pews separated by a center aisle of stone running straight toward a massive pulpit on a wooden platform that crossed the room from wall to wall. Above and behind the pulpit, set into the back wall, was a colorful stained glass window depicting the four brown stakes of the God-Son neatly arranged on top of the Golden Chest of Promise, showing the connection of old history with history much older than that.

In late afternoon, when the drizzle ended, and the familiar sun once again began to blaze down, drying the puddles and making the tall wet grass sparkle, Galen appeared at the tunnel opening with his first load of tapestries. Everyone had pushed hard, not wanting to be seen as slacking. He laid them on a rock and strode to the wall. Mira, only seconds behind, with a load too heavy for her smaller frame, collapsed against the tower. Her long dark hair fell across her face. She gasped for breath. Not once had she complained. Galen hurried to where she sat, reached down and took her hand. She winced. Then he saw the ugly red blisters.

"Mira, I'm sorry!" He withdrew his hand. She pushed the hair away from her face. How beautiful her dark eyes were! And sad. Galen tried not to stare. What was she hiding? He felt himself redden.

"Oh…it's nothing," she said. "Nothing that won't mend. Your hand didn't hurt me, really." It was her turn to blush.

Lightly he took her fingers and helped her up.

"I…when I catch my breath" — he breathed out more deeply than he had to, and when she smiled at his overdoing, he laughed — "I'm going to check out the chapel. Come. Four eyes are better than two." Deliberately, he spun around, walked briskly to the tall oak door, pulled it open, and stepped inside. She followed, tiptoeing in his shadow. As soon as he let the door go, it groaned, and on its own swung back in place. The latch clicked shut.

Galen's arms shivered with goose bumps. He would kneel for a moment at the altar and pray. Silently, he moved to the front. Maybe the girl would join him. Then they could…

"This…this place bothers me!" whispered Mira. She started inching her way back to the door. Whatever had she seen or sensed that he hadn't? Galen wondered. The only light in the shuttered room was very dim, and came from the stained-glass window high in front, on the wall of the building that was closest to the mountain wall itself.

"Give it more time, Mira. The room, it" — he glanced around to see if he was missing something — "it…it only needs some more light and air. The beams and supports of the tall roof of the tiny room were almost hidden in darkness. He tried to whisper from where he stood, but with the echo in the empty stone room Galen found quiet conversation difficult. "I see this just as a room…a room for quiet meditation and prayer, for worship of the God of Heaven. That's all."

"I…I'm sorry, Galen. That picture up there…it's scary!" She pointed to the window. "And there's no priest to help us."

"It would be a lot scarier if there was a robed figure up there," offered Galen. He tried to imagine one. "We've a stone mason and a weaver, but no priest!"

"Then who will stand behind the pulpit on the Sabbath?" asked Mira.

"In the absence of a priest, it's the leader of the people."

"You?!"

"Yes, me." Galen glanced at his feet before looking up. "I have a copy of the Holy Book and I can read. I will read aloud every Sabbath. God can tell us what it means. Then we will sing and pray."

Mira's eyes were riveted on the high window. He sensed she wasn't listening.

"Surely, you know that's the Golden Chest of Promise — you know, the wooden box that was covered with gold that once belonged to God's people long before the God-Son came and died. In it, carved on stone, were the first rules God gave to his people. Rules that also appear in the Holy Book. The Golden Chest has always reminded us that God would keep the promises He made. The Holy Book, you know, says He's coming back to Zareba to rule...rule at his Second Coming."

"But the Golden Chest was lost, wasn't it?"

"Yes, it was — many years ago after God's people kept sinning and sinning. Pagan nations from the south conquered Zareba City, not unlike days ago, and destroyed the Great House of Worship there. That's when the Golden Chest and everything else in the Temple was carried away and destroyed — but not what it represents. That's the important part. Years later, when Zarebites recaptured their city, God's people rebuilt the Great House, but since the Chest..."

"But," interrupted Mira, "the Shrine in Zareba City...it..."

"It," said Galen, "holds only a replica. And from the fires we saw just days ago, even that's probably destroyed. But many years ago,

310

when the God-Son was born of a virgin woman, the Golden Chest became less…"

"I know, I know," Mira interrupted. "Everybody's taught that." She backed all the rest of the way to the door, her eyes still riveted to the window. What did she see there? Galen wondered. Was he overlooking something important?

"And the God-Son preached repentance and salvation before being taken by hateful Zarebites who cruelly staked Him out in the sand to die only to…"

SSSQUEEEEERRAAAWWK. SLAM!

Galen jumped. He turned just as the bolt dropped back in place like before. Mira was gone. In an instant he too was back outside. Mira was staring at several heavily laden fruit trees that stood in an unusually thick patch of grass in front of the chapel. Her long, almost raven-colored hair tilted back against the warm breeze. Below the trees came the tinkle of a tiny copper bell from a sheep collar. The smell of the patient animals was comforting.

"I'm sorry, Prince Galen. In there I…I just felt too closed in. I'm sorry. I didn't mean anything. You'll make an excellent priest—you know, in the absence of a real one.   Look…look at how tall the grass grows here! And the apples and pears!" Ten wild-looking fruit trees stood in front of the chapel, and toward the sides. Apples and pears overwhelmed sturdy branches, fruit twice as large and plentiful as that of any tended orchard he'd ever seen. Was it the height, the abundant sunlight, perhaps the minerals in the warm ground underfoot? Several other wild-looking fruit trees stood near the faraway eastern wall beside the miniature olives. But fruit there was of more ordinary size.

"With a good pruning we could get even more!" said Master Weft, emerging from the opening that led to the bottom. He was carrying a spinning wheel. Right behind him was Storie with a load of dishes. How different her hands were from Mira's. The young climber's eyes danced this way and that, seeming to take in everything. Then she fixed them on Galen. "Just look at that fruit!" said Weft. "Wait till you see what we'll get next summer after a bit of cutting."

Next summer!

What was Weft saying? Would they...could they ever stay here that long?

Storie interrupted his thoughts.

"Prince Galen, King Stulk knows that if any people have gotten up here, that they probably don't have much food...or anything else."

"Meaning?" interrupted Galen.

"I'm guessing—he'll try hard to find a way to get in. If we got in, why can't he? If he fails at that, he'll try to scare us or wait us out. Winter's not far off, and I doubt if he thinks that the few of us here could survive that. Or would even try to. So he'll be expecting us either to sneak out or surrender. And if we can get out, he can get in! And, knowing his curiosity, and how tired his army is, I'll bet he'll plan to stay for a while. He'd promise his daughters in marriage, his mother's head—anything—to get up here to claim an Emperor's daughter and find the treasure."

"Remember," interrupted Weft, "he may leave some of his army here and continue east and west. There's not much to the north."

"That's something we can't let happen," said Galen. He ran his fingers through his hair and stared at the wall. He recalled the Emperor's letter: His greatest prayer was that Mt. Zareba not be taken.

"Can't let that happen?" Storie wrinkled her brow. "Can't let King Stulk leave? Why not?"

From the corner of his eye Galen saw Lady Millicent appear in the doorway.

"Millie, come here. I've an idea." The two looked over the edge of the wall. The entire western plain seemed filled with soldiers, weapons, and tents. It broke Galen's heart to see what had become of their beautiful village. But there was more. Down at the base of the mountain, spelled out with carefully placed large rocks was a message:

LET US IN
GIVE US PRINCESS OR DIE

"That's interesting," said Galen.

"Meaning...?" asked Storie.

"Somebody down there can write and spell," said Galen. He stared at the girl. "As *you* will by next year! Storie, how many do you think are down there?"

"A least a thousand, Prince Galen. And...and remember, Prince Galen, I *can* count. All climbers must count and figure very quickly, as their lives depend upon it! Words will also become mine very quickly. You'll see! Now as to the enemy, unless they're forced to do otherwise, they'll stay near the western side because they know about the bees, and I'm sure some stories about them have been exaggerated."

"That's because you people here are superstitious and haven't received the Elphian scratches," said Mira. "All the Emperor's family and servants have received them." Maid Mara glared.

"Well, I haven't," said Galen. He glanced at Mira, then Millicent.

"None of us in the village have," said Master Maleg. "And we're not superstitious. We just wonder if they work...and why."

"I'm sorry," said Mira. "I didn't mean to be rude. I...I just didn't know." The girl lowered her eyes and seemed to study her shoes. "But the scratches do work. No one who's received them and been stung has died!"

"A thousand soldiers," muttered Galen, changing the subject.

"But they're a thousand from the *south*," said Master Weft. "There may be a few skillful individuals like the climbers, but don't count on

313

them as a group to be well organized."

Now everyone but Saren stood on the platform by the wall.

"And they're probably restless," said Millicent, "and superstitious."

"And when their food runs low, they'll be hungry," said Mara.

"And eager to move on," said Galen, "which is something we don't want them to do right away!"

"We don't?" exclaimed Soren.

"Right! My bet," said Galen, "is that King Stulk's whole army is down there. Our best chance to end this rebellion for once and for all is to keep them here—angry and quarreling, if possible—for as long as we can to give the Emperor every possible day to rebuild his army and return."

"And just how will we do that?" asked Master Weft. "We're just a little bit outnumbered—1000 to 10, or 100 to 1—and even more if we count only the men."

"Count only the men!" Lady Millicent rolled her eyes in disbelief. "Galen, you can rest assured that every woman here will do anything— everything—that has to be done. Right, Storie?"

"Right!" said Storie.

"Ab-so-lute-ly!" said Maid Mara, emphasizing every syllable, with a strong voice that belied her age.

"You can count on me—for *anything*," said Mira. "Uh…you know what I mean. I am your servant, and from a royal court, but I'm not your slave."

"Excellent!" said Galen. "Because I am counting on the women, especially you, Mira, but you may find what I'm going to ask you to do—now—quite difficult!"

"Just try me!" said Mira.

"Okay, Mira, I need the 'Emperor's daughter,' and you're it. The Emperor's daughter to give King Stulk!" He paused to let the words sink in. The servant girl became wooden. "Nobody, Mira, would make a better Princess than you. But you must agree. Will you be our first line of defense? We were able to save most of the dead Princess's possessions. Now they're yours. I want you to have them and use them. I want you to wear her clothes." Again he paused. "I want you to wear her clothes and pretend you're the Emperor's daughter."

"Wear her clothes? Pretend? Why?"

"Mira, the Princess is dead. Her soul is with God. Nothing is sacred about her clothes. Besides, you loved her. I want you to have what is hers. I'm sure she'd agree. Right now I want you to put on her most dazzling gown so you can stand with me on the wall. I want you to help me keep King Stulk from wandering off. Okay? We have just an hour before it's too dark."

Once more the girl stared down at the hundreds of soldiers now looking up. Without a bow or a nod, she bounded down the steps and ran to the tower. Maid Mara followed as quickly as she could.

Master Weft shook his head and glanced at Master Maleg.

"Just might work…" Master Maleg muttered, smiling.

But the Prince was far from done.

"Soren, get Pinrut and your brother and gather as many easily 'throwable' stones as you can, and bring them up to the wall. We may get quite a reception! Our army shouldn't disappoint them! Go!" What he asked was clear and doable. It was a plan, some kind of strategy. The three sprang into action.

Storie stared in amazement. Then her face broke into a thin smile.

Weft looked stunned.

"Millie, I need a bow and arrows and a pen and paper."

The Prince prepared three notes — showing them to no one — and tied them to three arrows. Hundreds of stones soon lay in long piles against the wall. The shock of so many soldiers below seemed to discourage questions. What could they do against so many? At least everyone had a break from carrying things up.

"Everyone, to the wall," the Prince said at last. "Everyone, watch for arrows. Three hundred feet up is a long way, but still, they probably will answer us with arrows—and we can sure add to our supply! Tell us, Master Weft, when we should take cover."

Suddenly Maid Mira appeared in the doorway of the tower in a scarlet silk dress. From her shoulders fell a pure-white fur-edged cape and on her head was a jeweled tiara. No one moved or said a word as she lifted the hem of her dress and silently made her way past the rocks to the wooden platform.

※　　※　　※

Later that night, Millicent told Galen what Storie said at that very moment.

"She walks like a Queen!" she had whispered.

"She's worked in a palace, Storie, something we've never done, except for Maid Mara," Millicent had returned. "But remember, it takes much more than a chest of clothes and jewels to make a lady."

"I think she has more," Storie had said, "more than we realize."

If play-acting could go a long way, no one was better to recognize that than the Prince. Whenever he'd thought about all he'd said and done in the last few days, he wondered if somehow he'd entered a dream, one in which he'd wake up with sunlight streaming through his bedroom window. How brave – brave and foolish – to say so much in the presence of such wise master craftsmen – and Millicent, who knew so much for her age. But whenever he'd held back, there had been silence, silence that could easily have been filled. And so far, he'd not been challenged.

"Why do they let me go on so?" he'd privately asked Millicent.

"That's easy to answer," she'd replied. "We're in an impossible situation, Galen, and they're not used to impossibilities. Which, of course, doesn't bother

you. Add to that the facts that Weft still has his precious weavings a while longer, and Maleg, his sons and iron tools. We don't have many choices.

"And we're still alive.

"Now Galen, help me," she'd continued. "What do you think of Maid Mira?"

"She's beautiful, Millie…and troubled. And I'm certain she's not lied to me, even from the first time she stood beside the dead Princess."

"Maybe, Galen" — Millicent rolled her eyes — "maybe not. But I'm afraid I agree with Storie. There's something more about Mira — something important that she's not told us yet. So be careful!"

＊　　＊　　＊

Galen waited on the platform. Then came Mira. With the confidence and poise of a queen, she approached the steps. But once again her eyes seemed reddened from tears that had to be wiped away. Her blistered hands no longer shook.

Mira was doing her part. Galen prayed that in the next few minutes he could overcome that great fear he never discussed, and do just as well.

CHAPTER 37

11

THE FIRST SABBATH

aid Mira stood on the platform. Prince Galen took her hand. Together they peered over the wall. In minutes the sun would begin to fall from view.

BAAAHHHNNNGG   BAAAHHHNNNGG BAAAHHHNNNGG. Maleg's brass gong echoed off the stone.

From their second day in the mountain fortress the haunting sound would signal what would become a daily appearance—except on the Sabbath—of the Emperor's daughter atop the wall.

The gong would also call everyone to evening dinner and morning prayers, so at times it was a weapon, at times a schoolmaster, and at the first hint of daylight a tool, chipping away at what would soon become the "frosty dawn." But the sound meant there was some sense of order; and that was reassuring, even though the metallic ring, soon to become a part of everyone's blood and bones, eventually would toll out the deaths of several defenders.

Prince Galen shuddered as he stepped up from a bench toward the top of the stone wall, that was only two-feet wide, so he could be seen. Mira followed. At first he stayed so close to the inner edge that his greatest danger was falling backwards. From behind, the twins held their legs. Mira took his hand, and he was seized by a strange comfort that comes when a lesser fear blocks out a greater one. Oddly, no one had even questioned his plan. Were things that desperate? He must be loud and clear.

"BEHOLD!" he yelled as loud as he could. He raised both his hands, and she her hand that he held, and squinted his eyes to fight dizziness. All movement below stopped. Deliberately pausing at each word, he went on:

"BEHOLD... THE... DAUGHTER... OF... THE... EMPEROR!"

He forced himself to glance down. Sweat soaked his clothes. The breeze chilled him. Mira squeezed his hand. She knew. His terror was no secret.

"I... AM ... PRINCE... GALEN...   THE... PRINCESS...
AND... I... SERVE... THE EMPEROR... AND... THE
GOD... OF... HEAVEN.   LEAVE... KING... STULK... AND...
THE... EMPEROR'S... MOUNTAIN...
GO... HOME!.........GO... HOME... OR... DIE!

"And," said Galen in just above a whisper, "since you're all as stubborn as goats, we could use many more arrows, so fire away!" All the way from south to north dozens of archers slowly raised their weapons. After Galen's last word, Master Weft let fly the Prince's three arrows, each bearing a written message and a streamer of silk.

Then, as if prearranged, a great groundswell of shouting and cursing rose from below. Galen felt goose bumps.

"Get down — close to the wall and under the platform!" cried Maleg. "A hundred arrows are coming! Heaven help us if only 99 miss! You have four seconds... 3... 2... 1!"

Galen and Mira leaped down to the platform and ducked just as the first arrow went high and hit the tower before harmlessly falling. The twins assisted their father. Before he could object, Maid Mira had raised Galen's hand to her lips and kissed it, so he would release his iron grip. Rubbing her fingers, he gave a quick smile and scrambled off the platform.

With one accord, all ten huddled close to the wall and gathered stones that were piled there. Most arrows crested just feet above the wall arching over it before ending their upward journey and curling downward, dropping slowly with little danger, if one kept his eyes overhead and stood ready to dodge any shaft that fell too close. And if one kept to the inside of the outer wall there was no danger from fallback.

After the first volley of arrows, came a second with dozens more. Master Weft was then stationed in the tower window to view any further danger from arrows and to shout warning. Then came his "All clear!"

It was time for the counterstrike.

"Let the mountain rain!" Galen yelled. Then, from the inside of the entire western side everyone who was able at the same moment hurled down all the rocks that had been piled there. According to Weft, while their response was hardly devastating, it had caught the enemy by surprise, ripping tents, destroying equipment, even seriously injuring and killing a few soldiers who were crowded and unable to scramble out of the way. "Now they know we're here!" said Galen.

"It'll make them wonder just how many of us there are," said Weft. "I'm sure that they'll now think that at least twice as many of us are really here." Maleg chuckled. Galen smiled.

"Then we've gained some advantage," said the Prince. "And we'll take all we can get."

After the harmless rain of a few more arrows, probably fired in frustration, the battle was over. "It's getting dark, if you help me gather arrows, don't touch the points," Storie said.

"Why?" asked Mira, already holding two arrows.

"Poisons," said Storie. "Southerners have been known to use them that way." While others helped gather, the young climber was put in

320

charge of gathering and storing the enemy arrows.

"We've time for two more loads from below," said Galen. Maleg and Mara moved to the kitchen to lay out food ahead of the growing darkness. Suddenly, Soren leaped like a cat, plucking an arrow out of the air just as it made it over the wall and started its downward fall. His brother cheered. A final arrow struck the chapel wall, breaking its iron tip. It was then that the defenders realized that no matter how peaceful life in their new world became, that whenever they were outside their buildings, they must always watch the sky.

Mira, again in servant clothes, stood in the dark tunnel just behind Galen. Her glistening hair was already brushed back as a palace maid's. The Emperor's daughter was gone. Suddenly she took his arm and, while seeming to pull away, buried her face in her other blistered hand. Her legs were shaking. Again she was that strange mixture of sorrow and meekness, punctuated by unexpected moments of hesitation, even fear.

Master Weft patted her on the back and gave her a handkerchief. And from the weaver, it wasn't just an old rag. "You did well, Mira. You could've fooled anyone!"

"Galen," he said, "just what did the messages say that I sent on those arrows?"

"I told them I was Galen, Prince of Mt. Zareba and that my army and I..."

"Your *army*!?" interrupted Weft.

"That my army and I were holding this mountain for the God of Heaven and the Emperor. And I told them..."

"Told them what?"

"Told them to give us King Stulk's head."

"YES!" shouted Saren, punching the air with his fist.

Weft laughed. "Isn't that going a bit far?"

"No," said Storie. "Trust me—those are words they understand."

"I hope so," said Galen. "I can't believe how many arrows we collected!" Storie smiled. "Arrows we can use! Master Weft, you wonder what we're doing? God only knows, but I want to get the word out—to travel far—that we're here. I know my parents and they're worried sick. And the Emperor needs to know what we've done. So far, Mt. Zareba is ours—and his. We must give him as much time as we can to gather reinforcements."

"Maybe we should put more stones over the opening where we came in," said Master Weft, staring down the steps into the darkness.

"I think," said Storie, "that King Stulk's first move will be to try to open the entryway just in front of where he's camped. It looked full of giant stones, but can't they be removed?"

"I...I'm not sure," said Galen. "But years ago, several men, with my father's blessing, tried hard to enter there and died in the process. Ever since, by royal edict the Emperor has declared the opening off limits. My father even built a fence around it. The entrance is 'booby-trapped,' say some, or isn't a real entrance after all."

"Well, in case you haven't noticed," said Storie, "the fence has already been torn down, and King Stulk seems determined to find out things for himself."

"King Stulk may become his own worst enemy," said Galen. "And I won't make things any easier for him! Still, I don't like it. If there's an entrance down there"—he pointed back to the wall—"we haven't a clue where it comes up here. If there's a secret entrance to the top, we have to find it first. But right now, if he's determined to move rocks, he's got a lot of dangerous work ahead before we're in any real danger—I think."

After the second bone-weary trip of hauling things up, work stopped—for the night.

One more day—just one, which would include a quick look for a second entrance at the top—and they could rest.

The end of that day came and absolutely everything that was down was up. Their precious food was carefully preserved and put away. Weft's tapestries, blankets, and looms were stored in the large building with the flat roof. The rooms in the tower were decorated with colorful tapestries and curtains. Rugs—covered with pictures, scenes, and important symbols—were laid out everywhere. Zareba Village was alive and well, but with fewer people and 300 feet higher than it had ever been! Even the existing water pipes had been temporarily mended so both warm and cool water could run through them.

It had been work with a frenzy, everyone spurred by the differences they saw they could make.

And, ahead was a day of complete rest they could dream about.

All during this time, at the hour chime of the clock on the fourth floor of the tower, they took turns walking the platform. So far, no one seemed to be attempting to climb.

But far below, a flurry of activity surrounded the blocked western entryway, if that's what it was. Galen sent more arrows with messages demanding that King Stulk give up his attack, encouraging the southern soldiers to turn against their selfish leader, and warning that the Emperor had forbidden moving rocks on the western side; and if they continued doing so, they risked death.

King Stulk and his soldiers ignored this, of course, but Galen, over the quiet objections of Maleg and Weft, insisted he had to do it anyway. Some may be spared. He hated to kill. But if it were surrender or fight to the death, he could do it.

But first he must warn them.

Killing the first soldier still hurt. At first, it had burned in the pit of his stomach. But with the arrival of arrows over the wall, his sorrow strapped on armor. More death would come. If he was wrong in his actions, God could take him. And the sooner the better. People would die, hopefully not them. There was no other way.

323

Galen added to the enemy's risk by letting the twins and Pinrut heave larger rocks over the wall. While these were dangerous and annoying—one stone actually bounded away from the mountainside to roll into Stulk's camp and destroy a food wagon and several tents—there were no signs of retreat. Perhaps moving farther from the wall was not permitted or considered weakness. Galen never knew. The legendary bravery of the southern soldiers was frightening, though often foolhearty.

In return for the stones, occasionally without warning a volley of arrows would arrive, as if from some contest. Each defender quickly developed the habit of watching, and staying close to some wall when outside. But in their early days there were no close calls. To lessen their fear of arrows, Maleg and Weft taught every defender—old or young, man or woman—the skill of archery, which they would regularly practice, and each defender was provided with a handmade personal bow and a collection of arrows.

Arrival of the enemy might come, but not without risk. And not from just one direction.

In addition, as Galen and Storie collected the arrows, he noted that each one bore the distinctive marks of the archers who shot them and, according to Storie, the towns and realms from which they'd come. This Galen recorded, as a possibility dawned that might be useful later. He would keep it to himself. As to how they'd fight back, Galen insisted they'd do what they could—and at odd times—to keep those below guessing. As to weapons, for now they would use rocks, for unlike anything else, rocks were abundant as well as dangerous when thrown from a high wall.

Galen's biggest worry was what would come of the digging in the—real or false—entryway on the western side. To those below, life was cheap, and what the Zarebites had failed to do, the brave southerners might actually accomplish.

Rest at last came.

The third day of occupation was the Sabbath that fell on the 28th of Solun, the 6th month, eight days before the traditional birthday of the God-Son on Aulius 1 when night finally equals light. On this first Sabbath on Mt. Zareba Prince Galen would try to lead his people in worship and quiet celebration. Weft was amazed that no arrows actually fell on that day, as they occasionally did on the following day and the day after that.

By early morning on the Sabbath, as Galen had ordered, everyone dressed as best as possible in whatever clothes were available. Mira and Millicent made provision for Storie, and Galen was amazed at how the young climber looked with her light brown hair brushed and combed, and probably wearing the first dress she'd ever put on.

The rising sun, of course, at last broke above the eastern wall and entered the small window above the Chapel door, striking the colorful window on the far end. Oddly, thought Galen, both the shutters and door of the chapel could be securely bolted from the inside as if one would want to lock out the peaceful mountaintop.

Perhaps, it had been considered a last line of defense.

When Galen flung open the shutters, he was astonished at how the tiniest bit of daylight brightened the inside. Together they found places on the short narrow pews, freshly scrubbed by Master Maleg. Mira, wearing another of the Princess's dresses, sat alone at the very back by the door. Together they sang and prayed to God.

Then Galen, carrying the Holy Book, mounted the platform and stood behind the great pulpit. Leafing through the pages he found the selection he wanted. When he looked up, Mira was gone.

Without comment or explanation, the Prince read about the Golden

Chest of Promise so vividly lit by the sun in the window above him. A refreshing breeze from the north reminded him that fall was coming, and also that the lamb dinner prepared the night before was waiting to be eaten.

"Give us, O God, a day of peace," prayed Galen, "that we may think of you and rest. Amen."

When they'd finished, the nine made their way to the dining room on the second floor of the brick tower. Mira met them there, and together they ate, rested, and talked about how with God's help they'd done what for years and years — all Galen's lifetime and much longer — everybody thought was impossible.

The table cleared, the dog given precious scraps that remained, everyone scattered to relax — no work was to be done except for the patrolling of the wall — some to the second tower, some to the chapel, some to the overgrown garden in front of it. There was no wind, the sun shone brightly, and the slightest nip in the air reminded everyone that winter was coming.

Galen, Millicent, Mara, and Mira climbed the circular steps to the fourth floor, where the clock stood, and books and documents waiting to be shelved lay where they'd hastily been piled on the colorful carpet Weft had already put down.

The Prince pushed open the shutters of the one window on the mountain which, except for the King's Room one level higher, provided the best view of the enemy camp below. Already a curtain decorated with the flag of the Horse and Sword of his grandfather's old kingdom at Aeron hung at the window's sides. Facing the window was a short wooden pew he and Saren had carried up from the chapel. Thrown over it was a large, creamy fleece.

Here Galen sat and took up for the first time the volume which Mira had given him, *Inside the Hollow Spear*, the diary of his Uncle Colin's strange quest and the shocking end of his life on Emryss. Fortunately,

326

the account was finished by another and passed on. Galen settled himself on the fleece and Mara handed him a cup of hot cider.

Behind him, Mira and Mara sat on the floor among the piles of books they'd saved from the coach and the village. Happily, they could read, and apparently enjoyed books as much as he and Millicent did. As Galen read, he stole glances back again and again at something that would command his attention nearly as much as King Stulk.

As Maid Mira sat holding a book, her hands would begin to shake. At first she seemed to ignore it, and pour herself more deeply into reading. Then all would be well. Then her hands would shake again and, once again she would force herself into the pages. Then all would be well. Four times the cycle was repeated. Silently, Maid Mara stood, and tapped Millicent, who was deeply engrossed in an old map, on the shoulder. For several seconds the two whispered. Mira's legs began to shake and drops of sweat appeared on her forehead. Suddenly, the servant woman went to Galen.

"Please, Prince Galen" — she paused and bowed — "I beg you to leave." Behind her Millicent nodded.

"But...but..."

"Please," said Millicent, "go!"

Without another word, Galen walked to the steps and went down. In seconds, Millicent was behind him. Two floors below in the dining room Millicent spoke:

"I don't know what's wrong, Galen, but Mara says it's something that's happened before, and sometimes as often as once a day. By sitting with her and holding her Mara can help her get over it. It began after something awful happened. Mira finds it embarrassing."

Galen went outside and found himself searching the sky and staring into the garden. Just as he finished an apple, he heard the rustle of a silken gown. He turned and found the girl calmly approaching. It was as if once again she were coming to the platform to be the Emperor's daughter and nothing had happened.

"I'm sorry, Prince Galen. Please don't worry. I...I'll be okay." Then she smiled and changed the subject to the fruit or the weather—Galen couldn't remember.

The remainder of the afternoon went without incident. Though the time of rest was welcome, by evening a general restlessness elbowed in.

The next morning everyone was in ordinary clothes and ready to get busy, but at what they seemed unsure.

After the gong summoned everyone to morning prayer, and then breakfast, ideas were exchanged and duties were passed out.

Their first goal: Hold Mt. Zareba until the Emperor or Lord Fairold returned, however long it took and by whatever means.

Their second: Keep King Stulk and as many of his troops as possible in their camp, instead of pursuing the Emperor and his father.

Their third: If there were any other ways into the mountain and up to the top, they must find them—and find them quickly.

CHAPTER 38

12
PINRUT'S
DISCOVERY

f life on top could ever be considered ordinary, it was at this point. But in the routine days that followed, a few discoveries, and some observations and thinking of the defenders should be noted. Soon enough an explosion of unexpected events would come one after another to end the siege, as well as lives on both sides.

Safety was a first concern.

And, of course, being able to eat and stay dry as well as warm.

Cool winds that began the countdown to winter were a sharp reminder.

According to Storie—who must've had ears everywhere—King Stulk and his captains reasoned like this:

As she'd already said, if any people suddenly found a way into the mountain, it had to have been recently and under desperate circumstances, since wagons, livestock and other animals were nowhere to be found, and evidence left behind indicated a quick departure.

So probably only a handful of people, and perhaps a few soldiers, were on or in the mountain. If there were many, that would put pressure on food. And if only a few, they should be easier to scare and safer to fight. If food ran out, they would try to sneak out. And if the defenders could come out, outsiders could get in. With a little patience, King Stulk probably thought, this mysterious fortress finally could be his.

His cruel army had been enormously successful and was rich with plunder. But it was weary. Time to rest and regroup. What better place than at the foot of mysterious Mt. Zareba occupied by at least one daughter of the Emperor, a tiny band of her protectors, and, perhaps the hiding place of gold, jewels, and other treasure — a plum well worth waiting for! Something a less patient leader might not take time to do. More than anything, according to Storie, King Stulk wished to be regarded as wise — a "king of kings" — which, he definitely was not, said the girl.

As to food, here's how things stood:

Their first Sabbath feast would be their last "generous meal," as Galen put it, for six months and one week — if they had to stay that long — until the traditional Resurrection Celebration on New Year's Day, Maenus 1, when once again "light equals night." Then they would feast "even if it took them down to their last loaf of bread."

As to meat — there were eleven large sheep, five soon to bear lambs; a dozen goats, creatures that acted as if they could eat the rocks themselves if the grass ran out; occasional foot-long lizards which appeared (considered a delicacy); and a few gulls and geese now and then would drop down to rest for what proved to be their final landing thanks to Weft's newly trained archers (for whom hunting for food, instead of people, was a pleasanter goal to train for). Fortunately, the new Mt. Zarebites had brought smoked meats and several large bags of salt and flour considered too heavy for the fleeing wagons.

As to fruit — altogether there were twenty-two trees, counting the ten in the chapel garden with unusually large apples and pears. With winter approaching, the fruit would be picked and carefully saved. The half dozen gnarled old dwarf olive trees could add to the precious barrels of oil they already had. As to water — both hot and cold was in abundance, even for bathing. Food could be made to stretch out for several months, though no one dared guess how many.

* * *

After the first Sabbath on Mt. Zareba things began to happen — both on the mountaintop and down below.

For whatever reasons, Storie was right, the enemy seemed to be digging in for an extended stay. King Stulk was more able than Galen first thought.

Much had to be done on the mountaintop, and the defenders found themselves facing ordinary but unfamiliar tasks. "We must divide things up," Galen said, "put people in charge of things, and all of us take turns at jobs, especially undesirable ones. Patterns and routines will help us feel safe, give us hope." That lesson received from his parents he'd not always practiced, but he'd never forgotten.

Millicent, Mara, and Weft identified what had to be done and assigned duties. Most included a turn for the Prince, and whether it was needed or not, he gave formal approval of what they decided. But his turn at patrolling the wall — just walking the platform below it, not on the wall itself — still bothered Galen, and his daily appearances on top of the wall with the Emperor's daughter, which just the two of them did, filled him with absolute terror, which he tried to hide.

One routine involved the Sabbath, which Galen declared would be a day of complete rest. There were no objections. Pains were taken to even prepare food ahead of time. On that day, as well as every evening, they would eat together as a single group.

There was defense, and there was "Weft's Band of Archers." Very soon the master weaver — who understood wood for the purpose of making looms, as well as archery — equipped everyone with a bow. All had pledged to defend the mountain until death, so there was daily instruction and archery practice. No exceptions. Bows were the only weapons besides the three swords taken from the dead soldiers, a dozen daggers or long knives — which apparently the women knew about — and Maleg's iron bars.

And, of course, rocks.

As to time away from duties: There were books and maps on the fourth floor of the tower and, again at Weft's insistence, everyone received instruction on the looms, and a few on the spinning wheel, so the making of cloth and clothing — for some — became a satisfying diversion.

✳ ✳ ✳

During Aulius, their first month there, watchers on the wall witnessed down below the recovery of five bodies, one per week, from where the Ember River exited on the southern side of the mountain. The twins reinforced the already secure entry with even more stone slabs.

At the same time, King Stulk tried to enter what he considered the blocked western opening (which will be described later).

It was also during Aulius, more than twenty days after they first arrived, on the day after the middle Sabbath, that they discovered the **secret passageway.**

It happened this way.

Since rocks were the best, and most expendable weapons, Pinrut and the twins had cleared away nearly all of the "throwable" surface debris, and large piles of rocks were made in many places near the wall.

And while Pinrut was helping the twins, he was the one who found the passageway.

About midway between the rubble of the northeast tower and the chapel, and beside an oddly placed shallow man-made pool about three feet across, which seemed to be for collecting rainwater, was a walkway of perfectly flat stones. So even were the stones that Maleg had even mentioned it. Then came a time when no one was looking that Pinrut, for reasons known only to himself, pried up one of the stones with an iron bar — something the others probably wouldn't have thought of.

"Hole! Hole! Pinrut find hole!" The huge boy danced in a circle rubbing his hands together. Saren and Soren came running.

And indeed there was a hole, a tunnel in fact, irregularly chiseled nearly three feet wide and more than twice as high, with stone steps twisting and turning endlessly down to within fifty feet of the base of the mountain. What skill, what hard work had accomplished this! Maleg was impressed.

Fifty feet above what turned out to be the floor of the mountain was a circular stone door, about one-third the size of the one they'd rolled back at the river opening. But this stone was much thinner, and two men could easily roll it to the side in a groove that had been specially cut.

And when the stone was rolled to the side, before them down below was a huge cavern illuminated by only three or four pinpricks of light that somehow got past the huge boulders blocking the western entrance. Just past the door, along a sheer wall, ran a three-foot-wide ledge about twenty-five feet to the left. Up, back into the mountain, ran several dead-end tunnels filled with rocks. The ledge was edged by a carefully stacked stone wall almost four feet high.

By torchlight Galen looked up into dark emptiness, and then over the wall straight down about fifty feet to the nearly flat stone floor. His stomach knotted. In battle, would such an ancient wall hold?

The cleverest construction in the new entryway were the narrow steps that sloped down from the opening along a steep ridge of rock that projected up like the fin of a fish. Dozens of perfectly cut steps, which by design had no railing, which could only be ascended or descended in single file, led fifty feet down to the flat bottom of the cave — and the mountain.

At the bottom, at the far western end of the cave, just within sight of the ledge lay a mound of boulders that apparently had accidentally, or deliberately, been dropped from somewhere in darkness above and somehow moved slightly downhill to cover the westward opening to the outside.

So the westward opening was real — and probably ingeniously booby-trapped by the last occupants who'd left another way. Storie helped Galen down the narrow steps and he pressed his ear to several great stones still plugging the opening. He could hear the digging and cursing of King Stulk's men.

In times of peace, the western entryway would be a blessing. But in war, it put the defendants at great risk, especially when overwhelmingly outnumbered. Nevertheless, the ridge of steps and the tunnel to the top would always be dangerous to attackers, especially when defenders from above were expecting them.

But, still, for a brave enemy trying to sneak in it provided great opportunity. If the tunnel were unguarded, and the stone door were somehow rolled back from the outside, it was the perfect way to the top of the mountain.

On the way back up Galen discovered the significance of the artificial pool at the top of the mountain. Nearly hidden at its base, he discovered a large plug leading to a huge pipe that emptied into the tunnel. Another defense to be carefully remembered.

Removing the rubble and huge rocks plugging the western entryway proved slow and painstaking, and when snow soon came, a minor rebellion must have occurred and King Stulk had to cease further work. Through his spyglass Galen saw several heads of rebellious soldiers impaled on the ends of stakes outside near the entryway to discourage others from leaving before the entryway was breached. A spring melt would come.

Stulk would wait and take residence in the comforts of Galen's family's home. Generals and other leaders took refuge in the village. According to Storie, King Stulk was known to promise great reward, including knighthood in his new empire to those who showed great bravery and courage.

Endless wagons of supplies made the trek to Zareba Village and the huge encampment. Food and entertainment would be no problem to an army so rich with the spoils of war. Would King Stulk dare to try to establish a permanent outpost at the base of the mountain? Even a residence at the base of the Holy Mountain? Galen shuddered at the thought.

As the weather turned cold, and a few days were bitter, a few troops did desert, and those who were caught added their heads to those who'd balked at removing stones. But most attempted to build makeshift lodging to stave off the cold, and those who attempted to build too close to the protection of the mountain often paid with their lives as the twins would hurl down rocks at night.

If Galen had hoped for an early retreat from a discouraged enemy, and not just a stop of their advance, he was wrong. But in keeping them from moving further to the north, east, and west, especially in pursuing the fleeing villagers, he'd been completely successful.

And, as Storie reminded again and again, she "knew" King Stulk was still hoping for a quick and easy surrender of the defenders. But if so, Stulk also was mistaken.

And so month after month passed.

The days, of course, had been full: Brief appearances on the wall by the Emperor's Daughter and the Prince were daily, except in poor weather and on the Sabbath. The time of appearing deliberately varied, though it coincided exactly with the first strike of Maleg's gong.

Occasionally, the enemy answered with a few arrows that presented little danger if carefully watched. These were collected, carefully cleaned to remove any possible poisons and were added to their supply.

Down below, at least two dozen more soldiers had been observed to have drowned, trying to enter by way of the river. Two brave climbers, carefully watched by Storie and Soren, without any hostile challenge, had fallen to their deaths.

Before the first snowfall, the chapel garden had yielded a generous harvest of fruit, and the trees had been pruned and readied for the next season. Thousands of rocks of all sizes had been collected and piled. Archery skills had gotten better and better.

But midway through this time, one important, and puzzling, thing must also be mentioned:

The **tent in the east**.

It's hard to say much about this. While most of the enemy's efforts seemed directed at removing the enormous rocks blocking the western entrance, which was a hated chore, a small group of men pitched a huge tent in a dangerous brushy area in the east, just out of rock-throwing range, and began some sort of feverish work inside.

According to Maleg, the walking bees said to live there hadn't always spoiled the brushy countryside. Decades earlier, the insects with banded, swollen bodies seemed to arrive at the same time as several Elphians, who also were not native to the land. When disturbed, the bees would buzz furiously with tiny useless wings and drunkenly zigzag across the ground as fast as fire ants or snakes. But they were completely unable to fly or even jump. They couldn't cross water. And they climbed poorly. This made defense against them possible; otherwise, even larger portions of the countryside would have been spoiled.

Most thought the bees to be somehow connected to the arrival of a handful of Elphians, a quiet, pale race said to have come from far away, and, according to Maleg, upon whom the deadly stings had no effect. According to Lord Fairold, these bees had once stung his mother and him. While his mother died instantly, they had only made him sick and he'd survived unharmed. In fact, Lord Fairold was the only Zarebite without Elphian scratches known to have survived the deadly stings.

So all Galen's life everyone in the village had been taught to stay alert. But having grown up with this caution, which prompted everyone to wear short leather boots outside, he didn't give it much thought. If the bees were left alone, they stayed in the brush and were hardly a bother. Their spread could be contained in many ways, but the only sure barrier was water. And they'd never been seen west of the Ember River.

All brushy areas for several miles east of the river and village were off limits and presently uninhabitable and dangerous to even casually travel through. Or so it was said. Those few who had meditated on the Walk of Monks to the north on the east side of the river, did so with caution. The possible encounter with bees reminded worshipers that even paths of life ordained by the God of Heaven were fraught with danger.

Still, from the middle of winter a handful of men seemed to work day after day in and about a tent in the center of the most dangerous area for miles around. Or so Galen was told, though he'd never set foot at the place where the tent was pitched, and he didn't know anyone who ever had.

Yet none of King Stulk's men in the tent seemed to die, or at least die and be carried out in one piece. If this seems odd, from time to time crude wooden boxes much shorter than a coffin, that reminded Galen of the Golden Chest of Promise, were carried between the tent and the village on long poles, like the poles that once carried the Chest. But what was in these boxes no one could tell.

At first, Galen suspected another secret entrance to the mountaintop had been found inside the tent and that soil was being carried out. But after repeated checking, the defenders could detect no soil or rocks being carried out and dumped. Perhaps the stories about the bees had been exaggerated just to keep people away — away from something like a special tunnel entrance!

The tent in the east occupied the defenders' dreams at night, but try as everyone did — and Pinrut lifted so many stones that his hands bled — no one could discover another entrance leading down.

Or discover another reason why so much time had been spent in the mysterious tent.

At least not then...

CHAPTER 39

13
SOREN'S PROPHECY

fter almost six months, the long-dreamed-of feast on Resurrection Day on Maenus 1 approached. Little did the defenders realize how soon everything would forever change.

Winter had brought some light snow, much cooler than normal weather, and a couple of weeks of bitter cold. Master Weft expressed amazement that most of King Stulk's men still showed no signs of heading further north or returning home. And there'd been no serious attacks, other than a few arrows now and then.

What did they know that held them there?

Winter had relaxed the defenders' vigilance, and bone-chilling patrols on the wall had become fewer and were done quickly. No one, said Storie, would climb in such weather. Inside the tower sleepy cozy hours were spent talking and reading, crowded around the sparingly fueled fireplace in the kitchen or library. (The other fireplaces, even the one in the restored King's room were unused.) Several enjoyed happy and puzzling dreams under thick quilts. There were simple, but meager, meals because of the shrinking food supply.

At last winter seemed to come to an end.

Seemed to.

Seemed to, because winter weather hadn't quite finished. And

339

weather played a key role in the series of events that would soon follow.

King Stulk's first attack—his first real attack—involved warfare unlike anything Galen, Millicent, Weft, Maleg, or even Storie had ever discussed.

On the morning of Resurrection Day, Maenus 1, the first day of spring and the first day of the New Year, everyone bundled up and assembled in the newly opened Chapel (that had been closed for cold weather). The air was unusually frosty. Behind tiny clouds of his own breath, Galen read the resurrection story from the Holy Book, and everyone prayed, thanking God for saving them through the long days of cold.

As the Prince closed the Holy Book, Soren suddenly stood and asked to speak. Galen nodded.

"All of you sitting here, listen to me!" He paused. Everyone turned. Was this really the quiet stone mason's son, always eager to do more than his share? The younger twin held his chin high. His knuckles whitened as he pressed his hands down on the pew in front of him. Once again Storie had managed to sit next to the handsome boy, who was several years older than she. She slipped her hand over the top of his fingers. His arm flinched but he stood fast. Millicent glared, but Storie's eyes were elsewhere.

"Go on," the girl whispered. How fast she was becoming like her new mother! thought Galen.

"It is part of a dream I had before." His voice was large and clear. "Last night these words came to me. I'm not sure what they mean, but here they are: 'Strange trouble will be immediately upon you. Before the sun again rises, the olive trees must be covered by the leader himself. And you, that's everyone here, you will be safe only in the tower.' "

"Safe from what?" asked the boy's father, raising his bushy eyebrows.

"From what's coming. But I don't know more than that."

"Thank you," said Millicent in an accepting voice that discouraged further conversation.

"I believe you," whispered Storie.

From the great pulpit — that later was to prove so important — Galen looked from face to face trying to measure reactions.

"Anyone else?"

Then it was Master Weft's time to startle:

"Let me share certain words that came to me as I awoke and was reading this morning: 'Do not overly mourn your great losses on this mountain, for as it says in the Holy Book, "we do not sorrow as others who have no hope," and "If you look to Me I will never leave or forsake you." ' "

"And?" asked Galen.

"And nothing. That was all I was given."

It was then that Galen realized someone was missing. Mira. Mysterious Mira. Shamelessly, even eagerly she always took his hand in their daily appearances on the wall — but was it only in the line of duty? To keep him from throwing up, or falling over? She, too, had always worked hard, been cordial, correct. But was there more? And if so, more of what? Mira had come into the Chapel with them. But now she was gone. And he never saw her leave.

Since coming to the top of the mountain, there had been death — death of the enemy below, death that wouldn't have occurred if they'd left with the others. But it was necessary. He had to tell himself that again and again. He was obeying the Emperor and his father. And, he'd given them a chance to leave and live, as if any of them would listen!

But Galen realized at this moment that, despite the servant girl's strangeness, he could not bear it if anything happened to her. Even if the Emperor's other daughter, who was still alive, suddenly appeared

341

and complicated everything.

*　　*　　*

After the brief service was over, the long-awaited time of feasting had arrived. To Galen's relief, Mira was waiting in the dining room on the second floor. She looked beautiful. Questions could wait. The table was laden with precious food. *Although no one would say so aloud, their food supplies were nearly gone.*

But foolish or not, Galen long ago promised a feast on this day. And, strangely perhaps, no one now suggested otherwise. If they were to die of hunger, they would die with the memory of celebrating the miracle of the God-Son being raised from the dead, the very God who'd led them into the mountain and preserved their lives so far.

Together the ten joined hands and prayed before being served. And once again they asked the God of Heaven to provide their "daily bread." Those who worked closely with the food spoke aloud about the need for vegetables and especially meat. The longer prayer also included thanksgiving for health, new friendships, the completion of many repairs with few supplies, and for new skills learned.

On the table was the last of their lamb and goat meat, and except for two goats still giving milk, the last of the animals themselves. It was the last bread from the last flour, and the dried fruit was from their dwindling supply carefully saved from fall. There were generous helpings of potatoes, the only vegetable not scarce. While Mira helped serve, Galen noticed she ate little.

It was a happy and memorable time.

The remainder of the day they had to rest. And rest they did, not knowing that it was the last day that the ten of them would ever enjoy together.

CHAPTER 40

14
THE
FALL

alen awoke the next morning to a scream.

Sunlight was pouring through the crack in the window of the room in the stone tower where he slept. Large weavings—the only cloths big enough to cover the trees—were laid out by the door. But it had been no easy job to find enough cloth. Feasting and endless conversation had dug deep into the night. They would awaken early, said Galen, and he would cover the olive trees before sunrise.

But with the sudden abundance of food, he'd stuffed himself and overslept! The sun was already high. It was mid-morning. No one had wakened him.

"GALEN! COME QUICKLY! WE'RE BEING ATTACKED! THE TWINS HAVE BEEN SHOT AND SOREN HAS FALLEN OVER THE WALL!" It was Millicent. Never had she sounded so frantic.

Storie was first to the platform. Saren, with an arrow deep in his shoulder leaned against the stone, looking down, pointing. As Storie bent over the wall, an arrow whizzed by her head. Ignoring it, she ran back to the tower, passing Weft and Maleg going the other way carrying bows and arrows. She disappeared inside and emerged with her coil of rope.

It didn't take long to learn what had happened. Hidden behind the one narrow pinnacle that rose to within a dozen feet of the top of the mountain, an archer and master climber (as Storie later noted) had shot his bow. A fat quiver of arrows lay in readiness, suspended in a make-shift harness attached to the back side of the needle of rock.

The archer was between twenty and thirty feet away. Down also about thirty feet, where a narrow ridge of rock connected the pinnacle to the mountain — and where they'd first seen Storie — lay Soren. Apparently, while patrolling the wall both twins had been surprised by the archer. After being hit, Soren, less seriously wounded, had also tumbled over the edge, but somehow had cheated death by sliding to the ridge.

His left arm was obviously broken and his head was bleeding. Unless the nearly hidden archer was dealt with, his death was certain.

Maleg and Weft spread out in opposite directions along the wall with arrows nocked. Mira, carrying a quiver, assisted the lame man.

"He'll have to lean out one way or the other to shoot," yelled Weft, stating the obvious. An arrow whistled by his head, answering him. There was a roar of cheering from far below.

"Just let him stick out an inch in my direction," growled Maleg.

Other arrows were arriving from below presenting danger, but nothing like that from the man behind the pinnacle. Oddly, on the arrows from below were tied small knotted bundles of colorful silk. Messages? Galen wondered. If so, why so many?

The Prince swallowed his fear and looked down. How far it was! His head spun and his stomach turned. Why had he eaten so much? He was going to be sick. Leaning over the wall, with a loud retching sound he vomited. And just when he thought his stomach had emptied he vomited again.

"GET DOWN!" screamed Weft. Galen opened his eyes just in time to see Weft's arm smash back against his face as an arrow whizzed over his head. Blood trickled from his nose down onto his shirt. Weft had saved his life.

Then Galen heard the buzzing.

"BEES!" Weft yelled. "WE'VE GOT TO KILL THEM!" Several silk bundles on the arrows that had made it over the wall had burst open; in other bundles furious- sounding bees had burst through fine slits cut into the cloth. It was ingenious, but deadly!

"GALEN, GALEN! DON'T MOVE!" said Mira. "THIS IS FOR PINRUT, MARA, AND ME! WE'VE HAD THE SCRATCHES!" Never had she talked so boldly! He leaped down from the platform.

"But...but..."

"DON'T ARGUE, GALEN! I KNOW WHAT I'M TALKING ABOUT!"

"Mira raced to the tower and reappeared with three brooms. At once she, Mara, and Pinrut were pounding the grass and stones. It was a job Pinrut relished.

Just as Storie knotted her rope around an apple tree next to the wall, Saren screamed. Like his younger twin, his left arm was also useless, but from an arrow deep in his shoulder. With his good arm he swatted his leg. He'd been stung. Storie jumped up to the wall.

"WHAT...WHAT ARE YOU DOING?" screamed Galen.

"GET READY TO PULL!" she ordered.

"STORIE, YOU'RE GOING TO GET KILLED!"

"GET DOWN!" ordered Weft, pushing the Prince back. "MALEG, WATCH OUT!" The archer was leaning the stonemason's way, an arrow nocked on his bowstring.

Galen forced himself to look again over the edge. Again, his stomach knotted, but there was nothing more to come. His eyes fell on Storie's taut rope that seemed welded to the stone. Incredibly, the girl was already down to the connecting ridge. Both she and the twin were safe from arrows below. From somewhere she'd produced a knife.

Quickly, she began cutting pieces from her precious rope. Whatever was she doing? In only minutes a crude rope harness ran from Soren's shoulders to his knees.

Weft shot at the enemy archer and barely missed. The archer saw his chance and leaned to the side and fired down. Just in time Soren, who could do little more than watch Storie work around him, pulled the girl down on his chest. The arrow tore through her hair and shattered on the cliff face just above their heads. Like a squirrel, Storie was back up the rope almost to the top.

The archer leaned out with another arrow ready. It was then that Weft dropped his bow. Maleg sent an arrow from where he stood, but it struck the cliff harmlessly. The archer pulled himself back and leaned too far toward the other side of the pinnacle. Then his harness rope caught on a snag. He struggled to lean back out of sight.

Then from nowhere, Pinrut mounted the platform with an armful of rocks. The first went wide. The second was closer. The third found its mark.

The brave enemy archer and climber never knew what hit him. Releasing his grip, he fell backwards. For an instant he simply lay back into the air. Then his harness ripped away and his legs broke free. Still holding his deadly bow — all master archers, said Weft, pray to die with their hand on their weapon — the man floated downward, behind the pinnacle out of sight. What courage! Galen marveled. What foolish, ill-spent, misdirected courage!

"GALEN! WEFT! MALEG!" Like a cat, the girl stood on the wall over him.

Galen stared. She slapped him across the cheek.

"Galen, get one of Maleg's bars! NOW! We've got to have something smooth to pull the rope over!"

In seconds, the bar was in place on the top of the wall and under the rope. Slowly the dark cord began rubbing up over it. Eagerly Pinrut lent his strength, and Storie reminded everyone pulling to be slow and steady so the rope wouldn't break. Periodically, she ordered Soren to push out from the cliff so the rope wouldn't rub against the stone. Fortunately, the few arrows still arriving from below had no success.

Just as Soren was pulled over the wall to the platform, Maleg yelled. The stonemason peeled away a bee from a red blotch rising on his bare ankle. Mira and Mara, holding the remains of their brooms came running. Each had several red blotches on their legs. Mara stopped and knelt by the older twin who lay silently. Pinrut gently dragged both Saren and Maleg to the tower wall and came back for Soren who'd fainted from loss of blood.

Galen and Storie walked to where the three lay. The older twin's head was twisted awkwardly to the side. Neither Maleg nor Saren moved a muscle. The bees' poison was working. Storie grit her teeth, and together with Weft, pulled Soren's arm to set the bone in its proper place. Soren groaned and bit his lip until it bled. Quickly, they applied and firmly tied a piece of broken broom handle as a splint. They would soon add two more pieces. Tears, still new to the young climber, once again wet her cheeks.

Mira and Mara showed little effect from their red stings. Galen studied the scene. Nowhere was he needed for anything. And all that he'd done was worse than nothing. He wiped the blood from his nose and spat to clear his mouth and throat from the foul taste. Overhead, a dark thundercloud rose in the southern sky, and began spreading east and west. Angrily he spun around and stared at a southern portion of the wall that was away from everyone. In a flash, he sprinted toward it, climbed to the wooden platform just inside it and, without hesitation, pushed himself to the very top of the wall. Millicent froze. No one spoke.

"STAY!" Storie ordered the remaining defenders. "He's not going to hurt himself. I...won't let him. Please, stay here, all of you!" She flew to the wall where the Prince stood looking down. Then slowly, like the 'walking dead' of old tales, said Storie later, he turned and began taking steps toward the east farther and farther away. There was the rumble of thunder. She climbed to the platform.

"Prince Galen," she called, just loud enough for him to hear, "I'm just below you. Now please listen. The top of the wall is two feet wide all around. And smooth. It is not slippery today. If it were a road on the ground, you could walk it for miles with ease. You wouldn't ever even get a speck of dust on your boots."

The Prince continued walking.

"Look down only on the stones before you. Count them. Do not step on a crack. Don't forget!" Then she was silent.

Galen continued, slowly and steadily, his circular path to death gradually bending north. It was as if the girl who stayed just below him didn't exist. At last he reached the eastern side. Slowly, he sat, letting his feet dangle down over the edge toward the rest of the world. He stared down at the strange tent that was no longer strange. Somehow Stulk's men had located and captured hundreds of walking bees, perhaps hibernating or sleeping from the cold. And had "wrapped" them in angry bundles and sent them up and over the wall. Two defenders had been taken down, and another was seriously hurt. As for his part, he'd only vomited, and in his foolish fear he'd almost killed Weft. It had happened so fast! He started to stand.

"Prince Galen" — again the girl's voice was soft — "when you stand, bring your legs over the side you have come from with the top of your head facing up but in the direction you want to walk. Then roll slowly to the inside of the wall so you are facedown with your knees under you. Put your hands down in front like a small child does when trying to stand. Then slowly push up into a standing position with your hands. Don't forget!"

Galen said nothing, but did exactly as he was told. Step by step he continued north, bending northwest, then west. The girl kept pace on the platform beneath him.

"Prince Galen, you're coming to a place that's uneven, so slow down and stoop with your ankles soft so that you can drop to your knees if you have to."

And so he did.

Soon he was plodding methodically west along the top of the north wall veering southwest, and then south. Of course, proceeding south in full view on the western wall presented the danger of enemy arrows. The sky even darkened more, and there was rumbling thunder, but the rain still held back. Silently, Millicent, Weft, and Mara stood on the western platform making room for Storie, always just beneath Galen, to quietly pass by and ready to shout warning if necessary. But no arrows came. Maybe those below were too astonished. Perhaps the mountain was ruled by a madman! They were superstitious, Storie had insisted. And madmen they feared. Let them ponder that!

Heading south became southeast, and then east. At last he was back where he started. He'd circled the entire mountain on top of the outer wall. He sat, this time dangling his legs down toward the platform instead of the rest of the world. Every stitch of his clothing was soaked with sweat. A chill ran up his back. Storie, who he'd never glanced at once, now stood beside him. No one else was in sight.

"I didn't throw up," he said, sounding like a proud child.

"There was nothing left to come up!" she returned. "Still, you passed your first lesson in moving on rocks. Master Alpin would have been proud. No one else up here has ever done that!"

She paused and they at last looked at each other.

"Except for me, of course." She smiled.

"That was my first and *last* lesson!" he said. "Thank you. I'll never look down the same way again...Thanks, Storie, for becoming one of us!"

"Forever," she said, smiling. Suddenly, she reached up and kissed

Galen on the cheek. "My first and *last* kiss for a Prince."

"Uhh...Why's that?"

"Two reasons," she said, matter-of-factly. "And yes, I know I'm sounding like my mother." Galen shivered. "The first is...that Mira loves you."

"And...and the second reason?"

"I love someone else."

She spun around and took several steps away. Then she broke into a run for the tower.

Like a hammer, the horror of their losses raced back. He reached the tower just behind her, keeping his eye to the ground for more bees.

Mara met him in the doorway.

"Prince Galen, Maleg—he doesn't answer me."

Maleg was dead.

And Saren was dead.

Pinrut was crying loudly and openly. The huge boy had never been more useful. A dark red blotch stood out on one of his ankles, but as with Mara and Mira, the stings seemed to have little effect.

The storm still held back. Immediately Weft and Pinrut carried the two bodies to the large building that held the looms. Storie hovered over Soren who struggled not to cry out in pain. She and Weft reset the splints. Mara was not feeling well, but she insisted it wasn't from the stings. The air was tense.

"Come, Mira, the Emperor's Daughter and I must immediately appear on the wall!"

"*Now*, Galen? Can't it wait?

"Now! We must do it now! They've no idea about our tragic losses. And we don't want them to know! And, it's just minutes before rain." He pointed to the sky.

In only seconds, it seemed, Mira was splendidly arrayed and they were on top of the wall in their usual place. Weft and Millicent stood behind them on the platform out of sight. Back on the ground, drops of rain began.

Storie raced to where Galen stood.

"Prince Galen, Soren is beside himself. He insists I remind you about the olive trees."

The olive trees!

Galen raced to the southwestern tower where the curtains and tapestries had been laid out the night before. Angrily, he refused all help and raced with two armloads to the miniature olive trees in the eastern side. He recalled Soren's words when they first entered the mountain and later in the Chapel. "The leader must do it alone." Why, he'd no idea. And what a miserable leader he'd become!

"No!" said Millicent. "This can wait."

"IT CANNOT WAIT!" thundered Galen.

"And why not? There's danger from the bees. We're not sure we've killed them all!"

"I'm covering the trees NOW!" He looked at the others. "If I die, Millicent leads. Is that clear?"

"The coverings are NOT needed!" declared Mira forcefully. "The coverings are FOO...LISSH!" There was something strange about her voice! As she spoke, a soft rumbling of thunder made the ground vibrate. He turned to the girl who played the Emperor's daughter so well. Why the hint of a smile? And at such a terrible time! The hair stood on his arms. Her lips were moving but the thunder made the voice seem unlike hers! Was he losing his mind?

The rain began. Grabbing two more armloads of coverings he raced to the trees. Frantically, he climbed and draped and "tented" the upper branches of short trees, tying the material in place. By then, the rain was pouring. Water sank into the deep-colored cloth, making it cling to the branches. Whatever was he doing? And why? What must the others think? He must be losing his mind...but no one stepped out to

351

stop him.

Too much had happened at once. The others moved into the kitchen with its warm fire to dry out. There, Mara had to lie down. Millicent covered her with blankets. She was feverish.

His job finished, Galen was soaked. He headed for the kitchen, realizing that so much water should easily protect him from the bees. He had covered the olive trees before anything happened to them. But whatever could happen? "O God of Heaven, I'm a fool! Forgive me! Stay with me! I'm lost without you!"

Just as he stepped up to the kitchen door, he reached down to untie his filthy boots. The battered brooms used to kill the bees stood against the wall by the door handle. Just as he untied the second boot he heard a buzzing. Down from the broom dropped an angry bee between his sock and his boot. Frantically, he tried to pull off the soaked boot, but the soggy leather clung to his foot.

Then came the fiery sting. And immediately after, a second sting. He pushed open the door and tumbled into the room. Just as the boot finally came off, the two blotches were already growing on his ankle. Those inside who could move gathered around him. His head began to spin. He felt Pinrut's arms under his shoulders.

The Prince rolled his head. He was by the kitchen fireplace, beside Soren. Mira knelt and loosened his shirt.

"Talk to me, Mira!" he said.

"Tell him!" Storie ordered Mira. "Tell him how you feel!" The young climber, kneeling next to her, was already attending to Soren. But Mira ignored her. Storie turned to Millicent. "He hasn't had the scratches, has he, Mother?"

The white-haired Lady sadly shook her head. Galen smiled. "Mother," the girl had said. How unusual! But how natural!

"Galen," said Mira. "I'm sorry, so very, very sorry!"

It was her regular voice! He must have been imagining things earlier. Her tear-stained face slowly circled above him. She rearranged the pillow under his head. He held out his hand and she took it. It was warm. She looked into the fire and began to cry.

"Hold the mountain!" said Galen. Several heads now were spinning above him. "The Emperor will come…My father will come…When I die, lay me beside Maleg and Saren. Bury me with them. I am at peeaa…ce."

He felt Mira's lips gently touch his, and her tears fall upon his cheeks. Her long dark hair tumbled into his face, cutting off what little he could still see. His arms were like stone. He could not lift them to put around her.

Suddenly, he felt Mira stiffen, and her lips become deathly cold, and her hand like stone. Was he dying and was she dying because of him? Or was it the other way around? No, there were the stings… The girl's arms fell away like broken tree limbs and he heard them bang to the floor. Once again he could see. Slowly, her body seemed to drift up, her face twisting into a mask of death! And then her heel, it seemed like her heel, slowly ground into his chest. Everything began to spin.

"Mira, Mira, where are you?" His words rang in his ears. Then there was the sound of a scuffle, which moved farther and farther away. It was replaced by the sounds of spring birds. Gradually, everything turned calm but black. He felt no fear. Had God somehow answered his prayer?

CHAPTER 41

15
THE RING
ON A
CORD

alen dreamed.

And he knew he was dreaming. Images of his mother, Lady Lambith; and his father Lord Fairold, a Prince by birth of the royal house of Aeron, flooded his memory. Then came his childhood—weeding his mother's garden, but never quite to her satisfaction; his watching the young weavers nervously sending their shuttles back and forth under the watchful eye of Master Weft, eager for approval; his looking up at the mysterious mountain again and again with friends and wondering what was up there.

And now "there" was "here," here where he lay.

And now he knew. Knew much about the mountain. But not all. Of that he was sure.

And he knew that he was not dead and, unlike Soren, he wasn't having a vision. There was no clue about what lay ahead.

✳   ✳   ✳

Honk Honk Honka Honk Honka — Bong Bong Bong Bong Bong Bong — Honk Honka Squaw—ooooooonnk.

354

THUD

Galen's eyes opened with a start. Daylight peeked in through otherwise tightly closed shutters. Whatever was going on? He lay on a makeshift bed in the round kitchen. Red embers glowed from the hearth behind him. There were two, no three, fuzzy bright spots—no, they were lamps, small lamps, lit elsewhere in the room. The dog Silk slept uneasily near the hearth. The room was crowded. Small tables had been brought from other rooms, and people sat musing over charts and books. His eyes began to focus.

The lamp on the floor across the room caught his attention. Storie sat on the stone next to where Soren lay with his bandaged arm. The twin was reading softly from a large book she was helping him hold. The blackness of Galen's vision was now gone. His head no longer spun. He was wrapped in blankets. Master Maleg and his son Saren had died. But he…he had not. There was a strange but delicious smell of roasting meat in the fireplace behind him.

Meat! But all their meat was gone. And nearly all vegetables.

First, he would look and listen. That's what a leader would do. And, young as he was, he was Prince here, appointed by his father under orders of the Emperor. But the day before had gone badly. They had suffered a surprise attack. Two of their number had died, and another nearly had. Would anyone again take him seriously?

Squawooonk Honk Honk.

A strange honking and other birdlike sounds broke into his thoughts, and every now and then the sound of something small smashing against the tower wall outside broke the silence. Something odd was happening but nobody seemed surprised.

Across the room, Storie was whispering excitably to her companion and pointing to the book he held.

"What's that word?" she whispered too loudly.

" 'Grandson,' " said Soren. Slowly, she traced the word with her finger.

355

"Read that part again," she asked. The twin did, but Galen couldn't hear the boy's words. "Read it again," she whispered. And he did. And when she looked puzzled, he began some explanation. She stood and slipped away to Millicent.

The Lady received the girl with a moist towel and would not let her speak until her hands passed inspection. Then the two whispered together for several minutes. Then Millicent kissed the girl's cheek and Storie returned to the twin's side.

Galen pulled away his blankets and tried to stand.

"Millicent, he's awake!" whispered Mira. The girl, buried in a book of her own rose from the table and slowly approached the wobbly boy. She extended her hand and Galen took it. Every eye turned their way.

"How long have I been asleep?" Galen asked.

"Three days," the servant girl replied.

"Three days!"

"Yes, I...Lady Millicent, Master Weft, and I...took care of you. Your sting marks are nearly gone, Saren and Master Maleg have been buried, and Soren is mending well if he can survive all the attention he's been getting." She smiled. "And if you wonder why our eyes are dry" — her voice started to break — "we...we've used all our tears up."

"Maleg and Saren buried?"

"Master Weft insisted he do it himself, and he got it done just before the blizzard hit."

"Blizzard?"

Squawronk Squawronk Thunk.

Galen jumped.

"Look for yourself." Together they tugged at the balky window latch. Suddenly, the shutters sprang open and a gust of swirling snow and frigid air poured in blowing a chart off the table. The ground was covered with several inches of snow, more than Galen had ever seen. On the snow hundreds of geese were walking aimlessly, many of them injured. Galen and Mira watched as another bird attempting to land was blown into the bottom of the tower wall.

"It's migration time and they've been forced to land," said Millicent. "I don't think they've ever seen anything like this."

"It's a once-in-a-lifetime storm," said Weft, "and at the beginning of spring it's caught everyone, every creature off guard. All we can do is wait it out."

"*And we will be safe in the tower*," said Soren from across the room.

"We've had a lot of sorrow, but we must go on. There is a ray of blessing here," said Weft, "but it's going to mean a lot of hard work. And it'll be messy!"

"We've already had the blessing," said Mira. "Prince Galen's okay!"

In an hour the storm abated and the master weaver, Pinrut, and Storie bundled themselves up as much as they could and Millicent and Mira began boiling a huge pot of water. The Lady and servant girl would remain inside doing the messiest work, and the other three who were most able — Millicent forbade Galen's going outside and Storie threatened to tie Soren down, which she could, if he moved from where he lay — would go out into the frosty air and, for the rest of the day catch, kill, behead, and bleed more than a hundred geese. Inside Millicent and Mira scalded, plucked, and cleaned all that was brought in. Piles of feathers were set aside for arrows and pillows. With the next thaw they would be smoked or dried.

Again, there was meat for dinner.

And for the first three days anyway, roast goose was a welcome ending to the day. Most meat was saved and, after the third day, not quickly requested.

The diminishing firewood would soon become a problem, and so heating rooms other than the kitchen was rarely done. The bitter weather, of course, was a wonderful watchman, and patrols of the wall temporarily ceased. Until the weather warmed, everyone would live, eat, and sleep in the kitchen, insisted Weft. It was a time to mourn, to physically heal, to reflect.

But Maid Mara's health, not good to begin with, had begun to fail. The old woman grew feverish, tossing and turning at night, talking deliriously. She and the women moved to the second floor where a second fire was built.

Late during the third night after the storm ended, Millicent and Storie descended the steps to the kitchen. The girl's eyes were terrified. Millicent spoke, just loud enough that those above wouldn't hear:

"Wake up, Galen!"

Instantly, Galen and Weft were on their feet. Silk sprang up from where he lay by Pinrut and joined them. The hair rose on his back.

"Mara…Mara…is she…" Galen stopped.

"No, no. She's still alive though I… She insists on talking to Mira alone and…and the girl is…well, she's just not herself. I'm afraid she's going to have one of her…"

Suddenly, Millicent was interrupted by loud words overhead. Galen had no idea that the older woman, who apparently had trained the girl, could talk so loudly. And the voices—three voices, not two! Silk growled. Millicent reached down and grabbed his collar. Weft reached for and lit a lamp.

"Storie," said Galen, "Get Soren up!"

"But Galen—"

"NOW!"

"I think"—Millicent's hands were shaking—"we should pray NOW."

Pinrut's eyes were large. "Good God"—the boy's voice boomed—"help me to be good. Help everyone to be good. God, come to us! God, protect us!"

"Thank you, Pinrut," said Galen. " 'God come to us! God protect us!'

358

Now keep praying that, over and over, over and over, but more softly so we can think. Do it until I tell you to stop. Do you understand?"

"Pinrut will!" And he began immediately.

How the twin finally reached Galen's side so quickly surprised everyone.

"Soren, you were reading *Inside the Hollow Spear* last week? And *Death in a Tavern* several nights ago?"

"Yes."

"We may see..."

"Yes, Galen, I understand," the twin interrupted.

"I need you beside me."

Suddenly, there was an explosion of shouting and screaming upstairs. Then a loud scraping of table legs. Then a crash and the sound of breaking glass.

"That was the lamp," said Weft.

Soren and the dog sprang up the steps, Galen just behind them. The others followed. Immediately, the dog slunk back to the wall. The Prince, holding back at the top in the darkness, saw in the center of the room something he'd never forget as long as he lived. Mara, in bedclothes, was standing but leaning heavily against the table. In her hand was a long dagger. Mira, sideways to the stairs, stood only a yard from the dagger. Slowly she inched her way back to the wall.

"You can't marry him!" declared the old woman. "I'll kill you first! And now just may be the time!"

Millicent started to move forward, but Galen, still in the shadows, pulled her back. The Lady began trembling.

"God come to us, God protect us. God come to us, God protect us."

"Don't stop," whispered Galen. Pinrut nodded and continued. No one excelled more in repetition, and the boy's words, never wavering, formed a backdrop to all that followed.

What happened next was chilling.

"I'll marry whoever I please, old hag!" The deep throaty growl came from the mouth of the servant girl. Millicent thrust forward the lamp Weft had given her. Mira glared back at her. The girl's lips twisted with the words as if a horse's bit were pushed against her teeth. **"Get back, White Hair!"** said the voice. **"This doesn't concern you!"** Millicent's trembling grew worse. The dog growled, then whimpered and backed out of sight. The servant girl's eyes, as if held captive, struggled to agree.

Though Mara trembled, the knife in her outstretched hand was surprisingly steady. She pointed it at the girl's neck.

"My life is over. I've nothing to lose," she said. Suddenly she doubled over as if punched in the stomach. Still she held her ground.

"Old hag," said the voice, **"don't you value your soul?"**

"How dare you speak of souls!" said Mara. "I love God, this mountain, and the Emperor too much to let you—"

It was then that the girl turned and first saw the Prince.

"Oh, Galen!" The same lips now moved naturally and the voice was hers. "Don't worry, Galen. Everything's fine. Mara's just having another bad dream. Go back to bed, all of you." She turned back to the old woman. "Come on, Mara, hand me the knife." She extended her hand. This time Mara inched back, still holding the knife in front of her.

The old servant from the Emperor's Palace turned to Millicent. Galen could see she was in agony.

"Please, Millicent, trust me! Don't try and stop me. Too much is at stake! You just don't understand!" Then the old woman whirled back and confronted the girl.

"You, you Prince of Evil, you'll never rule this mountain! I thought I could wear you down." Her voice quavered. "Okay, I was wrong. I know what you're up to and I'll never let it happen!"

Then she lunged forward, but at the last second tripped on the table leg and crashed to the floor. The knife fell and skittered to Mira's feet. The girl scooped it up.

"Here, Galen. Now you can see who's wrong here." The voice, however, was not right. And if Galen knew anyone's voice it was hers. Mira stepped forward and, holding the knife by its blade, held it out to Galen.

"She's not who you think she is!" said Mara, weakly, from where she lay.

"Mira, speak to me!" ordered the Prince.

"I am talking to you," said the girl. The knife was easily within reach. As Galen reached to take it, Pinrut stepped up beside the Prince and gazed straight into the girl's eyes.

"*God come to us, God protect us! God come to us, God protect us! God come to us, God protect us! God —*"

"**Ohhh!**" The girl spat at the large boy chanting. "**Stop it! Stop it! you fool!**" The more she complained, the louder Pinrut prayed. Her servant disguise falling away, she raised her other hand to her forehead, squeezed her eyes shut as if in pain, and took a small step backward. As she did Mara grabbed the girl's ankle.

"**Get back, you old hag!**" ordered the girl, wrenching herself free. Her face began to distort hideously.

"May the God-Son be praised and glorified!" said Soren matter-of-factly.

With these words the girl threw herself back at the stone wall. Then she turned the knife around and pointed it at her own stomach. Tears came.

Oddly, rather than race forward, Millicent, with Storie right behind her, dropped to her knees and began praying.

"Galen, don't stop me!" This time the voice was Mira's. Galen was sure of it. "I love you, Galen, I'm doing this for both of us!" She started

361

to push the knife in.

"STOP! IN GOD'S NAME STOP! Why kill yourself if —"

Galen felt a slap in the side of the head. "Galen," whispered Soren, "you stop! Stop and say the words!"

"EVIL SPIRIT! COME OUT OF HER!"

"Don't say that, Galen!" — the voice again was Mira's — "Don't say it! The Great Dragon is in me. He wants you. He wants you, but you're hardened. He can't get to you. And I won't let him! He wants a child from…from us…so he can…uuuuuhhhh." The girl clutched her stomach, and for a second, Galen feared she'd pushed the knife in. Instead, it clattered to the floor. The girl fell on top of it, then rolled over on her back. Her mouth opened with a hideous grin. Then came a peal of hideous laughter.

Behind him, Millicent and Storie began praying louder along with Pinrut.

"Galen" — it was Soren again — "say the words, *all the words, all of them!*"

"EVIL SPIRIT, IN THE…THE NAME OF THE GOD-SON, WHO IS GOD OF EMRYSS, GOD OF ALL WORLDS, GOD OF ZAREBA, THE GOD OF THIS HOLY MOUNTAIN, COME OUT OF HER. COME OUT! AND…AND NEVER, EVER RETURN."

At once the girl's eyes closed, and she seemed to rise against her will into a standing position. Her lips curved into a sneer. Her next words were deep like a man's but mechanical.

"And where should I go? I am a great spirit who can only leave one living creature for another. I will go. I am perfectly willing to go if I can enter one of you! Your Holy Book says 'blessed is he who lays down his life for another.' Now which of you will 'save this girl' and take her place?"

"The spirit is lying," whispered Soren.

Galen looked down. Such a spirit had to be a liar, a child of the

362

father of lies. The Holy Book taught that. But perhaps…just perhaps this evil spirit had extended itself to a point of weakness.

"Pinrut, open the window!" In a flash the large boy, still praying, had the shutters open.

"You're a liar, O creature of the Great Dragon!" said the Prince. "No spirit must do what you say. And we, of course can do nothing of ourselves. But God lives in us. The God who made all worlds. May our God, the God of *Truth*, hold you accountable for the foolish thing you've said on His Holy Mountain!"

"EVIL SPIRIT, I COMMAND YOU IN NAME OF THE GOD-SON TO LEAVE THIS GIRL AND, IF IT NOT BE AGAINST GOD'S WILL, TO ENTER THIS DOG COWERING BACK THERE IN THE DARKNESS, AND TO LEAVE AT ONCE!"

"NOT AN *ANIMAL!* NNNOOOOOOOOO!"

A low guttural cry followed that ended with an ear-splitting shriek. Never would Galen forget the sound. The girl collapsed again to the floor. The dog, hair rising all over its body, leaped straight up as if standing in hot coals. He sprang to the center of the room and gave a terrifying howl.

"GO, EVIL PRINCE OF THE AIR! IN THE NAME OF THE GOD-SON, LEAVE THIS MOUNTAIN!"

In three bounds the cowardly dog was at the windowsill. Without hesitation, the creature leaped up and out, even far enough to crash on the platform just below the wall. A second leap brought him up to the top of the wall, and a third leap sent him over it.

In seconds, Galen was outside and peering over the wall. Screams and strange sounds Galen could never identify came from a row of enemy tents nearest the mountain. More than a dog had landed. Of that Galen was sure.

And more than a dog had left.

Back on the second floor, Millicent spoke first:

363

"Inside the Hollow Spear—that prophecy of the dying witch, who would have thought, but…"

"It fits what the Queen was told in *Death in a Tavern*," said Soren, "but still I don't understand how…"

"And neither do I," said Galen. "But something definitely evil is missing from here, and something definitely evil has been added below."

"But, Galen," said Millicent, "why the dog? It was Pinrut's dog. We're not really commanded to do things like that. Did you have to…"

"Let's not forget," said Weft, "we've all seen, in one way or another, an evil that's been with us from the beginning. And we saw it leave. I think we needed that."

Since the animal left, Pinrut, without being told, had stopped praying. Everyone was silent as he started to speak.

"OK, Lady Millicent. Pinrut OK. Silk is dog. Dog. Pinrut is person. Person not long here. God is God. Silk, dog. Pinrut, person." Then one by one he eyed each one in the room. "Lady Millicent, person. Master Weft, person. Mara, person. Storie, person. Soren, person. Storie love Soren. Soren love Storie—maybe." Everyone laughed. Then they looked at each other and laughed again, partly because they were embarrassed for laughing after what had happened. How long since they'd laughed? Pinrut smiled broadly. His words over, he stood rubbing his hands as if washing them.

Mira quietly brushed the dust from her nightclothes and knelt by Mara, who still lay quietly on the floor. Millicent brought the lamp closer.

"Mara, I'm free! Totally free! I know it! Is it okay to love Galen now?" Though the girl was obviously released from her distress, she began to shiver.

Galen knelt beside her.

"Is it okay?" Galen asked the woman.

"Why ask me?" The old woman's voice was barely audible. "You rule here. I'm just a…"

"God rules here, Mara," said the Prince. "I ask because I think you know. Besides, I want to give her this." Galen reached up and removed a cord from around his neck. On it was the royal ring from his father's Kingdom that was no more. It was the ring, just like his, that had arrived with the book, *Inside the Hollow Spear*.

The old woman looked at the ring, then at the boy, then at the girl in her thin long nightgown.

"You need a robe on!" she said.

Millicent, obviously agreeing, but waiting for the right time to intrude, placed a cloak over the girl's shoulders.

"I'm dying," said Mara, "but don't mourn me. My time has come and I'm going to a far better place. But you" — she quickly scanned everyone in the room, missing no one — "your work here on the mountain is far from done."

"Tell me, Mara, can she wear this ring?" interrupted Galen. He held it up in the light.

"Let me talk to the girl alone," she answered. Everyone edged back into the darkness, but only so far, not wanting to miss what would happen next. "While I talk, Prince Galen, go get the Holy Book," Mara ordered. Galen disappeared, and returning with the book stood back with the others. Mira was bending over the old woman now under a blanket next to the warm hearth. The two whispered together for several minutes. "Come back, Prince Galen," Mara ordered. She coughed and Maid Mira wiped her mouth.

"Tell me, Mira," said Mara, "loud enough so everyone can hear, and let me see your eyes when you answer." The girl, still kneeling, called for the one burning lamp to be brought closer. Her eyes sparkled in the new light. She fixed them on the woman. "Mira, do you love the

365

God of Heaven and his only Son?"

"Yes."

"Are you sorry for the wrong things that you've done?"

"Yes, I am sorry. Very sorry," she repeated.

"Do you want the God-Son, and only Him, to live in you and be your Savior?"

"Yes."

Mara turned her head to the Prince. "Galen, come and kneel by me and look into this girl's eyes."

Galen did. The girl smiled, but immediately turned her eyes back to the woman.

"Mira, do you want to be God's child?" said the woman.

"Yes, more than anything, I want to be His child."

"Enough to die for Him on this Holy Mountain, if necessary?"

"Yes."

"Bring me my dagger." From somewhere in the silent darkness she received back the dagger they'd first seen her with less than half an hour ago.

"I am done with questions," she said.

"May I ask one?" asked Mira.

"Of course," said the woman.

"Am I safe from that knife you're holding?" Again there was laughter.

"Only if you don't cut yourself with it," Mara returned. "You see, though it's served me well, I have no further use for it. I'm giving it to you." Holding the blade, she handed it to the girl, who received it tenderly like a silver brooch.

"I will treasure it always." Somehow she quickly tucked it away.

Galen would treasure the old woman's patience, her wisdom, something he seemed now to lack. He was astonished that the girl's old hesitation was gone, replaced by a new eagerness that almost seemed frightening.

"Mira, the angels in Heaven have heard you and are rejoicing."

"And?" asked Galen.

"And, Prince Galen, the angels know what you're thinking."

Galen struggled as never before not to move and remain expressionless. He kept his eyes on the woman.

"And?" Galen repeated.

"Oh yes, the ring…" She paused for a full minute. "She may wear your ring—but around her neck, not on her finger. That's something for the Emperor to decide. Galen, you've helped this girl more than I ever thought possible. She's been through terrible torment. I beg you in the name of the God of Heaven not to hurt her further."

"Galen"—tears suddenly filled the girl's eyes—"Prince Galen… This…this ring is from the House of Aeron…I'm just a…I'm not worthy of this." Never had Galen seen her this way.

Galen circled the girl's neck with the leather cord. Afterwards, his hands shook so much that it was less embarrassing to put them around her. Lightly, he kissed her lips. His heart raced. And he could feel hers. At last he turned to the old woman.

"I will never hurt her—or you," he said.

"Me?" said the woman, "I'll not be a problem much longer. Please, if you would, Mira, even though it's late, I'd like you to read to me from the Holy Book. There're no other words I'd rather hear."

As Galen knelt to stay alongside the girl as she read, Millicent reminded him that the dining area on the second floor was now women's quarters, and that he was needed below.

CHAPTER 42

16
UP
FROM
BELOW

alen awoke to someone tapping on his shoulder. A sliver of faint light pushed through the window. Mira was kneeling next to where he lay, and Millicent stood behind her.

"Prince Galen, it's…it's over…Mara's dead."

The servant girl's eyes were red and puffy but wiped dry. The room was smoky from the last ember in the fireplace. Outside there was no sound of wind or from geese making their final landing.

"Galen, we — Millicent and I — read to her nearly all night. How alert she seemed, how she enjoyed it. Then, somehow, early this morning we both drifted off, and when we awoke, she wasn't moving…she… she was dead."

"Dead…" He paused to let the word sink in. How many more? He wondered. Perhaps she was fortunate. "I think it's how she would have wanted, Mira. Maybe the best way it could happen." How matter-of-fact he sounded! His sleep had been deep. Now everything raced back, the night he would never forget, the words he couldn't believe he'd said, Pinrut praying, Soren by his side continually helping. Mara — never one to complain. Now she was gone. His eyes moistened. Absently, he put his hands to his neck and traced his fingers around his throat and chest.

"It's here," the servant girl said, putting her hand to the ring around her neck. She smiled and took Galen's hand. "You don't have to say anything. But I have to tell you. For the first time last night the words of the Holy Book rang in my ears. They are beautiful and deep! The old pain is gone. Thank you, Galen. Thank you! Thank you!"

"And you've thanked him enough, milady!" interrupted Millicent. "Go back upstairs!"

" 'Milady,' you say!" The girl, still on her knees, turned to Millicent.

"You heard me correctly! Around your neck hangs a ring from the Royal House of Aeron, the line from which came the mother of the God-Son so, servant girl or not, whether you feel like it or not, you will act like a Lady. Is that clear?"

The girl turned back to Galen, trying to hide a smile.

"You heard her, Mira. The High Counselor of Mt. Zareba speaks with my voice." He extended his arms as if nothing more was to be said.

The girl stood, brushed off her dress, and made a curtsy.

"Yes, Your Majesty." And just as quickly she was back upstairs.

Had he climbed into his father's skin? No, his father never would have walked on top of the wall around the mountain. He had too much common sense. But what if he'd had the chance? Memories of Lord Fairold, his mother Lady Lambith, and Lady Millicent, not long ago playing a far different role, flashed into his mind.

❋   ❋   ❋

Three days later the seven defenders of the mountain awoke to a brilliant sun. Maid Mara had been buried. The meat from the geese had been dried or smoked. The olive trees, now uncovered, had been

369

spared. Water supplies had been replenished. The weather had finally broken. Just as quickly as the unexpected cold had come, the air became warm, if not hot. Spring had arrived.

With spring came danger and endless duties—more because of the loss of three defenders, and Soren's injury. There was little time to grieve. Except for a variety of seeds for planting, and the remaining corn that now had to be saved for making bread, potatoes were the only vegetables left. Did planting really matter?

Loss of life, however, was not confined to the mountaintop.

Down below, the blizzard had also taken King Stulk by surprise. Galen studied the vast camp with his spyglass. Many tents and makeshift shelters had been totally destroyed. Apparently, those who could, or who were strongest, had displaced the less fortunate in crowded buildings in the village. There was the digging of dozens of graves. Exposure to the cold had claimed many lives, and perhaps fighting over limited resources. Several men were flogged, perhaps for stealing, and one man apparently was even executed. Some less fortunate dead were burned without ceremony as garbage.

When Galen saw a dozen soldiers quarreling over a supply wagon, he recalled an idea he'd had after collecting the first arrows. Food was not just low on the mountaintop. The seven defenders—though Stulk still probably never dreamed there were so few—couldn't continue much longer, and the enemy probably knew that. Laying siege in winter was almost unheard of, but it had occurred, and at least 700 soldiers still surrounded them. In six months the odds of 100 to 1—counting the women, of course—had not changed.

King Stulk must not leave, unless to return home in the south where he came from, Galen insisted. The Emperor should return and soon. And should arrive and attack on his own terms. Better for him to fight here, out of others' way. Perhaps more lives of the innocent could be saved that way. Quietly, Weft questioned this though Millicent agreed, or at least seemed to. Galen scanned the horizon—north, east, and west—day after day, but still, there was no hint that help was on its way.

Once again the "Emperor's daughter" and Prince made daily appearances on the wall, and Galen wondered how the Emperor's dead daughter compared to Mira. Again, enemy arrows arrived at odd times and from different points, just enough to be annoying.

But there were no more bees.

Search as they did, not a single living walking bee was found. And down below, the same thing seemed to be true: perhaps the walking bees in the whole region were also dead—hopefully for more than a season. Perhaps the once-in-a-lifetime harsh cold that surprised everyone, had finished the bees. If only this curse from years before his birth was over. If only it had come weeks earlier...

But if true, it was a mixed blessing for the defenders.

Great stretches of uninhabitable land suddenly seemed to be open for use. Bit by bit, King Stulk's men began cautiously clearing away the brush and moving step by step north and south away from the crowded campsites of the west, but still near the base of the mountain. The effect was disturbing. Now the defenders were truly surrounded. While climbing up from the north and south and eventually the east was much harder than in the west, the enemy now had to be carefully watched everywhere. Guard duty doubled, and with the women now dressing as men, Galen insisted they make themselves visible often. King Stulk must never conclude that only seven defenders were left.

This led Galen to put together a far-fetched plan. Nearly every collected arrow had identifying marks that indicated the city or kingdom it came from. These he grouped in special bundles that he lay on the ground in different directions. When early one morning Storie asked him what sort of divination he was practicing, Galen laughed and said he was doing nothing of the kind, but instead was planning an attack that she could help with. When for the first time ever she looked totally bewildered, Galen was delighted. He told her his plan and she laughed.

"Prince Galen, you're crazy! But it...it just might work! And it will make Master Weft roll his eyes again and shake his head! I'll help, and you'll not be disappointed."

"Then let's begin—now!" For the rest of the morning he and Storie worked alone in the library on the fourth floor with Storie doing most of the talking and Galen writing notes on scraps of paper and attaching them to arrows with pieces of yarn. When they finished, they carried the arrows outside and lay them on the ground pointing in the directions Storie indicated.

Two days after the weather broke, soldiers were busy once again trying to clear the western entrance. In the huge cave the sounds of men digging and removing rocks grew louder. More and more beams of light pierced the darkness in the great cavern. Soon armed soldiers would be elbowing their way in.

Jars of oil from the olives had been carefully collected, and saved for use in battle. Galen ordered dozens and dozens of rocks, as big as they could carry, and pot after pot of oil to be placed along the short balcony wall just beyond the stone door at the end of the tunnel. The shallow pool at the top was also filled with oil.

Last but not least, three large boulders found in the blind-end passages were moved down to the end of the ledge, and positioned almost directly over the blocked entryway.

Several days went by.

Five days after King Stulk's men resumed work, one of Galen's worst fears came true. Four hundred fresh troops arrived from the South, and with more climbers, Storie emphasized. Now the enemy numbered 1100, more than ever. If the Emperor returned, could he face so many? Oddly, most new soldiers set camp in the west and close to the base of the mountain, perhaps ignorant of the risk, or perhaps eager to be first to get their hands on the "treasures" above them. And King Stulk did not discourage them.

At dinner that night Galen made an announcement:

"The time is coming to make King Stulk's soldiers work for us! And make them his worst enemy!" Millicent and Weft glanced at each other with puzzled looks.

"I agree!" said Storie just loud enough for everyone to hear. "It's about time." No one else said anything. They finished their meal in silence.

Later that evening everyone gathered by the wall.

"Notice," said Galen, "there's a vast army down there, but everyone's camping in tight groups according to their cities and kingdoms."

"And," said Storie, "although they're all on the same 'side' they don't trust each other. You can trust me on that!"

"We're going to use that against them," said Galen.

The boy then shared his strange plan. Weft did roll his eyes and both he and Millicent shook their heads, but said nothing. What else could they do? After all, barring some miracle, it was only days before they would all die, and even if the Emperor returned, would he be prepared to face so many? At any time the western entryway might be opened.

Galen and Storie's attack with the arrows would depend upon perfect timing, and upon how much the young climber actually knew.

❄   ❄   ❄

Three days later it was warm and sunny.

"I think this is the day," Galen announced. "And let's make things happen—sooner rather than later!" He told Mira to put on the dazzling red dress she'd worn the first day. In the early afternoon light she stepped up to the platform. He whispered into her ear. She smiled. After Weft rang the gong, she removed her red slippers and climbed to the top of the wall.

Yelling and taunting came from the new soldiers below. Mira raised her hand and waved. More jeering and cursing. At the last second she threw the slippers out from the wall and stepped back down. Galen watched the slippers catch in the breeze and float down to the screaming sea of men.

And Galen was right. Whether patient King Stulk had finished what he wanted to do or not, which he probably hadn't, they would enter the cave that very afternoon.

Down at the stone balcony wall the army of Mt. Zareba waited. Two small torches were lit.

From the balcony wall, Galen at first saw nothing, but the scraping of spears and helmets against stone couldn't be missed. Finally, when two enemy torches made it inside, Galen counted two dozen men. The opening they had squeezed through was tiny, barely large enough to admit soldiers in armor on their hands and knees one at a time. Galen smiled. Stulk's hand had been forced. With only a few days' more work, the entry — and exit — would have been much safer, and changed everything. But so many soldiers had waited so long. And the newer arrivals had yet to learn patience.

Those first inside scurried under a low protective overhang just above the cave floor, farthest from where the defenders were hidden. No more than 30 men, Galen figured, could be safe there, waiting for the right time to climb the stone steps and attack. That, of course, would be very dangerous to both sides. Many more must enter if his plan were to work. Of course, that was also very dangerous. Just as if the enemy were hearing his prayer, soldier after soldier continued to squeeze inside. The cave floor finally filled. But still more pressed their way inside until everyone was elbow to elbow. There was cursing from those who'd first arrived, but they could do nothing. Several had begun to test the narrow steps that led up.

It was time.

Galen stood. He was only fifty feet above them. Mira held up a torch so he could be clearly seen. When in front of groups, according to his father, if you can't be silent, always be loud and clear.

"Listen, everyone of you!" — he couldn't believe the echo in spite of all the people — **"I am Galen, Prince of this mountain and servant of the mighty Emperor Charlayn III. In the name of the God of Heaven, I beg you to immediately leave this mountain! If not, you will pay with your lives!"**

There were several seconds of silence.

Of course, their actually leaving was out of the question — but he must let them know what was at stake.

"It's just a boy!" said a new soldier. **"Let's get 'im!"**

"Silence, fool!" growled a deep voice just loud enough to be heard. **"Continue, Prince Galen!"** The voice came from the safety under the ledge. The Prince struggled to keep his legs from shaking.

"Galen!" whispered Storie. "It's Stulk, King Stulk himself!"

The Prince couldn't believe his good fortune. "Fear is to be shown; fear is to be hidden," His father had said. "But do each at the right time." Galen hid his fear. As they talked, still more men entered. Now cursing came from the back. He must bite his lip and continue. In the shadows, Weft nocked an arrow and waited for anyone to raise a weapon. No one did.

"Okay, King Stulk, you've called our bluff. But listen carefully. I'll let you up, but only if you come with respect and bring the leaders you so masterfully command from the Kingdoms of Sparton, Belind, Gortran, Marford, Ultior, Franculin, Mordant, and...and..."

"Stelanz," whispered Storie.

"Stelanz," said Galen. **"Each leader may bring two men, fully**

375

armed, if you please."

"And if I don't?" boomed King Stulk.

"Oh, you may get up here one way or another. We know that."

"Whatever are you asking?!" whispered Millicent, her eyes wide.

"That's the same question, Millie, I hope Stulk is asking!" Galen whispered back. "I want to see him reach for control of this rabble!"

Even more pushed their way inside. Everyone was in place.

"BUT IF YOU FORCE YOUR WAY IN, KING STULK, OR WHOEVER IS IN CHARGE, YOU'LL COME AT A TERRIBLE PRICE! YOU HAVE BEEN WATCHED! WE KNOW WHO YOU ARE! Let them think about that. They may have second thoughts about entering by impulse, not plan, and led by new soldiers. Their first battle may be among themselves. **"All we want is peace. Peace. Peace in the South. Peace here. Peace everywhere. But we're ready to die for it! Make no mistake!"** There was not room now for one single more person. Galen's knees were shaking so hard Storie wrapped her arms around them. Let flattery and seeming safety do its work.

"King Stulk, I am waiting, BUT NOT ONE FALSE MOVE! ONE LIE AND YOU DIE! Or have your generals left you? Or are they afraid? ANNOUNCE YOURSELVES. Or are you afraid of a 'boy'?" Two soldiers in the far back laughed. By now King Stulk was so hemmed in by men shoulder to shoulder he couldn't even see where the boy stood.

"I'm Lord Brighton, commander of the forces of the Kingdom of Mordant," said a voice to the right. The words sounded sincere.

"I'm Lord Norby, commander of the Kingdom of Gortran."

Then except for whispering and the scraping of armor at the entryway, there was silence.

"Anyone else?" asked Galen.

"I'm Lord Willernoot commander from…uh…the Kingdom of Stelanz." This was followed by several snickers. **AND I CURSE**

376

YOUR GOD OF HEAVEN!"

"AND I CURSE THE GOD OF HEAVEN!" said another.

"AND I!"

"AND I!"

An archer from the center of the room raised his bow. Thwwaaaat. But the weapon slid from his fingers and his hand rose to the feathered end of Weft's arrow sticking out of the front of his neck. The archer's scream had an eerie effect, but because of the crowding, only those nearby saw.

"King Stulk, you surround yourself with liars and cowards!" Suddenly an arrow struck rock and shattered above Galen's head.

The time had come.

"FIRE!" screamed the Prince. Mira lowered the light out of sight, and with one motion, from seven different points on the wall sizeable rocks rained down below. Again and again and again. In most cases the rocks—even large ones—fell silently, not even hitting the floor because of the extreme crowding. From every direction they landed came screams of agony, cursing, the sound of splintering bones. There was a rush for the entryway which made it impassible.

"The stones! Pinrut, the big ones!" ordered Galen. Down rolled the biggest stone, blocking the exit. Then a second stone. The screams were deafening.

"CHARGE THE STAIRWAY!" someone yelled. There was more screaming as rocks on the stairway fell one by one claiming more victims, first on the stairs, then on the floor below. The big rocks were now gone.

"NOW FIRE! RELEASE THE FIRE!" shouted the Prince.

In seconds, six oil-soaked blankets already set ablaze were hurled down. Then six more and six more. Light flooded the huge room. Soldiers were soon afire everywhere, and many not yet injured found themselves pinned under layers of bodies and being smothered by those who were. With fists and knives those who were able tried to cut their way past their companions. Blood was everywhere. But there was no escape. Only the smell of burning flesh. Except for the growing plumes of choking black smoke, the advantage of darkness was gone.

An arrow grazed Storie's arm. In a fury she rained down a dozen more rocks. More screaming. Three tried to storm the stairs at once, but Soren was waiting. Two fell by rocks, the third by an arrow, only the second shot by the defenders. Three large fires were burning below and Galen ordered whole pots of oil thrown at them. Greedily, flames leaped several feet high.

Galen screamed at Pinrut. The third huge stone remained on the wall. The boy struggled against it. At last it moved, dropping away and taking part of the wall with it. More deafening screams. A shower of smaller rocks also fell, and the entrance to the outside again was sealed, cutting off fresh air. Huge clouds of smoke filled the cavern.

Everyone was coughing.

"BACK TO THE TUNNEL!" screamed Galen. "OR OUR NEXT WEAPON WILL CLAIM US ALONG WITH THEM!" The stairs below now were slick with blood. With arrows, Galen and Weft kept those few still able to navigate the slippery stones at bay while everyone else scrambled back up.

Pinrut was last. Galen was horrified to see an arrow rising from his back. Blood streamed from his tunic. Just before entering the stone doorway, Pinrut fell. A lance from the direction of the stairway pierced his neck.

"Back up the tunnel!" ordered Weft, who was struggling with the stone doorway. "You can't help him now! There're others to think about!"

Just as it seemed Weft had sealed the opening, a spear landed and blocked the rock from rolling into place. Try as he did, Weft couldn't budge it. With bloody hands he rose.

378

"Up the stairs!" yelled the weaver. "No time to lose!" And up they hurried, Weft at the rear.

Running up the narrow tunnel was noisy, but Galen heard, to his horror, the stone door roll back open. Smoke poured up the tunnel like a chimney, confirming this. Everyone began coughing. At least three of the enemy were behind Weft.

Then came a sound Galen would never forget—distinct, clear, echoing through the rock. Somehow, the stone door rolled back shut. And without smashing the great stone, which would require the best of circumstances, opening the door from the other side seemed next to impossible. Whether Pinrut had pulled the spear out of the opening and somehow got the stone back before dying, no one knew, but the door was shut and the entrance once again sealed.

But between that door and the defenders of Zareba were three of the enemy.

At the top of the tunnel, Storie set afire the waiting oily rags and tossed them down the steps. It was she who saw the first enemy soldier.

"It's King Stulk himself!" she gasped. The man's clothes were ablaze. So were his eyes. How he'd cut his way through his own men to be first into the tunnel, Galen refused to consider.

Just as Stulk approached the last burning rag, a huge piece of old tapestry, Galen pulled the plug that emptied the oil from the pool at the top. Down poured the oil. Then the buttery yellow glow began to grow and grow. Stulk stopped, slid on the slippery steps, and screamed.

The smoke pushing out the opening like a chimney burned the eyes. The passageway became hotter. Everyone backed away from the opening. The smell of burning flesh was overwhelming. Slowly, so the fire wouldn't go out, Weft and Galen slid the stone on top halfway back.

Millicent turned to Storie's wound, which was slight, and which the girl had ignored. Mira moved into the kitchen. Weft, Soren, and Galen sprawled out on their backs exhausted on the new grass behind the chapel.

The loss of Pinrut was bitter. No one spoke.

Then came slow grinding as the stone half-covering the secret entrance to the mountaintop slowly slid the rest of the way back. As King Stulk emerged from the opening he faced three drawn bows and a spear. Quickly, Weft slid the stone cover back.

"Prince Galen?" Stulk asked.

"I am he."

The man's skin was blackened and shrunken in places beyond recognition. His head and right arm were wet with blood. His hair and beard were nearly burned away. What was left of his clothes still smoldered. The stench was terrible. How the man could walk, let alone move the stone? He carried no weapons. The pain he must be in! With his hand he pointed in the direction of the boy's voice.

"He's blind!" Storie whispered.

"The wall!" — the voice sounded as if his mouth was full of gravel — "Prince of this mountain, take me to the wall!" the King ordered.

"Follow my voice," said Galen, refusing to touch the man. With few words Galen directed the King to the steps of the platform on the western side. Mira slipped from the kitchen and followed closely. Stulk ran his fingers along the stone, and finding the railing pulled himself up the steps to the platform. There he turned.

"How many of you are there?"

"Six," said Galen.

"Six..." King Stulk turned his head to the side and looked down. "Six," he repeated. "And the Emperor's Daughter?"

"I am she," said Mira.

"My eyes are badly cheated!" said the King. "Prince Galen?"

"Yes, I am here."

"And so am I—at the very top!" His face cracked as he half-smiled. Fresh blood ran down his cheek. "Prince Galen, this mountain is in good hands."

Turning back to the wall, again he fingered the stone. With effort he pulled himself to the top and stood, facing the sun that hung low in the western sky. With his back to the defenders, he groaned and for a full minute began to whisper words to himself too softly to be heard. Slowly, he raised his hands. Then, perhaps from injury, his right leg buckled, and without any apparent effort to fight back, he tilted forward and without a sound, fell over the edge.

King Stulk was no more.

CHAPTER 43

17
GALEN'S
ATTACK

ing Stulk and possibly 200 soldiers had been killed, or would eventuallly die in the cavern, if no one below had escaped. But one defender, beloved by all, had died. Died, most likely, so the rest could live. And for the time being he must remain where he fell. The stone covering the entrance at the top was slid back in place with a dozen large rocks stacked on it.

Galen could say nothing. He had to be alone.

When the slow-witted boy was told what to do, he'd done it, always the first to take action and the last to back away, even when things were difficult. Never had he complained. If only...if only he hadn't asked him to move that last great stone, as important as it was to seal the entrance. So many enemy deaths! So 1100 were soon to be 900, what difference did it make? Safety for a few more days perhaps, but most rocks that could be thrown and nearly all of the oil was gone.

"I'm going for a walk — alone," the Prince announced. He turned and headed off for the same stairway on the south that had once taken him to the top of the wall.

"Not alone!" announced Millicent raising her voice.

So much for his authority, but what did it matter now?

"Mira, come here!" said Millicent. Instantly the girl was there, Storie at her heels. "Mira, follow him, closely!" "And Storie, follow Mira and never be more than ten feet away." The young climber understood numbers. And Millicent had learned that being specific helped. "You three are to return together while the rest of us fix the evening meal.

"And Storie, do not let..."

"Don't worry, Mother!" the girl interrupted. "He's got nothing more to prove, and besides, we won't let him!"

"Thank you, Millicent!" said Soren. For a second, Galen glanced back. The twin was smiling. At least he could have a few moments of peace and quiet. "Thank you!" he said again.

Storie turned and glared.

Soren smiled back.

"Storie, take care of Galen," said the twin. "You already know I'm your slave. I'm only here because of you." His smile widened. He extended his good arm. "You saved my life. And I'm yours."

Startled, Storie allowed a weak smile.

"Now when you grow up," he continued, "who knows, maybe we can—"

Weft slapped Soren on the back and doubled over, trying to hold back laughter.

"Not in a 100,000 years!" she hissed. Turning quickly, she started toward the other two and joined the smiling servant girl.

"Storie, isn't that a bit extreme?" asked Mira. "How about a 100,000 minutes instead?"

"Two months? No way, Mira! *He's* not that ready!"

"Storie! Two months? How do you do numbers like that? Is it really—"

"It's about half a day more than two months, really, Mira, but climbers learn to measure, guess at sizes and distances and do numbers quickly. Or else they die. Their lives count on it."

"Well, now Millicent's 'counting' on us!" said the servant girl.

383

"Really"—Storie pointed at her companion and cocked her head—"she's counting on *me*!" Both girls laughed and Galen tried to increase his distance from them. Mira put her fingers to her lips and the girls were silent. At the steps on the south side, Galen climbed to the platform. Since the boards would allow only two side by side, Galen led as if he were alone, the girls following several yards behind. Now and then, he would stop and peer over the wall. Automatically, the girls would stop, too, keeping their distance the same until he began again. No one spoke.

On the second circle around the wall, Storie stepped forward beside the Prince and took his hand. The boy flinched.

"Relax, I'm just your sister," Storie whispered, brushing her long hair away from her face.

"Sister?" said Galen.

"Yes, Prince Galen, like Millicent is my mother. And you made that happen. And after all we've been through, I declare myself to be your sister. And, as it happens, I—*usually*—enjoy being sister to a Prince." Storie felt a poke from behind. The young climber was silent for the rest of the time around.

At the beginning of the third time around the circle, she finally spoke again. "Mira, it's your turn with the Prince, and since I'm so tired of walking slow, I'm going ahead." She placed Mira's hand in Galen's, which neither seemed to object to, and she led the way not once looking back.

At the end of the third circuit, Galen descended the steps and sat in the grass against the wall, a girl on each side of him.

"You know, Pinrut was the lucky one," he said, staring ahead and offering his first words. "He was faithful in life and faithful in death, and he's *already* dead." How silly the words came. Mira began softly crying.

"I...I've been trying to put it out of my mind," she said. Galen turned and let his arm circle her. Tears fell upon the magnificent ring on the cord around her neck. Mira and the boy had come in the coach to Zareba together. How were they connected? Never had they discussed Mara's, Mira's, Pinrut's, and the dead Emperor's daughter's past. Mara had forbidden it and Galen honored her request.

"I'm sorry, Mira. I shouldn't have—"

"Prince Galen," interrupted Storie, "we're going to win."

"And how do you know?" asked Galen.

"Because Soren thinks so. Now he hasn't quite said it that way, but I know how he thinks. Would the God of Heaven bring us this far and then abandon us? I don't think so and neither does my mother." Galen shook his head and glanced over at Mira and smiled. How quickly she'd come to trust in the God of Heaven and his Son. "Oh, and Prince Galen"—almost always, it seemed, she used the word "Prince"—"there's still another reason."

"Which is?"

"We still haven't seen what the arrows will do!" Galen smiled.

His "private" walk was over. His grieving could wait along with theirs. The two girls, each taking one of his hands, led him back to the tower.

They were met by the smell of roast goose. There may not be any more vegetables, but there still was some goose…

✳ ✳ ✳

The table had plenty of space now with only six chairs around it. Despite everything, the meal was welcome, and eagerly eaten. "Nothing," said Millicent, "was to be said about losses or battles" until the plates were cleared. By prearrangement, Galen had asked the weaver to "add everything up."

"Master Weft, where do we stand?"

All eyes turned his way.

"First, Prince Galen, we did win the battle, and, setting aside our personal loss for the moment, our battle plan was magnificent and brilliantly carried out. We won, and won against tremendous odds! Let us never, never forget that! You were faithful to the Emperor and your father. And as unpleasant as it sounds, within three days, all who are not dead but trapped and injured down below will have died. They were warned in so many ways, but they acted like fools and have paid with their lives. And those next to clear away the rocks — whenever that may be — must first face the grisly task of removing the bodies in a place where foul odor is growing by the minute.

"How long that will take I'm not sure.

"We must never forget that it was our obedience that led to all this. We have pledged to God our lives and He may soon claim them.

"We have won the battle, but the war is far from over.

"The enemy has fallen from maybe 1100 to perhaps 900. Most important, their leader has been killed. But don't think he won't be replaced! And by someone perhaps even more evil who will trumpet that 'the hard work has been done,' and that the 'treasure' in here is just waiting to be taken.

"Yes, they *could* break up and leave — and quickly — as a few have already done after so much suffering. But the word must be out and circulating by a few at the entrance mouth who must have escaped and who may have concluded that we are few and must be running out of food.

"Which we are — of food, we may have two or three few weeks' worth of normal rations.

"Of wood for fuel, precious little.

"Of water — that will never be a problem.

"Or courage.

"In our favor are these things: First, our enemy is highly

superstitious. They don't know what forces are behind what we've done — or just what's inside here, for that matter. Second, the Emperor, if he's still alive, may return with an army, but I doubt if he suspects so many soldiers are here. Third, and most important: We're not fighting a holy war, but we are defending a sacred place, as well as our own land, from people who hate the God of Heaven, and we do this under orders from the Emperor.

"Lastly, I believe God has been with us. It's no accident that we had the oil we needed in battle. It is no accident that we sit here tonight with full stomachs. Or that we have a leader with purpose and brilliant strategy that I would never have expected." He glanced toward the Prince. "Or" — he pointed to his own chest — "an 'orator' now standing before you that would speak now like he's never spoken before.

"Yes, four of us have died, and so may the rest of us. But so be it! Things are far better than I ever thought they could be. We've lasted longer than I thought possible. And we serve the God of Heaven and his Emperor Charlayn III.

"That, Prince Galen, are the words I have for the people of your realm, and the army of Mt. Zareba."

Everyone smiled. And everyone stood. Galen called for water to fill everyone's cup.

"We drink today to the God of Heaven into whose hands we place our lives!"

They all raised the cups and drank the sweet water of the mountain.

And, despite sorrow and loss, they all cheered.

"The time has come to shoot the arrows!" announced Galen. Weft shook his head and smiled.

"There hasn't been a better time to shoot the arrows!" said the weaver.

As darkness drew nearly complete, the six studied the enemy below. King Stulk's body had been recovered and burned to ashes. And with new activity near the entrance at the base, almost everyone was now back on the western side. And no one was trying to climb up from the outside.

Everywhere in the west, people were talking, arguing. As the sun disappeared, several campfires sprang up. Their leader was dead. The sense of order of the past was unraveling. Comrades and friends had suddenly disappeared inside the mountain and were presumed dead. Drinking was more open, though with darkness everyone seemed to melt back into the safety of the campfires and tents of their own people, the locations of which had not greatly changed. Kegs of ale were visible everywhere. Conversations grew loud and bawdy.

"This is the time of their greatest weakness," said Galen.

"We need another hour," said Storie.

"For what?" asked Millicent.

"For them to get more drunk. They're fools to start with," said Storie. "But when drunk, they become even more stupid. And more darkness would be helpful."

At the last minute the arrows were carefully "aimed" and laid out on the platform instead of the ground. Weft and Galen were in place with their bows. Millicent had a pot of burning oil and a handful of rags.

"You're thinking this makes sense, aren't you?" said the Lady.

"Worth a try!" said the weaver, "What's to lose?"

"Our arrows," she said.

"Which is why they're here," he said. "Let's send them back points first! Why let them reclaim them up here in piles beside our dead bodies."

"The time has come, Prince Galen and Master Weft," said Storie. "They're all drunk, nasty drunk, something King Stulk would have never allowed."

"Pray for your *brother*," Galen told her.

"Thank you, Prince Galen!" She smiled. He'd accepted their new relationship. "I will. Now just wait and see what happens."

One by one, with Mira holding a light to erase the darkness, Galen and Weft shot the arrows over the wall. First the ones with notes, then, minutes later, arrows with fire.

It was the first hostile arrows sent down by the defenders.

Silence.

Had no arrows hit their mark? Could nobody find the messages and read them?

Then, from the centermost gathering of tents there was an orange glow as a pocket of flame began to get larger. Next, from both sides of the flame came loud cries. From a group of tents about thirty yards from the base of the mountain came the rattle of swords. Then arrows began to be shot from below — not up at the defenders, but at tents only yards away on the ground!

Millicent looked down.

"Okay, now about these messages. What message went there?" she asked, pointing to a tent at the left where yelling was coming from.

"Remember the roll call of the eight kingdoms?" Galen asked.

"How could I forget!"

"Well, down there on the left are the warriors of the Kingdom of Mordant and just to the right are those of the Kingdom of Gortran."

"So?" asked Millicent.

"Well, there's a rumor that the King of Mordant is not the Queen Mother's child, but the son of a prostitute from Gortran."

"And?" interrupted Millicent.

"And I used a Gortran-made arrow to remind those in Mordant

about that."

"That story's hardly a fact!" declared Millicent,

Down below a great blaze leaped from a tent in the Gortran camp, followed by yelling.

"What difference does it make? They're drunk and angry. And that *is* a fact!" He pointed down toward the tents of Ultior.

"And, Storie, what was it you had on the Kingdom of Ultior?" asked Weft.

"Oh, I have at least a dozen stories."

"Aha! At last I understand your name!" said Galen.

"And," asked the weaver, "do you have all the spicy words to go with these tales?"

"Master Weft" — the girl jutted out her chin — "I have all the words they need to understand, thank you."

"I remember Ultior," said Galen, who pretended to ignore the exchange. "Ultior happens to be an illegitimate kingdom stolen a hundred years ago out of the larger Kingdom of Sparton by a band of brown dragoons. The man who became the first King of Ultior took a Sparton princess by force and bore a son by her. That is a fact and a festering sore between these two kingdoms. Am I boring you?"

For several seconds there was silence. Galen pointed down to the right toward the tents of Belind and Franculin.

"Okay...see if I remember this right, Storie...in the case of Belind, thieves in the service of the King of Franculin are said to have stolen crown jewels from the Queen of Belind, who was said, because of the size of her ears, to have descended from a wild donkey. And — "

"Preposterous!" declared Weft.

"But they're DRUNK!" emphasized Galen, "and mad, and upset, and scared. With the right words drunken young men like these would fight to the death! Right, Millie?"

"I've seen them kill themselves over much less," said the white-

390

haired Lady, "but you're looking at an army down there! You're asking for an awful lot!"

"I am because I'm still able to," said the Prince, carefully sending out two more arrows.

"But can they *read*?" said Weft.

"They can usually read when they want to—or find someone to do it for them," said Storie. "A mysterious scrawled note on an arrow from another kingdom is too irresistible to ignore. Not only will they fight, but they'll try to outdo each other bragging about who'll do what to whom. They're from the south, you know. It's like throwing oil on fire."

"Like we've already done!" said Storie.

"And can do no more," said Weft.

"But won't they figure out what we're up to?" asked Millicent.

"That might be a little hard for them, Mother," said Storie. "And they know where those arrows came from—at least when they were first shot. Don't forget, they may be against us, but they don't trust each other! Not for a minute! And they're DRUNK!"

Ten minutes passed.

Suddenly from below came the loud ripping of tent canvas, followed by several men yelling. Five minutes after that, a fire rose from a tent roof in the west, then another from somewhere in the south. Then fire from a tent in between. To the rear, one commander's headquarters burst into flame. Soon, because of the smoke, little could be clearly seen, but much was heard: the clash of metal upon metal; the splintering of wood, perhaps as horses broke through a corral; the sound of broken glass, probably from windows in the village. From everywhere came cursing and yelling which led to more cursing and yelling. Hour after hour into the night it continued.

But not a single arrow arrived on the mountaintop.

"Unbelievable!" said Weft. "It's working! But how well though, remains to be seen." He turned to the boy and offered a slight bow. "Once again, it's an honor to be in your service! We've earned at least a few more days!"

For the time being, the mountain was safe.

✳   ✳   ✳

The day after the shooting of arrows Galen awoke and discovered that Weft, Soren, and Storie had used ropes and had removed the bodies of the two other enemy soldiers who'd made it into the passageway. Since burial had proven difficult on the mountaintop, the bodies were pushed over the wall. With the Prince's help, they cautiously rolled back the stone at the lower end of the passageway, and recovered the large boy's body. Already, the vast underground opening was silent. The great stone was rolled back in place and other stones were placed against it.

On the top of the mountain a proper grave was dug for Pinrut.

Afterwards, Galen, Storie, and Weft stood on the platform to determine the results of their second battle, where they convinced the enemy to fight against itself. Of the eight armies at the base of the mountain, three—Stelanz, Belind, and Gortran—had headed back for the south or were in the process of leaving. They'd had enough, and nobody seemed willing to stop them. According to Storie, those leaving were the "best of the worst." Galen prayed other kingdoms would follow, but that was not to be.

At least a hundred men lay dead or badly wounded. Men killed by jumping to the wrong conclusions. Dozens of graves were being dug by men with swords, bows, and spears nearby. Did they distrust each other that much? Some of the wounded were leaving on litters or in carts. Many would die because it was "the will of the gods," said Storie, and others still alive with serious injuries would be "discarded" along the way. That was their way, she said.

If that weren't bad enough, the circumstances of many soldiers within sight were even more horrible.

For reasons that escaped Galen, nearly a hundred men had been stripped, tied, and herded into a small fenced enclosure. Somehow they'd offended during the confusing night, and somehow those below with swords had won control. In a single night and the morning that followed, these soldiers had become slaves of their comrades — behavior strictly forbidden by the Emperor. The reason to keep these now-naked captives alive was obvious: to reopen the mountain entrance at any cost.

Most disturbing was a new leader who had appeared. Through his spyglass Galen and Storie studied this busy, energetic warrior who wore a white helmet with brown edges. Storie had no clue who he was. As the defenders watched, several warriors, probably leaders, knelt in a circle around the man and bowed while a screaming young woman was tied to a stake and burned alive. Millicent pulled Galen away from the wall.

"He's a brown dragoon," said the Prince. His hands were shaking.

"I've heard of them," said Storie, "but have never seen one."

"Occasionally, my grandparents faced them in the east. Somehow they're in allegiance with the Great Dragon and seem to have great power without the conscience of ordinary men. Some say they are possessed by the Great Dragon himself and are capable of great evil. Fortunately, there are only a few of them, say my parents, and the only one I ever saw wore the same helmet."

The Emperor's Daughter would no longer appear regularly on the wall.

"We've been successful," said the Lady of Zareba, "so successful that the Great Evil that hides behind ordinary evil has been forced into the open. We've not been wrong to fight. I pray to God that others may see what this rebellion has brought and now join us!"

Again, Storie reminded them about the new climbers, but their ropes and climbing harnesses were not hard to overlook.

And, according to Storie and Weft, the 900 warriors had been reduced to 400—including the new slaves—but the 300 hardened men with swords who were left would stop at nothing, and think nothing of spending the lives of their 100 slaves to reopen the entrance and force their way up to the mountaintop.

Two things seemed certain to the defenders:

First, they'd stopped the southern invasion from spreading further. Second, the war to capture the mountain was far from over.

CHAPTER 44

18
THE
BEGINNING OF
THE END

O n the fourth day after shooting the arrows, the new slaves, or what was left of them, finally cleared away enough stones to reenter the cavern.

But when Galen saw that the slaves who removed the first bodies through the narrow opening had to be flogged to crawl back inside, and he smelled the odor from the opening easily detected now at the top of the western wall, he knew that further attack wouldn't be immediate. But barring a miracle, their days were numbered.

Climbing the side of the mountain was easier now, but by no means a sure thing. Storie and Soren continually watched everywhere for anyone foolish enough to try.

Regular formal meals ended. People began to eat, sparingly by necessity, in the grass under the trees by the Chapel. From there most of the top could be seen.

As to the tunnel that led to where they'd fought: the oil and rocks were gone. There could be no more defending from the ledge. Rocks were piled against the closed stone door that led there. It could be broken through eventually, but not easily. The shallow pool at the top that once held oil was refilled with water.

Nearly all throwable rocks on the top were gone. With Maleg's bars, smaller rocks were broken from stones in the rubble of the third stone tower.

Everybody began to sleep in their clothes in the Chapel garden. The ground there had always been warm, and the first place to be free of snow. To everyone's surprise, the recently pruned fruit trees seemed to be growing rapidly, months ahead of schedule! Blossoms opened overnight and pollination by bees — ordinary ones — that suddenly appeared began the countdown to lining the tree limbs with fruit. But how soon? And would it matter?

Galen, Mira, Millicent, and Weft carefully observed the enemy at the western side. Galen watched and counted. The new leader, "King South" they called him, was patient. And therefore dangerous. He must know that time was on his side. Methodically, the bodies from the cavern were stacked and burned. At the cost of three slaves' lives, the opening was enlarged so that people could walk through standing.

Late in the afternoon on the seventh day after the shooting of arrows, the day the 110th body had been removed, dust appeared on the horizon from the east!

This didn't escape the enemy. Quickly, according to some prearranged plan, 250 soldiers, leaving 50 behind to guard the slaves, took up their weapons, and in three ranks, fanned out almost as far as Galen could see. What discipline! And with southern soldiers!

What the Prince saw next, at first couldn't have made him happier. But then almost broke his heart.

First, a flag appeared in the distance — the Emperor's flag with the familiar red X and stakes over a gold bar! No mistaking it! It was the same flag as atop the northwest tower. Behind it was a column of soldiers led by half a dozen knights. While still in the road a couple of hundred yards away, the Emperor's men fanned out into a long row, the flag held at the center. Slowly, they moved closer. On either side of the flag rode three knights. From the shine of their armor, it had to be remnants of the Palace Guard.

Quickly, 30 soldiers fanned out beyond the knights on each side. Galen raised his spyglass and counted again. No more than 70 men! They would be slaughtered. Was Sir Kerky or his father with them? Why was the Emperor so undermanned? Until recently, rebellion came from only small groups. But never in recent memory, said Weft, had the south been so unified.

"The Emperor's going to be caught off guard!" groaned Weft. "We see, but he can't!" Weft ran for Maleg's gong that until recently had only signaled supper or the appearance of the Emperor's daughter. He stood on the platform. Over and over he pounded out the signal of warning.

At once the Emperor's men stopped. They had heard! Methodically, they arrayed themselves, holding position. Weft and Galen could do no more.

But that wasn't all.

From the south, from the direction of the ruins of Zareba City rose more dust! Galen raised his spyglass.

Flags.

Flags from the south! From southern kingdoms. Flags, the same as those that had surrounded them for seven months.

There were hundreds more soldiers, many on horseback! And wagon after wagon of supplies. No wonder "King South" (whoever he was) was so confident! Reinforcements were on the way.

As the sun dropped down to set, the climbers ceased what seemed to be half-hearted activity. War again was threatening. Darkness forbade beginning any new battle before tomorrow. By this time tomorrow it would all be over. The Emperor himself along with any troops that survived would be the next to burn at the stake. And soon after, Mt. Zareba would fall.

Galen refused to eat. Or talk.

As darkness deepened, the six gathered in the garden, held hands and prayed. Weft reminded them that they'd been faithful and they'd done far more than anyone dreamed they'd ever do. Including him. The rest was in God's hands. Galen would fight until he died. He sensed everyone else felt the same.

Then they all lay back in the warm grass of the chapel garden and stared at the stars. There was a warm breeze. The moon was full and rising, bathing them with light. Pale shadows of swaying limbs of the mysterious trees played back and forth on the wall of the chapel.

One by one they all fell asleep.

Everyone but Galen.

Silently, he rose and made his way to the front side of the chapel. Pulling back the massive door, he entered and walked down the aisle. At the rail in front he knelt.

He lifted his eyes to the familiar stained glass window overhead. With moonlight behind it, he stared at the simple rendering of the blood-stained wooden stakes of the God-Son lying on top of the Golden Chest of Promise that had been lost centuries earlier.

The Chest had been the focus of attention for the race of people, Galen's people, from whom God had chosen the mother of the God-Son. It was the centerpiece of worship — not that the box was worshipped, but God, who was said to dwell immediately above it in a hidden room in the old Temple.

But the Chapel window was also deceptive, pulling together symbols that were centuries apart. Never had the stakes rested on the Chest.

Later the stakes had become prominent because of how the God-Son had died. First beaten by whips, he was pinned to the sandy ground under the hot sun by stakes driven through his hands and feet. There he died, and was buried only to rise again three days later. It was these stakes, attached to an X showing how the God-Son's arms and legs were spread out, over the bar of gold representing God's promise of Heaven, that was displayed on the Emperor's flag that was so despised by those below.

The gold bar, and symbol of Heaven. How many hours until he was there?

"I've tried, God. I've tried. But I've failed. Why...why have you let us come so far only to fail?" Tears rolled down his cheeks.

When he wiped his eyes with his sleeve, he was aware that someone was kneeling beside him.

"You haven't failed, Galen. You've been called to do hard things, but you've always been faithful to the God of Heaven...And...and I love you." Raising her own sleeve, she wiped his cheeks.

"I love you too, Mira. I'm...I'm so sorry that..."

"Sorry about what?"

"It doesn't matter now. That silly promise my father made to the Emperor who, if we lived, would make us...me...obligated to... But I'm sorry too about dying. We're going to die, you know. Whether we fight or surrender. And so many have died already. Perhaps we deserve it."

"Galen, look at me." She turned his face toward hers. The ring around her neck bumped him on the chest.

"Dear sister..."

"No, no, Galen, ring or no ring, I'm not your sister! Storie's your sister. I heard her announce that herself! And you never objected. And from what I've—we've—seen of her she's all the sister you'll ever need! Are we clear about that?"

"Okay." He smiled, carefully holding back other words. She looked deeply into his eyes.

"Now listen to me. You did what your father asked. You did what the Emperor asked. Even far more than they asked or expected. Look how you delayed King Stulk and spared the dozens of towns and cities to the north. Many women and children probably live today, and live with their honor, because of what you did.

"And as for us—yes, Pinrut died. And Mara. And I loved them more than you did. And Maleg died and Saren. They all believed as you, and chose their way. Now they're in a far better place. We who are left are on a beautiful mountain. There's no place I'd rather live. Even with a wall that needs to be watched, dishes that need to be washed, as well as clothes, books that can be read, and even dirt where Storie can forever scratch out words.

"Yes, we may die, Galen. But I've already seen a beautiful girl die instead of me." Now her eyes filled with tears. "But, Galen, I'll join those wonderful people because of you!

"As to the others down below, Galen, you always gave them a choice, a chance. The Emperor loves the God of Heaven far more than you may imagine. And you did what he wanted more than anything: occupy and defend this place that is Holy to God."

She glanced up at the stained-glass picture.

"And you...you defended me."

Then, as if a cloud had crept over the moon and suddenly danced away, a beam of light burst through the window, illuminating the Golden Chest, and falling on the pulpit just above them. Mira was staring and Galen could see her dark eyes.

"Why do you trust me so?" he asked.

"Because...maybe for the same reason you trust me. You do, don't you?" Gently she pushed away and seemed to stare at the window even more intently. Then she glanced up to the massive pulpit looming over them. "Galen, I want to see you one last time behind the pulpit."

"Okay, but you come with me."

She fingered the ring hanging from the cord around her neck.

"If you think it's okay."

Moonlight penetrating the colored window was their only light. Slowly their eyes adjusted to the dimness. She lifted the hem of her dress and together they ascended the almost hidden step to the platform.

Behind the pulpit lay a small, thick rug that had been woven by Master Weft's own hand. As Galen shuffled forward, his boot caught under the rug's edge just as Mira's foot came down on his toes. Off balance, he stumbled, slipping out of his boot and falling sharply forward, pulling Mira on top of him.

On the way down his shoulder crashed against the pulpit.

As his hand slipped down the wood, his fingers caught on an iron bar, which he supposed was a brace anchoring the great pulpit to the floor. To his surprise, the bar pulled away from the wood and bent down to the floor.

Suddenly, there was a loud scraping, and slowly the massive pulpit began to move, grinding its way across the floor turning around a similar-looking vertical iron bar on the pulpit's far side, which served as a pivot.

A rush of air struck Galen's face.

Where the pulpit once stood was a large gaping hole! When Galen reached for his boot, it slipped from his fingers over the edge.

Thumpa thumpeta thump thump thump thump.

"Stairs!" said Galen. "There are stairs that circle down…and…and there's a railing!"

CHAPTER 45

19
DOWN FROM ABOVE

mmediately, Galen started down. The vertical passage was pitch black, but the stairway was narrow, dry, and the railing solid. By extending his arms he could, in most places, touch the wall on each side.

The girl followed.

"Mira, it's filthy—your dress—it...wait, I'll just get my boot and..."

"Don't worry about my clothes, Galen, I'm coming! You're not leaving me!"

"Are you afraid?" he asked.

"No. You?"

"No. Not yet. My fear's about used up! But, I can change my mind!"

Around and around the stairway, holding tightly to the railing they descended, into the air rushing up the stone chimney. The rubbing of her dress, his jacket and single boot against the black stone sides and the steps, and the weird echo of their voices erased any chance of undetected entry. But entry to where? And who would be there to listen?

About 20 feet below the chapel floor, they came to what seemed like a bottom. Reaching down, Galen fingered something soft. Mira came down beside him and with one hand on the railing and another on his collar, Galen bent to use both hands to put on and tie the boot. Just as he slipped it on, there was a loud scraping overhead. They looked up and watched their faint and only light scissor shut ushering in complete darkness as the great pulpit slowly slid back in place. His ears rang. The air rushing up immediately stopped.

"Galen, did somebody do that?" He circled her with his arm, partly to steady himself.

"But who it could be?" he said. "I think it went back by itself."

"You're sure?"

"No. Afraid now?" he asked.

"No." She reached up and accidentally poked his cheek. She found his hand.

"Why not?"

"Galen, the pulpit may be many things, but it just can't be an instrument of death to someone who believes. That's one reason..."

"There's another?" he asked.

"I'm not alone," she answered.

"You mean because I'm here?"

"God is here, Galen!"

"Oh..."

"Oh, nothing! You're my *third* reason, Galen." She laughed and squeezed his hand. "Okay, my breath's come back. Let's go on!"

"Then it has to be *down*," said Galen. "We've nothing to gain if we just go back."

"Of course we must go down."

With hands always glued to the railing, they shuffled forward several steps until once again the railing dipped and the stairs spiraled straight down, down, down. Here and there was a short walk sideways on a flat surface, but overall the carefully cut tunnel seemed like a nearly vertical drop, adjusted maybe for safety if someone grew weary going down or climbing back, or perhaps it was because of the nature of the rock itself. When finally the stairs abruptly ended, they entered another tunnel, but one wide enough so they could walk side by side, joining hands, while Galen clung to the ever-present railing. The air was warm, but not hot, certainly not cool as most caves are deep underground.

"Galen, are we at the bottom of the mountain?"

"At the bottom? I think so, or at least close to it."

It was then that it dawned on Galen that he could see, but the light was so faint he couldn't tell where it came from. He stopped and turned the girl toward him and stared.

"Mira, you're the most beautiful girl I've ever seen!"

With both hands she started to push him away, but then she laughed, brushed her hair away from her face, pulled him close, and gave him a little squeeze.

"Galen, sometimes darkness isn't as bad as people think."

"Then the Emperor's Daughter loves me?"

"Maid Mira loves you, Galen—and wears your ring," she corrected.

With their next steps the tunnel turned abruptly to the right. And from the right side came the growing sound of falling water. Here the tunnel widened even more. On the right a sheet of steamy water poured down into a scoured-out bowl in the tunnel floor. From there it entered a trench at the edge before disappearing several feet later through a long crack. Otherwise, the tunnel floor was remarkably dry.

The "waterfall," which rose to seven feet and was almost as wide, didn't spill over solid rock. Oddly, the water itself glowed buttery yellow and was, as Galen soon realized, the source of nearly all their light. Though the tunnel went further straight ahead, the waterfall had to be a doorway to somewhere else on the right.

Galen thrust his hand into it, wetting his sleeve up to his shoulder. There was space behind it, how much he couldn't say.

"Look!" interrupted Mira. The Prince turned back to the tunnel that ran ahead to where the girl was pointing. To his surprise, it seemed to end just thirty feet ahead, yet light, very faint light, seemed also to be coming from the window at the end. She tugged his arm. "Look! A tiny window with small panes of glass!"

Side by side they crept forward, leaving the noise of the waterfall behind them. Finally, it dawned on the Prince that the light straight ahead came from the moonlit night sky outside! How brightly the light contrasted with the dark gray of the tunnel!

But just to the side of the window there was something else. Galen stopped. It was a man! A man crouched over with light just catching the top of his head. Mira's fingers tightened on Galen's arm. He drew his dagger and inched forward. Nothing moved.

"In the name of the God of Heaven, stand!" Galen commanded. "Stand and identify yourself!"

No movement.

"Stand!" he repeated.

Still nothing.

"I...I think he's dead," said Mira.

They inched closer. Galen bent over. The man's skin was paper thin and the skull and ribs and other bones seemed like tent poles holding up shrunken canvas.

"How did he die?" he asked aloud.

"There...there's no smell," said Mira.

"And no evidence of decay," added Galen. "Still, he was once living, and now he's dead. Something we should not ignore, I feel."

"Look, Galen, at his right arm! His hand—it's shrunken like it's almost withered away! And look at his clothes! I don't recognize them! And the layers of dust! Look, he's barefoot! Barefoot in a stone tunnel

405

of all places!"

"Mira, the clothes are from our own people — still they're strange-looking. They...they've got to be old. Like a hundred years or so. Maybe more. How did he get in? And when?"

The Prince tugged at the window latch. With a loud squeak that shivered him to his toes, the window came open. He pulled it all the way to the right side. His head just barely fit outside. The opening, too small to crawl through, was recessed deep into the rock, and a tangle of briers and rose bushes pushed out three feet further, hiding the window from view on the ground. Through the tunnel of briers he could just barely see the remains of Zareba City 20 miles away.

They had to be no more than 30 to 40 feet above the ground at the mountain base, where the rock was sheer and wouldn't yield to climbers. It wasn't another way in — or out. How fortunate briers grew there! Or had they been planted long ago?

The dead man was expressionless. He would give no clues.

So what had they discovered? The tunnel seemed a dead end. The answer, if there was one, had to be at the waterfall.

When they again faced the glowing water, Mira insisted it resembled a looking glass at midnight in the Emperor's Palace, one where you could see your whole self from head to toe. But no reflection of any kind was given here.

Then Galen saw the writing cut deeply into the stone on one side:

HOLY GROUND
REMOVE SHOES
ALL WHO LOVE GOD MAY ENTER

It was Mira's turn. She pointed to the floor at the right of the falling water. There, covered by grime, were ancient shoes unlike any Galen had ever seen. He picked up one and it fell apart. The two looked at each other, then he glanced back at the man, whose outline was just barely visible.

"Mira…I'm going in!"

"Galen—"

"Mira—" He felt a tap on his shoulder and turned. The girl was already barefoot. "You'll get wet."

"So? You're *not* going in without me! What do you think I am, an Emperor's Daughter?"

"You certainly talk like one!"

"Galen, how do *you* know what an Emperor's Daughter is like?"

"Well…well…opinionated, spoiled, I've heard."

"Puuuleeese, please"—suddenly she knelt and looked up—"The Emperor's Daughter that you have seen is one of your own creation. Now, Prince Galen, Maid Mira beseeches you to let her take off your boots." Her voice was so soft Galen shivered.

"Who am I talking to?" he asked.

"Who?"—her voice was still soft—"just one ordinary girl. Maid Mira's her name, Maid Mira, the girl who loves you and wears this." She touched the ring around her neck, then dropped her eyes as if embarrassed. Though she snapped them back up, her tongue was gentle. "You're not going in without me! Now give me your foot, my Prince. We must do it properly."

"I will enter properly, but I will put on and take off my boots myself. I am *not* an Emperor's son…" And so he did.

Barefoot, he took her hand, paused, and stepped quickly into and through the golden looking glass, pulling the girl behind him. The waterfall was no more than four inches thick, but just as Galen's foot landed on the other side, it skidded ahead, causing just enough delay for the water to pour down through his jacket and shirt. Mira, in her servant dress, caught the warm water full force.

It was a doorway and they were inside some kind of natural room.

407

Mira coughed. Water poured from their clothes.

"Sorry, I slipped!"

"Galen, it's okay."

She pulled the dripping dress away from her skin and pushed wet strands of hair out of her face, then smiled. How beautiful her hair shone in the golden light. He told her, and she looked at him as if he were crazy. He bent over to kiss her cheek. She gently squeezed his hand and pushed away.

"No, Galen, we don't know where we are."

Light! They were in a natural, nearly circular room somewhere in the center of the mountain and they could see each other! The cave, with its almost perfectly flat stone floor, was twenty feet across and more than twice as high, with parts of the ceiling lost in darkness. Mira pointed to the buttery beam of light rising from a huge stone crypt, or box, up against the far wall, if it were not part of the wall itself. The box seemed hollow, because over it, and shoved slightly back on one side was a slab of cut rock which, if in its proper place would seal the opening and cut off the source of light.

But whoever moved the lid hadn't slid it back properly. This allowed a triangle-shaped opening at the left front corner. And from whatever was inside, up rose a beam of golden light that spread out like a partially open fan on its way to the ceiling. The beam that tilted slightly to the side was what allowed them to see.

They tiptoed to the opening, leaned against the crypt, and looked inside.

"Galen, the light's coming from a box! Yet there's no fire, no lamp, no candle! It's from the box itself!...Just like the box in the window upstairs! Could it be—"

The intensity of the light made her look up. When she did, she saw something lying on top of the flat stone lid. It was wood, sharpened pieces of rough wood, four stakes darkened with age. Then her eyes rose to the wall above them.

"Galen, look at the words!"

Just above the stakes, ten rows of capital letters, written in the ancient way without any punctuation, were cut into the wall:

WORSHIP NOTHING HERE
EXCEPT THE GOD OF HEAVEN
FOR HE IS ONE AND HE MADE ALL THINGS
HE INVITES YOU TO HOLD
THE STAKES
FOR HE DIED AND ROSE AGAIN
THAT YOU MIGHT LIVE
WITH HIM
FOREVER
PRAISE HIS HOLY NAME

Galen reached for the stakes. For several seconds he just held them. Tears ran down his cheeks. Mira was crying, too. She bent over and started to reach down to the glowing chest inside.

"No, Mira, don't touch!" He pulled her back sharply. "The Holy Book is very clear about that! Here, hold the stakes. That's okay, even though...even though that may be...*must* be...the very wood that pinned the God-Son to the ground as he died for our sins." He handed her two of them.

"Why can't we open, or even touch, the Golden Chest of Promise now?" she asked.

"I'm not sure," said Galen. And maybe I'm wrong. I think the dead man at the end of the tunnel has given us a warning. Remember his hand? I think he's the one who moved the stone lid. And then touched the chest. In pain, perhaps dying, he ran back through the waterfall so, as God would have it, he wouldn't defile this place by dying inside.

"I…we, we've touched, even leaned against the stone crypt, and are unharmed. But the Holy Book says nothing about a holy stone crypt. This must be a place of hiding when the Temple with its Holy Place was destroyed. And later, as the carved words suggest, this became a secret place of worship. Not everything has an easy answer."

"Galen, the God-Son has come, lived here, and gone back to Heaven. So why does the Chest still exist?"

"Mira, I'm not sure. Perhaps to remind us of the holiness of God, which Weft says we often forget. Maybe it will be used when the God-Son comes back again to reign. The Chest reminds us of the seriousness of what God expects; the stakes remind us of salvation, the price it cost, and our future hope. Maybe the Emperor can explain it. Mira…I can't explain it… but…Mira, the Emperor's coming back!"

"Galen, as Prince of this mountain, you are guardian of the greatest treasures on Emryss!"

The Prince fell to his knees and began to cry. When he saw his tears fall upon the stakes he held, he jumped to his feet and started to wipe them off with his shirt. But it was already wet. Gently, Mira took the stakes from his hands and placed them and the two she held back on top of the stone slab where they'd found them.

"Galen, you've done nothing wrong. The God-Son let a doubter touch the scars in his hands that these stakes made. He wouldn't be displeased." Then after she realized what she said, she began to cry.

The Prince raised his eyes.

"I wonder if the Emperor even knows all this is here!" he said.

"I doubt it, but I think we'll soon find out! You said he was coming! And don't worry, I'll help you bring him!"

"Mira, we've got to get back up!"

"Not yet, Galen."

"What?"

"First, we've got to pray! See how well you've taught me?" He raised his eyebrows and she smiled. "See how well I know you? Better than any spoiled Emperor's Daughter could!"

Then, though Galen couldn't understand why, their smiles melted away and both began openly sobbing. There was no attempt to hide. They joined hands and walked back to the center of the room.

At first they took turns praying, raising their voices louder and louder above the continual sound of falling water. Slowly Galen felt a warm breeze. Wind from nowhere began to stir and circle the room as if it were alive, touching, swirling, sweeping the stone and making spray. The girl's wet hair whipped out and stung his cheeks. Both began to tremble as words of sorrow and regret escaped from their lips. How could they possibly be standing in the presence of God? Galen, horrified, pressed the girl and himself facedown on the rock floor. Moments of his past flipped through his mind, and as he learned later, hers as well. Together, they cried for mercy, for forgiveness for forgotten things that now burst into their minds, things a holy God should never see.

Mira was sobbing loudly. The wind began rushing faster and faster in the circle. Still on their faces, he locked the fingers of one hand with Mira's hand for fear that she, as well as he, would be blown back against the wall, though neither body actually moved.

For Galen, memories of Zareba Village raced back. Then darker closets opened. Things that no one should see. In his mind he flew to the mountain, stood on the high wall, only to trip and fall, pulling Pinrut, Saren, Maleg, and Mara after him. He had killed—killed hundreds to keep hundreds away. Or so he'd said. To serve the Emperor, or so he thought. How clever he'd been! How proud! How arrogant! How protected!

The girl also was expressing anguished words as loudly as he. He felt naked. A wave of shame swept over him and he begged God to just let him disappear from this holy place. How unworthy, how unworthy

411

to be in the presence of a holy God! Together they thanked God for his salvation and many, many things they'd forgotten about and had taken for granted.

They begged for the safe return of those they loved. Finally, they confessed how helpless they were, and pled for wisdom to live good and honorably in the years, or months, or weeks, or days, or hours they had left.

Then as quick as their words had first come, Galen knew the time for them had ended. Silence rang in his ears until time took away the ringing. And, though each had cried out in the presence of the other, the memory of all she said melted away. Later she would say the same was true about what he had said.

His forehead still pressed against the stone floor as if it were a pillow, and the girl also still lay on her face three feet away, with only their fingers locked together. A blanket of God's presence dropped over him. He dared not move an inch lest the invisible covering pull up at a corner and slip away. Would the girl ever speak to him again? But why would it matter! Then, as quickly as it came, the wind died away. The peace of God fell like a mist, and he melted into the hard stone under him. Then the words

"My child, my child, my child,
You are forgiven for My Name's Sake,
You are forgiven for My Name's Sake,
You are forgiven for My Name's Sake"

echoed again and again in his ears, and in the girl's too as he found out later.

Without moving a muscle, each fell into a deep sleep.

CHAPTER 46

20
AN
EXCHANGE
OF MESSAGES

alen slept.

But that was not all. In a vivid dream, a voice broke his silence: "Prince Galen, when the High Prince of Zareba comes to rule you are to tell him: *'Thus says the God of Heaven:* *'Within a year you will be mightily blessed. But that firstborn child of yours will be mine. At a time when you least suspect, I will take that child away to another world, to do my will. You will never see that child in your world again. But do not mourn, it is my will. I am more than enough for you. If you and your child follow me, I will never leave or forsake the child or you.'*"

How strange and disturbing! How glad it wasn't for him. His rule, if not his life itself, was at its end. After it was over, if he lived, he would pack what few things he had and—

"He felt a poke in his ribs.

"Galen, wake up!" He lifted his head.

"What?" His first thought was the absurd idea that he lay, where none of the defenders ever had, in the great bed in the King's Room at the top of the tower. But instead, a girl sat beside him on the stone floor where he still lay on his stomach. And they were alone.

"Galen, I've never felt more at peace!" Her face reflected the soft glow of the buttery beam of light. "I think I've even been given a prophecy!"

He rubbed his eyes and pushed up from the floor into a sitting position. The servant girl rose to her knees, carefully keeping her distance, and smoothed out her dress and pushed back her hair. He felt his cheeks redden. Never had he awakened like this! He scooted himself back a foot. She smiled. Such a disturbing dream and still feeling at peace! A peace they seemed to share. How deep had he slept! The girl as well, apparently.

He was embarrassed, yes, and it probably showed. But no guilt. That had been washed away.

And danger? Yes, he sensed that. But fear, no. Just peace.

"A prophecy, Mira? Tell me about it."

"I...I am to give a message to the High Prince and Princess of Mt. Zareba," she answered.

Could they've had the same dream? Or had he talked while he slept?

"A message, Mira? Did it disturb you?"

"Oh, not at all! It was a wonderful message! The message to both the High Prince and High Princess was, *'Thus says the God of Heaven: Within a year you are to be greatly blessed. You will be given a son. And if your firstborn son obeys me, he will reign on Mt. Zareba after you. Train up a child in the way he should go, and he will not depart from it.'*

"Galen, if this is true, the mountain will be spared!"

The Prince turned his head and felt the hair stand up on his arms. He stared into the strange golden beam rising from the corner of the crypt. *God, O God, O God, how can this be?* he said to himself. Slowly, the beam grew wider, but as the puzzled girl turned to see what held his attention, he sensed that she had seen no change at all. Words from the light soundlessly echoed in his head:

I will do what I will do. I am the Truth, the Way, and the Life. Believe in Me. And do not forget the words I gave you. They are from me. Cover the crypt and go. You and the girl are needed above.

"Galen! Galen! Are you okay?" She tilted her head and tried to look more serious. "Do you know where we are?"

The strange beam now looked as it did before, but from a tiny spear-like hole in the rock in the wall overhead, a ray of sunlight poked in from some crack that led outside.

It was morning! How late? How long had they slept?

"Uh…where we are? Uh…somewhere hundreds of feet under the Chapel, I'd guess, almost at the bottom of the mountain."

"Very good, Galen!"—she was imitating Millicent—"Actually, Galen, since we came almost straight down, then turned the way we did to face Zareba City through the window, I'd say we're *just in front of the Chapel,* unless my sense of direction is—"

"*Under the Chapel garden!*" interrupted the Prince. "Remember the fruit! And"—Galen smiled—"do you know what we're in?"

"The secret hiding place of the Golden—"

"Oh yes, that's very, very true," Galen interrupted. "But that's not all we're in!"

"What, Galen?"

"We're in serious trouble up above!" He offered a faint smile.

"I forgot!" The girl raised a hand to cover her smile in an attempt to look more serious. Her words in the Secret Chamber were finished.

He looked up.

"Help us, God, get back to the top."

"Amen." Though her lips moved, the word was silent.

Galen walked to the crypt. They hadn't been harmed by touching, even leaning on the stone the night before. Slowly, he carefully slid the lid back in place. The buttery beam disappeared and the spear of daylight was the only light that let them see to move around in the

415

great room.

In the dim light the sound of the water seemed to grow louder.

This time Mira, holding his hand, entered the waterfall first. Then stopping halfway, and moving slowly, she ensured that this time the Prince got a complete drenching. But on the other side, both were so wet that their shoes wouldn't go over their feet, so they carried them. With hands on the railing, they retraced their way back in the light from the tiny window to the "chimney" where the steps this time went up.

Galen sat on the bottom step.

"Your shoes, Mira."

She held them out.

"Your foot, please."

"No Prince will ever put shoes on Maid Mira!"

"Overruled!" he declared. Slowly and gently he drew up the girl's foot from where she stood. "And don't slip!" With little effort he eased the first shoe on and then the other. Then he put on his own boots and stood.

"Now it's okay," she said. "And it's far enough away."

"What's okay?" he asked.

"It just wouldn't have been right while we were in the Secret Chamber, and I wouldn't have wanted it."

"Wanted what?"

"You to kiss me on the cheek, remember?"

"But I can't do that!"

"And why not?"

"Because that stuff's for sisters like Storie and —"

"But, but you said —"

In total darkness, his hands found her cheeks. Then his lips found hers. They were warm. She trembled. Then he ran his fingers through her hair, stopping to squeeze some of the water out. Then he put his arms around her and squeezed again, and kissed her again. Water ran from their clothes like water spilling from a pitcher. He pushed away.

"No, Galen, you aren't done," she laughed.

"Not done?"

"I'm still very wet. You must squeeze me dry! Aren't you worried about what Millicent will say?"

"Millicent? Do you think she's in charge down here?"

She fell into his arms and he squeezed and kissed her again.

"I love you," he said.

"I love you!" she answered. Gently again he pushed away. "Why, Galen…?"

"Re…remember, it's not Millicent, not me, it's God who rules down here. What would—"

"O…kay, Galen"—she paused—"let me see…if I'm to love a GREAT PRINCE who loves God, as I do, let me remind you"—she stopped and laughed—"we must be 'honorable' and I must think differently, right? And not like the rest. So I think…I think—"

"'I think' what?" he interrupted.

"I think I'm probably dry enough!" She laughed again and gave him an obvious peck on the cheek as Millicent might, and pulled herself up a couple of steps. "We have to get to the top! But, Galen"—she pushed out her arm to keep him from joining her—"right before we open the door under the great pulpit, you must kiss me one more time. Promise? You know, it might be our last time. The Emperor's coming, I just know it, and he keeps his promises, and I'd be very surprised if his daughter isn't with him!"

Galen promised. It was surprising how quickly they made it to the top. Fulfilling his promise took a bit longer.

※　※　※

As Galen expected, there was a lever under the floor, and when he pulled it, the great pulpit slid to the side. With a little jump, the Prince stepped out and onto the platform.

What happened next, Storie loved to repeat with certain embellishments — but only to certain people who, like her, were sworn to secrecy.

As one would expect, the four defenders at the top had become frantic. Millicent had awakened in the garden in the middle of the night, and finding Galen and Mira missing, she — and everyone — had combed every inch of the mountain over and over. After first being angry, Millicent had gone mad with worry.

The Lady of the Mountain was inconsolable.

Barely fifteen minutes before the Prince had suddenly appeared at mid-morning, Weft, Soren, and Storie had led her into the Chapel. Up at the altar, they had knelt and fervently prayed. At the exact moment they finished, the great pulpit above them slid noisily to the side.

Everyone jumped back. Everyone, that is except Millicent who fainted dead away, which was something she was proud that she'd never done! Fortunately, Soren caught her. (Later when Storie asked if fainting was part of becoming a Lady, Millicent was furious.)

When the Lady of the Mountain opened her eyes, Galen and Mira were standing before them, Weft was struggling to catch his breath, and everyone was suddenly crying or laughing or both.

"Millicent," said Soren, "why be so afraid when you pray and God answers you? Where's your faith?" He extended his good arm. Weft, now able to breathe, laughed.

The Lady ignored them. Her eye caught the appearance of the girl's clothes.

"Where...wherever have you — "

Weft jumped as the great pulpit suddenly, on its own, scraped along the floor back into place.

"Is it a way to escape?" the weaver asked.

"Escape?" said Galen. "Why should we escape? The Emperor is coming!"

"Yes, he's coming!" Mira chimed in.

"From down there?" asked Weft pointing.

"I don't think so," said Galen. "What we've found is hardly a way out—at least in the way you're thinking."

"You know the Emperor is coming?" asked Soren.

"No, but I...feel it," said Galen.

"And I feel it too," added Mira.

"You feel it, you say!" snapped Millicent. "What else do you feel?"

"Who's guarding the wall?" Galen shot back, pointing back in the direction of the colorful window. Millicent glared. Her questions, which would be thorough, would come later if they lived long enough.

Weft interrupted:

"Galen, do you two have any idea what's going on down there?" For the first time the Prince saw fear in the man's eyes.

Leaving the Chapel, they ran to the wall. The sun had climbed to midmorning, and the sky, in contrast to what was going on under it, promised to be clear. From somewhere Millicent produced a towel and a comb for the servant girl, ignoring the Prince. Soren brought a handful of dried goose from the tower for the two to eat.

Telling about the adventure inside the mountain must wait, because down below, other disturbing events were taking place.

On the ground closest to Zareba City, more southern reinforcements had just set up camp a hundred yards away from the mountain base, probably stopping near where they first appeared. Now 200 men in armor—Weft had counted them—were slowly moving toward the mountain to join the 50 southerners who guarded the slaves. And alongside the new soldiers came supplies—even women! The old army of 250 that had left was nowhere in sight.

When the guards of the slaves saw flags above the wagons, they began cheering. One by one they secured the slaves and laid down their weapons. Several even began beating drums. Isolation and security was over. The discipline and drudgery of recent weeks had paid off. The defenders' days had become hours, numbered hours. Victory and celebration were at hand. One, then another and another, and finally all the remaining soldiers broke into a run to welcome the newcomers. There would be women, fresh food, new clothes, and wine.

Galen had never felt as shabby. And hungry. The handful of goose wasn't enough. His mouth was powdery dry. Mira, ignoring looks from Millicent, held Galen's hand. At the wall, Storie leaned against Soren and he circled her with his good arm. Millicent and Weft stared down over the wall in silence.

When the first of the guards reached the fresh troops, an animated discussion took place while the others caught up. Suddenly, when half had arrived, the soldier on horseback leading the column barked an order Galen couldn't understand. The men behind him fanned out in battle formation.

The cheering ceased. The new soldiers came closer.

Then the leader yelled a second command and something very unusual took place. Down fell the flags of the southern kingdoms. Up came a dozen new flags which had been carefully hidden away — white flags displaying the red X with the stakes of the God-Son at each point. Then coverings on the shields were pulled away, emblems bearing signs of the Emperor, and other northern kings were exposed. And, as Storie pointed out, not every southern flag was put away. Some still flew on staffs but under the Emperor's banner.

The surprise was so sudden that the enemy guards, not the best fighters to start with, threw down what few arms they still carried without so much as the drawing of a sword.

It was the slaves turn to cheer!

Millicent scanned the troops with an Elphian spyglass. But Sir Kerky was nowhere in sight, nor was Lord Fairold, nor the Emperor, nor anyone she knew. Was this some trick? It was almost noon. Before darkness, their control of the mountain would be over.

Galen made his decision.

Minutes later, Weft sounded the gong. The Prince stood on the wall for a final time with the Emperor's Daughter. He held and waved the Emperor's flag. Everything below stopped. All eyes were on the top of the wall. Though many seemed to be talking to each other, there was no cheering! Weft and Millicent looked bewildered.

Then came an arrow with this message:

WHO ARE YOU?
HOW MANY ARE UP THERE?
WHOM DO YOU SERVE?
WHAT WOULD YOU HAVE US DO?
    – General Sarcrage
    of the Kingdom of Narland,
    in the service of Emperor Charlayn III

Narland, said Storie, was a southern kingdom. Millicent was irritated by the curtness of the note.

" 'Who are we?' Really! They never even told us what's going on!" she said.

"Maybe they really don't know," offered Weft. After all, Narland is far away, and we've done our best to confuse everyone about what's up here! Let's not complain that they know less than we do."

Fortunately, over winter the defenders of the mountain had learned to make ink of charcoal mixed in fine oil. Now, said Galen, an important moment had come. Without hesitation, he took a pen and one of the few sheets of blank paper they had left, and wrote the following:

421

WHO? I AM PRINCE GALEN, RULER
OF THIS MOUNTAIN BY THE WILL
OF LORD FAIROLD AND
EMPEROR CHARLAYN III

HOW MANY?   ENOUGH

WHOM DO WE SERVE?   THE GOD OF
HEAVEN AND THE EMPEROR

WHAT SHOULD YOU DO?

1. ANY SLAVE BELOW WHO WILL
PLEDGE ALLEGIANCE TO THE
EMPEROR SHOULD BE GIVEN
FOOD AND OUTER CLOTHES
FROM THEIR CAPTORS WHO
BROKE THE EMPEROR'S LAW
ON SLAVERY, AND THEY SHOULD
BE ALLOWED TO RETURN HOME
WITH NO FURTHER QUESTIONS
ASKED.

2. ONE TERRIBLE TASK REMAINS: MAKE
THOSE YOU HAVE JUST CAPTURED
FINISH CARRYING OUT THE REST
OF THE BODIES INSIDE THE
WESTERN ENTRANCE, FINISHING
WHAT THEY MADE OTHERS DO.
THEY MAY BE SENT HOME TOO
WITHOUT WEAPONS AND WITH
ONLY THE CLOTHES THEY HAVE
LEFT, OR WHAT YOU
VOLUNTARILY PROVIDE.

3. RUSH TO THE EMPEROR'S AID. HE'S
IN DANGER IN THE NORTH. GO

**TO HIM AS A REPRESENTATIVE
OF PRINCE GALEN OF AERON AND
HE WILL WELCOME YOUR HELP.**

Galen held out the sheet. Softly, Soren whispered the words quickly to Storie as she followed them with her finger. Millicent shook her head, but smiled.

"Prince Galen, with the shot of one arrow," said Weft, "we will win all or lose all." Then he beamed and patted Millicent on the shoulder. "It's crazy, of course, Millicent. But it's not as crazy as you might think! They may have had no idea that the Emperor controlled Mt. Zareba, that his 'daughter' might be there, or that holy forces of the God of Heaven may be awakened from a long sleep!"

"Master Weft, if you'd only been where we've been!" said Galen. Mira smiled.

"Galen," said Weft, seeming to not hear, "let me send the arrow with your message."

And he did.

"Now," said Galen, "we must prepare for the arrival of people who've never been here before—we hope, of course, we haven't been deceived. Rocks must be removed from the stone door down below, and the mountaintop itself must be put in order.

"But we must do one other important thing first."

"What's that?" asked Millicent.

"Eat!" said the Prince. "All together like we used to! But up on the platform so we can watch. I'm starved! It will take time to ponder and act upon our message. And for them to finish dealing with the horror in the cavern. I bet they'll get rid of the slaves as fast as possible, whether they do it our way or not. Disposing of the bodies will take longer. While they do, we can take care of some things up here."

The mid-day meal was simple, small, but most welcome. Galen

raised a cup of water thanking God for their success. Though it was hard to be silent about the Golden Chest of Promise, they said nothing about it. Until certain the enemy wasn't arriving, Galen told Mira, they must not reveal their secret which could fall into the wrong hands.

The Golden Chest must be spared at all costs. A time of dying, or a time of delightful sharing if the Emperor came.

One or the other.

But for now, too many other things had to happen first.

CHAPTER 47

21
PRINCESS LUCIA

ithin minutes of Weft's arrow, there were whoops and yells as the slaves began to be released. In less than an hour, all slaves were gone with little more than the clothes on their backs — to God knows where — perhaps fearful that their fortune might again change. The grisly, but thorough, clearing out and burning of bodies by the old enemy guards occurred less fast, but faster than before probably for the same reason.

Two of Galen's orders, or requests, had been carried out.

But no one had shown any signs of heading north. Had something gone wrong? Hadn't they sensed the urgency? Were these strangers, many from the south, true servants of the Emperor? Or was the Emperor dead, and they didn't want the defenders to know about it?

Something wasn't right.

No further messages were sent up. Galen resolved to send no more down. In all their discussions about what might happen, something very important had been overlooked — and that was determining events now. And it was something Mt. Zareba's defenders were unable to think about.

But revelation about that would come.

And the Emperor was coming, Galen insisted. He decided he had to tell them that below the pulpit, that they had seen move, was a place of temporary safety. After they ate, they gathered in the chapel. Everyone carried weapons.

"We've something more than just a hiding place," he found himself telling them, "but exactly what has to wait." Oddly, no one challenged him. He showed them the lever at the pulpit. "Use it only in a life-and-death emergency and follow the railing. *Tell no one about this for any reason!*" he emphasized.

Galen was interrupted by the sound of a bugle. Everyone raced outside. In the north, several hundred troops were approaching. Galen raised his spyglass.

It was the Emperor's colors! But still no sign of the Emperor, Sir Kerky, or Lord Fairold. Who were these people? The decision to shoot the arrow had been made. If they were now to die, it would be his fault, but whatever he'd done, if wrong, had given them only a few more days at best. Still he must be cautious and act in good faith. Galen, Weft, and Soren entered the tunnel to the cavern and pulled away the last of the rocks behind the stone door. Then they opened it a little, so those coming up from below could easily roll it back.

Galen slid back the stone slab covering the entry at the top. But even though the bodies had been removed, the open tunnel acted as a chimney to the great cave and foul air still rose, reminding everyone of the horrible battle. Galen shivered. Though the end was now determined, they mustn't become careless. After a final clearing of the area on top, they all, said Galen, must dress in their best clothes and wait with weapons ready.

The troops from the north had finally arrived. Down below they quietly mingled with the others already there. Minutes later, there was the sound of armor and weapons against rocks down below as soldiers pushed into the great cave.

The first soldier up the tunnel to the top of the mountain no one recognized. Bravely, he stood with a raised shield and sword.

"Not one step further!" ordered Galen. The man stared into the business ends of five arrows and a sword aimed at his head. "Bring us the Emperor!" said Galen.

Carefully, the soldier surveyed the six standing before him: the old weaver with a fringe around his ears; three well-armed women dressed in silk; and two young men, the smaller one talking, the other handsome and muscular, holding the sword, with his left arm in a sling.

The newcomer's jaw dropped.

"Where are your soldiers?"

"I'll ask the questions and give the orders," snapped Galen. "In God's Holy Name, bring us the Emperor! Do you understand? Now go!"

Without another word, the soldier backed down through the entry, and though it wasn't easy, he at last turned in the narrow tunnel loudly scraping his shield and disappeared.

A half hour passed. The next man up was a large priest in a robe smudged with soot, an older man with stringy, grayish hair, gray eyes, and, as Storie put it later, a "bookish look and voice." Galen wondered how with his bulk he'd managed the narrow stairway.

"We asked for the Emperor!" said Galen.

"And you did so in God's holy name, did you not? Well, I come in that Holy Name on the Emperor's behalf." Boldly, he hoisted himself out of the opening and stood. He, too, surveyed the group and tried to conceal a puzzled look.

"Don't play with words!" snapped Galen. "We want—"

"How dare you say I play with words when I mention God's Holy Name!" interrupted the priest. His eyes suddenly blazed. But just as suddenly the priest's tone softened. Slowly he eased himself forward. "Where's everyone? I'm searching for your head...uh...for one called uh…Prince Galen. Where is he?"

"I am he," said Galen. "And your name?"

The priest arched his eyebrows. His mouth fell open.

"Well, my, my…" he said, edging closer and glancing from side to side.

"One more inch," interrupted Storie, "and they'll search for your head after we throw it over the wall!" She lowered her bow and pulled a long dagger from her belt. "Now bow to Prince Galen!" From the corner of his eye Galen saw Soren wince and Millicent slip her heel over the girl's foot. But Storie ignored it.

"I'm Father Stephan and I bow to no man, peasant or Emperor! Only to the God of Heaven. I am his priest." He stared into the Prince's eyes. "Let fly those arrows and I'll quickly join my Lord and Savior, and later you'll explain to him what you did and why!" He turned to the girl climber, now disguised in a beautiful dress, holding her blade an inch from his belly.

"Get ready to be introduced!" hissed the girl. The priest's eyes grew large, he raised his hands in mock surrender, and smiled.

"But, milady, you do have a point, and I dare say, a sharp one. I come no further."

Galen motioned the girl to move back, which she did but for only a foot, and though he fought not to show it, he immediately liked the man.

"You mean this is all of you?"

"All you can see!" snapped Galen.

"Sir Rengel was right," continued Father Stephan. "Two ladies and —"

"*Three* ladies!" snapped Soren. At once his sword point was parallel to the climber's blade.

"Uh…three, of course," said Father Stephan. "Three ladies, two boys, and an old man!"

"*Three* men," said Weft, "who're getting tired of one nosy, fat old priest, who's given us nothing but words!"

"And up here is the God of Heaven," said Galen, "whom you will not mock on this mountain!"

"The God of Heaven, you say. Then let me bow to him!" Father Stephan suddenly dropped to his knees, and openly began thanking God for opening the mountain and for bringing him, the Emperor, and the Emperor's army inside. The defenders lowered their weapons halfway and bowed their heads. After several minutes the priest ended and suddenly stood. "Sir Rengel, the brave soldier who first came up—you've no idea the confusion his report stirred."

"Bring the Emperor, NOW!" said Weft. "Don't question our resolve. We're pledged to defend this mountain for him."

"For the *Emperor* you say!" boomed a new voice.

Suddenly a large, powerfully built man stood before them. He wore armor without any coat of arms or markings whatever. Immediately, two magnificently clothed knights leaped up from the opening to face arrows drawn back in bows.

"No swords!" ordered the large man. Each lowered his blade and stood in a ready position on either side of him. The man in the middle fixed his eyes on the white-haired lady. His jaw fell. He removed his scarred helmet and moved toward her. "Millie, can that possibly be you?"

The Lady of the Mountain put down her bow, stepped forward, and bowed low.

The man reached down and swept her up in his arms.

"Millie! Little Millie!"

"Your Majesty! Your Majesty, God bless you! But my Kerky...Do you have news of my Kerky?"

Sir Kerky Greenwald was next to appear in the opening, and after him Lord Fairold. Millicent flew into her husband's arms. Galen into

429

his father's. All except the Palace Guard had worn clothes without markings to disguise themselves, Galen later learned.

"Sir Rengel said he saw only six of you!" said the Emperor. "Where are your soldiers? Some said at least two dozen were here. Where are they? Bring them out. I'd like to meet and thank these brave men. Wait! I see only *five* of you…"

It was then Galen noticed that the servant girl had somehow slipped away.

"There's a servant girl, Mira," said Galen. "She…she pretended to be the Emperor's Daughter so we could try to hold King Stulk and his army here. Stulk's now dead. Your coach arrived just before we entered the mountain with a large young man named Pinrut, an older serving maid called Mara, and a young maid named Mira. Your daughter… your daughter"—Galen felt his throat catch—"your daughter was thrown from the coach and she died, but we killed the three soldiers chasing them.

"That's not all—"

"*Mira* you say?" interrupted the Emperor. "Pinrut, God Bless him, is my son…my only son. Maid Mara is a highly trusted old servant. But *Mira*?"

"Pinrut is dead, Your Majesty. There was no braver a warrior. He saved the life of Soren here"—he pointed back to the twin—"by killing his attacker. Later he died bravely defending this mountain and saving the lives of all the rest of us.

"Mara…died of illness."

"Pinrut helped you fight?!" interrupted the Emperor. Tears filled his eyes. "Pinrut helped you fight?!"

"Not only did he fight," said Galen, "but he found the entryway you came up—we arrived another way, you must understand — and we now stand before you because of him. He bravely fought, saving us before dying himself."

430

"Died…died in battle," mumbled the Emperor, staring sideways toward the wall. He wiped his face with the back of his hand.

"Found another way up?" asked Lord Fairold, changing the subject. His eyes were large, his jaw unnaturally slack.

"Yes, Father. But that's only a small part of everything. Your Majesty, we had great losses, too."

"Yes," said the Emperor as he turned to face the boy. "Your brave soldiers, how did they—"

It was Galen's turn to interrrupt.

"Master Maleg, our stone mason, is dead.

"His son Saren—Soren's brother—is dead." He paused. "They attacked us with walking bees." For several seconds he could say nothing. "They died after they were stung by the bees.

"This 'Lady-to-be' Storie climbed the mountain and came over the wall to join us and has become the new daughter of Lady Millicent"—he glanced at Sir Kerky and smiled—"and Sir Kerky Greenwald." The girl, standing beside Millicent, bowed to her new father.

"These…and those you see"—he extended his arms—"are your 'soldiers.'"

For a whole minute the mountaintop was unnaturally silent.

"But what of…what of my daughter—pretty, headstrong, silly, sick little Lemerah?" said the Emperor. "What about her? And what about Maid Tillnah, her constant companion?"

Galen dropped his eyes.

"Your Majesty," said Millicent, "we know nothing of any servant girl named Tillnah. But Princess Lemerah…she…she was killed…she fell from your coach just before it got here. Or…" The Lady held back her next words. It was her turn to look away.

"Lemerah *killed*!" The word obviously stung. "We were told again and again that the 'Emperor's daughter'—my daughter—regularly presented herself on the wall! I expected some trick, but…"

Shamelessly, tears began to run down his cheeks. "Since she was little she's lived under a curse. Never did I allow her to leave the Palace. And now my precious Lucia who's been promised to..." The Emperor interrupted himself and paused. He stared at Galen. "Princess Lucia has just become ill."

"Your Majesty," interrupted a soldier, "look!" From behind a tree in the Chapel garden stepped the raven-haired servant girl attired in a glittering blue gown, a long dagger in a slender scabbard inconspicuously attached to a golden belt about her waist. As every eye turned her way, she walked soundlessly, seeming to glide toward them, her eyes fixed only on the Emperor. Ten feet from him she stopped. Her face was also wet with tears.

The Emperor's eyes grew large.

"Lemerah!" he gasped.

"Father!"

The Princess and the Emperor fell into each other's arms.

"Lemerah, whatever has happened to you! You...you're alive! How did..."

"Father!" She pushed him away. "I've a thousand things to tell you! But...but Father, did you say Lucia is ill?"

"Yes, but..."

"How is she ill, Father?"

"She...she suddenly began acting...acting like..."

"Like I did, Father?"

"Yes, yes, Lemerah, but worse, much worse." The Emperor looked down at his boots. "It's just happened. She says strange and terrible things in a voice that is not hers. The physician with us has tried everything..."

"Father, please listen." She reached up and took the man's head in her hands. She gazed deep into his eyes. "Don't be...you know, what Mother used to say. Everything else must wait. Everything. Bring her

432

up here at once! Tie her if you must. Use soldiers if you have to. But bring her!"

"Now?"

"Your majesty," said Millicent, "trust me! So much is happening so fast! But think back. That old prophecy that Lord Fairold and Lady Lambith told you about, where Galen's grandmother was warned in a vision that a witch had pledged her life to marry her grandson for reasons that were never told."

"You're saying my daughter is a witch?" thundered the Emperor.

"I'm saying no such thing, Your Majesty!" said Millicent. "Please, listen carefully. Very carefully. First, we know nothing of Prince Colin, Lord Fairold's brother. He may have a son which the prophecy applies to, but we think not, for we've read how the story of his life ends.

"We think this prophecy applies to Galen, this Prince who stands before you. Princess Lucia is not a witch, no more than Lemerah was! But she may be under a spell, one that we on this Holy Mountain understand."

"Your Majesty, where is she now?" asked Galen.

"Where? Down below with the other women," said the Emperor, "babbling strange things and unable to walk."

"Bring her here immediately!" said Galen.

"You're ordering me to do what!" exploded the Emperor. Lord Fairold buried his face in his hands.

Galen fell to his knees.

"Your Majesty, I'm begging you!"

"*We* are begging you, Your Majesty!" added Millicent, dropping to her knees and folding her hands. "In the Name of the God of Heaven. Take me and your best soldiers immediately down where she lies." Quickly she stood, leaned over, and whispered into the Emperor's ear, then Galen's. Lord Fairold, Sir Kerky, and the soldiers exchanged puzzled glances. Then she whispered to Weft, who looked stunned but said nothing. Finally, she ran to her husband Kerky, and kissed him, before gently pushing him away and returning to face the Emperor, where she bowed low, and then stood tall before him face to face. "We await your orders, Your Majesty."

"Follow me," he shot back. He spun on his heel and walked back to the opening that led down. Millicent and two soldiers followed. The priest fell in behind them.

"Father Stephan," called Galen, "you're to stay with us." The priest looked toward the Emperor for direction. At that moment, a low indescribable howl or moan, came up from somewhere down below over the wall.

"Stay!" ordered the Emperor.

Galen walked to Lord Fairold, hugged him, and privately dropped the royal ring that he had worn into his father's hand.

"The mountain is yours, Father." He offered the puzzled man a rare smile. "That is, after two more things, maybe three, that I have to do." Lord Fairold slipped on his ring and studied his son. Galen called Princess Lemerah, or Mira, and Storie, Master Weft, Soren, and Father Stephan to join him in the warm grass in front of the Chapel. Then the six formed a circle, Galen urged the priest to set aside any discomfort he sensed, and at the boy's direction they lay on their faces before God and prayed.

The newcomers who'd only witnessed what had been leftover from the horrible battles below, kept their distance and began whispering. Whatever had happened here? How could so few have slain so many and survived so long? And how did they get up here?

And what about the young Prince who led them?

Sir Kerky, the Emperor's soldiers, and even Lord Fairold paced back and forth, turning this way and that, as if convinced that at any second smiling soldiers would spring from hiding, laughing at everyone's gullibility. But no one wandered far from those praying loud enough for everyone to hear.

Answers would be forthcoming when the Emperor returned from the mission the young Prince had sent him on.

✻   ✻   ✻

These things Sir Kerky told Galen later.

*As to **Princess Lemerah**:*

Since many things will quickly follow, it's a good time to explain the Emperor's youngest child's curious deception which surprised even Galen— though not entirely.

In time, everyone would learn about how war came to Zareba City. But days earlier when the Palace had been attacked, plans were already in place to save the royal family. One coach was to carry Princess Lemerah, her brother Pinrut, Maid Mara, and Maid Tillnah; a second coach was to carry Princess Lucia, Queen Brilena, and two of their maids. But the Queen and her maid died first. Lucia and her maid, however, made good their escape.

It was the first coach that came to Zareba Village.

Princess Lemerah, who'd seen little beyond the walls of the Palace was terrified by the bouncing and jostling in the fleeing coach. Soon she became frantic and her companions feared that one of "her spells" was coming on. To calm her, Maid Tillnah, whose main function was to serve and entertain the Princess, suggested that she and the Princess exchange clothes and switch roles as they'd often done playing as children. The girls, who strikingly looked alike, never of course played this secret game in the Emperor's presence, and each was delighted that they could "become each other" and fool many.

Maid Mara not only tolerated this, but privately agreed with the young maid, who loved Lemerah, that this game might one day protect the Emperor's Daughter.

Which tragically it did.

It was Maid Tillnah "in disguise" who'd not been thrown, but actually

435

jumped from the Emperor's coach.

As to why the royal identity was kept secret from the defenders, Mara made "Mira," a short form of "Lemerah" that Tillnah always used, promise to say nothing till her father arrived. Revealing this, Mara warned, might be dangerous and mean that Tillnah's death was for nothing. Privately, Mira deeply mourned her friend, and as Mara lay dying, the Princess-in-disguise had renewed her promise.

*As to **Pinrut**:*

He was a year older than Mira, but soon after his birth it was clear he could never follow his father on the throne. Prince Pinrut, the long-hoped-for son of the Emperor could not learn to read, and he spoke with difficulty; however, he was strong for his age, and could be taught to do simple things. That was as far as his responsibilities would ever go. His sisters, however, loved him dearly.

*As to **Princess Lucia**:*

She was two years older than her only brother. After the birth of Pinrut and her sister Lemerah, the Emperor began to groom Princess Lucia, his oldest and only other child, to become Empress and rule after him. Of the three, Galen quickly learned later that it was commonly agreed that she was the most poised, best mannered, the best looking, and the best educated of the royal children. And someone who, with the proper husband, just might be able to follow her father on the throne.

But now she was ill.

❋   ❋   ❋

Less than an hour after the Emperor and Millicent left, there was the sound of scraping and loud voices in the tunnel. A frightened soldier was the first to appear, immediately followed by a second soldier carrying the front end of a litter, on which lay a beautifully dressed woman tied down by a rope wrapped at least a dozen times around her body and fastened securely. The Emperor himself, with grim resolve, carried the back of the litter. As soon as they stood on the surface at the top, Millicent came along the woman's side. There were scratches on her arms and on her cheek. Vile words in a deep husky voice poured out of the bound woman's lips. After that a long howling rose from the tunnel below. And soon there was the clicking of nails from animal feet.

Millicent took the front of the litter from the hands of a very grateful soldier, and without a word, led the way to the garden. With Millicent's direction, the circle opened and Princess Lucia, still bound, was laid in the center. The Lady of the Mountain and Emperor knelt alongside the other six who, following Galen's example, had risen to their knees. The Princess on the litter screamed that the heat from the ground below was burning her.

Then, most horrible of all, a dark black dog surfaced, howling and growling at the same time and headed for them.

"Father, Kerky, in the name of the God of Heaven, grab and bind the dog! DO IT ONLY IN THE NAME OF THE GOD OF HEAVEN!"

Kerky quickly had a rope in his hands. Calling on God, he and Lord Fairold tackled the muscular beast, and to their surprise, easily managed to tie his body. With the other end of the rope they tied the struggling creature to a post, where he left off growling and barking, and fell into a low, continual howl. To their surprise, neither Kerky nor Lord Fairold had been injured. The dozen or so soldiers who stood nearby with drawn swords, and three of the Princess's maids with two bags of her belongings circled the group warily, careful to keep their distance.

"**Princess Lucia,**" said Galen, staring directly into her eyes. "**Do you want us to help you?**"

"**Untie me, you filthy beast of the mountain!**" spat the Princess, in a deep voice.

"That's not my daughter speaking, Prince Galen!" said the Emperor, his eyes tearing up again.

Father Stephan's eyes seemed to nearly explode out of his head. He looked to the Emperor for some sense of direction. But the High King's eyes were fixed on his daughter.

"**Pray aloud, Father Stephan,**" said Galen, "**that the Princess herself will speak.**"

"**Pray,**" added Millicent, "**in the name of God of Heaven.**"

"In the name of the God-Son," added Soren, "the one who shed his blood that we might..."

At the word "blood" the Princess on the litter shrieked. The surrounding soldiers and maids edged back.

"**You know the words, Stephan,**" ordered the Emperor, "**say them!**"

The priest did.

From where she lay, the Princess thrashed and spoke in a strange language no one understood.

"**In the name of the God of Heaven,**" said Galen, "**speak only in words we all understand. Princess Lucia, do you want us to help you? Answer us! We will wait here all night if we have to! Father Stephan, tell us how the shed blood of the God-Son took away our sins. Say the words again!**"

The priest, finally losing himself — all but his voice — ably began again, and as he continued, as priests often can do once they get started, familiar words about the gift of the God-Son at last poured out strongly and with conviction.

Again, the Princess thrashed, straining against the cords. She was drenched with sweat.

Then there was silence. Even the dog left off howling.

On his own, while everyone else was privately praying, the priest again said the words: "**Dear girl, in the Name of the God of Heaven** do you want us to help you?"

Daylight began to fade as the golden sun began to rest on the horizon.

No one moved.

"Please, someone help me." The words were soft but clear.

"It's...it's Lucia!" whispered Mira. "She's come back. Talk to her, Galen."

"Princess Lucia," he said, "will you give the God of Heaven and his Son all that you are and have?"

She twisted under the rope and water seemed to flow from her skin.

"Yes."

Galen turned to Mira and raised his voice.

"Princess Lemerah, say the words for all of us."

"O God," said Mira, **"in your Holy Name we cast out this evil spirit that torments my sister. May it forever leave this mountain, and never torment any creature, and may your Holy Spirit enter this woman fully, and may peace reign again on this mountain. Amen."**

"Amen"

"Amen"

"Amen"

"Amen"

"Amen"

"Amen"

And the evil spirit which had arrived in such an odd way, tore at Princess Lucia's body one final time and was gone.

At the same instant the strange dog fell over dead. Or so the soldier who cut him loose thought. At the freeing of his bonds, his eyes opened and he licked the man's hand. The fierceness was gone.

Mira took her long dagger — which caused the Emperor to suck in deeply — and cut her sister loose. She helped her to her feet. The woman yawned as if waking from a deep sleep. Then she smiled. Despite her disarray, there was no mistaking her as an Emperor's daughter. The High King held both daughters in his arms. Then he pushed them away and faced the boy who had held the mountain. He glanced at Lord Fairold, then back to the Prince.

"Prince Galen," said the High King, "I'm a man of my word. We have much to talk about!" He smiled. "Let me present you my daughter, Princess Lucia."

Though wet and stained by grass and dirt, her hair askew, and clothing in bad repair, Princess Lucia stood tall, with the bearing of royal blood which could overcome such handicaps. She was now well, completely well, and everyone knew it. Though years older than the Prince, she bowed low before him. Color raced to her cheeks. And to Galen's. The Emperor beamed. Lord Fairold smiled.

But Lady Lambith, who had arrived during all the confusion, pulled at the High King's arm and whispered in his ear.

CHAPTER 48

22
THE
HIGH
PRINCE

nly so many could be comfortable at one time on Mt. Zareba, so the friendly invasion was finally curbed by the Emperor himself. Besides, entry through the tunnel was risky. But the Royal Cook and his assistants—unusual participants in a war party, but now homeless except for their food wagons and tents—were among the privileged to witness what would follow. Immediately they began preparing a feast of celebration for later that night. The Emperor hadn't arrived emptyhanded.

Galen struggled to keep his eyes off the endless meats, breads, and vegetables coming up through the tunnel, followed by narrow tables and benches that could be put together and taken apart, and stools. The odor of cooking foods that months ago had disappeared was pleasant but distracting. It would be late, but they would eat that night—and well.

The defenders, Father Stephan, Princess Lucia, and the Emperor along with several knights and advisers stood in the Chapel garden. (No one dared sit in the High King's presence though the tall grass was inviting.) A warm breeze ruffled the white cloths bearing His Majesty's seal that now covered several camp tables being set up in two long rows. About some things the Emperor didn't dally.

Nor did Prince Galen.

"Your Majesty, please know that I claimed to be Prince of this Holy Mountain in your absence only because my father ordered me to. I've given my father back his ring. Now, before I step aside, I beg you before God to grant me two favors."

The Emperor glanced at Princess Lucia, then Galen and Lord Fairold. He smiled.

"Granted, so long as it doesn't change an old promise."

"First," said Galen, "while dinner is being prepared and before we eat, Princess Mira — 'Lemerah' will take some getting used to — and I and the defenders of this mountain, request your uninterrupted presence immediately for two hours in the Chapel, that is you, Princess Lucia, Father Stephan, my father Lord Fairold, my mother Lady Lambith, Sir Kerky Greenwald, the six of us and no one else." Master Weft, Storie, Soren, and Millicent exchanged puzzled looks. Galen and Mira were on their own.

"Granted," said the Emperor. "And second?"

"Second," said Galen, "at this final great feast, I want your daughter Princess ... Lemerah to sit at my side."

"Granted," said the Emperor. Long ago, Millicent and his mother had emphasized that when the Emperor found his direction, he didn't hesitate.

Princess Lucia, standing next to Mira and Galen, pointed down to her soiled dress and whispered to her younger sister.

"Not now, Lucia," Mira whispered back. Somehow, she'd already slipped away and was already in a servant's dress. "God knows you're still the most beautiful girl in the world." She stepped back gave a quick head-to-toe inspection. "Hmmm. Besides, where we're going is going to be very, very dark."

"I'm in your hands, little sister...You are Lemerah, aren't you?" She tilted her head. "Or is it 'Mira'?"

"It is!" The younger sister laughed.

"That sounds like what a priest would say!"

"Maybe, but with fewer words!" said Galen. The sisters laughed. He wondered when they'd last done that.

"Trust me," said Mira, "before supper you'll have plenty to think about. And I WILL get us *both* a comb and towel!" She laughed.

As the twelve entered the Chapel, a dozen soldiers with shields and swords circled the building and stood guard. Security had come to the mountain.

Inside, Galen and Weft closed and locked all the shutters and bolted the door. At first, the only light came from the disappearing sunlight entering the stained glass window above the pulpit. Conversation became a whisper. Unseen to all but Galen, Mira tucked away a bundle of several towels at the end of a pew. She, herself, carried an empty serving bowl. With Storie's help, Soren at last secured two small torches in brackets. The flickering light cast dancing shadows.

"Finally, we have a priest," declared Galen. "Go, Father Stephan, stand there behind the pulpit." Without hesitation, the huge man inched his way through dim light up to the great pulpit where he silently stood, hands at his side. Galen and Mira stood in the center of the floor two feet lower, in front of the pulpit on the platform.

"Pray for us, Father Stephan," said Galen, facing the nine in front of him.

"For...for what?" asked the priest.

"The Princess and I wish to take the ten of you on a journey."

"The *twelve* of us? On a journey?"

"A journey that can't wait!" It was an order. Galen's legs began to shake. Mira took his hand and the shaking stopped. Together they bowed their heads, and waited.

Silence, welcome silence fell for a whole minute. "Journey" — Father Stephan later told of how he puzzled over the word. Any "journey" in the cramped Chapel had to be some "journey of words or ideas." So he must be careful of his.

"O God" — the priest's studied voice echoed back from the high ceiling — **"O God, you are our God. We come boldly into your — "**

In mid-sentence Galen pushed back the secret lever. Suddenly, with a loud grinding, the great pulpit lurched to the side.

While the defenders were prepared for this, the Emperor and the five others most certainly were not. Those below the altar jumped backwards, falling into the front pews. Father Stephan, apparently lost in his thoughts, leaped back, his heel digging into the small pulpit rug he was standing on, which skidded forward, propelling him back and down like falling timber. With a crash he was flat on his back.

"Galen," Mira whispered, "did you have to — "

"Probably not," he whispered back.

Galen climbed to the platform and helped the man up. The priest worked his way to his feet, at first shaking uncontrollably, and from then on was never again quite the same. Galen detected the hint of a smile on the Emperor's face. For the next half hour or so, Father Stephan was silent.

"Lead us safely down for your Name's sake, O God," said Galen. **"Amen."**

Several barely audible "Amens" followed.

✳   ✳   ✳

After nearly a half hour of carefully descending the narrow spiral stairway by the light of one of the torches, the twelve stood before the waterfall doorway. Princess Lucia was first to spot the dead man nearby. She grabbed the priest's arm, and the poor speechless man remained so.

"He's dead, Lucia," said Galen, raising his voice to be heard over the falling water, "but he doesn't smell, and has been sitting there since long before you were born."

"Are there any—"

"No, at least he's all that your sister and I have found, and we're the only ones who have been down here"—he paused to let everyone think about that—"so you may want to keep your eyes open! Now, everyone"—he turned to the rest—"remove your boots or shoes and join hands and follow me. We're all going to get wet, so watch your step!"

Taking Princess Lucia's soft fingers, so unlike her sister's now, he stepped quickly before she could protest, into and through the waterfall, much darker this time because the light from the crypt had been covered and Soren's torch didn't show anything behind the water. Deliberately, he pulled Lucia behind him, but Mira who was behind her sister, held back so the older Princess caught the full force of the falling water. Then pushing her forward and quickly following, the others entered one-by-one.

All were soaked, but Lucia was sputtering and gasping for breath. Galen asked everyone to stand in the back of the room as water trickled from their clothes. Storie was last in, trying to shield the torch under Mira's bowl. But halfway in, the sure-footed climber slipped, wetting the torch, and startling everyone—because she, of all people, was the most surefooted.

As the torch began sputtering, Galen moved everyone to the center of the room. Again the room was warm, not cold, and a light fog clung to the warmer floor. Just as the torch surrendered its last light, the Prince stood beside the crypt. All was silent, except for the falling water. Galen stood motionless in the darkness.

"We're not alone down here," he said, raising his voice just loud enough. Slowly he slid back the stone slab to the way they'd first found it. Immediately, a golden beam of light pierced the darkness. "Come, look but don't touch," he instructed.

Viewing the long-lost Golden Chest of Promise through the opening was overwhelming. Galen picked up the four stakes.

"You may hold these." Taking turns they did.

Father Stephan was the first to lie face down on the stone floor before the crypt. The Emperor was next. Without shame, both men began to weep quietly. One by one the other eight lay down beside them. "It is okay to pray," said Galen, "and several at once if you wish." Without shame they did. Once again, a warm wind began to circle inside stirring the foggy pillows. Behind the others and farther away, Galen and Mira lay on their faces side by side again with just their fingers touching. They were the only ones silent, and this time the peace of the Holy Presence wrapped them like a fleece from the beginning.

For the others, it was as for the two of them earlier, a time to confess and ask forgiveness. Words simply poured out without shame, no one later remembering what another said. Tears that came were not wiped away. Nearly an hour later the words ended as everyone seemed to know that the time for praying was over. Slowly they backed away from the crypt and found themselves in a circle facing each other. Together they sat.

"I think we all have questions, Your Majesty," said Galen. "I think it's okay to talk. May we ask questions?"

The Emperor nodded, looking a bit puzzled.

Princess Lucia was first. Her voice was soft, almost as if she were intruding. As was everyone else who spoke.

"You know, before the slab was moved away, the crypt and this cave reminded me of a tomb, but while it scared me, I had no feeling of death."

Lady Lambith was next.

"Could this be the tomb of the God-Son, where he lay before rising from the dead? But don't they say this happened 20 miles away in Zareba City?"

"So they say, my lady," said Father Stephan, "or so say the curio makers, the sellers of relics, the moneychangers in the City—but all without one shred of proof! The name Zareba has been used in this whole area for centuries, and ancient ruins have been found everywhere. Just where the tomb was, in my view, doesn't matter at all, only the fact that wherever it was, it was empty after three days. Now why the Golden Chest of Promise still exists and is hidden here, I'm not sure. But it certainly has been hidden well! We'll ask the God-Son about this when he returns."

"I think the Tomb is here," whispered Storie.

"I think you're right," whispered the Emperor back, "but back then I think the Tomb was easier to get to." The High King turned to Galen's father.

"But let me point out, Lord Fairold, it was not my ancestor but yours, your ancestor King Merceon who was anointed the first guardian of the Golden Chest of Promise, that right now is giving me light to see you as I speak!"

"And gives warmth to this room!" added Storie. "I've been in many caves, but never in one where I felt comfortable when soaking wet!"

"And, I believe, the chest warms the ground directly above on the mountaintop," said Weft, "and causes the fruit trees directly above us to prosper so well."

"And even the stakes exist, too," said Princess Lucia, "which remind us of our sin and what we've been saved from."

"But why, Father Stephan, are these here?" asked Galen.

"I don't know," said Father Stephan, "but I can guess. The God-Son promised in the Holy Book that he'd return to Emryss a second time, not as a servant, but as—"

"Return again?" Storie interrupted.

"According to the Holy Book," said the priest, "the God-Son said he had come briefly for 'a lifetime' to seek and save that which is lost, but much later he would return to Zareba for a **'lifetime times a lifetime'** to rule Emryss as King."

"A lifetime times a lifetime?" asked Storie. "Rule as King or Emperor?" Millicent glared, but the girl's eyes were riveted on the High King. Sir Kerky squeezed his wife's hand and put his finger to his lips.

The Emperor, not known for patience in interruptions, then surprised everyone.

"Millie, important things demand our attention, or they should. Your new daughter—and so far my kingdom is blessed to have people like her—has chosen the good way. It reminds me of a child I once knew, one who couldn't rest until she could read!"

"*You*, Mother?" said Storie.

For the first time ever, even though the light was dim, Galen saw Millicent's cheeks redden. The Emperor smiled triumphantly.

"Now as to Storie's question—what is 'a lifetime times a lifetime'? I know climbers are good with numbers, so let me go on a bit. According to the Holy Book, the God-Son lived from conception to death and resurrection almost exactly 29 and ½ years. The measuring rod for a 'lifetime' is that short period the God-Son actually lived. And, as is commonly said, a person who lives 'two lifetimes,' or twice that, has been unusually blessed. Now if what's meant here is not that, but a lifetime *times* a lifetime, he'll come back and rule for quite a while. You can figure that out for yourself!

"And when he comes to reign, it will not be as Emperor or King, but as King of All Kings!"

"In what part of Zareba?" asked Storie.

"Storie," interrupted Millicent, "now is hardly the time to—"

"The Holy Book doesn't say," said Father Stephan. "It could be the City, the Village—"

"Or," interrupted the Emperor, "even this mountain. We have already seen God's power here." He glanced at his daughter Lucia. She smiled. "Many believe the Holy Book teaches that when the God-Son finally rules, even the old animal sacrifices, which his ancestors offered and which foreshadowed his death, will once again be offered as a memorial to the once-for-all sacrifice for sins of the God-Son himself."

"Of course," said Father Stephan, "not all believers see things quite that way." Weft's jaw dropped, but the Emperor smiled.

"It's been a long time since we've talked about such things, hasn't it?" said the Emperor. "You're right, of course, but it is something to think about. The God-Son is coming back again. Agreed?"

"Most certainly, Your Majesty," said the priest.

"Maybe some more things are hidden here that we'll find later!" said the Emperor. "This day's certainly been full enough! Now about the Chest—it's been hidden for good reason. I can see nothing gained by displaying it now. So for now it will stay here...as well as the knowledge of it being here. Please realize"—the Emperor glanced at each person—"we've been entrusted with a great secret. But...it's time to get back to the top."

One by one they went through the falling water, Mira leading the way, Galen last, sliding the slab back in place before he left. Side by side they stood in total darkness, holding the rail and letting water drain from their clothes. With some difficulty, they gathered their shoes. Most would walk barefoot on the trip up.

✳   ✳   ✳

Back in the Chapel they sank into the pews and dried themselves with the towels and sat silently. As the Emperor started to speak, the

449

chief bodyguard knocked at the door.

"We are well, Sir Blane, and the twelve of us will join you shortly," said the Emperor, "and we'll be quite hungry, I might add." Galen heard Soren's stomach rumble as if commanded to and, sure enough, his was next.

"Your Majesty," said Galen, "now the mountain's all yours. I give it back." He smiled. "The King's Room on the fifth floor of the tower lies in readiness for you, and the person you choose to rule here. Now I'm finished, though"—he looked into the High King's face—"I sense you are not!"

"I am not? Just what should I do, Prince Galen? I seek counsel," said the Emperor. Lord Fairold raised his eyebrows.

"Please, Your Majesty, I don't know much, but I've thought about a lot of things here," said Galen. "But some things not so much because they've happened so fast." He glanced at Mira. Millicent and Lady Lambith exchanged glances. Galen smiled. For once it was his turn to speak and theirs to listen. But would this satisfaction last long enough to hold back his growing panic? He was now advising the great Emperor! Galen knew about games. Was the man playing games with him now?

"Your Majesty," said Galen, "at the very least I believe we must promise never to tell what we saw here. That would only increase the danger of someone trying to steal the Chest. There's no reason now, as you said, to make public what we've found. If you agree, Your Majesty, you should make us promise that. And make some provision to keep the Secret Chamber of the Open Tomb safe." It was Galen who first called the hidden room by that name.

"I see," said the Emperor.

For a minute there was silence.

Then the Emperor stood, walked to the front, staying on the main floor. He pointed back and up to the great pulpit, the top of which was at the level of his head.

"I will not stand up there because I do not rule here, not directly. Besides, we've a priest of God who can stand up there if necessary — and if he's able." He offered the hint of a smile, humor that only an Emperor could get away with after what they'd just been through. Weft's eyes dropped to study his boots, Storie beamed, Millicent clamped a hand over her mouth, and Galen grit his teeth.

How glad he was these months were over. His father was home to lead, and the Emperor could set the rules. His own play-acting was over, probably forever.

But what lay ahead? Not for a minute had he thought about it. There had been no time. Or courage to aim his mind in that direction. He felt his shoulders melt and go soft. When was the last time he'd done that? Then, in spite of the closed shutters and door, he smelled the food. His stomach growled again.

But the Emperor was far from done.

"As your Emperor, I can *stand successfully* down here. Father Stephan, please join me. The rest of you stand before us."

A line of ten immediately formed across the front of the Chapel.

"This day I am forming **The Order of the Holy Mountain**. I'm going to ask each of you to do something: to stand before me, then kneel.

"By kneeling before me and the God of Heaven, if you choose to do so, you will be agreeing to the following: (1) to defend this mountain with all your might, even though it cost you your life.

"(2) to never reveal the secrets here, except at the 'right time' to one of your children, or a suitable person you choose, who in turn will be instructed years later to similarly pass this on to someone else.

"(3) to meet here once a year, insofar as possible, on a day designated by the High Prince or High Princess of this Holy Mountain, which will be one of you. Further, though that Prince or Princess who rules will

451

live in what you've called the 'King's Room,' there will not be a king of this mountain until the King of Kings himself arrives.

"And lastly, (4) to strive to obey and follow the words of the Holy Book while we wait for the God-Son's return.

"Father Stephan, as a priest of God, and Priest of this Order, you will be given no additional title, but I expect you to select a suitable priest to follow you.

"Does anyone here NOT agree to do what I've said? If so, speak NOW!"

There was a full minute of silence. The Emperor examined the eyes of every person. If there was ever any question why the Emperor was the Emperor, that question was quickly answered.

No one objected.

"Kneel!" he ordered.

Everyone knelt, except Father Stephan, who was not expected to, and who stood at the Emperor's side. One by one, the King placed the blade of his great sword upon the shoulder of each.

"We must begin the Order of the Holy Mountain the right way.

"Arise, *Sir* Weft of Zareba.

"Arise, Lady Lucia, already a Crown Princess and Royal by blood.

"Arise, Lady Lemerah, already a Princess and Royal by blood.

"Arise, *Sir* Fairold, already a Prince and Royal by blood of the ancient House of Aeron.

"Arise, Lady Lambith, already a Lady of the Empire.

"Arise *Sir* Galen, already a Prince and Royal by blood of the ancient House of Aeron.

"Arise, *Sir* Soren of Zareba.

"Arise, Sir Kerky, already a knight of Zareba.

"Arise, Lady Millicent of Zareba."

"Arise *Lady* Sto—"

"Your Majesty," Millicent interrupted, "my daughter's not of age, not ready to—"

"Don't *you* interrupt me, Millie!" The words were sharp. Galen shivered. The Emperor turned and stared into the girl's eyes.

"Storie, do you love the God of Heaven...love him enough to die for him?"

"Yes, Your Majesty."

"Can you read?"

"A little, Your Majesty."

Suddenly, the High King drew himself to full height as if facing an ambassador who was holding back important information. His eyes were fiery. He raised his voice.

"You will read and write *perfectly* in one year from this date—when I return for the meeting of our Holy Order. Is that understood?"

Though the girl's fingers trembled and her knees shook, her back was iron. She met the Emperor's gaze head-on, rare for someone her age.

"Yes, Your Majesty."

"And you will obey your father and mother. And you will conduct yourself with dignity and not marry without their permission. Is that understood?"

"Yes, Your Majesty."

The Emperor glanced at Lady Lambith and turned to Millicent.

"The girl and I understand each other. *I* say she's old enough! Arise Lady Storie." As she stood with tears quietly streaming down her cheeks, she became the youngest commoner in Charlayn III's realm to ever be given a title.

"The first meeting of the Knights and Ladies of the Order of the Holy Mountain has come to an end. We will meet here briefly, and privately, tomorrow after the noon meal to work out details. But remember carefully these things: I will announce, and publish, your knighthood, and with the ladies, your rank throughout my kingdom.

If you must, you may mention that you belong to this Order, the Order of the Holy Mountain, that you are committed to the God of Heaven and preserving this Holy Mountain, and that you report only to me, or the person who follows me or the one I designate.

"But no other details are to be told. You must certainly talk about this with God, and you may talk privately about what you've seen and heard among yourselves, but not even to those you marry, so I suggest, but do not require, that you marry among yourselves. A great trust has been placed upon us. When you speak to any other person you always do so at risk. Remember, the walls have ears!

"Is that clear?" The Emperor walked by and studied each face. He stopped in front of the young climber. "Is that clear, Lady Storie Greenwald?"

"Yes, Your Majesty." The girl, now seeming to be in agony, nonetheless stood firm. Galen feared she might tip over and fall. It was then that Crown Princess Lucia exercised a bit of liberty that no one else would have dared. She slipped from her place in the line to behind where the girl stood, put her arms around her and whispered in her ear.

"It is clear to *us*, Your Majesty," said the Princess.

The King over other Kings in this part of Emryss loved God and was wise. Galen had heard his parents talk. But when the High King acted, he could strike like lightning — as now — where a more cautious person would take more counsel, more deliberation, more time. But Charlayn III, probably knew better than most that time could erase the power of the moment. One could be too cautious. The Emperor would have to leave the mountain soon, perhaps right away. After all, the capital, Zareba City, and much of his world was in ruins. Other things demanded attention.

The next rulers of Mt. Zareba would be Galen's father and mother. It made perfect sense. They were wise; they knew and loved the area as he did. But if so, then would he, the firstborn son, be stolen away? And taken by whom? How would that affect the foolish promise his father had made? The Emperor knew nothing about the strange prophecies he and Mira had been given. Would his parents "be blessed within a year" with another child — his brother or sister — to follow them ruling here?

All his life he'd dreamed and thought and planned. By himself. But in the past year he'd had to act. Had to. And nobody stopped him. Now that was over. But what next? Returning to the village, helping repair it, and wandering the surrounding fields? Or should he regularly walk the Monk's Walk, preparing himself to be stolen away? And, on other days, even sleeping long into early morning, as he'd often dreamed of doing?

He'd no idea.

Just before Sir Weft unbolted the Chapel door, Galen saw his father and the Emperor whispering. The transition of rule on the newly occupied mountain was starting to take place. That was good.

* * *

The darkness of night had settled in.

Outside, in the orchard in front of the Chapel, two rows of camp tables had been put together end to end. On each table a lantern of glowing light cast shadows among the fruit trees. How splendid after so many evenings of only one or two small lights! Just beyond the tables, set with great care, more lanterns hung from branches, or were attached to poles. These led to tables of prepared food even farther away. The Emperor had been generously resupplied at his northern palace, which Stulk and his soldiers had never reached. And, in gathering his new army, he took pains to bring at least some of his palace with him.

Plentiful good food made better soldiers, and extra provisions made

455

possible special ceremony to cement new beginnings along the way.

Now was such a time.

After a quick change of clothes — how princesses and ladies could do this so fast, Galen didn't dare guess, but the smell of roasting meat and vegetables (other than potatoes) must have helped — the twelve members of the Order of the Holy Mountain were escorted to the long table closest to, and parallel to, the front of the Chapel. The **Emperor** (now in royal clothes and wearing a crown) stood in the center, his back to the closed Chapel door. Millicent directing, seated the diners in the following order:

The Emperor sat in the center, the door behind him. Beginning on his right, closest to him at the table was **Lord Fairold**, then **Lady Lambith, Sir Kerky, Lady Millicent, Lady Storie**, and at the end facing the length of the table, **Sir Soren**.

Beginning at the Emperor's right, from the people's point of view, closest was **Princess Lucia** (stunningly beautiful with glistening dark hair pulled back and up in a knot), then **Prince Galen** (who'd only managed to put on a dry jacket), **Princess Lemerah** (hair still damp and held in place with a thin silver tiara), **Sir Weft**, and on the end **Father Stephan** facing Soren far down at the other end. Somehow, the black dog found his way under the table undetected. He lay with his jaw across Galen's foot, his tail slowly wagging.

Two other long tables ran — one from near each end — in front of the first table but out at an angle leaving a wide opening in front of the Emperor, the three tables forming sort of a triangle, open at the top. At these two tables, sat generals, officials, a scribe and recorder, and selected knights from the Palace Guard, all facing the first table.

Beyond these tables, crowded in the grass, sat several dozen others who were privileged to stay and hear what followed. Food from heaven, and plenty of it, was quickly and efficiently served, first to the tables, and then to everyone else seated beyond them. Lady Storie was hardly recognizable in the beautiful dress Mira had given her months ago, that she had carefully tucked away. Millicent quietly urged her to eat slowly and to "watch and follow" what the others did, and not—in this case—to jump up and help to clear things away when the meal was over. But long ago the young climber had mastered watching and following, and was still alive to prove it. As long as darkness hid her rough hands, her humble beginnings were still secret.

Galen ate slowly as plate after plate was passed his way. It was the best meal of his life.

After the last food was cleared away, the Emperor stood. He raised his cup.

"Ladies and knights, soldiers and citizens of the Empire"—his voice boomed—"today is a day I have long dreamed of. For the first time in many years we have courageously entered, successfully occupied, and mightily defended the Holy Mountain of the God of Heaven!"

The Emperor was interrupted by cheering and applause. Those seated in the grass rose to their feet.

"And our flag now flies from atop yon tower!" He pointed to where the flag was almost lost in darkness above the King's Room in the first tower.

More cheering and applause.

"This was possible, not because of anything I did, but because of a daring band of ten defenders, four of whom lost their lives: Master Maleg the stone mason, his son Saren"—from the end of the table Sir Soren bowed his head and under the table Lady Storie found his hand—"and from my palace, an honorable maid named Mara, and… and my only son Prince Pinrut. We will remember them now with a moment of silence."

And they did.

"We are here tonight because Lord Fairold and Sir Kerky successfully got almost everyone safely away from the Zareba Village before the enemy arrived.

"Commanders, knights, and citizens of our vast Empire, know this: The uprising from the South has been crushed, and we are here today because of the cleverness and bravery of the four defenders, including my son, who have fallen, and the four villagers who remained behind, and one 'warrior from the south' "—Soren smiled at Storie—"and my younger daughter who survived. These ten, now six, against all odds found entry to this mountain fortress when for decades no one else could, and courageously defended it, holding off more than 1000 soldiers, and killing hundreds of the enemy. Will you six please stand?"

The six stood, and immediately afterwards, so did everyone else not already standing. Many looked at the six with expressions of unbelief. Then the clapping began.

When Galen sat, the others at the tables followed suit. The recorder wrote furiously.

The Emperor raised his hands for silence.

"Please… please let me finish. Now has come a day I have long dreamed of," he repeated, "a day when Mt. Zareba can be at peace, and can forever fly overhead the flag of our Empire, and be a place of worship of the Son of the God of Heaven. However, for this to continue, we must have *three* things.

"*First*, to look after this place itself, I have established the **Order of the Holy Mountain**, and we are they who sit before you. As I call each member's name I will ask that person to stand, and remain standing. Hold your applause until I have called everyone."

And so he did, the people applauded, and the twelve—except for the Emperor—sat down.

"*Secondly*, we must have a wise and Godly person to rule."

Galen looked at his father and smiled. Their time had come. He reached down and patted the dog's head. But Mira's hand was already there. "I miss Pinrut," he whispered. She raised her hand and secretly

458

took his. A wet dog nose pressed against their fingers.

"I love you," she whispered.

Galen looked up and found the Emperor staring at him. He straightened in his chair, and returned his gaze, as was proper. He must look suitable for his father's sake. He tried to pull his hand away but failed.

"Prince Galen, of the ancient House of Aeron, has renounced his title as Prince of this mountain," said the Emperor. "I accept that. Now I will appoint the next High Ruler of this mountain and the royal companion to that person…May their children and their children's children rule this mountain until the King of Kings, the God-Son himself, returns." He looked back to Lord Fairold and Lady Lambith. Galen sighed with relief.

For ten full seconds there was silence.

"Citizens of Zareba, knights of the Empire, and especially Lord Fairold and Lady Lambith, it gives me great pleasure to present to you the new *High* Prince of this Holy Mountain — Prince Galen of the House of Aeron." Galen's jaw dropped. The Emperor turned back to him.

"But…but, Your Majesty! I…I'm too —"

"Too young?" interrupted the Emperor. "Sorry, Prince Galen, but this can't wait, and neither can I. You've more than proven yourself and I trust you. So does your father, who will rebuild the village down below. As to age, don't worry, you'll pick up years faster than you care to receive them, especially when you marry."

"*Marry!*" Suddenly, Mira released her hand and Galen found himself standing, the silence of the mountain swept away by a cheering louder than he'd ever heard. His knees began to shake. Then the Princesses on either side of him stood followed by the others at the table. Above the noise he heard a whisper on his right. He turned to face Princess Lucia. She bent her lips to his ear.

"Help is nearby, Galen. Just hold on!" Lightly, she kissed his cheek.

More cheering. That fateful promise! But Princess Lucia—who was she?—a woman groomed for a Palace, to rule an Empire, not a country outpost. Of course, the Emperor still had many years to rule. She could get experience here, maybe have a child, a child who—Galen suddenly began to sweat.

"*Thirdly*, for this special mountain we must have a High Princess. The High Prince must marry! And, marry on the second day after this one since I must leave." Galen's knees started to buckle. The Princesses on either side crowded close to keep him from falling. Father Stephan, of all people, was smiling.

"Let me present to you the new High Princess of Mt. Zareba, my own beloved daughter"—he paused—"Princess...Princess Lemerah!"

Lemerah?! Had he heard it right? The Emperor was going to marry off his second daughter first? Trust his pretty, headstrong, silly, wonderful younger daughter with all the responsibilities of the Holy Mountain? He looked at his mother who was tight-lipped but smiling. He caught Millicent's eye. She was beaming. How had they done this behind his back? But hadn't the two of them privately had the ear of the Emperor before?

"Galen..."—it was Lucia—"See, I told you help was nearby. My sister is most blessed. I owe you so much. If only I can find a husband half as fine as you. Now kiss her properly because everyone's watching, and so will I to see if you do it right." The Emperor's older daughter was enjoying this too much! What had she known? She bowed low to the High Prince and backed away towards her father. But her eyes were wet.

The cheering began. He turned to his bride-to-be, who now alone was keeping him steady.

"It's you...Lemerah!" he whispered.

"It's me, *Mira*," she whispered back. "Up here I'm Mira—Galen, are you okay? Can you stand by yourself?" Holding his arms, she leaned back a few inches, looked deep into his eyes and smiled.

"I love you, Princess Mira — High Princess Mira — Princess Mira of the House of Aeron! Aren't you glad we practiced in the tunnel?" he found himself whispering. "Your sister said she'd be watching." Together they stood face to face. The cheering became louder.

"Practice?" She answered a bit louder. "I don't remember *practicing!*"

"But, Mira, remember you're now a High Princess of the Holy Mountain."

"I will never, never forget that, Galen. And you must never forget that I can also play-act! But not quite as well as my father — or you!" The cheering now was deafening.

"Play-acting? What's that?" Methodically, he reached down, picked up her cup and handed it to her. Then he picked up his own. Together they held out their cups to the cheering people. Then, turning, he pressed his cup to her lips. She drank. Then slowly she raised her own cup to his lips and he drank.

He set the cups back on the table. He circled her with his arms and squeezed.

They kissed.

His knees finally stopped shaking (for a moment). Then they looked up. The roof of the tunnel had melted away. Pinpricks of light salted the sky. By moonlight they could see the flag slowly waving above the fifth floor of the tower.

"Two days..." he began.

"...from today," she finished.

"So much for my old plans," he said. "I'll have to start making new ones."

"I'll help," she said matter-of-factly, keeping a straight face.

He touched his lips again to hers, but lightly. They sat, nudging away the face of the dog under the table, so they could sit as close as possible without seeming obvious.

They glanced at Princess Lucia. Tears were streaming down her cheeks, but she was smiling.

"I think she approves," said Mira.

"I love you," they both said, laughing that their words came at exactly the same time. There was a tap on his shoulder. One of the food servers quietly approached and handed him a note, which indicated that this was not the end of surprises this night.

"A toast for our new High Prince and High Princess!" yelled Sir Kerky, standing and saying his first words. Everyone raised his cup and drank. It would fall to Millicent's husband to lead the High Prince the next day on a long journey along the Monk's Walk. And with Sir Kerky only would he share the strange conflicting prophecies that he and Mira had been given about children to be born.

"High Prince Galen, is there anything you want to say?" asked the Emperor. At once all were silent.

"Yes, Your Majesty" — how automatic was his father's training, and yes, he had rehearsed his words — "just two, no three things." He put down his cup. "First, I do love Princess Mira, as she wishes to be called on the mountain, with all my heart.

"Second, I will do my best to serve the God of Heaven and do all you expect of me.

"Third, my counselor Lady Millicent wishes to have a word."

The white-haired Lady rose.

"Your Majesty, Knights and Ladies of the Holy Mountain, commanders, leaders, and villagers just returned, I want to announce a future marriage. Our ablest defender, Sir Soren, must leave with the Emperor for several months of training after which he will return and marry my daughter Lady Storie one year from this date." She turned and whispered to the girl beside her, "not one day earlier! I'm not finished with you and Lady Lambith hasn't even begun. What I have done I can undo, and trust me, you don't want to tempt the Emperor about what he said!"

Lady Storie stood ramrod straight, and bowed to the Emperor, then the people. Her tears were gone. With a quick flourish so her rough hand wouldn't show, she reached down to the rough hand of the former stone worker, Sir Soren, and pulled him to his feet. For the first time in many days he wore no sling. He took her in his arms and they kissed.

Again there was applause, too much for what had been said, according to Millicent.

But peace had long last come to Mt. Zareba, which held precious secrets about the history of Emryss and God's people there. A sudden unexpected marriage between the new High Prince and High Princess would celebrate this peace and the fact that an old chapter of Zareba—Mountain, Village, and City—was over, and a new chapter was about to begin.

THE END

✳   ✳   ✳

EPILOGUE
(found attached to the story)

It was my grandfather, or great-grandfather—perhaps both—who said it was important to write down important things before they're lost, so I, Galen, wish to add a few more sentences to our story. I write this four years after High Princess Mira and I were married.

As to **Lady Storie** and **Sir Soren**: First, they were married in a bit less than a year, but on the first day that Millicent permitted it. When the Emperor returned for his annual visit, which was exactly a year after he left, he said he'd never encountered a woman who learned

463

so fast and could read and write so well, though it was her skill with numbers that was unsurpassed. The two lived both in Zareba City and Zareba Village, but also in the Royal Court where they tutored and taught at the Emperor's request.

As to **High Princess Lemerah** and **High Prince Galen**: We were hardly more than children when we began life together in the King's Room on the fifth floor of the tower. But memories of all we'd faced together defending the Holy Mountain, and especially our time in the Secret Chamber, had cemented our love, regardless of what lay ahead. We'd already overcome tremendous obstacles and knew how it hurt to suffer great loss. And we'd already learned one of life's great lessons: Things are often not what they first seem.

Now about the confusing prophecies? Would the son promised to arrive within a year rule our tiny world after me? Or would our firstborn be stolen away?

Though we were young and seemed to have been forced together, it was hardly against our will! Loving Mira was at first scary, and later she confessed it was the same for her, but actually it was one of the easiest and most wonderful things that could happen. After all, how many are encouraged to make love by a prophecy from Heaven! Nearly a year after our marriage, the midwives prepared my dear Mira to give birth. Never did I pray longer and harder!

But never did I expect what happened. If *I* was a child on the morning of my dear Mira's delivery, I was a much older one by evening. Soon after I heard the baby's first cry, I was presented with a beautiful *daughter*! "Her name is **Triana**," said Mira, "She is Ann of three Zarebas." It was an unusual name, but I had no objection, for I had no name in mind for a girl.

But that wasn't all.

The midwife smiled. "Prince Galen, your wife as usual is full of surprises, for our work is not finished!" In several minutes I was

464

handed a second child, a handsome son.

"His name will be **Prince Corban**," I said, feeling it was my turn.

Most important, my dear Mira survived in good health, and two years later gave birth to another daughter, and just last year to another son, but I'm certain that's more than you care to know.

In our beginning years of life on Mt. Zareba, with frequent visits to my parents in the restored village — now with a wall — down below, many from far and near have come to see the work of the weavers as well as the Holy Mountain, so long cloaked in secrecy. Again and again, my dear friend Sir Kerky and I have secretly prayed about what may lie ahead and the precautions we should take. But as of this writing, High Princess Mira and I couldn't be happier about the life that God has brought our way.

END OF EPILOGUE

NOTE WRITTEN AFTER EPILOGUE

Emris grohw smaal lik pohnt. Girrrll nowe leffft oft criing, hav al books in haanfd, Saffe liftoff once agin.

CHAPTER 49

A Critique of The Secret of Zareba

THE STORY EXAMINED

TIME: AEMP 01, 1 AM, Day 319

PLACE: Dr. Harwell's Study

  Susquehanna Territory, northeastern PA

(This chapter picks up where Chapter 26 ended on p. 212.)

What book club ever had such a story to consider! Talk about "The Secret of Zareba" went far beyond the complexities of "Death in a Tavern." And it put people's reputations, if not their very lives at risk.

The hand-wound Regulator clock in the corner of Harwell's office struck one o'clock. The minister earlier had removed his coat and tie, familiar to all who knew him. Dim light radiated from an oil lamp, augmented by a thick homemade candle surrounded by a glass globe at the end of Harwell's desk, where Michael and Triana had pulled up their chairs and done their reading.

Michael had raced through the story "Death in a Tavern," taking two hours, making notes here and there while Triana turned the pages of "The Secret of Zareba" as one might thoughtfully consider a book of pictures. Her eyesight was mainly troublesome for distances, so Michael knew she'd missed little.

How peculiar their problem with Mr. Cample! Nearly a year ago the world suddenly had been crippled by an electronic plague, presumably isolating people into self-contained "walled worlds," at least it had in their world, and probably had killed untold millions.

Now in one of those worlds, their teacher had seemed to throw all his energy into accusing his two best students of an absurd act of cheating, something that nowadays most other teachers would have paid scant attention to.

But Michael knew Marvin Cample was not just any teacher.

The oddity did not stop there.

Were the stories, really, more than just imaginings put down on paper — one tale recorded by the girl, the other somehow obtained by his adopted father? If Triana had actually written the first story, what amazing talent! What passion for detail for both teller and recorder! And the intricacy of the plot of the second story was profound.

The discussion of "Death in a Tavern" with its unique calendar and genealogies had just ended. Michael ran his fingers through his curly brown hair. A connection between the stories was obvious. It was clear why Mr. Cample, so passionate about honesty, was upset! But then, that wasn't the "whole story" here. Somehow Cample had two more stories with important details that Triana and Jonas knew nothing about.

And, Michael? He, of course, knew the least of all.

What Triana had said had gone far beyond fascinating. And his teacher was taking things far past an accusation of cheating.

Marvin Cample tugged at the collar of his faded plaid shirt.

"Now let's look at 'The Secret of Zareba,' which is the most un-Christian Christian story I've ever read!"

"Come again?" said Harwell, leaning forward from behind his desk. Again the swivel chair squeaked. The lamp flickered and the minister's shadow danced eerily along the shelves stuffed with books. When Triana stood to stretch and smooth out her skirt, Michael took the opportunity to pull his and Triana's chairs even closer together, and a bit farther back from the imposing desk and its lamplight.

"The parallels to Jewish history and the church almost overpower the story," said Cample. "The Golden Chest of Promise is just like the Biblical Ark of the Covenant. The stakes that killed the God-Son correspond to the cross of Jesus. A virgin birth is mentioned, and even the coming of a 'suffering Savior' who will someday return and rule as king. I could go on and on. It's just like your Bible. Everything's the same, but different."

"Why do you have a problem with that?" asked Harwell. "You're certainly familiar with Lewis's Narnia stories and allegories that have Jewish and Christian parallels."

"Of course! But Jonas, this isn't being presented as an allegory!" Cample paused to let the words sink in. "This is being presented as 'truth,' as if it really happened."

"You mean," said the minister, "that it's made to look like real *history*, right?"

"Exactly."

"What's so disturbing about that?" asked Michael, wondering at his own words.

"Like I said earlier" — the teacher shifted in his seat — "the problem should be yours, not mine! You believe, I take it, that 'The Secret of Zareba' is historically true, that Jesus Christ *literally*, and I underscore that word, was born, lived, died, and rose again in several places, but at *one point in cosmic time*. Correct?"

"Yes..." said Harwell. "But we've already touched on that before... Yes, you do have a real concern, and so do I. So let me go a bit further. What I say will be based on science. But I warn you, it'll sound a bit wild!"

"Try me."

"As to 'one place.' Scientifically, what we see — here on Earth, of course — as something in one place is not really in one place at all.

"And why? Because every solid thing we see, even touch, is mostly empty space. Now let me take a little liberty to make a point. This empty space is 'shaped' by the kind of matter within it into, let's call it, 'race tracks' for atomic particles that continually move at mind-boggling speeds. This motion is so fast and predictable that everything solid looks solid and feels like it's at rest.

"But these particles are never at rest. On a submicroscopic level, if we tried to net and pull out one *particular* particle in the solid in front of us, it would be impossible to — "

"*Dr.* Harwell," Cample interrupted, "you're starting to lose me! Just what are you driving at?"

"Marvin, what I'm saying is simply this: *The stuff of matter in a particular thing can be in many places though, as far as our eyes are concerned, it rests in one place.*"

"Say that again."

At that point Triana cupped her hand and leaned towards her companion to whisper something. Michael, lost in his own thoughts and not seeing her, accidentally tilted sideways and his ear touched her lips.

"Uh …sorry!" He pulled himself upright.

Triana covered her mouth with a feigned look of embarrassment, but her startled eyes were also smiling.

"Pardon me," she said loud enough for all to hear, "I'll try again." She leaned forward a second time and behind her cupped hand whispered, "Want me to explain this to you later?" Then in the dim light, ever so subtly, but this time deliberately, she touched her lips to his ear. It was a kiss. How could she so quickly have converted an accident into this!

"Sure," said Michael, "I'll be glad to explain what Jonas is saying!" surprised at his quick comeback, before realizing how silly it sounded.

Triana stifled a giggle, which for the moment seemed, especially

469

for her, so out of character. Cample laughed, Harwell searched the ceiling, and Michael — his world, from molecules on up — struggled to pull back together.

"It's just flirting, Mr. Cample!" said Triana, "At Grace Alliance we're awfully strict, but it's something we single Christians are permitted at least to try if in the presence of two mature adult chaperones." So much for wondering! Or was it? Harwell closed his eyes and Cample laughed again, which, thought Michael, was perfect for the late hour of what might become an all-night marathon. He struggled to get back on track while the girl continued without missing a beat, *"that the stuff of matter in a particular thing can be in many places though..."* she turned to her foster father and waited.

"Though as far as our eyes are concerned," said Harwell, *"it is static and solid, resting in one place."*

"Okay, go on." Cample uncrossed his legs and leaned forward.

"Now God as *Spirit* and as *Father* exists everywhere. Hardly any Christian would challenge this mystery — though he'd be hard pressed to explain it. Now *just suppose* somehow, in some way, the Son of God — perhaps known by different names in different places — can and did exist in the limits of human flesh in more than one location.

"If this sounds strange — and I'm sure it does — just remember that, apart from faith in some act we can't understand, we can't explain the Virgin Birth of our own Savior Jesus. And few attempt to. It's a mystery, which — "

"Which" — Triana placed her glasses in her lap — "is another way of saying we don't *presently* understand it, right?"

"Yes...except we might never understand it with the limits of our human minds. But please realize that scientists don't like to say that. I'm simply trying to say that maybe...*just maybe, the eternal Jesus appeared in the flesh simultaneously in other worlds*...and I do this by talking — superficially, I'll grant you — about some science we do understand.

"Just suppose that God-the-Father desired God-the-Son to go in the flesh as Savior to several places for brief 'lifetime' face-to-face encounters with fallen humans, who—let's say—live on other planets besides Earth. Perhaps, just perhaps, he, the Creator of everything, caused the matter, or energy—and Einstein showed the two were related—of his body to move at infinite speed, infinitely 'vibrating,' across light years of distance from place to place—wherever the Father wanted him to be."

"Can science explain this?" asked Cample.

"Absolutely not," continued Harwell. "No more than it can explain the Virgin Birth or the Trinity that I accept for nonscientific reasons. I'm just trying to use a known phenomenon from science as a springboard to consider certain possibilities. God has given us laws of matter and energy, but perhaps there are deeper laws behind the laws we know. After all, he created all things, and many scientists have even made a case for that. We are the stuff of creation, not the planner or engineer of it.

"*If* the matter which the Son of God once took upon himself could somehow infinitely vibrate from planet to planet, then he as the God-man could be in several places as a *human person* at the same time. By the end of the 20th century, science had clearly demonstrated that time was linear.

"And that by using science that we know, we can trace back to a fixed point many, many years ago when everything began. To go further, then at one specific point in cosmic time—if a perfect clock started at the beginning of time could mark it—there could be one Holy Conception; at another point, a Holy Birth; at another, a Holy Death; at another, a Holy Resurrection; and at still another point in comic time, One Second Coming—"

"You're saying the Bible *teaches* this?" interrupted Cample.

"Ab-so-lute-ly not!" Harwell reached over and gently lay his hand

471

on the well-worn leather volume which in the dim light looked almost the same color as his desktop. "But…the Bible does declare that God is the creator, sustainer, and savior of all the universe. Other than that, it says nothing about what I just said. Nor does it suggest it."

"Then why," said Cample, "are you suggesting it?"

"Good question, Marvin, and it goes to the heart of things. Sometimes we—even us preachers—must look beyond the Bible to find answers to questions life forces us to ask."

Michael and Triana glanced at each other.

"Doesn't sound like what you heard in Sunday school?" He glanced at each of the other three and smiled. "Well, some things just aren't meant to be learned there! And we must recognize that! But don't jump to conclusions. The Bible doesn't explain molecules, microwaves, microorganisms, or the EMP that's suddenly fractured our world. Yet all these exist.

"Nor does science explain everything that emerges from matter and energy. Science can tell us very clearly how to make nuclear bombs, but it *can't* tell us *if* we should make them or how we should use them. It *can't* tell us why we love or hate, or why we even ask questions about all these things."

"I agree," Cample broke in. "That's one reason we have folklore and stories—because science can only go so far. But let's get back to Jesus. Let me see if I follow—you're saying *we need* to think about the Son of God going to worlds far beyond the orbit of Earth?"

"No and Yes. No, earthlings don't have to consider this for their own needs—at least I don't think so. But…what if there are other *fallen* people created in the image of God on other planets? And, what if you had good reason to believe they needed and wanted our help? And further, what if science found a way to leave Earth and get to them?"

"An interesting problem, Jonas." Cample reached up and scratched his ear. Michael smiled when he imagined him inspecting to see if he was hearing right. The teacher continued. "But let me back up. You're trying to say, if I'm hearing you right, that one religion—our own Christianity—cuts across the cosmos and that there are parallel Scriptures that tell about the same 'Father-Son-Holy Spirit-God'?

"And you're also *insisting* that everywhere the Son of God appeared in the flesh that he was conceived, born, died, and resurrected at *the exact same cosmic moments?* Presumably, then, he's going to come back again at the same cosmic moment?"

"I'd prefer to say that I'm *open* to that."

"Okay…but *if* 'The Secret of Zareba' is a true story, doesn't your argument conflict with the Bible and break down? For example, look at how ages and times differ in the story. The Emperor says the God-Son is said to have lived 29 ½ years from conception to resurrection…"

"And," interrupted Triana, "you're implying, although the Bible doesn't say exactly, it's generally accepted that Jesus lived from birth to death and resurrection about 33 years."

"But look," said Michael, "years are longer on Emryss—420 days to be exact." He reached up to the edge of the desk where his notes lay and began scribbling. "Look at this! 420 days divided by 365 days times 29 ½ years equals 33.9 years, and since on Emryss the God-Son's age was measured not from birth but from conception, as the Chinese once did, to death and resurrection, the length of his lifespan in each place is almost exactly the same!"

"I saw that," said Cample. "Quite frankly, I was taken aback by that discovery. But how do you handle the strange way the God-Son's future rule as King is treated?

"The story says that he'll come back and reign

'a lifetime times a lifetime'

and there's confusion about just what that means. The Emperor seems to think that 'lifetime' refers to the God-Son's lifetime of 29 ½ years, and if that length of time is taken literally, he will reign 29 ½ squared, or 29 ½ times 29 ½ years.

"According to your theory, Jonas, if Jesus or the God-Son were to return to rule on Earth or on Emryss or anywhere else, wouldn't he have to return in the flesh at the same moment and reign for the same length of time? And doesn't the Bible say that he will reign for a *millennium*? Doesn't your reasoning about Jesus-being-at-several-places-at-one-time break down here?"

"Wait a minute!" It was Michael's turn. He stood at the desk and for a full minute scribbled in silence. "Look...look at this! Let's take things literally. If the 'lifetime' referred to is the lifetime of the God-Son, or 29 ½, and we square it, we get 870 years. But since years there are longer, or 420/365 or 1.15 longer, and we convert that reign to Earth years, or 870 times 1.15, we get almost exactly *1000 Earth years,* and that, Mr. Cample, is what a millenium is!"

"Let me see that!" gasped Cample. Sweat suddenly began to bead his forehead. Michael handed him the paper.

"Now Marvin, to be fair, not all Christians see Jesus reigning here for a thousand years, but I and many others do, and we believe the Bible teaches this."

But Cample wasn't listening.

"Now there, 870 years; here, 1000...but Jesus' age was 33. Multiply 33 times 33 — "

"And," interrupted Michael, "you get an answer much bigger than a thousand. But then our Bible doesn't talk about Jesus' return that way."

"O my God!" said Cample.

"Oh he can be," said Harwell, "if you're serious! But don't be taken in by just an interesting pattern of numbers. There's much more than that. And...and there are still things here that, quite frankly, I don't understand."

"Same for me," added Triana.

"Oh...make no mistake"—Cample wiped his brow with his sleeve—"I'm far from 'out of the woods' on this."

"Cliché," whispered Triana, just loud enough. "Which drains away the meaning of what you really feel." She offered a thin smile. "You were so insistent about this in class I can't let it pass!"

"I'm far from out of the woods," repeated Cample seeming not to hear. "And my real feelings? I don't know." He smiled and again wiped his brow. "I feel weak."

"We all do," said Harwell.

Michael suspected the man was grateful for a turn in the conversation.

"But," Cample continued, "you don't know everything I know, and Jonas, if you're puzzled—and especially you, Triana—I'm certain I can show you some interesting things that can—"

"Answer my questions?" asked Triana. She brushed away a strand of hair that had fallen across her face.

"Oh yes! I can give you some answers, but watch for the questions that come with them...bigger ones!" He shook his head as if startled by his own words. He lifted his briefcase to his lap. "But before I show you anything"—he focused on Harwell—"you're going to have to answer at least one of my questions." He paused. "What do you mean, Triana, when you say you 'translated' the story, 'Death in a Tavern'?"

Triana looked at Harwell.

"Tell him," said the minister.

The End of Part IV

475

PART V

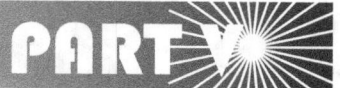

THE RESOLUTION

"When the blood of three worlds mingles in a child, many will once again believe."

ancient prophecy from the
I-Rex Code of Elphia

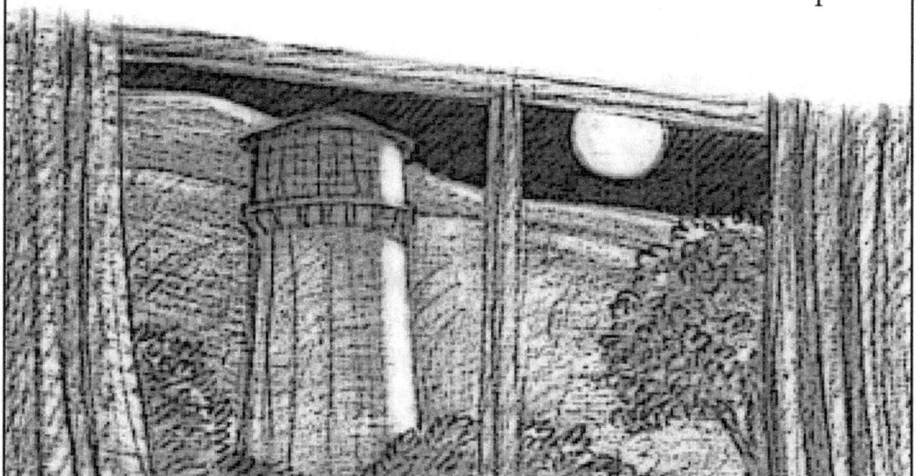

CHAPTER 50

A CALL TO GO?

As Triana started to explain, Sally Ferguson appeared in the doorway with a tray of bowls of steaming oatmeal, and where she'd gotten brown sugar to put on it was anybody's guess! She laid them on the desk, called Harwell aside, wiped her already clean hands on a large apron, and whispered silently. Michael saw she was troubled.

The minister returned to his chair.

"Marvin, as you probably know, we've got company upstairs."

"Long-time company?" asked Cample.

Michael stiffened. Now and then circulated the story that a man had lived there upstairs for about three years. But he'd never seen him. When Jonas had sat Michael down and told him that there was a man without a family, that he was "special," and not well, that Sally who was also a nurse, and Triana as her aide were trying to bring him back to health, and for the present he required privacy, Michael accepted and dismissed it as one of those things people live with.

But "long-time company"? Long-time questions came flooding back.

"That's right, Marvin and, unfortunately, things aren't looking good. It's 2 AM. We'll have to wrap up things sooner rather than later, but don't worry, Triana can and will have her say."

"I hope she can answer that question before I leave," said Cample.

"Let's talk while we eat," said Harwell, fixing his eyes on the tray.

Michael quickly passed around the bowls and milk.

"Mr. Cample," said the girl, "remember our agreement?" She rearranged her hands in her lap and leaned forward.

"Yes, all things said here will be confidential—insofar as legally possible."

"Well then, let me be direct. I consider you honest and fair. And you certainly care about the honesty of your students!" She glanced at Michael. "You may believe or disbelieve my words. That's your privilege."

"And my responsibility," added Cample.

"And," said the girl, "let me be frank. While I don't mind if we disagree, I don't care to be laughed at."

"Triana, if three years ago you'd try to tell me that EMP was coming and what it would do to us, I would've thought you were crazy. But even then I wouldn't have laughed. Now with all I've seen and heard—today—how could I ever laugh? I can still smile though....Can't you see"—he extended his arms—"I'm on my knees?"

Triana put her glasses back on and studied her teacher as if he were marble on display in a gallery.

"Not quite..." She declared. "You're still very much in your chair. Mr. Cample, that man upstairs is a friend named Igneal...a dear friend who isn't well. And as you can see"—she slipped her glasses off and turned to her companion—"Michael also knows nothing about him, no details anyway. Igneal, who's older than Jonas—and that's in Earth years, Mr. Cample—Igneal and I...have, separately, come to this kind home here from far...perhaps very far away.

"Igneal is brilliant, like no one I've ever met, but his mind now"—she blotted her eyes and put her glasses back on—"is failing along with his body. He knows things, Mr. Cample, that nobody else knows. He can say things in detail very precisely, and a week later repeat what he said—word for word.

"Some have called him a mad man, I've been told, and strangely that protected him for years, and that's one reason why he's now here. I talk to this man and write down what he says, some things in English, which he can speak perfectly, but for only minutes at a time, as well some other language that easily falls from his tongue. And...from my tongue as well, even though I can't identify the language!"

"Things," interrupted Cample, "like about a 'meteor' that fell in Kansas about twelve years ago?"

Silence.

"And becoming a *meteorite* as it landed," interjected Michael, again trying to be disarming, but again feeling foolish after the words slipped out. Cample had obviously struck a nerve. How long could she stay in control? Michael reached out and covered her hand with his. She looked at her foster father. He nodded.

"Some people called it a meteor," she said.

"Falsely?" asked the teacher.

"Mr. Cample, I don't know where you got your information, but yes, falsely, I think."

"Well" — the teacher shifted in his chair — "maybe I can erase those doubts."

Harwell scooted to the edge of his chair and Michael sensed that the girl was struggling to gather new courage.

"If you can help me, why have you waited so long?"

"Triana, it wasn't until you and Michael handed in your stories that I knew enough to intrude. And you Christians — I didn't know how you'd react to questioning, how you'd treat me, or what might be at stake for you. Triana, it probably sounds silly, but I sensed your pain. And please forgive me, in spite of my curiosity, I didn't want to hurt you. Can you believe that?"

"I can."

"But submission of the two stories actually forced my hand — and, quite frankly, gave me the excuse I'd been waiting for. I'll bet if you had one wish, one wish in the world, you'd wish you never handed in those stories. Right?"

"Mr. Cample" — her eyes riveted on his — "there's a lot in all this that I don't understand, there's much I'm quite confused about, but maybe, just maybe something's going on that's larger than we all realize, and maybe *you* are a part of it. If I had *one* wish, it would be that you'd stop fighting and come to believe as we do."

The teacher's head snapped back as if hit by a stick. Tears welled up in his eyes and began to trickle down his cheeks, but he made no sound. Triana handed him a napkin and continued talking as if nothing had happened.

"Mr. Cample, you're not afraid to express emotion — I value that — and you love stories of the mind, folktales that people create, stories that help us understand the way people have thought for hundreds and thousands of years. And so do I. But for me — the girl sitting before you — I've the strong suspicion, but no real proof, that *I was in fact born in another world, or had parents who were, and have come to Earth.* I wasn't joking earlier. I have faint memories of a gleaming silver spaceship, of seeing everything clearly without glasses. I have occasional nightmares of a flaming explosion.

"About two years ago I learned that a man who supposedly came with me on that silver ship still lived, but was old, slowly dying, and very confused, having been locked away for years in several mental institutions — the safest place, by the way, for the federal government to hide people who say the things Igneal does. Who in an institution cares about the ravings of an odd-looking old man who mostly speaks in an unknown tongue?" She paused to let this sink in.

"And — you may find this strange — he insists he believes in Jesus, though often he calls him the God-Son, and insists there's only one God. So perhaps he's a religious crazy — but if so, then I'm one also. If you question his sanity or mine — or even Jonas's — I don't blame you. Igneal and I haven't been the first who've claimed to be from different worlds.

"Igneal lives bedridden upstairs, where I've spent countless hours with him, and where Sally and I have tried to nurse him back to health. Oddly, though he knows English — which he can only speak for a few minutes at one time — this brilliant man talks to me endlessly in a strange language that he patiently teaches me and that falls so easily from my tongue," she repeated for emphasis. She glanced at Harwell. "Igneal is the one who continually reminds me of the haunting words that somehow I'd heard as a young child:

> *"Triana, always remember,*
> *you are a child of **Emryss**,*
> *the stolen daughter of Galen,*
> *High Prince of Zareba.*
> *Though the Golden Sword is lost*
> *the Flying Horse is dead, and*
> *the Kingdom is destroyed,*
> *the royal blood of the House*
> *of Aeron flows in your veins.*
>
> *And also, Your Highness,*
> *you are a daughter of **Elphia**,*
> *so the blood of two worlds flows*
> *in your veins.*
>
> *And even more, dear girl,*
> *according to an ancient prophecy*
> *from the lost Holy Book of Elphia,*
> *'when the blood of three worlds*
> *mingles in a child, a remnant of*
> *people in Elphia will once again*
> *believe.'"*

"From the words I've heard from Igneal I painstakingly wrote down the story 'Death in a Tavern,' going over and over it with him several times. I've tried to be accurate with every word.

"Oddly perhaps"—she glanced at Harwell—"in all this time my foster father has never shown me the story, 'The Secret of Zareba,' which he must have obtained elsewhere."

"Correct," interjected Harwell. "Marvin, I've never shown 'The Secret of Zareba' to either child for reasons of my own."

Triana continued:

"In 'Death in a Tavern,' according to Igneal, Prince Fairold is declared to be a descendant of 'Great King Agnon' of the House of Aeron. The frustrating part is that in his perfect bard-like telling of the story, mostly in English, partly in his own language, he doesn't once mention the Queen's name or her husband's name! Nor does Igneal seem to know them! It's just like in the Bible where we know the names of the faithful Jewish midwives who saved the babies, including Moses, but the name of the oppressive ruling Pharaoh has been lost!

"So I'm supposed to believe I'm a real princess from a real world called Emryss. Why? What's my evidence? A memory of sometime years ago hearing some of what I'm now told in greater detail. My source? A dying old man—a wonderful, confused, bedridden genius whose pale skin is not too much lighter than mine. A man who may have come from a planet scientifically advanced enough to send a spaceship to another planet called Emryss, and then here to Earth.

"And, with a strange story and strange information from one of those worlds.

"And he swears over and over again that he and his 'friends' are in no way related to me, and I wasn't 'stolen back' or reclaimed for some Elphian ancestors. Yet his language, unlike any other on Earth as far as I know, is music to my ears!

"Fortunately, language, and translating is unbelievably easy for me.

483

I'm a language savant, I've been told. Remember my words to Jacky Fenton this — I mean yesterday — afternoon? He was speaking demonic words in Igneal's tongue. But why of all people was Jacky speaking it? I've no idea, unless something or someone is trying to force me to give up secrets. What Jacky said — and I don't want to repeat it — was evil and had to be answered.

"But were those words really from Emryss, or perhaps Elphia? I'm not sure. Igneal says he's Elphian, or an 'Elph' as some say, but remember, he's lived for years around people who think they're from Mars! My connection to him? Nothing I can prove, though it's quite probable that we arrived at the same time, perhaps in Kansas.

"But I do have the story, 'Death in a Tavern,' Mr. Cample — which I trusted you with. Now I also have 'The Secret of Zareba' which is brand-new to me. Its Epilogue, said to be tacked on four years later, is obviously startling, but is consistent with everything I remember. And I'll show you why.

"Still, I have so little to go on." She reached for and unfolded a piece of paper. "Let me summarize everything I think I've learned from Igneal and these two stories. Since I have to start somewhere, I will be chronological:

TRIANA'S CHRONOLOGY

"1. _King Merceon_ of the Royal House of Aeron, in long ages past, is anointed by Eldon the prophet to be guardian of the **Golden Chest of Promise** [told to me by Igneal and supported by both stories]. Sometime after this, due to war, destruction of Zareba, or some other cause, the House of Aeron probably relocates far to the East.

"2. _The God-Son, born to a woman from House of Aeron who now lives back in Zareba, lives, dies, and rises again many, many years after that_ ["The Secret of Zareba" (TSOZ)].

"3. _King Agnon, the Great_ descendant of King Merceon of the House of Aeron comes to the throne many years after that (presumably back in the East). [Personally "told" about Agnon; also supported by both stories].

"4. IMPORTANT UNKNOWN PEOPLE. Let me group them. Agnon's son? Agnon's grandson? We know nothing about them. Agnon's granddaughter, all 3 of these, by the way, from the H of A, is the unnamed "Queen" who bore 4 sons. ["Death in a Tavern" (DIAT)]. There seem to be a lot of important things that are unknown in this time frame!

"5. _Lord (Prince) Fairold_ 2nd son of unnamed Queen of H of A and great-grandson of Agnon (above) [DIAT, TSOZ].

"6. _High Prince Galen_ 'great-great grandson of King Agnon' and _High Princess Lemerah_ (or Mira) daughter of Emperor Charlayn III (house or lineage unknown) [I was "told" this and it is confirmed by TSOZ].

"7. _Princess Triana_ daughter (firstborn of twins) of High Prince Galen and High Princess Lemerah, and great-great-great granddaughter of King Agnon, who was, according to God's will, stolen away by strangers [I was told this and it seems confirmed by the words that seem like gibberish tacked onto the end of TSOZ]. I would translate

'_Emris grohw smaal lik pohnt. Girrrll nowe leffft oft_
Criing, hav al books in haanfd. Saffe liftoff once agin.'
as
'**Emryss grows small like (a) point. (The) girl (has)**
now left off crying. (We) have all (the) books in hand.
[maybe this refers to the stories that were stolen with the girl]. **Safe liftoff once again.'**

END OF CHRONOLOGY

"Why was such a note put there? Because her life on Planet Emryss, especially to the girl, was over, and whoever left Emryss with her and the story wanted to make clear that the prophecy about the stolen Princess had come true.

"Just one more thing about the strange-looking ending. I've no idea what happened to 'The Secret of Zareba' after it got to Earth — that's for Jonas to explain — but the ending, written in imperfect English, had to be written *on Earth*, where English is spoken, though the story probably was first written on Emryss in the language of Emryss.

"And whoever first wrote it, I don't think was Igneal. Perhaps it was Galen, my alleged father."

"All I can add is that 'Princess Triana,' who was kidnapped not just from her home, but her planet, is said to be me — Triana Simms, now foster daughter of Dr. Jonas Harwell.

"Now, let's suppose this is true. Then I'm the last of seven listed in a genealogy that goes back many, many generations: Merceon, Agnon, Fairold, Galen, and Triana. About the first two people we know almost nothing. That leaves Lord Fairold, Prince Galen, and…and me.

"But let me emphasize one very important thing: Even if everything I've said here is true, *I have no evidence whatsoever that I carry blood from a second world.*

"Now how am I supposed to think about that?"

"Triana, you're forgetting an important part," interrupted Michael. "Remember the vision on the beach? That unnamed Queen, who was Lord Fairold's mother, was clearly told" — he reached for 'Death in a Tavern,' and flipped through the beginning pages — "here it is, Vandor from Elphia says 'My gracious Queen, from your children will come a child *who is also from this world* — that's Elphia — who will return to my people with the lost message of the Son-of-the-Highest-God's great act of salvation, which is for everyone who will believe.' "

"Yes, Michael, but remember, *first*, where is any evidence or even a suggestion that I have a real, *genetic* or *blood* connection from Planet Elphia? And *second,* how do we know that the promise is for the Queen's child Fairold and his child Galen? What about the mysterious Colin that no one knows about? Could the prophecy have been for him? Or was it open to either of them? And, *third,* shouldn't we step back and realize that travel from Earth to another planet — especially now — is scientifically, and practically, impossible?"

"Triana," said Michael, "back to the *blood connection* to Elphia thing. That doesn't necessarily have to come from those in the spaceship. Remember, Elphians were said to be *immune* to stings from walking bees. Now six of the ten defenders on the mountain were stung — Maleg, Saren, and Galen (all from Zareba) and Pinrut, Mira, and Mara (from the Emperor's Palace). The last three had 'Elphian scratches' said to protect them. But none of the Zarebites did. And they died, except for Galen who, unexplainedly, only became sick and recovered.

"Also in the first story, Fairold and his mother the Queen were stung, and while she died, Fairold got sick but didn't die. Perhaps they carried immunity from an unmentioned ancestor from Elphia?"

"But what about Crown Prince Gavin who died?" interjected Harwell.

"It was a snake, not bees, that killed him," said Michael. "And snakes were a whole different thing." It was a little scary when Jonas overlooked a detail like that. But how many mistakes was he making?

"That's only a tiny shred of evidence," said Triana.

"Jonas, Triana, Michael," said Cample, matter-of-factly, "I have more than a shred." His hands were shaking. "In fact, I think I have good evidence here — that is, for the Elphian connection."

All eyes turned toward the teacher.

"But Jonas, let's say that my evidence is 'good.' And let's say for the sake of argument that 'Providence' has somehow brought us together — "

"Which I believe it has," interrupted Harwell.

"Well then," said Cample, "Jonas, suppose one could go to Elphia, just what would a person say to the 'lost people' there?"

"If I knew their language, I'd do the same thing as here — preach Jesus." He extended his hands. "He's the one we know, and to anyone else created in God's image who's looking for answers, we would preach about him. The Christian Gospel, I feel, would resonate with what they know and what the Holy Spirit stirs within them."

"And if it doesn't?" asked Cample.

"I'd probably soon become a martyr — a martyr that no one on Earth would ever hear about."

"You really believe that, don't you!" exclaimed Cample.

"I do, Marvin, and of course I may be wrong.

"But I have to be true to what I know. We can't always sit and watch. When we learn something new in the natural world, the world of the mind, or the world of the spirit, our faith has to consider it — if possible, test it — whether it's subatomic particles, the Big Bang, the possibility of multiple dimensions, or the presence of spiritual forces that may be good or evil, or even T.O.E. Real faith can't afford to hide. It's joyfully open to understand more. You know I'm confident in what the Bible says about —"

"Toe? Or is that 'T dot, O dot, E dot'?" interrupted Cample. "Come on! You're pulling my…uh…"

"Well, your shoes are off and it's tempting" — Harwell laughed and Michael and Triana glanced at each other utterly bewildered — "but T.O.E. is simply the 'Theory Of Everything' that involves String Theory, that involves multiple dimensions and suggests that absolutely everything can eventually be explained with numbers and equations. But String Theory is highly controversial among scientists, still a 'tangled ball' — though less so than ten years ago — and it doesn't add anything to what we're talking about.

"But *if* we could go somewhere beyond Earth we should take what we know, share what we have, and be what we are. I think the agreement expressed by those three on the beach is exactly right. The question, of course, to us on Earth is just how big is the world, and how far can we all go across or beyond it? Never before the possibility of 'curled dimensions' have we had to use the word 'beyond.'"

" 'Beyond,' " repeated the teacher, "hmmm...and what if some alien from 'beyond' came here and asked about all this? What would you say?"

"Same thing—preach Jesus." Harwell winked at the girl and smiled. "And I just may have already done that. Triana knows Jesus as her Savior." The minister eased back his chair, stood, and stretched his arms. The others, as if taking his cue, did the same.

"I do," the girl added, loud enough to be heard above the moving chairs, "and the Gospel 'resonates' perfectly with what I know and feel."

"Jonas, we still haven't addressed one of Triana's big questions," said Cample. "The part about Colin...I, for one, *if you knew what I know,* don't think it really figures in here. But as to determining where the Elphian connection is..." He hesitated and seem to check himself. "Is there...is there some way to actually leave Earth for another planet?"

Harwell looked at his wind-up Timex watch. He began to twist the tiny knob.

"I think we'd better 'wind up' this evening... er...morning."

"Jonas, is there a way to..."

Suddenly a blinking blue light began flashing through Harwell's left front pants pocket. Since everyone was standing, there was no hiding it. Conversation ceased. The minister pulled out the tiny phone and spoke into it.

"Marcus, tomorrow at 9, same place. Later, okay? Goodbye." He returned the phone to his pocket, as if this were an everyday occurrence.

489

Michael and Triana stared at each other. Cample broke the silence.

"Jonas, I haven't seen one of those in almost a year! Not even a broken one!"

"Maybe I'm playing games," said the minister, smiling.

"I suppose that's your pilot," offered Cample.

"It would be more accurate to say, 'my space pilot,' don't you think?" returned Harwell. He laughed, the others joining him uneasily.

"I'm not sure I'd approve of your substitute teaching in science at the high school, even if you volunteered with no 'string theories' attached," said Cample.

"Then I'll resist a temptation to try that!" Harwell laughed. "Really, it's nearly 3 AM. We must stop. Remember your promises! And my children's problem at school?"

"If they'll ever forget I made charges, they'll both get A's."

"It's a deal!" said Michael and Triana together.

"Supper again at 6 in two days?"

"That's also a deal!" said Cample. "And now for my part. Here are the other two stories, 'The Fourth Prince' and 'Inside the Hollow Spear.' I can hardly wait to hear your reaction to these!" He handed the minister two volumes that were about as thick as the stories Michael and Triana had handed in. "They may change your lives forever, Harwell, if Marcus the space pilot is as talented as you think!"

"Oh, he's pretty good!" Harwell laughed. "But we'll see!"

Just as the teacher disappeared down the long sidewalk, Michael confronted his father.

"Jonas…what…is…going…on…here?"

"Sounds like a lot of things to me!" returned the minister as if everything were business as usual. Michael glowered and Harwell returned a half smile. "Son, I may have sounded lighthearted, but if that was a mask, unlike the two of you, it was the only one I wore this evening. Every word I said was true. We must pray like we never have before. Do you think Cample can be trusted?"

"I do, I really do," said Triana.

"Jonas," interrupted Michael, "about *physically* going to other planets like Elphia, that's impossible, right? And T.O.E.?"

"Let TOE go, Michael. We've got enough going here without that.

"But about going into space—we are talking about real possibilities here! I said 'possibilities,' " the minister repeated. "So far, I've done everything I know to do, but terrible decisions lie ahead. I need your prayer. We'll keep the new stories in the office. And, Triana"—he smiled—"you get the same 'privileges' as Michael—you can look at them without asking. Just don't remove them. I'm exhausted. We'll need to study them right away. Now, it's bed for me."

He turned to Sally in the hallway. "The meal, the food, everything was wonderful. I'm sure you can wrap things up better than I." He disappeared around the corner and out of sight.

The clock chimed 3 AM.

"Oh my goodness!" said Michael. "I've got to get home. Aunt Steffi will be—"

"Aunt Steffi," interrupted Sally, "will be asleep. I already sent a message to her, I did." The stocky woman's large apron was as fresh as it was in the morning. Her graying hair was still tied neatly in a bun, and she stood with her hands on her hips. " 'Michael will be staying here tonight,' I said. And I told her again to make sure she heard. Now come on into the living room. Your bed is made up on the sofa, it is."

Michael lay on the overstuffed cushions and pulled up a comfortable quilt. So much to think about.

A strange encounter of people said to be from two other worlds.

Mount Zareba. How could it be a mountain? Yet an old, old book that he'd just recently stumbled across said that an essential, yet indefinite element in the definition of a mountain involves its "conspicuity," or how it contrasted with its surroundings. Mt. Zareba, small as it was, was certainly conspicuous. He'd have to try that word out on Triana tomorrow.

But why did the river run *to* the mountain, not away from it? That was certainly strange.

And the way they climbed mountains in Emryss seemed strange, but could it be done that way?

The Golden Chest of Promise — what was its source of light? And how did it warm the orchard at the top and accelerate the growth of the trees? And what role did the chest have in the future?

The distracting X-shaped symbol on Triana's medal…but only here on Earth. What would they learn from "The Fourth Prince" and "Inside the Hollow Spear" that Cample had left?

And what was behind the EMP that had devastated Earth?

Could someone really get to Elphia? Would Triana finally be convinced she should go? And would she? Would Marcus the space pilot take her there?

And would he also go along?

What in the world — the world of Earth — was he thinking about? He'd never met Marcus and he'd rarely talked personally with Triana before today. But she seemed to know him. And he, her. Or did he?

Through the window the huge water tower poked up into a full moon. Why did the water tower he'd so carefully painted hold his attention now?

Suddenly he smelled the perfume. He turned and could see her figure standing in the darkness of the doorway. She came toward him. Pulling the cover away, he turned to a sitting position.

"Sorry, Michael, but here — " The pillow in her hands was where the smell came from. He held it to his nose. "Sorry, I didn't mean to — "

"No, no, it's nice."

"I make this perfume myself. Sometimes it's hard to get away from.

I'll get another pillow." She wore a comfortable oversized terrycloth robe and matching slippers.

"No, no! I...I like it. This will be fine. Triana"—he turned to the window—"why can't I take my eyes off that tower?"

"The tower is important," she said, "very important and *you* helped to make it that way."

"I did what?"

"Here, Michael." Her glasses were off. She extended her hand as if meeting a stranger. "Thank you for helping me at school."

"At school?"

"You know, Michael, that box I dropped, like the one Marcus called on tonight."

Marcus. What a terrible name.

"The box! Oh yes, I'd almost forgotten. Where did you—"

"Not now, Michael—just thank you. Thank you for everything. I trust you." She extended her hand further. "Thank you for loving me." So much for the stranger part. Did she hear what she was saying?

"But how did you know—I mean...I mean why do you say—"

"Michael"—she smiled into his eyes, as if she were reading the thoughts that led to his accidental words—"sometimes aliens see things that poor earthlings don't have a clue about." He sensed her struggling not to laugh. Or was she trying to cover something up?

"Triana, why are your knees shaking?"

He pushed her hand down and slowly circled her with his arms. The hair of the Princess stolen from Emryss was soft and silky. He drew her close.

"Michael, Sally's watching from the doorway."

"Triana, how do you—"

"I see things, I told you!"

He made himself start to push her away, but she held onto his arms.

"No! Michael, you just don't understand. Sally's not like you think.

493

But you must be proper about things." He sensed her gently pulling him back. He made himself resist.

"Be proper about...uh...Now you're going to tell me you know how I think?!"

"Michael, silly, that's easy with you...but just now" — she paused for half a minute — "Sally just told me Igneal has finally gone into a coma. He's really dying!"

"Triana, how can you be so lighthearted and then jump to something serious so fast?"

"Michael...I...I'm sorry. Some things I'm so...so very new at. But he's going to go home to our Lord."

"Okay, now it's my time to be sorry. Please forgive me."

Once again quiet tears began to flow from the eyes of the girl who seemed never to cry before today. She leaned toward him and he wrapped her in his arms. She could change the subject or her mood back and forth as often as she wanted.

"Michael, I have no one, no one now — oh, I shouldn't have said that! Sorry!"

"Look at me!" He put his hands on her shoulders and gently pushed her back. "Triana, you're not alone. You have me. *For always.*" As soon as the words were out, he wished he could reel them back. Several times, yes, they'd been together in the same room in school or in church. But...but today they'd easily played games with Cample and Jonas. Maybe the surprising way she'd 'publicly' announced that 'he loved her' made him talk so foolishly. But never before today had they ever touched. And now he'd said that! She would think he was an idiot. How Marcus What's-His-Name would laugh! Or would he warn him to stay away?

"Michael, you...don't be silly. You don't even know me...don't even know what's going...but thank you, thank you."

"*Always,*" he heard himself repeat.

494

Spinning almost out of her slippers, she turned and walked briskly back to the doorway. Only seconds after she got there, he saw her coming back.

"Sally sent me back. She said…she said I didn't let you kiss me."

"She…what? Do you really —" He stood and mechanically she put her arms around him. He drew up her face to his and with very little extra effort they kissed. Pulling back, she looked at his face.

"Michael, my knees aren't shaking anymore!" They kissed again. And one more time after that. Finally, she pulled back. Sally was tapping on her shoulder.

"Michael needs his sleep, he does, and so do you! So off to bed with you!" Sally gave Michael a peck on the top of his head, and before she left, she tucked in the quilt around him.

"Pray for Igneal, Michael — pray. He's dying, he really is. And going to the hospital is out of the question. You probably don't see it, but Triana is beside herself. And… and Marcus has told her he loves her. He's brilliant, but… Please don't think she's crazy. Be kind to my girl now. There's none like her — in this world or any other."

In seconds the woman was gone. The long day was over. But much was happening beyond the walls of the parsonage and Territory. The tower was unbelievably clear in the moonlight. Perfume from the Princess from Emryss remained. Much would soon follow. Things that in his wildest imaginings he would never have even dreamed about.

THE END

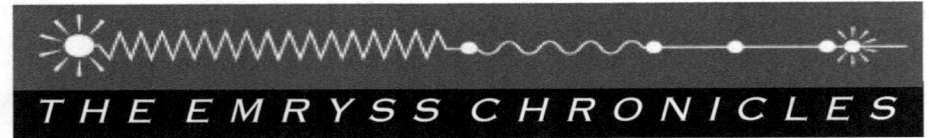
An Excerpt From
THE BLOOD OF THREE WORLDS
by John Knapp II

THE KING IN THE IRON CAGE

"I had a dream last night," said the teacher, "that I must confess was as vivid as it was strange and dark."

"Tell it," said his companion.

"Once a good king on an island in a sea of islands had three children, and all seemed to share many of their father's good traits.

"Now the sea became filled with fierce and terrible creatures, though a protecting iron fence was quickly built to keep the creatures from coming ashore, as well as anyone from leaving.

"One day several holes appeared in the fence, and on this same day the King was walking in the meadow to once again consider the God who made everything.

"Suddenly, an enormous bird arose from a pile of ashes and stood before him.

" 'Don't be afraid, Your Majesty,' said the bird. 'I'll do you no harm. But I must warn you. Your iron fence has been ripped apart, and fierce creatures nearby have come ashore.' The bird paused and drew his

496

wings closer. 'The world as you know it is doomed. There's nothing you can do,' he continued, 'but I can do one thing.'

" 'What is that?' asked the King.

" 'In my talons I can carry those three you call your children up and over the iron walls to a place where you'll never see them again...but only if you let me.' "

"Can you tell me more? Anything else?" asked the teacher's companion.

"Only this," said the teacher. "At some point the spectacles will be smashed beyond repair."

EPHEMERON PRESS

About content and style: Four things in, or influencing, this manuscript are not typical. Here they are and my reasons for them:

1. Where there is <u>dialogue</u>, it <u>almost always *begins* the paragraph that it's in</u>, followed by the speaker tags and any necessary descriptive detail. This energizes the text, I feel, makes for snappier paragraphs, and for smoother oral readings by those new to the story. And parts of this story have been read aloud several times.

2. There is <u>generous use of stylistic "road signs"</u> — italics, boldface, quotation, underlining, numerals (in place of numbers expressed as words), generous use of capitalization, occasional double punctuation (e.g. ?!) much shorter paragraphs, and occasionally the repetition of key details that might be overlooked or forgotten. These features also help to clarify and, again, make oral reading easier and tone changes easier to detect.

3. <u>Clotting the text in places with more-than-usual detail.</u> For too long I've been put off by heroes and heroines running unscathed through a hail of bullets or arrows, gathering, if any, only superficial wounds that for the females leave no scars. If 6 to 10 defenders hold off a 1000 attackers in a mountain fortress, I want you to know how this is possible. And here you learn how! Details, details, details, running the risk of narrative overload.

4. <u>Being fusty in places with use of Scripture and Biblical interpretation.</u> Making Scripture fit into and energize action in uncharted territory beyond centuries-old interpretation terrifies me. Yet such has always occurred with the gaining of scientific knowledge and the passage of time. I accept the interpretation of the International Council on Biblical Inerrancy, and declare to the dreamy-eyed that this story is fiction, fiction, fiction. In these pages, only four major characters, and one minor one, enter directly into any part of the extra-planetary encounter. The plot does not require more, nor does it get it. What happens in this story, and its sequel, does not involve the church body dividing its interest, loyalties, or responsibilities between planets.

I have three hopes for each person who reads this tale. First and second: At night I hope you forever after look a little differently at the stars that God created, and in the day, that you will read the old classic fairy tales (which are loaded with good things) and take them a bit more seriously. And third: I hope both day and night you read Holy Scripture and follow God in every part of your life.

John Knapp II (PhD in sci. ed.) is
former Professor of English at SUNY-
Oswego and writer of science text-
books for Silver Burdett. His volume
of poetry, A Pillar of Pepper, won
the first C. S. Lewis Gold Medal in
1983. A former department editor for
School Science and Mathematics, he
founded (and edited) The Westigan
Review of Poetry and the Endless
Mountains Story Club. He and his
wife Karen divide their time between
the (future) "Susquehanna Territory"
and Florida.

www.ingramcontent.com/pod-product-compliance
Lightning Source LLC
Chambersburg PA
CBHW071215250626
47163CB00001B/1